Water Beyond the Bridge

Water Beyond the Bridge

Sue Allen

a novel by
Sue Allen

Mackinac Memories Books

Water Beyond the Bridge
Copyright © 2016 by Sue Allen
Fourth Printing 4/2022

Printed in Michigan, USA, by a company
that's committed to the environment and maintains
certifications with the Forest Stewardship Council©,
the SUSTAINABLE FORESTRY INITIATIVE©, and the
Programme for the Endorsement of Forest Certification

Author
Sue Allen

Cover design by
Lily Porter Niederpruem

Published by
Mackinac Memories Books
www.mackinacislandmemories.com

ISBN-10: 0-9973847-0-0
ISBN-13: 978-0-9973847-0-3

Ebook - EPUB
ISBN-10: 0-9973847-2-7
ISBN-13: 978-0-9973847-2-7

Copyright Registration
TX 8-338-858

Library of Congress
2017905982

To the people and horses
of Mackinac Island and
all who have ever loved
this beautiful isle.

~~~~~~~

All water has a perfect memory
and is forever trying to
get back to where it was.

- Toni Morrison

~~~~~~~

1

Nick had planned this trip in secret, the way one plans a suicide, but with a different objective: rather than ending his life, he hopes to rebuild it. So here he is, aboard the old ferry clunking its way across the wide waters of Lake Huron to Mackinac Island, on a mission to reconnect with Ella, his summer lover of bygone years.

He's driven seven hours straight, coming down from Duluth before sunrise without even stopping in Marquette to see Mama. That can wait until later, on the way home.

For now, he has business to attend to. Never mind that Ella doesn't know a thing about this; never mind they haven't communicated in three decades; never mind what a friend had warned Nick about re-unions with old lovers: "Don't expect too much. Sara's boobs were hanging down to her navel and her hair was half silver" is how he'd described his high school sweetheart.

Not until this moment has Nick allowed for the possibility of a failed mission. But as he stands on the top deck peering through the mist for a first glimpse of the island, pesky doubts slink in. Hell, will she even remember him? Running his hand through a crown of thick, wavy hair—proud plumage on an old rooster—he wonders what she'll think of him. There's plenty of wear and tear on that young man of yesteryear: the old six-pack has gone a tad gelatinous, and his hair turned as silver as the towers on the Mackinac Bridge to the west.

And what about her, his lovely, horse-driving Ella? Will her little breasts have sagged, her luster and rebellious soul dulled? And after all this time, her intense libido surely has waned. His has. Perhaps he should stay on the boat when it dumps its load of tourists at the island and take it right back to the mainland.

As Nick paces the deck debating his decision, a kid with a shock of red hair poking out from a Detroit Tigers cap breaks free from his parents seated on a bench, grasps the railing with both hands, screaming, "I see it. I see Mackinac Island!" Nick spins and leans into the rail, squinting. There it is, the island, straight ahead, rising from the fog. First the bluffs, spired in cedar, laced by whorls of departing mist; then one by one, white buildings appear on the green hills, like polished teeth. As the boat approaches the break wall, Ella's cottage, Cedar Bluff, appears—at least what he thinks is her house—that rambling, white Victorian with green trim, and a tower poking up on the east side. Then he notices that the neighboring homes look almost identical. Nick scratches his head. He'll find it tomorrow, for sure. *If* he stays.

As the view brightens, resurrected ghosts emerge from his time-darkened memories. Those sun-spangled days with Ella, her tomboy style and loud laugh that swelled up from her belly. Those starry nights up on the old fort wall, he with his guitar and rock star imitation voice, she exuberantly off-tune. Those three decades suddenly seem short, the span across the years a footbridge.

As he stares at the house, a last swag of fog descends, enshrouding the sight as if it had never existed. Nick sighs. He can't remember why he and Ella drifted apart, their relationship vanished, *poof,* following the course of most summer loves that bloom brightly as annuals, then shrivel at the first frost. One day she and her family departed their cottage without a word to Nick. She had not written, and later, had stood him up on a promise they'd made to meet on the island in the winter. Even so, to Nick, their relationship was always more than a summer romance. There had never been anyone like her before or after, not even his ex-wife, Katie. He's thought about Ella off and on for years, and lately these renascent longings, once an occasional tug on his heart, had upgraded to an obsession. It was finding that letter that did it, near the bottom of one of his green plastic bins with the dreaded "Miscellaneous" label to assure it would be the last bin he'd ever open.

Nick's last contact with her family had been a note from Ella's father years ago in response to a photograph of Ella that Nick had mailed her. It captured her perfectly: wading into the lake in a pair of cut-off jeans over a red bathing suit, her face turned slightly toward him, golden-brown hair flowing around her shoulders, and that smile—never the big-grin toothy type—both welcoming and secretive, her blue eyes drilling straight into him, the way they did when they made love. Sometimes it unnerved him, but more often, excited him, those huge eyes staring into his.

Ella's father must have snooped through her mail because he sent back a polite but terse note:

Thanks for the photo. I'll pass it on to Ella. Stop by next time you're on the island. Truly, Henry Hollingsworth.

Nick had thrown the letter on the floor. Old Henry, a quiet, glum sort, with his head in a book; why was he replying and not Ella?

Four months ago, Nick finally opened the plastic bin in search of a college transcript. That's when he'd found the letter, that's when the obsession had begun. It had gnawed at him every day since; planted the seed for this trip today. But he should have done his homework better, not just some half-assed searching around on the Internet ("such a chintz" Katie, called him), finally paying $10 to some people-finder site to pin down the fact that a 48-year-old Ella Lynn Hollingsworth lived in Ann Arbor, Michigan, though he'd have to pay extra for her address and phone number, which he didn't do. On the electronic white pages he'd learned there was still a Henry Hollingsworth with a residence on Mackinac Island, confirming his hunch they still have a cottage there. Nick wonders if Henry has changed, and if Ella married, did he approve of the guy. She might be married to a tweedy, pretentious English major, a William who refuses to be called Bill, or a James who shuns a plain Jim. He can't picture her with a country club sort of fellow with a name like Sherwood who wears pink linen pants, but you never know. Maybe she's divorced. Or widowed. Or gay.

Nick feels the boat slow as the captain eases the ferry up to the big pier. With one toss, a young dockhand in khaki shorts lassos a rope around a splintered piling. The kid has an eager, open face, tanned by the northern sun, unclotted by disappointment, the way Nick's used to be.

Nick moves away from the rail toward the stairs where the excited boy from the top deck has already made it to the bottom, his parents close behind, his mother clutching the back of his T-shirt.

Decision time.

Squaring his shoulders, Nick marches down the stairs. He'll follow through on his plan, damn it.

As he waits on the stern in a line of restless and mostly overweight tourists, he looks around anxiously, wondering if Ella is on the pier. *Crazy thought.* He notices the woman in front of him is wearing stilettos. Big mistake. She'll have to walk on those things all day, spiking manure and succumbing to a torn Achilles tendon before her visit's over. She stands close to a man who appears a decade older, her butt pressing into his thighs. Nick looks away.

Finally, two beefy teenagers yank the ramp from the boat like a stubborn colt, its clang causing a dray horse on the dock to flatten back its ears. "All ashore!" shouts the worker on the right. When it's Nick's turn to stomp up the metal ramp behind three carts of luggage, he's shocked at the steep grade: *lake must be down three feet.* Superior, *his* lake, has been also been hit by climate change, but not so dramatically.

On the pier, a young dock porter wheels by Nick, his bike basket a tower of four suitcases, with two duffle bags, one sprouting a tennis racquet, swaying from the handlebars.

"Hey, watch it, mon!" shouts the man, swerving to avoid Nick.

"Sorry," says Nick, jumping out of his way, the tennis racquet clunking him on the arm. It stings, and Nick rubs his arm, cursing softly. Back when Nick worked here, the only accent was that of a Yooper, a guy from Michigan's Upper Peninsula—UP—like him. He'd envied the dock porters, pumped-up macho college guys who got all the women. He'd aspired to be one, but was stuck as a dockhand and general all-around wharf slave, never cool enough for the dock porter ranks. And these fellows bantering about the dock today, hawking their hotels and B & Bs, "Anyone here for Mission Point?" "The Island House?" "Iroquois Hotel?" are an older, hungrier lot with pattern balding and special work visas.

Straight ahead, a *Duck Dynasty*-looking guy in blue jeans sporting a full beard and a red bandana hoists a wagonload of boxes onto a dray, reminding Nick that not only horses work hard on Mackinac. A terrain without cars requires old-fashioned hard-core physical labor. He'd been one of them, sweating and stinking, earning big biceps right along with his meager paycheck.

As he steps into the street, the stench of horse urine and manure rises, blending with the aroma of chocolate pouring from fudge shops that line the street, an olfactory oxymoron. Nick takes a whiff. *I'm back.* Ella used to joke about the parallels between fudge and horse manure: *One goes in the mouth, both come out the south as shit in the end.* Now that would be a good description of his flat-lined marriage.

He's forgotten how clogged the downtown could be: bicycles, strollers, carriages, people everywhere. Main Street reminds him of those pictures in the Busytown books he used to read to his daughter, Melina: peripatetic tourists pawing through carts for their luggage and asking all the same questions they did when he'd worked there: *Where's the Grand Hotel? How far to the fort? Where's the closest bathroom? Yuck, why's there poop in the street?* Folks on bicycles thread through groups of gawkers. Three towheaded children break free from their parents and race toward a carriage parked next to the dock where two pintos stamp their feet and flick flies with their tails. "Stay back, kids, they kick," cautions the driver.

Nick feels the island effect, an instant slowing down: everything is dictated by equine pace, a five-miles-per-hour lifestyle. After a day or so, most people ease into island time, tossing the minute hand off the clock, and a few days later, shucking the hour one, too. The others go back to the mainland or stay glued to their electronic gizmos. Well he won't; he's barely mastered flicking and scrolling on his new touchscreen cell phone. And social media? That's another universe.

Although he's brought only one carry-on suitcase and a backpack, Nick decides to splurge on a horse-drawn taxi. He spots a team of two bays standing patiently on the street while the driver texts on a pink cell phone, holding some 2,500 pounds of horse with the reins in her thin fingers. Nick sighs. The driver reminds him of Ella—her perky posture, a brown ponytail popping out the back hole of her baseball cap, the casual way she commands two enormous beasts. Leaning over the driver's seat on the front of the carriage she asks, "Where to?"

"The Maples B & B." Although he'd never heard of the place during his summer there, the brochures said it had the lowest rates. Such a pricey place, this island.

"First time here?"

"Nope. Used to work on the dock, but it's my first time back in years," he says, proud to prove he's not just another fudgie, the islanders' term for tourists.

"You're lucky. Wish I could get off this rock. This place sucks."

Maybe the island would lose its magic if you were stuck like her on a hard wooden seat fully exposed to all sorts of weather with two pooping, farting beasts before you. Tossing his bags on the rear luggage rack, he climbs in and sits back, listening to the rhythm of horseshoes hitting the pavement, equine rap: *clip clop, clip clop.* The sound brings him peace, like rain on a cabin roof. With eyes closed, he leans back on the seat as the breeze rustles his hair.

As they head east along the main street the driver shouts: "Horses coming through!" dodging her way through a tangle of tourists walking in a curb-to-curb line in the street, oblivious to the carriages and bikes around them. "Would you walk in the middle of the street back home?" she barks at them. Turning to Nick she says, "They're gonna get themselves fucking killed. Pardon my French." Nick chuckles.

They pass a large, grassy park, where up in the center, a statue of the French missionary Pere Marquette looks out to the harbor, a seagull roosting on his head, tourists scattered around his robes at the base. Nick figures there must be inches of bird poop on the statue's head. Two boys toss a yellow Frisbee, a couple nestles in the shade of a lilac bush smooching, and an Amish family checks out the horses. Staring from the carriage, Nick straightens his back and cranes his neck. This is where he'd first met Ella, there, by the corner next to the drinking fountain.

It had been a brilliant June day, the sky a Michigan blue, lilacs bursting like purple balloons on bushes everywhere. She was perched on the driver's seat of a fringe-topped surrey, second carriage from the front, gabbing with the other drivers. Nick, who'd recently celebrated his twentieth birthday and taken a job as a dockhand, was sitting on the short stone wall wrapped around the park, eating his lunch. There was something different about her, the way she sat so upright and regal, how her hair rippled down her shoulders and lifted in the breeze; pretty, more natural than most of the island girls who loaded up on makeup.

"Got two suckers on that last trip," the driver parked in front of Ella had called back to her. "They fell for it when I said the Mackinac Bridge swung over to the island at night. Tipped me ten bucks."

"You're going to have to return it tonight when the bridge doesn't swing over," replied Ella.

"Hey, did you hear about the lady who gave up her husband for a horse?"

"Uh-uh."

"Said nothing can beat seventeen hands between your legs."

At that moment, one of her horses farted so loudly everyone sitting on the wall laughed. "Jimmy," said Ella, turning to the driver behind her, "I told you to lay off those beans." Her horses farted again, louder this time. Nick guffawed, and Ella stared at him. "Queenie, Duke, mind your manners. You're ruining this poor guy's lunch."

"No problem," said Nick, seizing the excuse to meet her. "I don't usually get live entertainment with my lunch around here." He stood up and extended his hand. "I'm Nick." Ella leaned forward and extended hers. "Ella." Her hand was soft, warm, and a little moist, smelling of leather.

Jimmy, a middle-aged man missing half a mouth of teeth, turned in his seat and said, "Now remember, we're all just farts in the wind."

Ella winked at Nick. "Don't mind him. He always talks like that. A Yooper." She stuck out her tongue in Jimmy's direction.

"I'm a Yooper too, connoisseur of deer camp humor," said Nick. "By the way, I didn't quite get that joke about the hands."

Rolling her eyes and leaning down she whispered, "You measure a horse's height in hands. A hand is four inches. Get it?"

"Got it." Ella stared at Nick a moment, a small furrow in her brow. "I—I haven't been around horses much," he stammered.

"No problem. Aren't you the guy who plays a guitar up there at night?" she nodded toward the statue.

"Yeah."

"I've heard you."

What did that mean? He considered himself pretty damn good on the instrument. Back home in Marquette he'd played in a band and had booked plenty of gigs.

Ella held his glance before turning away from him toward a young couple approaching her carriage. A little boy toting a plastic bow and arrow from a souvenir shop pointed it toward Queenie.

"Kid, please don't aim that at my horses," said Ella.

"Put that thing away right now, Danny," snapped the father. "Can you take us for a tour?" he asked with a hand on his son's shoulders.

"Sure," she said, pulling in the reins. "Hop on." As her carriage moved forward, Ella turned and looked back at Nick.

"Come down and visit me on the dock sometime!" he yelled to the departing carriage. He felt he'd blown it, but wasn't sure why. Maybe she hated his music. Maybe he'd been too dense about the joke. Anything that started with a horse fart was bound to be stinky and short-lived; yet, despite its stalled beginning, their relationship turned sweeter than a slab of Mackinac fudge.

2

On a bluff above the harbor, Ella hunches on her knees, scraping last year's gray enamel paint off the steps of the front porch of her family cottage, clenching a paint scraper in her right fist, a cup of tea in her left. Steam swirls from the cup, but it will soon turn lukewarm in the chill Mackinac morning. Cranky from her early awakening by the wail of the foghorn, Ella scowls at a seagull eying her teabag. "Scat!" she yells, waving a scraper at the bird. It raises its wings and screeches, then flies into the mist.

Her scraper slides under a long strip of paint, loosening more than a foot that easily peels from the wood. This small act pleases her, the way stripping a long layer of skin after the first sunburn of the summer did when she was a teen, before anyone thought about melanoma. She moves with the athletic ease of a tomboy, her strokes smooth as she establishes a rhythm—*five pushes, a tap, a shake, five pushes.*

Fog hovers in the cedars, a shawl wrapped around the cottage, unusual for this late in the season. Ella loves it; in such conditions, no one can pin her down.

Out on the road her neighbor Gary breaks the spell. Up early walking his black Labrador, Bernie, he's close enough to see, standing right next to her wrought-iron fence. And that damned dog of his squats and pees on the strip of grass between Ella's fence and the road. Pushing her hair off her forehead over a bead of perspiration, Ella sits back on her heels, dagger-eyeing him. Surely he'll stop that animal from pissing on her lawn—that's what she calls the nearly grassless spread of vegetation—once he sees her.

But no, just a casual smile as he shouts, "Morning! I see you're back at it. No easy job on Mackinac, you know." Easy for him to say—with a full-time caretaker to keep his cottage in shape, chores are a gentleman's sport for him. She'd seen him mowing his lawn, a lush mass of chemical-coated greenery. Ella wants to run the scraper down his tanned face.

"Hey, Gary, are you yearning?"

"Huh? Yearning for what?"

"Urinating dogs are not allowed on my lawn."

Gary's smile fizzles. "Oh, sorry." Then he breaks into a run toward his cottage three lots up the hill, a massive Queen Anne with a turret resembling a rocket poised for launching from a bed of bright-pink petunias. Ella watches his retreating figure, noticing his calves bulging beneath his knees. She's always had a weakness for ripped calves. Then she remembers he doesn't believe in global warming. *Really? Just wait till the big lake dries up, that will show him.*

Taking a swig of tea, she frowns at its tepid temperature before resuming her work. Porch scraping's a job she's performed for forty summers. Grandfather started the tradition when he resolved the cottage must stay in the family forever, or until the last Hollingsworth dropped dead, relegating the task to his two sons; Henry, Ella's father, and Stu. It was Stu who had the good sense to bail out when Grandfather died, and Henry bought out his brother.

When she was eight, Father demanded she work on the house right by his side, a scrawny little apprentice. "In case you ever get to thinking it's easy to maintain this place," he'd said. It certainly isn't. Not that she has to do one lick of this tedious porch work; it's self-assigned labor. Sometimes she wonders why she continues the tradition. Must be in her blood, along with a few other scrambled notions. But it makes her feel virtuous, shoulders above her younger sister, Sara, who always weaseled out of the tasks of maintaining the Hollingsworth place. That and loyalty to Father, now that he's passed on.

In Ella's mind, summer doesn't officially begin until the porch is repainted. Now summer will be over before that happens, what with all the commotion: Mother breaking her leg, her nephew Charlie dumped on her by his mother, Sara, off overseas. So here it is, August 2, and she's just starting. She returns to her task, making no bigger dent in the job of keeping up this house than a quart of strawberries can fill the Grand Canyon. Mother always said the place would keep the family together, but Ella has her doubts on how a dysfunctional family is supposed to keep up a dysfunctional house.

Cedar Bluff is her family's obsession: a leaky, rambling survivor of a century of beatings by Great Lakes' winters, lumbered with solid Michigan white pine. Like the other showy bluff houses, it started out more plainly toward the end of the nineteenth century: vernacular style with symmetry and regularity, a vertical box with pieces of gingerbread tacked on here and there to break the monotony. But when the Grand Hotel came along in 1887—*the newest, most fashionable resort hotel in the Midwest*—cottage owners went into a remodeling frenzy, trying to outdo one another with belvederes, verandas, third stories, porticos, towers, and all manner of exterior ornamentation. The simple designs vanished as homes were torn to the ground and replaced with the big, trendy Victorians, most loosely labeled as Queen Anne or Stick Style, prime examples of the cluttered complexity of Victorian architecture. The first owners of Cedar Bluff slapped on a tower in 1894, a third story the next year. When Ella's grandparents bought it in 1935 at a tax sale, the place was a wreck. The owners had made some poor speculations and went bust, leaving the place uninhabited for three summers before Grandpa picked up his *bargain*. His casket business prospered—"A booming underground market" he'd say—so he took advantage of the opportunity mortality brought him. When he passed on in 1969, he gave it to Henry. The other son, Stu, wanted no part of it, fleeing to California, where he raised a family who had no desire to visit. "Michigan?" they'd say. "What on earth is there?"

The house frightened Ella when she was a child: massive, with its unpredictable architectural features, the cupolas, gables, and balconies threw her off balance. That and the dark-paneled rooms, such a contrast to the brilliant light on the porches. She wanted rectangles and squares, regularity. Ella's mother, Audrey, told her a story about the house. "Once upon a time there was a little gazebo."

"Like ours?" asked Ella, referring to a small gazebo behind the barn.

"Yes. Although it was a lovely little gazebo, it wanted to be bigger, more like a small house." According to Audrey's story—Ella later figured out her mother borrowed liberally from folklore and Indian legends—a great blue heron flew down and gave the little gazebo a whitefish. "If you eat just one bite of this you will grow very big," said the bird. "But don't take more than one bite." But the gazebo was greedy; it gobbled up the entire fish, and then fell asleep with a tummy ache.

When it woke up it went into a frenzy, expanding from four hundred square feet to six thousand with cupolas, porches, and a tower sprouting out from it within minutes.

"The gazebo went berserk?" asked Ella, relishing her new word, *berserk,* that she'd learned that spring when a teacher explained that's what happened to people who got bit by tarantulas.

"Yes."

Audrey's story jolted Ella's imagination. She drew a cartoon of a gazebo chomping on a fish, then expanding wildly. She called it *A Gazebo Goes Beserk,* overlooking the "r" before the "s." Audrey hung the unframed picture on four white thumbtacks in the pantry for decades until the paper furled hopelessly and the thumbtacks rusted. Years later, when studying the food chain in middle school, Ella wondered where a carnivorous gazebo fit into the puzzle of who eats whom.

When Ella turned ten, Mother converted the gazebo into a playhouse where Ella hosted tea parties with her stuffed animals—Lambie always served the tea—and later, she'd read book after book there, escaping the tension inside the house. Then there were the encounters with boyfriends. Oh yes, the boyfriends.

Ella scrapes a little harder, gouging a strip of pine. A few gray paint chips fly into the grass. How would her life have been without those young men, had she stayed out of that gazebo with its sweet pleasures. She'd experienced sex before love with a pompous jerk who went on to become a real estate attorney in Baltimore. The guy had deflowered her in a puddle of blood and pain with no apologies. She had just turned seventeen.

But a few summers later, she discovered the delights of lust when it came harnessed to love. She should have stuck with that fellow; sensitive, handsome, and musical. They'd had a bright summer romance, the kind that lingers in you, even when you forget your lover's face and name. What was his name? She sees his face, golden-brown eyes and a mess of hair. Nick, that was it. His last name was Greek sounding, she remembers that much. Whatever happened to him, anyway? At summer's end he took off to go back to Northern Michigan University, living at home to save money, and soon she was off to her sophomore year at the University of Virginia. They'd talked on the phone once when she called, and she'd mailed him a letter, then another. He never wrote back. Life brought in replacement characters, new preoccupations. And that little hole in her heart patched up just fine.

Now here she is at forty-eight, divorced, fired from an environmental consulting job she loved, and stuck managing a business she loathes—the Hollingsworth Casket Company. Time's gnawing away at her. Make that chomping. Before you know it she'll be needing one of those caskets too, though hers will be biodegradable and no embalming fluid, thank you very much. At a recent meeting her financial advisor had said, "We've got to get more funds into your retirement portfolio. Actuarially speaking, you've only got about thirty years left."

"Thirty years?"

"The average life span of a female in the United States is 78.2 years."

"But I'm not average. I'll live to ninety."

"Then save even more."

She knows she looks years younger, with a thick crop of light-brown hair bossed in silver threads, lanky rock-solid arms and legs, slightly flabby tummy, but taut abs and glutes. A light net of wrinkles web the edges of her mouth and eyes. *Time's tiny footsteps* her mother calls them. *Time is beginning to wear combat boots across my face*, she thinks. What was that her friend Beth said? "You've got class reunion syndrome."

"Whaddya mean?" she'd asked.

"You want to win the 'least changed' award at your high school reunion."

"But I don't give a damn about their opinion—and I've only attended one reunion. I'm not vain."

"Sure you are. You've just been cruising on good genes, but we all wear out eventually."

Leave it to Beth, her friend since childhood, to talk straight. Beth herself had changed, a good twenty pounds heavier, and she couldn't blame her gene pool, not with her tall, thin father and petite mother. The truth, plain and simple, was that Beth was an unapologetic Foodie, and she didn't give much thought to others' opinions. She loved to cook and she loved to eat.

"OK, I confess that I just dumped over a hundred dollars on some anti-aging cream," said Ella. "Heroin would have been cheaper. But no animals were used to test it."

"See, I said you were vain. And the next thing you'll get is a bathing suit with a little skirt on the bottom. Cottage cheese thighs are problematic."

Now how did Beth know she'd looked at some swimwear a few weeks ago?

Several women she knew had face lifts or endured needles jabbed in their foreheads to achieve that tight Botox look. Wendy, a running buddy back in Ann Arbor, stopped exercising outdoors after plastic surgery. "I need to protect my investment," she'd explained. No, Ella would keep her face for now.

The cockiness of her taken-for-granted health has vanished, replaced by its pernicious nickel-and-diming; little things like twisting around to back out of a parking space could deliver a stiff neck for the rest of the day. Then there's the sneeze-and-pee problem; if she sneezes hard, she has to squeeze her pelvic muscles to prevent urine from trickling down her legs. She stakes out bathrooms whenever she's away from home, and dives behind shrubbery on her runs.

She's becoming invisible, zapped, like an old magnet sliding down the side of a refrigerator. Worse are the euphemisms; the one she most despises is "well-seasoned." That's how Harry, a man she dated a half-year back, described her. A forty-five-year-old art history professor with a whiskery face, sweaty hands, and a seductive, made-for-radio voice, he came across as intelligent and witty. They'd met at a volunteer river clean-up day in Ann Arbor and had several dates. After a long, winey dinner—one and a half bottles of a fruity Cabernet from a Leelanau winery—they'd tumbled into her bed.

"I like well-seasoned women like you," he whispered to her after flopping about on her belly, 185 pounds of dead weight, sticky with semen. *If he starts snoring I'm going to kick him in the balls,* she thought. Instead, she nudged him gently. "Please don't make me into a pineapple."

He lifted his head. "A what?"

"Crushed pineapple. I can't breathe. Move." She pushed him off, rolling over on her side.

As she lay in the dark beside him, stars flickered in the skylight above the bed, their brilliance diminished by the city's light pollution. She yearned for the stars over Mackinac, chunky and radiant; longed to be lying beneath them with that gazebo boyfriend, fresh as a northern Michigan night.

So here she is, scraping away on the porch. The wind has picked up, the mist completely evaporated. Waves etch white rickrack across the blue canvas of the lake. Ella watches a three-tiered white ferry packed with tourists round the break wall, its wake forming a rooster tail plume behind it, a swarm of seagulls circling above. Before you know it, the island will be teeming with fudgies.

Inside the cottage the phone rings, but she doesn't answer; waits instead for Father's gravelly voice on the answering machine to announce, "You have reached the Hollingsworth residence. Sorry I cannot come to the phone now. Please leave a message." *Click.* From her sea of brittle paint chips, Ella sets down her scraper and sighs. *Father, check out my good work.* Oh yes, she'll feel the paint scraping in her bones by morning.

3

The Maples B & B is a quaint yellow building with dark green trim on a back street, with no water view. Definitely on the downslide. Red geraniums fringe the front railing, giving the place a cheery look while diverting attention away from the peeling paint and splintery porch floor. A small investment in flowers is cheaper than the costly work old places require. Nick has played this trick, too. Nick pays his driver and leaves her a good tip.

"Enjoy your visit," she says. "And don't romanticize this place. Trust me." She lifts the reins and moves on.

In his musty room on the third floor, Nick surveys his face in the patchy mirror above the antique oak dresser. After a week of camping, the dark stubble on his chin has morphed into a cross between a beard and industrial-grade sandpaper. His skin has darkened over the summer, the creases around his eyes deepened. He sighs. *I'm withering up like a raisin.* Part of him wants the picture of the young Nick and Ella to be suspended in time, forever unchanged. If she sees him now—and vice versa—it will destroy that past perfection, the way viewing a corpse erases a lifetime of seeing someone vibrant, alive.

Quickly, avoiding another glimpse in the mirror, he steps into the shower, where the puny spray of lukewarm water never achieves a hot enough temperature to soothe his sore muscles. After toweling off he pulls on a pair of khaki shorts and a clean button-down shirt. Never one to care about fashion, he'd fussed over this one, wavering between checks, stripes, or solids. He'd opted for an orangish peachy one. Katie once told him the color looked great with his skin. Checking his watch, he remembers how Melina teased him about it: "Daddy, just use your cell phone. Nobody wears watches anymore." He can't imagine going without his.

It's not yet one o'clock, with the sun riding high in a clear sky, every lick of mist transformed into a lingering humidity. He'll try to call her house again. Punching the number on his cell phone, again he gets no answer, just the message with Henry's voice.

He'd picked up a copy of the local paper. Might as well learn a bit of news and show off his island knowledge when—well, *if*—he sees Ella. Maybe there's some news about her family.

A color photo splashes across the page showing a high-stepping horse pulling a polished wood carriage beneath a headline "Horse Parade Enjoyed by All." Nick smiles. Breaking news.

His finger scrolls down to the hard news: *Bicycle Mishaps Cause Police Concern*

Police Chief Stan Marko recently witnessed a bicyclist ride directly in front of a horse, which could have caused a runaway. "People just aren't paying any attention to what they are doing," he said. "They're looking around, looking at different things, the horses, the shops. They need to pay attention to where they are going."

He skips over a column devoted to horses, this week's story explaining the difference between snaffle, curbed, and hackamore bits; skims a nature column informing the reader that the best place to find Yellow Lady's Slipper is along Sugar Loaf Road. Stopping at the gossip column, *News About Us*, the big revelation is that Katie Coldwell hosted six cardinals at her birdfeeder last week, while Lucy Tippins will celebrate her 95th birthday on August 5. Not a word about the Hollingsworths. He's killed about fifteen minutes. Time to go out and conquer the world.

As he steps out on the porch, the owner, Judy, approaches him from the hallway. A short woman, fiftyish, with straight shoulder-length gray hair pulled back in barrettes, her pumpkin-round face with green eyes set wide apart gives her a look of being in a state of perpetual surprise. When he first signed in she asked him if he was alone and stared at his barren ring finger. "Nick, enjoy yourself. And if there's anything you need, I'm usually always here." He'd backed away and clambered up the stairs. God knows he didn't need that. But here she is again. "Just want to tell you a few of our house rules. First, no loud noise after ten. I get people up here who like to read, looking for a wireless vacation, so we don't have any Internet service."

That's no problem. He didn't bring a computer, and likes the idea of being away from all that.

"And no taking coffee in the china cups up to your room." Her smile offsets the stern words and she pats his shoulder.

"Absolutely not," he replies and hastens out the door.

Turning the corner onto Main Street, there's a phony feel to some of the buildings, a Disneyland aura he hadn't noticed on the carriage ride. He taps the big stones on the fence rail by the yacht dock. Hollow. When he rubs his hand on the wood rail, he detects plastic. Well, well.

At the park wall he's reassured that it is constructed of real concrete and stone. A line of fringe-topped carriages with matching horse teams stand on the street just as they had that day he'd met Ella. There are four men and two women drivers; one scrolling on her cell phone, blonde hair pouring down her shoulders, looks younger than twenty. Her pinto team matches perfectly, their brown and white patches creating a dairy cow look. He stares at her, thinking of Ella.

She looks up. "Interested in a tour today, sir?"

"Nah, no thanks." *Sir, my ass. Am I that old?*

Nick moves on quickly. A block down the street he stops to buy an ice cream, one of those jumbo sugar cones piled with two scoops of Mackinac Nutty Chunk Fudge Parfait. "Our most popular flavor," the perky clerk tells him. It dribbles down his chin as he walks past the shops. Under a green-and-pink-striped awning he watches a young man in a white apron rolling fudge on a marble slab. His elbows flap up and down like a marionette as he sculpts the creamy mixture into a flat rectangle. There's something wrong with this picture—the fudge is green. Poking his head in the door Nick asks, "What's that stuff you're making?"

"Pistachio mint fudge. Wanna try it?"

"No thanks." He's never developed a taste for molten plastic. Whatever happened to plain dark chocolate?

Strolling down Main Street, he passes a window display of T-shirts, snorting at a blue one that says, "With a body like this, who needs hair?" At a bike rental stand he picks out a twenty-one speed with a big basket, remembering how handy a basket was in his dockhand days. The teenager who adjusts the seat looks barely old enough to be out of middle school and cautions, "Stay off Main Street. It's way too busy." Peering closely at Nick he adds, "If you go anywhere off the road around the island, it's hilly. Not one flat inch on this rock. You up for that?"

"I can handle it. Thanks." Nick pedals off quickly just to prove it, nearly crashing into a couple swaying from side to side on a tandem. *Damn idiot fudgies. That police chief is right.* He turns on a narrow side street in pursuit of a pub. Bingo, he's in front of Buck's, a bar that was popular with the locals when he worked there. They wouldn't serve him in those days since he was underage, but all the minors would hook up with a 21- or 22-year-old friend and sneak sips from their drinks all night. Today the place looks much the same and is nearly deserted, a few hardcore drinkers perched on stools hang over the bar like wilted sunflowers. The bar used to smell of smoke, but with the ban on smoking, today only the stench of beer and mildew permeates the air, a slight improvement. On the overhead screen the Tigers are in the eighth inning, losing again.

The bartender, a short man with a brawny build and sandpapery jowls, throws a bar towel down in disgust. "Their bullpen is nothing but a bunch of losers." Looking at Nick he nods. "So what can I get you?"

"Jack and Coke." A bit early, but he needs fortitude. The bartender nods and turns to prepare the drink.

"Tigers now down by three at the top of the eighth," drones the television. The bartender shakes his head as he plunks Nick's drink down on the bar. "That's seven dollars."

Nick gulps: back home this would cost three dollars. As if reading his mind, the man says, "Island price. Cost of doing business here is ass-tronomical, if you get my drift."

"Do you sell water?"

"Two bucks."

"One bottle."

Swigging the rest of his drink—which tastes a bit diluted—Nick grabs the bottle of water and heads to the door. As the screen slams behind him he hears a jubilant announcer shout, "Home run for the Tigers!" Maybe his luck will change, too.

Back on his bike, fortified by the booze, Nick, the brave knight, is ready to face whatever lies ahead up at Cedar Bluff: Henry, a rejecting Ella, even a happily married one. He pedals toward the hill leading up to Ella's cottage, past rows of small white shops with flower boxes sprouting red geraniums and, in their windows, lilacs and lacey things instead of the ubiquitous T-shirts on Main Street.

Then he hits the first hill, an asphalt fist in his face. A wide carriage with a three-horse team hauling several dozen fudgies, crawls up the grade like a slug, the horses straining on their harnesses. The driver speaks into a microphone, "So a horse walks up to the bar and orders a drink. The bartender sets the drink in front of him and tells the horse, 'So, why the long face?'" Loud groans from the passengers.

Nick's heard the joke a hundred times. Can't these guys get some new material? He dismounts behind the carriage, glad the fudgies can't see him. Taking a hearty swig of water, he rubs his throbbing right knee. The hill is worse than he remembered, steeper than it was that day when visited Ella's house for the very first time.

What a shock that had been. It was several days after he'd met her at the park when she'd showed up at the dock to pick up groceries with a cart hitched to her bike.

"Is that a hotel?" Nick had asked, pointing to the words *Cedar Bluff* painted on the side of the cart.

"No, it's my house. My parents' house—or cottage, I should say. They sent me down to pick up a load of groceries coming on the ferry from St. Ignace."

"Let me help you," Nick had said. "I'm off work in five minutes." As he'd hoisted two boxes of groceries into her cart, he realized they wouldn't all fit.

"I'll make a second trip," said Ella.

"No need to. I can get that last box in my basket," said Nick. "Would that be OK?" His bike basket was huge, and reinforced with extra bars.

"Sure, if you don't mind. It's all uphill. The bluff," said Ella, nodding her head toward the west. Nick had biked along the bluffs, remembered they had the fancy houses, but couldn't picture her in one of them.

They pedaled in low gear up the steep hill leading out of the village. Although Ella had been pulling a good fifty pounds of extra weight, she never dismounted or stopped chatting, just kept up a steady prattle. "This one guy I had today, what a jerk. Asked me to take a picture of him and his ugly kids at least ten times, tipped me two bucks." At the top of the big hill they turned and biked up a small grade before plunging down a short incline. At the bottom, Ella signaled with her arm to turn into a paved drive lined by cedars that led to a massive white Victorian house with green trim and a tower. Nick looked at the house, then at Ella. "Here?" She nodded. He couldn't connect this girl—this carriage driver with flatulent horses who complained of two-buck tips—to this showy specimen of old architecture.

"Would you like to come in?" asked Ella. Nick hesitated. He felt out of his league; he knew she could handle carrying the groceries, but it would be rude not to offer to help. "Sure."

They entered the house through a back door into a small mudroom that connected to a large, homey kitchen. The wallpaper patterned a plump woman in a long skirt rolling out cookie dough while a cat played with a skein of yarn at her feet. Nick had an urge to grab a hunk of dough from her bowl. Through a door at one end of the kitchen, a butler's pantry and hallway led into a vast, dark-paneled dining room centerpieced by a long table. A wall of small windowpanes formed a sunroom on the south end of the house. Beyond that was the porch and a view of the lake; even from back in the kitchen, it was spectacular, each nook and cranny fed by the light of the sky.

With its high ceilings and carved wood ornamentation, the house loomed large and heavy on Nick, the way a crown must feel. His growing-up house was a one-story ranch with a big basement, built for Michigan winters and low heating bills, stuffed with bric-a-brac, walls covered with family photos and a big painting of the Parthenon, cluttered and comfy. This place felt more like a museum.

"This was my grandfather's house. He bought it from the original owner. My father inherited it. Back then these places didn't cost much." She sounded apologetic. "When I was little I called it a gazebo gone berserk."

"More like a gazebo on steroids. It's fantastic," said Nick, seeing Ella in a new light. She looked at home here, just as she'd also looked comfortable on the carriage down at the park, blending easily into both worlds. He didn't.

He set down the groceries. "Come on. I'll show you the view," said Ella. She led him to the front porch.

"Wow," was all Nick could muster. "Nice." Ella offered him a soda, and they sipped them on the front porch sitting on turquoise wicker chairs topped with flowery cushions. Although after 8:00 p.m., the sky was still filled with light. It was late June, less than a week past the summer solstice. Nick loved the long, light nights.

"You should see the sunset from our tower," said Ella. "Want to go up and watch it?" Nick had finished his soda and felt lost for words. "Some night, yeah, but I've got to get back downtown. Thanks, thanks for everything."

"Thank you for helping me with the groceries. Are you playing your guitar tonight?"

"No, kind of tired."

"Will you be dining at the park tomorrow?"

She wants to see me. "Yeah, I'll be eating a sandwich there."

"I'm getting a different team. They'll have hay—not beans—for breakfast."

And that's how the best summer of his life had begun.

Now he is back again, a middle-aged man pushing his bike up the hill, unable to grind away in the lowest gear in a seated position, let alone haul a load of groceries. His hands shake on the handlebars and he stops for another hit of water before resuming his plod up the nev-er-gets-easier hill.

4

A few hours after finishing her paint scraping duties, Ella's back on the porch, this time rearranging the wicker furniture, a habit she picked up from Mother, whose anger management program consisted of rearranging the furniture. When Ella and Sara heard the scraping of chairs and tables against the floor, they knew Mother was on a rampage and kept as far away from her as possible.

How she wishes Mother could be on a rampage today rather than sitting around a nursing home waiting for her leg to mend and pestering anyone who will listen to her to drive her to the ferry dock. "Get me to my island!" she screams whenever Ella calls. She should get down there today, but can't bear it. She hasn't even started working her way through the casket business paperwork and e-mails, and there's the letter-writing campaign to persuade the city council to impose water restrictions. Sliding a chair back a foot from the porch railing, she looks west at the Mackinac Bridge slicing a silver "M" across the horizon. It's turned into one dazzler of a day. Next she pulls the rocking chair a respectable but not unfriendly distance from the other chair, slightly to the left. Shaking the seat cushion, she sneezes as a cloud of dust rises from the fabric where a faded red geranium spreads across a sea of green leaves. The cottage is sliding from shabby chic to downright shabby, and the whole place is on her shoulders. Sara's off in Sri Lanka working on production of a shoe design—so she says. But Ella is always skeptical about her sister. Mother is fuming at the nursing home, and all the good handymen are tied up with other projects. If she could get Charlie to help out more . . . well, never mind. He's just a boy.

Fresh from a shower, her moist hair frizzes in a halo around her head. She's changed from her painting clothes to a pair of beige capris with a drawstring and a sky blue linen top, the front cutting a V down her scanty cleavage. On her cheeks she's applied a few strokes of blush, and the Chapstick on her lips creates the effect of youthful dewiness. As a reward to herself for all her hard work she's made a pitcher of iced tea with fresh lemons to savor while plunging into a new book on water policy.

As she turns toward the front door to fetch her sunglasses, she hears someone say, "Hey, Annie Oakley." It's Boon, the family's on-and-off handyman, walking across the yard toward her. A shock of hair hangs over his left eye, and his shirt is splotched with dried paint blobs. Once handsome in a dangerous, cowboy sort of way, Boon has been weathered by time. He'd once bragged that he could ride any horse and any woman on the island, but today it looks like he'd have difficulty even mounting a pony.

For years, Father had a verbal contract with Boon to open and close the cottage, paint and perform small jobs on the house. A self-taught carpenter and painter, he worked brilliantly—when he showed up. The problem was his extreme unreliability and frequent drinking. Now he's standing in the yard smiling up at her with a twisted grin. Ella sighs.

"You gouged that wood there," he says, eyeing the area on the steps where she'd been working.

"Just a nick."

"If you keep at it, there'll be nothing left of those steps. Why don't you let me do it?"

Ella slams the book shut. "I've been painting these steps for more than forty years and no one's complained." She wishes he'd just disappear.

"How 'bout up there? Looking pretty bad," he says, pointing to the second-story tower where the paint is peeling off the windows. It's her bedroom. "Too high even for a tomboy like you."

"I'm not quite a tomboy, Boon. I'm a forty-eight-year-old woman."

"Whatever you say, Annie Oakley."

"You looking for work?

"Yep."

"If I hire you, are you gonna blast another paint can all over the lawn?" Years ago, Father and Boon had a falling out when, midway through a job, Boon took a long liquid lunch downtown, returning to the Hollingsworth's late. Ella had been reading in the living room when she heard shouting followed by a loud thud outside. She ran to the porch to witness white paint splattered all across the lawn and on her mother's prized pink peonies, as if an army of seagulls had just released their dinner simultaneously on the flowerbed. It was no accident, as Boon claimed, so there went the Hollingsworth's' handyman. Mother begged Father to give him another chance, but Father wouldn't hear of it. Shortly after Father died Boon resumed occasional chores for Mother. They got along famously, but Ella didn't feel Boon worked very hard under Mother's lax eye.

Now he stands in the yard looking anything but contrite. "Sorry about that. Wish I'd never done that, but I'm still pissed off at your old man, rest in peace." He crosses himself. Ella hesitates. Making a deal with Boon could get as sticky as dancing in a tar pit, no matter what boundaries she establishes, but she's desperate. Not just that—she and Boon go way back. He'd showed some unexpected kindness by helping her with Captain, the family horse, after a runaway accident where she'd nearly gotten herself and Sara killed. Father insisted they euthanize the animal, and she was near hysterical when one of the dray guys said, "They're gonna send your horse to the glue factory." Even Mother sided with her on this, but Father was adamant. Then Boon intervened, showing up one day and took Captain. Later she found out he'd sold the horse for five hundred dollars to a family in the UP. The next year they bought Jed, now twenty-seven years old and living in their barn out back.

"How's your mother?" asks Boon.

"She's fussing up a storm to be back on her beloved island."

"Why don't you get her?

"Her leg's not healed yet. And you know she won't stay put."

"You should bring her up. Must be killing her to be off-island in August."

Ella clenches her teeth. One more do-gooder worried about Mother. "Yeah, well then you try to take care of her."

Boon stares at her, his eyes nearly buried under his sagging lids. "You got PMS today."

"What?"

"Pissy mare syndrome."

"Whoa right there, Boon." He's crossed a boundary, but Ella can't refrain from grinning. Boon surveys the porch steps again. "Why don't you let me do that, too? You never get it right."

"Oh yeah?"

"Yeah."

"It's a tradition."

"Your traditions will destroy this place. Hollingsworths—you're all wacko." He looks up at the windows. "So when can I start? Today?"

Ella looks longingly at her iced tea and book. "It'll have to wait." Boon cracks his knuckles. "How about tomorrow?"

"Okay, Annie Oakley. Tomorrow."

"Say, can you mow the lawn?"

"Don't do lawns, if that's what you call that mess of weeds." He shrugs, then disappears as quietly as he'd appeared.

Sighing, Ella plops back in her chair and opens her book. At last.

5

~~~~

Having conquered the big hill, Nick turns off the busy road onto a smaller, and by island standards, flat one. Looking down at his shirt, now drenched in sweat, he scowls. *What a fine presentation I'll make, stinking and wet. Should have brought a towel or another shirt.* Patting his pockets, he extracts a comb and a tissue. Sweat from his hair stings his eyes. It'll have to do.

Two women in jodhpurs and riding helmets pass him on the left, moving up and down in the stirrups. He knows there's a name for that movement—Ella had told him—but he's forgotten. He would never attempt saddling a horse without a big pommel on the saddle to grab hold of, unlike this fancy English stuff. Those gals must have amazing thigh muscles. Their horses' brown coats glisten above solid girths, in much better shape than those scrawny wrecks they rent out downtown. Certainly these must be private horses, possibly neighbors of Ella. He follows them along the road, hoping they will lead him toward her house, but they veer off onto a bridle path into the woods.

Ahead he sees a wood-shingled roof, then a large white barn. Something familiar about it. The road splits, and he keeps right. Within a few yards he sees a smaller gravel road bearing left. Excitement ripples through him—this is the back road to Cedar Bluff. He follows it past a few houses veiled by tall cedar hedges. He doesn't recall the hedges, but things can grow mighty tall in three decades, even this far north. Moving slowly, straining his head for a closer look at the dwellings, he hopes he doesn't arouse suspicion. The bluffers are leery of fudgies and guard their privacy.

Better to approach the homes from the front road where there's a chance a sign will be posted. Turning his bike around, Nick retraces his course back to the paved road, makes a sharp right and proceeds. From the front the houses look completely different. The first, a white Gothic with loads of gingerbread trim, has a small sign that says

"Heron Cottage." Two doors down is "West Winds," proclaimed in a flowery sign with elegant script, then a massive, white-towered place with no sign. A hedge on its east side obscures the next house, a blue one with white trim. "They must have painted it." Nick looks up and gasps as he reads "Cedar Bluff" in a curly font swinging above the porch steps. Thinking back on the white house he realizes it's now painted blue. He has arrived.

A family walks by him staring at the houses, the mother pushing a stroller with two children walking like ducklings behind her, another duckling bulging inside the woman's protruding abdomen. "I want to live in that tower like a princess," says a small girl with a red bow slipping down her ponytail. On the porch, shadowed by its steep roof and wooden bric-a-brac, he spots wicker furniture and flower boxes brimming with geraniums. His pulse quickens as he realizes there's someone sitting on a chair partly hidden by a post and the flowers. *Oh shit.* It's a woman; that he can tell, with a glint of silver in her shoulder-length hair, long legs stretched out before her.

As if feeling his eyes on her, the woman looks up for a moment. Nick turns his head and pushes his bike forward. When certain he's out of her sight he stops, takes out the tissue, wiping his forehead and arms, and running a comb through his hair, its teeth sticking in the wet strands. His legs are shaking. Maybe the drink was a bad idea.

He's mulled over several strategies on how to approach her. Should he stroll past her place in the hope she'll be sitting on the porch— which now it appears she is, or simply knock on the door? Nothing wrong with that. It must look unplanned, certainly not the sole reason he's come back here, that yes, he is still deeply in love with her.

He practices a few lines, hoping the tourists around him won't hear. "My God, is that you, Ella? I just happened to be—" No, that won't do. "I was on the island and thought I'd see if the old Hollingsworth place was still here." Not quite. "Is that you, Ella? It's Nick, Nick Pappas. Remember me? I'm up here doing a little research, thought I'd see if your family still had this place." A middle-aged couple holding hands walk past and the woman shoots him a puzzled glance. Then he has a new idea. Puffing up his chest and taking one last swipe at his brow with the back of his hand, Nick whips his bike around and soldiers up to Ella's gate.

***

As Ella reads on the porch, a twinge of pain shoots down her right thigh through her sciatic nerve, and there's aching in her wrists, souvenirs from the morning's paint scraping. She looks out at the Straits; a freighter with the white lettering SS *Sheldon* on its side pushes through the narrow passage between Mackinac and Round Island, its rusty bow like a robin's breast. The captain greets the island with two short blasts on the horn. What a beauty of a day, the water a blue-sequined gown reflecting the sun on each ripple. She remembers seeing Grandmother in this chair gazing at the lake for hours. "This view is all I need," she'd once told Ella.

At the time it made no sense to Ella, who'd replied, "Don't be silly. You can't eat or breathe a view. You need food and air." But now she understands. Food and air could sustain one's body, this view, one's soul.

Getting back to her book, she flips the page to a new chapter about the contorted history of getting all the states and provinces surrounding the Great Lakes to sign a compact to save their hydrologic treasure. It's a complex story, and she wonders if the final shaky agreement can endure. Several new governors have already questioned it, and rumblings from drought-hit states about taking water from the Great Lakes have rippled through Congress. Seems someone understands the wealth of its water.

On the road out front a few tourists stroll by, ogling the house. With her nose in her book, Ella ignores them. A man walks by slowly pushing a bike, staring at her. He walks past, and she resumes reading. A few minutes later there he is again, this time at her front gate. She looks up. *Snoopy fudgie, can't get a moment of peace.* About six feet tall, with a crop of hair as thick as those found on a US senator, he's an attractive man, but way too intrusive.

"Ex-cues-a-moi!" he calls with a botched French accent.

"May I help you?" she asks icily. He should know better; tourists aren't supposed to do this.

"Madame, is it true that bridge swings over to the island at night?" he asks, a big grin on his face. Ella sets down her book, staring. There's something familiar about his face, his voice. "Remember me?" he asks, dropping the accent.

Could it be? Oh my God. "Nick?" She stands up quickly and walks to the top of the steps, patting down her hair.

"The one and only, my lady," he says with a bow.

"Well, come on up for goodness sakes!" She descends the steps as Nick opens the gate and moves up the stone walkway, his stride slightly gimpy, like a horse with a bad shoe. They stand face to face, Ella on the bottom step about six inches above him.

"Ella." He looks directly at her, studying her face and she backs away, suddenly conscious of her age lines. "Your eyes," he whispers.

"My eyes?"

"Bluer than Lake Michigan."

"Nick Pappas," she says, remembering his last name as a jolt of memories open in her mind and with them, a ripple of delight. Though crinkled around the edges, his eyes that now hold her gaze are the same amber brown, warm and deep, unlike the steely blue of the Hollingsworth clan. His skin is a coppery hue, much darker than the lobster red shade Kevin, her ex, would turn every summer. Nick's smile is immense; a little startling, this burst of enthusiasm, and his wavy gray hair reminds her of the silver platter on the dining room credenza. He opens his arms Papa Bear-wide to hug her. A trace of perspiration emotes from his shirt and he's breathing hard. Nick's embrace is so hearty her breasts press into his chest, and for one moment she allows him to hold her before pushing away, summoning up a half-century of WASP manners and says, "It's so good to see you. Come on up." She directs him up the steps, points to a rocker and says, "Have a seat." Once they're both seated facing one another, Ella maintains her shield of good manners. "So, what brings you here?" She hopes he doesn't notice her knees trembling.

"Oh, had to do a little research for a history project. That, and a bout of *Mackinacitis*. Haven't been back to the rock in thirty years."

"You're kidding!" She can't imagine missing even one summer.

"No. Dead serious." He holds her look. "I've missed it."

Her mind races to recall the last time they were together, and whatever happened to pull them apart. Something gnaws at her, but she can't grasp it. She runs her fingers through her toweled-off hair, remembering her protest to Beth. *Not vain, right?* At least she'd rubbed some blush on her cheeks and a smudge of eyeliner.

"How about a toast?" says Nick, raising a water bottle in his right hand.

"Wait, let me pour you a glass of iced tea."

"Whatcha got in there?" he asks, eyeing the pitcher.

"Tea with a slice of lemon."

"Come on, Ella, I betcha put something stronger in there." He winks.

Oh God, not a drinking problem. "It's only two o'clock. A bit early for booze."

Nick laughs. "Is this the same Ella who pilfered her daddy's scotch and drank it on outings with me? That's okay, I'll just stick with my straight stuff," he says, raising his water bottle again. "To old friends."

Ella lifts her glass. "To old friends."

"And may I add happy birthday?"

She takes a sip of tea, jiggling the ice cubes. "You remember my birthday?"

"Not the exact date, but as I recall it's in July. And you're a spring chicken."

"Well, well. I wouldn't consider forty-eight a spring chicken," she says, studying her glass. "Hmm. This is better than that stuff you're drinking."

"Better than water?"

Ella clucks. "Not just any water. God knows where that stuff in your bottle came from. Mackinac tap water is some of the cleanest, purest on the planet. And that plastic bottle isn't very eco-friendly," she says, shaking her head and moving toward him. "Here, give me that," she says, plucking the bottle from his hand.

"Hey, what are you doing?" Nick asks as she strides toward the porch railing, loosening the cap. Ella pours the water over the porch rails into Mother's flowerbed. Nick sits up straight, mouth open. "You just dumped out my water!"

"Don't worry. I'll refill it with some decent water from the kitchen tap before you go."

"Christ, you'd think I'd robbed a bank. It's about 80 degrees and that hill was steep. Not like I'm some dock porter."

Ella pivots toward her chair so quickly she nearly trips. Then she lowers herself to the rocker, crosses her legs, the left one on top, pointing and flexing her toes beneath the straps of her leather sandals. What's gotten into her? This is no way to greet an old friend; but something about his dropping in like this has scattered her equilibrium. Glancing at Nick's legs, she has a clear view of his muscled calves—Roman statue legs, even better than her neighbor Gary's—which brings a tingling to her nipples, embers of sexual energy that never have been wholly extinguished. Her eyes follow the line of his leg upward to his belly, which pushes against the bottom buttons of his orange cotton shirt. Many men her age have that four-months-pregnant look, and he's no exception. But overall he's weathered well. Very well. She pours a glass of tea and hands it to him. "Try this."

Nick's eyes twinkle as he slaps his thigh. "Well, I didn't come all the way up that damn hill to pick a quarrel with you." He sits back in his chair and takes a swig of tea, smiling. Out on the lake the Mackinac Bridge flashes in the sun. "Now there's a million-dollar view if I ever saw one," he says. Turning back to her he leans forward, lowering his voice. "And you, Ella, you look like a million dollars." She rubs her nose vigorously, twirling a lock of hair with her other hand. "Boy, it feels great to be sitting on this porch with you again. Like old times."

"And you, you're looking—good. Not many men make it to fifty with all that hair. So, where are you staying?"

"The Maples, down on the east end."

Ella knows the place. Probably the cheapest rate on the island; a firetrap, too. She should invite him to stay here, or at least for dinner, but that would be awkward. She needs to sort things out. And then there's Charlie. "Yes, I know it. And this research project?"

"Oh, I'm uh, trying to gather more information on some little known aspects of the fur trading business."

"And you're staying how long?"

"Just two days. I leave Monday."

"We'll have to have you up for a meal." It's the polite thing to do, but Charlie will probably be none too pleased. In her best Miss Manners voice she asks, "Well, goodness, where do we begin? Thirty years is a bit of broad territory."

Nick smiles. "Let's just say I'm a lot like Zorba."

"Zorba?"

"You know, *Zorba the Greek*, Anthony Quinn in the old movie:

wife, children, house, the full catastrophe—except I'm divorced and renting." He leans back and chuckles.

A warning light with the word "rebound" flashes in Ella's mind. So that's why he's come up here. "How many kids?" "Just one, a daughter, Melina. Not really a kid—she'll be twenty-one this September." He stands up, fumbles in his back pocket, finally extracting a wallet. "My magnum opus. The fruit of my loins." Ella flinches at his words; she hasn't managed to bear fruit. He passes her the wallet, opened to a photo of a young woman who looks about seventeen or eighteen, a typical senior shot: too perfect, an air-brushed picture with an unnaturally sexy pose, one hand on her knee, the other on her hip, leaning forward. The girl has thick, light-brown hair outlining a heart-shaped face and gorgeous skin. Her eyes are like Nick's, deep pools that draw you to them. She's not pretty-pretty, but quite attractive.

"She's lovely, Nick." Carefully, she hands back the wallet.

"Outside and inside, too." He places his hand on his heart, gazing tenderly at the picture before closing the wallet. "Putting her right next to my AARP card." Leaning back in the chair, he takes another sip of tea. "I'm still up on the big lake, but over in Minnesota. Can't seem to get away from Gitchigumi."

"And what do you do up there?"

"Teaching, been doing it for years."

"History?"

"Yep."

"Which university are you at?"

Nick's eyebrows rise. "University? Thanks for the promotion, but I teach the youth of our nation—high school."

"High school?"

"Yep."

"But you were going for a PhD in history." It's all coming back to her. His interest in history was the main reason he'd chosen to work here, he was enamored with the island's historic ambiance. Unable to get a job at the fort, he'd settled for a dockhand job. She notices his left hand tighten on the chair arm.

"Oh, I got my PhD all right, if you mean Pretty Handsome Dude. But no, I'm actually an ABD—All But Dissertation dude. I went through the whole program, started to write my dissertation, never finished. I had some great ideas but—" He raises his shoulders and offers two empty hands. "Had to make a living, and when I started teaching I found I had some talent for it, so I just stayed with it. And then other things happened. Life."

"Oh." Ella pushes back a strand of hair, swirls her glass. She suspects by life he means love and marriage and kids. On the lake, with the mist gone, the air is crystal-clear, the view sharpened. "That's too bad. You were so passionate about it. But high school? How do you put up with those kids?"

"Actually, most of them are fine. Now as for their parents . . ."

Ella snaps her left fingers. "I remember—you were studying the Voyageurs."

Nick begins humming, then singing. *Dans le bateau, avec les hommes du bois.* His voice, once a sexy, modulated baritone, sounds low and gravelly.

"Les voyageurs."

"Mais oui, madame. The voyageurs, the missionaries, the whole French-Indian trading era." There is a long pause. "Ella, remember that night at Nicolet's Watch Tower?" He's watching her intently, rocking his chair toward her. She scoots hers back a few inches. "Nick-o-lay."

Oh yes, she remembers: the Watchtower, a small marker atop an easterly bluff erected in honor of the French missionary Jean Nicolet, the first white man to slip through the waters of Lake Huron, had once served as a love nest for her and Nick. "If they were so celibate, why do they call it the missionary position?" Ella had joked. She and Nick had favored that position one night, and after that she nicknamed him Nickolay.

That long-ago evening had begun with a starry sky that exploded into a full light show of the Aurora Borealis. They had stripped naked at that monument, then, in the little space between the bluff's edge and the marker, Nick had carefully placed his T-shirt and shorts on the ground and eased her gently down on them. As they made love, Nick touched different points on her body, kissing each, one by one. Finally they lay side by side, staring at the Northern Lights, pulsating shafts burning across the sky for hours.

But at this moment she's looking not at the heavens, but straight ahead, rattled by the truth that she and this man—a near stranger now—were once that close. Nickolay. He's no longer that boy beneath the shimmery sky; blue estuaries of veins rise on his hands, his neck is ringed with creases and he's bushed from the climb to her house. This is a different man, a worn-down one. His very presence reminds her that she is no longer a girl filled with chutzpah, expectation, and hope. All that has vanished, and with it, some essential part of herself.

"Remember? Yes, yes, it's hard to forget when you get about a hundred mosquito bites, half of them on your uh, southern half," she says. Such a bitchy response, but he's the one who started it, the one who marched right up here on the porch and opened a page in an old diary of her life.

Nick's brown eyes flash for a moment and his shoulders slump. "I was hoping you'd have a different memory."

"Well I don't." Ella stands up and strides across the porch, resting her hips on the white railing, facing him. She crosses her arms and studies his face. There's something fishy about him, something irregular, like a two-tuned fork.

"Why are you acting this way?" he asks, hurt in his eyes.

"What way? I'm simply stating a truth. Have you ever had mosquito bites all over *your* ass?" She can't refrain. She didn't ask him to come up here, to dredge up old memories.

6

W ho is this woman anyway, scolding him like some elderly aunt, an echo of her old self, his girl. *We're good animals*, she used to say, quoting that old running guru George Sheehan. At this moment she's behaving like a snappy little Chihuahua. Nick leans down and picks up his empty water bottle. Speaking very quietly he says, "I think I'd better go now. And I'll take this offensive container with me." Their eyes lock for a moment before Ella takes a step toward him, her hand extended. "Give me that bottle, please." He relinquishes it, touching her hand lightly.

"I'll be right back," she says, marching into the house. Maybe she'll fill it with poison, thus decisively ending this attempted liaison. Still, her hand felt silky and warm, and standing close he caught a whiff of fresh-pressed linen and pine.

Peering through the screen door listening to the *slap-slap* of her sandals retreat into the back of the house, an ache builds in the pit of his belly. He misses her already. That first good look at her today had startled him—the resemblance to her mother, and then the gap between the Ella he'd known to this one. Still lovely, long-limbed with flowing hair, but the girlishness gone, the innocence replaced with something harder. But he'd instantly readjusted the sight, like fuzzing up the binocular setting. It was the soft part of his heart that did the readjusting, that part that had always loved her.

A few minutes pass before she returns wearing a pom-pom girl smile, the kind he puts on when his students are driving him bonkers but he doesn't want to let on that they've hooked him; instead saying something like, "How can I help this class stay on task?" What he'd like to say to Ella is, "How can I help make you not such a totally up-tight little bitch?"

As she passes him the water bottle, he notices her trembling hand. "Oh for the love of God, Nick, please sit down. I don't know what's gotten into me."

A simple I'm sorry would be nice.

Ella plops into the center of a red poppy on the flowered cushion at the end of the sofa and sighs. "It's been a rough summer. Mother broke her leg four weeks ago and she's over on the mainland in a nursing home, hammering me and anyone who will listen to come back here. I can't put her off much longer. Then there's the family business, which has landed in my lap. Casket sales are way down since the Great Recession, and I'm no fan of unnatural burials anyway. And this house, a spectacular pain in the ass—guess who's in charge of the place?" She jabs her forefinger firmly into her chest. "Me. I bet you're thinking that sounds like caviar kvetching, but believe me, such blessings are not without burdens."

Nick presses his palms together in prayer. "God, please give me such burdens." Ella sticks her tongue out at him. "Don't you have help?"

"Getting good help up here is no easy feat. Even the one-percenters have to put up with certain—well, inconveniences—and we're certainly not in that tax bracket."

He seizes the opportunity to ask his burning question. "No husband or significant other?" That ring on the third finger of her left hand could be a wedding ring or one of those artsy things. Ella rarely wore jewelry, but he remembered a turtle of silver and agate she used to wear on a silver chain around her neck. Used to clunk him on the neck when she was on top.

"Not anymore."

"Oh." That sounds like divorced, but she could be widowed.

"And Sara, my sister—you remember her, right?—is off in South Asia, Sri Lanka, allegedly on business. So I have her kid to look after now. On top of that, since Father passed away two years ago, all the cottage issues have fallen in my lap. Caring for a one-hundred-twenty-one-year-old place is a full-time job. Not to mention Mother—not an easy task, if you remember her."

He does; how could he forget? Audrey had been up to plenty of mischief that summer. And he sees threads of Audrey running through Ella, the way she holds her head proudly but averts his glance, how she says "*Well, well,*" so crisply. "Sure do. Your dad wasn't around much, and I always felt he wished I'd disappear. By the way, why's his voice on your answering machine?"

"You called? I thought you—"

Uh-oh. "This morning, before I came up. Didn't leave a message though."

"How odd."

"What happened to him?"

"A stroke, then another and another. He was just eighty-one—I know that sounds like a ripe old age, but he was so immensely healthy. We thought he'd make it to ninety-something." She pauses. "We can't bear to take his voice off the message, and we're not the only family doing it. The Hathaways two doors up have their dad's voice on the answering machine too, and some folks over on the backside."

"My dad died twelve years ago, he was only sixty-seven." He shakes his head, looks down at his hands. Even now the wound feels raw.

"I'm so sorry." She reaches across the side table and rests her fingertips briefly on his arm. Nick leans down and adjusts a strap on his sandal, hoping she won't ask about the circumstances. He still can't discuss it without blubbering. In a casual tone he asks, "So you're here with your sister's kid?"

"Yes, Charlie, Sara's son, the only remnant of the Hollingsworth genes. The world can thank us for that. He comes every summer. One of the only teenagers I can put up with, unlike you, Mr. High School teacher."

Wonder if she lets the kid drink water from a plastic bottle.

"I don't have any kids." He'd figured that out already, yes ma'am. Is she infertile or was the guy? Maybe they chose not to have children. "I'm taking Charlie over to Round Island tomorrow. Perhaps you'd like to join us."

Round Island? Nick sits up straighter, remembering the day he and Ella sailed on her family's little Sunfish with its diaper-sized sail to a harbor at Round Island, a small undeveloped isle less than a quarter-mile from Mackinac. They had run around the beach naked that day. Nick blurts out, "Round Island, land of the apes."

"Apes?" asks Ella, breaking into a smile and jumping up on her chair and pulling herself taller. With curled fists she beats her chest and whoops: "*Ah Eeeee Ahh!*"

The chair begins to tip and Nick takes her hand to steady her. They stand looking in one another's eyes, laughing for a moment. The spell is broken by the pounding of energetic feet as a teenage boy bounds up the porch stairs, two at a time. When the boy notices them he halts and stares. Then Ella is all over the kid, hugging him, laughing. Her eyes brighten two notches. "This is my nephew. Charlie. Charlie, this is Nick, an old friend." Shaking hands, the boy looks hard at Nick. His hand feels soft, his grip light, unenthusiastic, a fish handshake. His eyes are Ella's piercing light blue. Charlie's built thick and a little porky, big for his age; the skinny Hollingsworth genes have skipped a generation. He wears the standard teen summer uniform: baggy khaki shorts, T-shirt, and grimy flip-flops. Nick pegs him as bright, a little geeky, a kid teachers love having in their classes but who are marginalized by the popular kids. But there's an angriness about him, and he sure doesn't seem happy about having Nick in his territory.

"Nick's one of you," says Ella. "A history geek. Teaches it, too."

"Cool." Charlie averts Nick's eyes before plopping in the rocker next to Ella and kicking off his flip-flops. The boy's toes are filthy.

"Charlie was the top history student at his middle school. Won an essay contest writing about the economic issues in the slave states during the Civil War." Ella sprouts the tone of a proud parent.

"There wasn't much competition," says Charlie. He glances at Nick, turns to Ella. "So, are we still going tomorrow?"

"Yes. I've invited Nick along. Be nice to have an expert with us."

The scowl passing over Charlie's face must surely be evident to Ella, but she races on. "Right, Charlie?"

The kid shrugs. "Why were you making that ape call?"

"For fun," says Ella, turning toward Nick.

"That was weird," says Charlie. "Can we take Benjamin?"

"Sure, but his parents will probably want me to sign a release form." She turns to Nick. "Helicopter parents, always hovering over him." Nick is well aware of this type, especially back at his former school in Wisconsin with the AP kids.

"I doubt you'd have room for me in that little boat, especially with another kid," says Nick. He'd hated Ella's tiny sailboat—more like a surfboard with a sail. It used to scare the shit out of him.

"We dumped that boat years ago," says Ella. "It took in so much water it turned into a sponge and sank right off the shore, remember that, Charlie? Your mom was furious at me, said I'd almost drowned you. We've got a nice little whaler with a good motor. You have nothing to fear."

Despite spending most of his life next to Lake Superior, Nick dreads being out on the Great Lakes when the wind kicks up. Something about the wide endlessness of it; what his father had told him when he was six: "Son, Big Daddy never gives up his dead (Papa had nicknamed each lake: Lake Superior was Big Daddy). If you drown you'll sink to the bottom and Mama will spend the rest of her life wondering where you went." Cold comfort for a six-year-old.

"Hey, man, Aunt Ella's the best. She's been going to Round Island all her life and she's an old broad," says Charlie. Ella glares at him; Nick can't refrain from smiling.

"OK. I'm in." Hell, he feels like he's won the lottery, even with the dreaded boat trip.

"What do you know about the 1840s?" asks Charlie, turning to Nick, a challenge in his tone. Nick rolls the words around in his mind, seeing a history text scroll up in front of him. "It was a pretty rough time. Andrew Jackson was president, nullification, Trail of Tears . . ."

"Hear anything about cholera back then?"

"Cholera? Sure, it was a huge problem." Nick's punting, can't remember much about the disease.

"I could use your expertise," says Charlie. "For my project." Ella strums her fingers on the tray table.

"What kind of project?"

"You'll see. Tomorrow." Charlie stands up and turns to Nick. "Nice to meet you." He shakes his hand with a firmness now transcending that of a fish, then walks into the house, letting the screen door slam behind him.

Ella's eyes sparkle. "I think he's beginning to warm up to you."

"If that's warm, I'd hate to see cold." The way to Ella's heart is through her nephew. He can play that game, but it won't be easy with a kid like Charlie. That and a bad feeling he has about this so-called *project*. What's the kid up to?

"Please, don't tell him any more about our Round Island adventures. He's a little paranoid about men." Nick wonders what she means. "It's a long story, but suffice it to say, his father screwed him over."

"Mum's the word, but you'll have to suppress those primal cries." With this Nick beats his chest and lets loose an ape call, deep and resonant.

Ella stands up and puts her finger over her mouth. "Shh."

Nick laughs. "The neighbors will be talking for days. Listen, can I take you out to dinner? You and Charlie?" He has to include the kid, though he has a hunch Charlie will turn down the invite. As for Ella, she seems more relaxed and friendly.

"I'd love to go," she says, her smile contradicting the sudden coolness of her eyes. "That's kind of you, but it's just been a . . . well, odd day. I need a little time with Charlie, to get things organized for tomorrow. I haven't even checked my e-mail and I've got a few messages to write. Not to mention a pile of bills to pay. I hope you understand."

Yes, I understand rejection quite well.

"I've got to call Mother, pick up some paint, produce, feed Jed . . ."

"Jed?"

"Jed. Our horse. Jedi Knight."

"May the force be with you."

Ella's eyes soften. After a long pause she says, "Before you go, would you like to see the house?"

Now that's a rhetorical question. Nick eagerly follows Ella through the front door. She leads him into the foyer with its wood-paneled walls and ceiling, a huge oriental rug spread over a tessellated parquet floor, and a curved-glass oak secretary against the wall. Nick shuts his eyes to adjust to the darkness. The air is redolent with old house odors: musk and varnish, the fusty carpet, a lemony trace of furniture polish. This has not changed. He remembers the carved finial atop the bottom post of the staircase, like a polished artichoke, how he and Ella climbed these stairs on their way to the tower where they'd sit for hours talking, and once, when her family was gone, making love. Nick peers up the stairs. "I'll never forget the view from your tower." His memory isn't so much the expanse of shining water, but Ella's creamy skin, her eagerness to get him inside her.

"I'd take you up there but we've closed it off since the roof is leaking and the steps are unsafe." She sighs. "Someone's coming to fix it this week, so they say." He trails her like a puppy as Ella moves brisk-ly, announcing each room in a docent's voice; "The parlor, the din-ing room," treating him like a tourist, as if he'd never set eyes on the place. The cavernous living room is filled with uncomfortable Vic-torian furniture—*bet I'd break that little velvet parlor chair*—and in the dining room a long cherry table, its polished top gleaming in a dust-mote-filled ray of sun; a marble-topped credenza, a tea cart and a crystal-filled vitrine feels formal and cold. He remembers his first visit here, how the rooms felt like vaults, and his little horse-driving gal so at home in them, one of the bluff tribe.

A hallway at the rear of the dining room leads to a pantry and the kitchen, where Nick finally feels at home. With its microwave, dish-washer, and hundred-year-old beadboard walls, the room is a study in anachronisms. The floor, faux-red brick seventies linoleum, the coun-tertops with aluminum edging and a beige Formica sprinkled with a cylindrical design that looks like UFOs. Everything feels uneven, like walking on a boat at sea. One wall is papered with the round cook-ie-baking woman and sleeping cat.

"You still have that wallpaper. It always gave me a craving for cook-ies," says Nick, patting his belly. "I mean, more than usual."

"Mother calls it visual comfort food. It goes back to the days when Grandma was the queen here. She picked it out. It's on my to-do list to rip down."

"Aw, don't do that."

"Not to worry. I probably won't get around to it for a few years—not with all the new projects like the tower popping up all the time. We live in fear of our next cottage Armageddon. Last summer it was the floor in the downstairs bathroom—completely rotted out. A house guest said she got seasick sitting on the toilet. We were so used to it we didn't notice. Then the water heater conked out. I was taking a shower and felt like I was in the lake in December. Charlie thinks the porch is starting to go. Our big project is a new roof next summer."

"How much will that cost?"

"Well, the last bid was $50,000. It'll probably go up by the time we get to it."

Nick whistles. That's more than two-thirds his salary. "Jesus. Ever think about selling the place?"

Ella pivots around so quickly Nick has to take a step back. Her face is flushed. "Of course, but every time I think about it, well, it's like heresy. You're being much too logical. This place is all about emotion. Grandpa called it the gathering place, said it would keep the family together."

Nick's only experience with inherited property was his grandmother's farm in Greece that pulled the family apart. Mama and one of her sister's still don't speak to one another. Mama inherited part of Grandmother's land, then turned right around and sold it, thank God. Since the country's economy tanked, a farm in Greece was about as valuable as a condo in Flint.

"Has it?" he asks.

"In our own crazy way, yes. I mean, we're all still coming up here, right?"

Nick shrugs.

"Look, it's a constant love-hate relationship with this old place. Sometimes, when I'm on the porch and a group of fudgies stand out there gawking at it, I want to shout, 'Go home and enjoy your life! Don't be a cottage slave! Buy a timeshare!' They have no idea what it takes to maintain these homes, with or without money." Ella brushes a strand of hair away from her forehead and clears her throat. "Everyone on these bluffs is a little nutty. When you have a Mackinac house you want to be here, not there, wherever *there* is. You have a foot in two worlds, but your heart's always on this old rock. Your emotional home."

"You mean the Mackinac of the eight weeks of summer."

"It's gorgeous in the fall."

"Sometimes. And November, December, January, and the rest of the months till June?" Having lived most of his life in the Upper Peninsula, Nick knows better. April still brought snow, trees didn't bud until Memorial Day weekend, streets were slick with sleet on Halloween.

"I get your point, but it's not a rational thought process."

"Sounds complicated."

"Tell me about it. Cedar Bluff is our troubled asset. Can't sell it anyway. Father followed Grandpa's example, made an airtight will that prohibits us from selling it as long as Mother's alive. Two alpha males trying to call the shots beyond the grave—attempted permanence."

"Like half the people in our history books."

There's a long pause before Ella turns to the sink and fills a glass with water. Standing there watching the liquid spill from the faucet, she looks tired and smaller. Nick moves a step forward, so close he can feel the warmth of her body. He aches to put his arms around her.

She turns around with the glass in her hand. "Want some?" she asks.

Nick nods and takes the glass. He swigs it down. "Ah, the pure water of Mackinac."

"Listen, I'm sorry to burden you with my cottage woes. I'll walk you back out." Now she's all starched-apron manners, private and distant. Nick would enjoy being burdened for hours more, but it ain't going to happen today.

As they pass through the living room, Nick notices a black-and-white photo on a side table with Ella wearing a formal pantsuit, pure white, holding a bouquet of flowers. A horse stands behind her, nuzzling her neck. She looks radiant, so young. Nick pauses. "What a great picture. But why are you wearing a white pantsuit at a horse show? Isn't that a bit dangerous, getting it all dirty, I mean."

Ella laughs. "A horse show, huh? Not quite. That was my wedding reception."

"Wedding? Then why were you wearing pants? And where's the guy, your . . . husband?" He struggles with that last word.

"Kevin. That's his name. By the way, Kevin is a synonym for—*excusez-moi*–asshole. He was there all right, but I cut him out of the photo."

"You? A Mackinac bride? It goes against your grain." They used to poke fun at the brides on the island. "Here comes the bride," Nick would hum when they spotted a bride with her groom riding in a white patent-leather carriage that a local livery provided for weddings at through-the-ceiling prices. Hundreds of Midwestern girls fulfilled their bridal a/k/a Disney movie fantasies on the island. But what amused Nick and Ella was watching the brides navigate the horse manure, hoisting up their dresses, their satin shoes stained brown at the toes. "Don't tell me you rode around on display in a buggy?" says Nick.

"Now don't sell me short. I drove my wedding carriage. Mother was adamantly opposed to it—she'd already thrown a fit about the pantsuit—but I won out. I had to concede not to harness the horse. Father ended up doing that job. When he walked into the reception he had a little mud on his tuxedo and a piece of straw in his hair. Mother was horrified."

Tickled by the idea of Ella driving her bridal carriage, Nick imagines her setting down the reins and strutting up to the reception. How different from Katie, buried in a sea of lace, who'd insisted on a limo to take them from the church to the reception hall less than a mile away. To Nick it was silly and extravagant.

"It was quite an event. My parents stole the show dancing like Fred Astaire and Ginger Rogers. Kevin and I barely made it through a botched box step, and Sara passed out at the reception after throwing up all over her dress. God knows how much she drank. Later I found out that Kevin was hitting on one of my bridesmaids. Our wedding day, it turned out, was the beginning of the end. It just took me five long years to figure it out." Nick looks from the photo to Ella, comparing the two. The creases from the edge of her nose to her mouth are new, and that steeliness in her eyes.

"I'm sorry. Divorce is—well, nasty," he says.

"Sometimes it's a blessing." Her eyelashes flutter in a series of blinks as she slaps her hands back and forth in a dismissive manner. "Well, well. Enough of that," she says, leading the way back to the foyer, sandals flapping with each step.

All that pure water has run to his bladder and he can't hold it much longer. "May I use your bathroom?" he asks.

"Of course. Do you remember it's through there?" she says, pointing to a door beneath the stairs. In the bathroom a sign on the toilet tank directs the user to push the handle right for pee, left for poo. When he finishes, Nick dutifully pushes it right, truncating the water flow in mid-flush. He peers dubiously into the toilet, but sure enough, everything has swirled down the pipes.

"What's up with that toilet?" he asks, exiting the bathroom, where Ella stands in the foyer next to the staircase.

"Just doing our part to conserve water."

"But you're sitting in the middle of the Great Lakes—no shortages here."

"That's one of the problems—complacency. That, and every place with drought eyeing our lakes."

"Whatever you say."

"I've formed a group, Save our Water Now, SOWN for short," she says. "Haven't had any time for it recently, not with all this."

"Well, you've got to set priorities."

Ella stops at a door in the foyer. "Do you remember our skeleton in the closet—the real one?" Before he can reply, she opens a closet door where a full-sized human skeleton, its yellowed bones rattling, hangs on a hook. Nick jumps back.

"This was Grandpa's prank. Used it to tease people back at his company.

"Look here," she says, taking down a wreath hanging above the skeleton. As Nick examines it he realizes it's made from human hair. He looks at the skeleton. "His?"

"Hers. It's a female, you can tell by the pelvis. We call her Fanny. But this hair is an authentic piece from the 1890s. One of Grandpa's enthusiasms, collecting odd Victorian pieces." A shudder creeps over Nick as she shuts the closet. Not until he passes through the front door back into the sunlight, the glimmering sweep of the lake and the smell of freshly-cut grass, does he feel warm again.

On the porch Ella turns to him, extending her right hand like a cocked gun. "It's been so nice to see you again. Such a surprise." So this is dismissal time.

Nick reaches to squeeze her shoulder with his left hand, feeling ripples of tension coursing up her arm.

"Tomorrow at the marina," he says.

"Slip number eleven. Bring a windbreaker. Wear those sandals." She points to his feet.

"You sure you want me along?"

"Of course."

"And Charlie?"

"He'll warm up to you."

And you? "Au revoir, madame," he says with a slight bow. At the gate he glances back where she stands by the door, watching him. He waves as she disappears into the house with its human-hair wreathes and cookie-baking wallpaper, its dark edges and bright flashes of beauty.

7

After Nick leaves, Ella races to the pantry where she's stashed a box of chocolate-covered raisins. Popping a handful in her mouth, she sits down in a kitchen chair and slaps the table with her left hand. *Get a grip on yourself, Ella. TMI. What were you thinking, telling him about the house, Kevin, everything! And that business about the Nicolet marker.* Still, she takes some pleasure in the fact that he remembered it, certainly more clearly than she, and that he's carried this with him all these years. A current of desire pulses through her as she thinks back upon that night, how close they'd felt, dwarfed by the intensity of the Aurora Borealis, the vastness of the sky. Can only the young share such exquisite tenderness? She closes her eyes, sighs, and pops a fistful of candy in her mouth.

This unexpected resurrection of memories is off-putting. *OK, I shouldn't have lied about the mosquitoes, damn it, but he had to be stopped.* He was getting way too fresh, acting like he'd never just walked away, never not called or written. It's all coming back to her, how she'd written to him, but he never responded.

Her thoughts are interrupted by Charlie who strolls in, flings open the fridge door, prowling for dinner. "There's nothing here but leftovers," he grumbles.

"There's some whole wheat pasta and quinoa salad."

"Why can't we just buy some real food? I can't even pronounce key-naw," he says, pulling out a milk jug and placing it on the table.

Ella pushes back her chair and exhales. The kid eats the worst diet, all processed and sugary stuff. Once she caught him with a spoonful of butter topped with maple syrup. "Do I have to go into this again? The food in the fridge is real food. That cereal is not." Charlie carries a box of honey-covered cereal to the table.

"What do you think of Nick?" she asks as Charlie pours milk on the cereal.

"Hmm. He's okay. He knows history and stuff."

From Charlie "okay" is as good as it gets.

"'Cept what was all that ape crap about?" he says, slurping a mouthful of cereal.

She can't refrain from chuckling. "Ah, just some college-age silliness."

Charlie grunts and continues scooping spoonfuls of cereal in his mouth. Ella walks out the kitchen door and turns her face north. Perhaps the Northern Lights will appear tonight.

***

As Nick pedals off, he notices the homes along the bluff seem in better shape than he remembers. These rambling mansions, built to impress more than shelter, are not to his taste; he prefers simpler, more rustic structures. The gardens appear brighter, in high-definition color, brimming with magenta and fuchsia petunias, snapdragons, and exotic annuals. He remembers Ella complaining about how annuals were "Showoff plants, totally useless." It perplexed him, for he always found the flowers beautiful, like jewelry lacing the necks of the big homes. And come to think of it, those big flowerboxes on her porch were swimming with annuals too. There's a lot about Ella he finds confusing.

With an empty agenda he decides to bike to Nicolet's marker, wondering if it has changed. He makes his way east, dodging piles of horse manure, and humming a Voyageurs' song. He pedals past the cemeteries, one on each side of the road, Catholics on the right, Protestants to the left. Henry must be up there on the Protestant side. *Think I'll check it out.* Nick leans his bike against the concrete fence at the entrance. The cemetery is empty, eerily quiet as he wanders among the graves looking for the Hollingsworth plot. *Emmanuel Lee Hudson, died the year of our Lord, December 10, 1893, 39 years, 1 month, 17 days.* On his right, Susan. *Wife, died 40 years, 2 months, 3 days.*

A few feet past, a white rectangle chiseled with a curvy vine reads: *Alexander McKay, Sept. 20, 1842, In the 50th Year of his Age.* A mossy stone to the right, *Adam, a son, 3 years & 9 months & 16 days.* With life so short and brutal, no wonder they counted each day. On a small rise to the east he finds it, a slab of polished gray granite with the word *Hollingsworth* carved in large gothic letters. Gravestone font. Four small headstones sit in a line in front of it, like children sprung from the big marker. Two are inches from each other in post-mortem intimacy: *William O. Hollingsworth, 1900-1971* and *Ella Lang Hollingsworth, 1903-1978. Love everlasting.* Nick remembers coming here with Ella to water the flowers, how she'd spoken about her grandma, her namesake, who had died the year before Nick came to the island. Ella visited her gravesite frequently, and Nick felt honored she'd invited him along that day. In a weird way it felt very intimate. She told him people thought her grandma shy and reserved, but she was a feisty fighter, tough on the inside, waging a five-year battle with cancer. He suspected Ella was closer to her than her own mother, as is often the case between grandparents and grandchildren—that two-generation gap leaves room for less drama between the adults and children. Staring at the grave, Nick thinks there must be a mighty fine coffin down there. *Quality forever,* the Hollingsworth slogan. A single pot of red geraniums and a small American flag in a metal holder provide the only spark of color on the plot.

Graveyards stir up his anxiety at a level that pierces far deeper than grief. It is this that he fears: that he will be forgotten. Not immediately, but eventually. Surely Melina would visit his grave with memories rich in imagery, and tell stories about him to her children. His grandsons and granddaughters, they would have memories, but only of him as an old man, never the young Nick. Never the one who had run naked with Ella, their bodies perfect, nor the young father who swirled baby Melina on one hand. The memories they'd have they might pass on to their children, like photocopies of photocopies. And that's where it would end: in the third generation, where he'd become an ancestor, someone you never met but to whom you were eternally connected, another branch on the family tree. Nothing more.

What if he'd had no children, like Ella? Who will remember her? If only he could keep memory alive, let the world forever know of her. Nick plucks a petal from a geranium and places it on the grave of Ella Lang Hollingsworth. "Rest in peace," he whispers.

Back on his bike, he turns left at the wooden sign that says *Arch Rock ¼ mile.* The massive rock forms a limestone arch above Lake Huron on the island's east side, a graceful arc over the water, believed by the Anishinabe to be a bridge between two worlds. The carriage drivers brashly hyperbolize that it's one of the Seven Wonders of the

World. The Watch Tower stands just above it, tucked into the woods at the top of a staircase.

After five minutes on the carriage roads he arrives at the bottom of the staircase, another one of Mackinac's vertical challenges. Good thing Ella refilled his water. Ascending, he counts the steps; this time there's a mere forty-four. At the top he steps into the small clearing where a marker rises from the center: gray, vertical, obelisk-like. Staring at the spot where he and Ella had lain, he closes his eyes, imagining the scene. This is sacred ground. Then he leans down to touch the soil with his fingertips, glancing around to be sure no one is watching. And what is there to see? Only a man with a memory, a sentimental old fool, his witnesses the cedars, wind, and water. As his fingers graze the earth, he feels the ache of nostalgia, memory's bittersweet companion. His gaze moves toward the lake; today it looks limitless, a vast sea with not one trace of development, neither house nor ship nor buoy in sight. It may as well be 1634 when Jean Nicolet slipped past here in a birch-bark canoe.

The fence enclosing the area is carved with modern names like Nikki, Tyler, Alex, and Crystal. Nick picks up a rock and inscribes "Nick & Ella" next to "JD and Megan." When he finishes he stands back to examine his handiwork. *Probably won't last through the winter.*

If only Ella had been more enthusiastic. How she has changed, become so agitated, defensive. She'd always been opinionated, in pursuit of some cause, but back then her little fits and uppityness seemed funny, part of her charm; this Ella could match the most skittish thoroughbreds on the island, the ones that shy at a piece of discarded gum glued to the pavement. Yet there was that glint of his girl, something in her eyes that tipped him off that he had moved her, too. And she'd invited him on this trip tomorrow. He's not ready to give up.

Nick walks back to his bike, thirsty for something stronger than iced tea or Mackinac tap water. Something to ease his smashed nerves. He knows where it is served, and the way there is all downhill.

8

That night Ella's dreams come in waves. She hasn't slept well in months, and has tried the usual soporifics: herbal teas, Melatonin, wine, even a meditation on YouTube. Tonight she's taken nothing and wakes up in the dark, grasping her mouth, feeling that her lips are twisted, as if she'd had a stroke. Like Father's last one, half his face frozen. He'd never left his bedroom after that, just lay in bed playing with his fingers and talking to his bony hands. "Go away," he'd told her. That hit hard; she'd always been his special one. Little rabbit, he'd called her. Only Mother was allowed into his space, sitting tirelessly by his bed, trying to spoon in food from her own shaky hands. Her father's pajamas were often covered in applesauce and red Jell-O.

In the dark she stares at the ceiling thinking about Nick. What's his real agenda? On one hand she wishes he'd just go away, vanishing as he did thirty years ago, taking his bullshit with him; yet, he stirs her up, arouses her curiosity, among other things. She falls asleep again debating whether she should wear shorts or capris tomorrow, annoyed with herself for such girly, trivial thoughts.

Ella is wakened by the freight boat's sevenish whistle, the piercing blare audible a mile back from the harbor. As she tussles with the sheets, the brass balls on the headboard spindles rattle. Sunlight splashes through the polygon of windows across from her bed. From there she can watch the lake, a wall of shimmering blue in the top panes, framed by the green of the cedars. She never tires of waking to this sight.

Mackinac birds, louder than city traffic, seem noisier this morning. A young ring gull, nearly all white with a spray of gray on its tail, soars above the bluff past the window. A warbling tru-lee resonates through the canopy of trees, the song of a bluebird out there.

Ella hastens down the wooden stairs to the kitchen, where she puts on a kettle for tea. As she paces the floor, the ripply linoleum chills her bare feet. When the water boils she pours it over a teabag, watching the steam rise from the cup. Even in August the kitchen remains cold, and she wraps her hand around the cup for warmth.

Leaving half the tea in the cup on the counter, she moves to the back porch and holds the screen door to keep it from banging shut, hoping her neighbor Darci won't spot her. The woman seems to pop out of her yard with her screechy "Yoo-hoos" whenever Ella opens the back door. (Replace screen door spring, she adds to her mental to-do list).

Moving stealthily down the terraced back yard to the barn, she stops to feed Jed. As she walks toward the hay bales, the pungent smells of horse doo, musk, and fur remind her of her carriage-driving days. She'd loved that job, rarely minding rising early to get to the barn, a soft world filled with shafts of morning sunlight, the stomping of horses, and the chatter of drivers coaxing their steeds, "Come on Prince," "Back, back," "Whoa." The silly jokes, crude stories.

There everyone accepted her; not at first, by any stretch—who does this bluffie think she is anyway?—but after her first runaway—no one hurt, horses okay—she'd earned their respect. That and the extra revenue from Grandpa sending down his cronies and friends for tours and most leaving hefty tips. To this day she knows the names of the horses and the majority of the drivers, and always checks out the teams when she's downtown. Now there's only one horse in her life, beloved old Jed.

He pushes his head through the fence and she scratches his forehead. His hazelnut eyes remind her of Nick's. "Good boy, Jeddy." Her hand lingers on his nose as he nuzzles her. "I'll be back soon." With that she takes off at a quick walk, then breaks into a run.

Rounding the curve on the road behind her cottage, she hears the scrape of a shovel on the asphalt and sees Bud, an islander who works full-time as a manure shoveler, his honey wagon beside him. He's full of one-liners. "I'll walk a mile for a pile," and, "What's the scoop? A lot of poop." She always makes a point to chat with him, especially this year. In remission from melanoma, Bud had endured a brutal winter of chemotherapy and radiation.

"How's it going, Bud?" she asks.

"Another beautiful day," he says, scooping a pile in his shovel.

"Busy day too, huh?" Manure spills over the side of his cart.

"Horses are putting lots of deposits in the bank."

"Guess they won't go under like the rest of the banks." Bud chuckles. "You feeling good?" asks Ella, jogging in place.

"Just a little stiff." He rolls his shoulders. "You keep praying for me. OK?" Fear flashes across his face, quickly replaced by his yellow-toothed grin.

Wonder if he's received more bad news. "I sure will, Bud. You take care."

Turning away from Bud she begins to run slowly, her pace a sluggish eleven-minutes-per-mile, way off from those days when she'd bust her butt to maintain a seven-minute-per-mile pace.

"When you going to start slowing down?" he calls.

"I used to walk faster than this!" she calls out.

Soon she leaves the carriage road, preferring the soft bridle paths that wend up and down through the forest; better on the joints than the paved roads. Toppled white birches and cedars litter the forest floor, their dead feeding the living. In the places where sunlight finds a path through the trees, the hillsides are covered in a brilliant yellow blanket of Hawk's Weed, punctuated by stalks of milkweed. She frowns at a sea of Norwegian Maple seedlings, bends down and yanks one out. It's near hopeless; the invasive species, introduced for mistaken virtues—fast growing with a huge canopy—is one of her quests to eradicate. The damn things will eventually kill off all the cedars if they don't put a stop to it. But she smiles when she spots a Yellow Lady's Slipper, a true native, in full bloom by the trail's edge, nearly a month past its expected time. A good omen. Once, when she was a child, Mother had scolded her for picking one and trying to slip it on her doll's foot. "Fairies dance in these at night," she'd said.

Leaving the paths for the carriage roads, she dodges a manure pile in which two crows are foraging. Though the tourists hold their noses around the stuff, Ella appreciates manure, considers it a perfect display of recycling. "What stinks more," she often asks, "fumes from your car exhaust or biodegradable droppings from the back of a horse?"

Stooping over a drinking fountain by Arch Rock, she gulps down water like a thirsty carriage horse before climbing the wooden steps up to Nicolet's marker. At the bottom of the steps she pauses for a moment, her hand resting on the railing, silkened by hundreds of hands sliding over it daily, year after year.

In a tiny clearing at the top, the granite monument pokes up, its backside stained green from lichen, but the plaque on the front is in perfect condition. There's the spot where she and Nick had made love, barely big enough for two adults to stretch out. She struggles to connect the image of the Nick she saw yesterday with the one she frolicked with here, two tectonic plates that have slipped apart to form new continents, new lives. Now they seem poised to collide again.

She turns from the marker toward the lake, now brightening from slate to baby blanket blue under the rising sun, dotted by the green chain of Les Cheneaux Islands to the northeast. The arm of the Upper Peninsula wraps around the water at the horizon, vanishing far to the east. The island's raw beauty never ceases to wow her.

Her eyes move from the view to the fence scrawled with names: Kyle, Alex and Kiki, JB loves BB, Crystal, and below that, Nick & Ella. What? Tracing the letters with her index finger, she shrugs. Just a coincidence. A blue jay lands on a limb above, turns its head to assess her, then flies off.

As Ella descends the staircase, two brown squirrels rummage in a trash can below that they've hijacked as their personal diner. She'd read that squirrels were extremely hospitable to one another, sleeping up to seven or eight per nest for warmth, although older females aren't allowed in due to the complications of sexuality. These ladies become loners, hardened by survival. As she takes a step toward them, the frantic squirrels soar out of the can, nearly flying to a nearby tree, their bushy tails quivering. She stands still, amused by her power, watching them race in circles up the trunk. The braver of the two descends a few feet, pauses—as much as a tail-shaking, mouth-quivering rodent can stay still. Their eyes lock for a moment until the squirrel leaps back into the can. She jogs away. Far up the road she can still hear its scolding.

9

Nick spots Ella on a dock downtown on the bow of a small outboard, looking like one of those intrepid British women in a movie filmed in somewhere with tropical heat, foliage, and a hero in a safari hat. The boat is tucked in a slip, sandwiched between a monstrous triple-decked yacht to the right—the *Miss Muffet* from Port Huron, and the *Wet Dream* from Cheboygan to the left. As he approaches the slip, he notices gray paint splatters on Ella's shorts. Well-packed biceps and triceps form little mounds on her spindly arms, and her legs look firm and tan, though a few purple lines crisscross the front of her thighs. Her hair is pulled up in a tortoise-shell fastener with curls spilling over the sides, more a younger woman's style, but it becomes her.

"Well it's about time," she says, glancing at a cell phone in her right hand.

"Sorry, I'm a bit late." Nick had overslept and missed breakfast at his place, but Judy kindly gave him a bowl of Cheerios and some sitting-on-the-burner-for-hours coffee.

"Well, climb aboard. It's a good thing you're well rested cuz we're in for an adventure."

Squeezing four people, a heavy cooler, towels, and cameras into the boat is tipsy business. As Nick lowers himself from the dock into a seat on the right, the boat keels to his side. Charlie switches places with Benjamin, a stick of a kid with stringy strawberry-blonde hair and pale, freckly skin, who's sitting on the far left. It evens things out. Ella sits regally at the steering wheel, her back straight, head held high. "Life jackets on?" She's not wearing one, but the boys and Nick hustle to strap on theirs. "Okay, we're off."

Maneuvering the craft through the harbor, Ella avoids the ferries that are backing up on both sides of them from three different docks. One approaches so close Nick swears he can touch it. "On your right!" he yells.

Ella shoots a disdainful look at him. "We call that starboard," she says.

"Okay, okay. Starboard. We're going to get run over by that ship on our starboard!"

Shouting over the motor's roar and the wind, Charlie explains that his project is a search for an old burial site. Every history-loving cell in Nick's body screams, "What the hell do you think you're doing disturbing a historical site, not to mention a burial site? This is sacred stuff!" But all he says is, "Hmm."

"I'm not looking for Indian artifacts, it's evidence of cholera victims—Europeans—who died in the early 1800s!" shouts Charlie. Benjamin nods. Nick suspects this boy would follow Charlie into just about anything. Charlie's clearly an adventurous leader, Benjamin a follower.

The bow smacks against small whitecaps, evenly spaced sets of dentures nipping them every few feet. The spray hitting Nick's right arm feels chilly, yet warmer than the water of Lake Superior. Even in August that lake numbs his nuts.

A few hundred feet ahead he spots Round Island's *sandy* beach, but it sure looks different. That boulder just a ways out that he and Ella had swum to years ago protrudes a good foot higher, and the rocks below the water are coated in slippery green slime.

They anchor the boat in hip-deep water, then take turns jumping into the lake, balancing their gear on their heads. Nick goes last, carrying the cooler with the food, the heaviest item.

"What happened to the sandy beach?" asks Nick.

"Lake's down," says Ella. "No such thing as global warming, right? Be careful. These rocks are slippery, like walking on eels."

Grunting, Nick almost falls on his face on the rocks several times. His rubber sandals feel clunky. Ella and the boys are well ahead, moving easily in skimpy flip-flops. He feels his heart rate jump. At the beach he sets down the cooler, breathing hard.

"Aah ee ahh!"

Nick looks toward the sound.

Charlie is up on the beach beating his chest, making an ape call.

"Aah ee ahh!" Benjamin has joined in. The boys run back and forth on the strip of beach like apes. Now Ella joins them, beating her chest, too. Nick feels a rising buoyancy. Even his soggy sandals can't drag him down as he moves toward them. *"Aah eee ahh!"* he shouts, but the sound is feeble.

The boys are beaming; Ella bends over laughing and Nick joins her. When they recover, Nick points out to the cove. "Hmm, I seem to recall something about that big rock out there."

That long-ago day in August had been a scorcher, the lake unusually warm. They had dragged Ella's old Sunfish up to the sandy beach at Round Island, then held hands as they ran into the lake. The water grew progressively colder as they swam toward a large boulder protruding from the lake about a hundred feet offshore. Ella, the better swimmer, was first to hoist herself up. "Yuk, it's covered with seagull poop," she said before diving back in, just as Nick heaved himself onto the boulder.

"Catch me!" she yelled, zooming headfirst underwater around the rock. A reluctant underwater swimmer—the pressure hurt his ears—Nick jumped in feet first, looking to his right and left for Ella. Suddenly she was there, grabbing him from behind, wrapping her long legs around him. Despite the chilly water, he felt himself harden. Trying to remain afloat with Ella on his back, her little breasts pressing into his shoulder blades, he turned, pushing her toward the rock. "Up you go," he said.

He nipped her calf as she pulled herself up, protesting, "But the seagull poop—"

"The hell with it." And then he was standing on the rock beside her, stripping off his bathing trunks. Ella peeled off her suit, placing it beside his. But as he turned to pull her toward him she pushed him away, then plunged into the lake. Nick watched her swim to shore, her pale butt and shoulders shining like three pearls above the surface. He stood atop the rock, dismayed, as he went limp. *Damn her.*

When it was too shallow for her to swim any longer, Ella stood up in the water and ran to the beach. There she turned toward him, beating her chest and ape-calling. Nick sighed, picked up her swimsuit and placed it on his head like a shower cap. Then he slipped into his and swam back to shore, where he joined Ella as they ran up and down the beach beating their chests, Ella naked, Nick with her bathing suit on his head. Finally they collapsed in laughter and made love on the sand. He completely forgave her, though later she complained about having sand in her crotch.

But today the water level around the rock has dropped to a few feet, and here he is, trudging through it with a heavy cooler and two boys.

"Hey, guys, can you give me a hand?" Nick asks, pointing to the cooler. Charlie grabs one handle as Nick takes the other. Benjamin carries a stack of towels.

"How long have you been doing this project?" asks Nick.

"Two years."

"The island's about three miles around, right?"

"Yeah, but it takes hours to walk around because of the rocks. We're not going too far."

Charlie is gabby, unrestrained. Round Island has loosened up all of them. He talks about the island's history, how Henry Schoolcraft visited there in 1834 and discovered an ancient Indian village site. "He found a burial ground and an ossuary on the southern side of the island. It's all written down in one of his journals."

Nick is impressed with the boy's knowledge of local history and his vocabulary. "Where did you learn all this?" he asks.

"A lot of it from my grandpa and the stuff in his library, listening to lots of stories. Living here in the summer. I read a lot, too."

"So what do you hope to find here?"

"I just want some evidence. Nobody's ever found anything."

Benjamin turns around. "Dude, we might get famous."

"Maybe."

At that moment Ella announces they have arrived at their picnic spot, a clearing between the north shoreline and a small rise of trees.

"Your nephew has quite a grasp of history," says Nick.

"He's always been that way," she says as she spreads two beach towels on the pebbled clearing. A squall of wind snatches the cloth, blowing it westward. "The wind's shifting east. We may have to cut our visit short." An east wind in the Straits was a bellwether for a storm.

"But we're just getting started," says Charlie.

"Right!" pipes in Benjamin.

"I didn't say we had to leave, just to keep an eye on the weather."

She places rocks on the corners of the towels. "Come on, help me out, guys. Bring me some firewood." Charlie, Benjamin, and Nick scramble away, chatting about cholera, soldiers, and boats. They hastily gather pieces of driftwood, so abundant on the island, and stack them in a pile by the towels. Ella scoops out a small pit in the stones, then crumples pieces of newspaper. The boys place the driftwood around the paper, teepee-style, and Ella strikes a kitchen match at the bottom of the paper. A small flame crawls rapidly up the dry wood. Within minutes they are toasting hot dogs—"Not Dogs" for Ella—until they are bubbling and juicy. Nick eats two. He dabs grease from his chin with a linen napkin Ella brought—"Don't want to waste trees, you know." She'd also brought thick reusable plastic plates and ceramic cups. No wonder that picnic basket was so heavy.

The main course is followed by s'mores, the soul of a Michigan picnic.

Nick nurses his marshmallow, slowly turning it near the flame until it reaches a light golden color. When he sets it on top of the chocolate bar between two graham crackers, the marshmallow squishes slowly, the melted portion soft but binding.

Ella and Charlie thrust theirs directly into the fire until the marshmallows expand like chubby ghosts before morphing into crisp black blobs clinging to their sticks.

"You should wait till they're slightly brown," says Nick.

"Nonsense." Ella slides the gooey mess onto her cracker. "Perfect," she says, easing it into her mouth as a stream of white oozes onto her hands.

Benjamin, more circumspect, roasts two marshmallows over the fire before one becomes barely brown. "Yum," he says, popping it into his mouth.

"Now it's my turn to tell you a story," says Nick, turning to the boys.

"Cool," says Benjamin. Charlie stares at Nick with a blank expression.

Looking around as if spirits are listening in the trees, Nick lowers his voice and begins. "A boat of ill soldiers came up here from Detroit during the Great Cholera epidemic in 1882."

"Right," says Charlie. "The ship started in Quebec. Rats from an infected vessel from Europe ran down the ropes to the wharf and into the nearby area." Ella shoots him a glance with a slight nod toward Nick.

"Excellent. You sure know your history. Now these soldiers on a British boat didn't know it, but they all got infected."

"That sucks," says Charlie.

"So they stuck them over here?" asks Benjamin.

"Wait. I'm getting to that." Both boys are watching him. "Anyway, the captain took them over here and ordered them off the boat. He wasn't a bad guy. He left them with food and blankets. It was August, so the temperature was warm, like today. No one knows what happened except they disappeared."

"Whaddya mean, disappeared? People don't just disappear," says Charlie. "I never heard this version. Are you sure about this?"

"There's a story—but it's only a story, you know—that someone on Mackinac was sent over to check on them. When he got here, all but one soldier was lying on the ground too sick to move. This one guy was caring for them, giving them water, even made a bed out of their uniforms. He was singing and praying over them, even rubbing the feet of one of the men who was moaning. When the guy from the island saw this, he felt so bad he went over and put his hand on the man's shoulder. The story goes that he told him he would come back and bury them."

"Did he?"

"No, he couldn't. When he returned to the island he, too, got cholera. But before that he told some island folks the story. On his deathbed he asked his wife to carry out his promise. But she never got there. She died, too. So did all his kids."

"Dude, you're making this up," says Charlie.

"Be quiet. I want to hear what happened," says Benjamin.

"This is the weird part. A group of men finally came back to bury the bunch. They beached right here with a boatload of shovels and pickaxes on account of all the rocks. But when they arrived, there was no one here. All the blankets and supplies were here, even a full pail of water. But not one person, not a soul. They searched and searched, but nothing. Nada."

"Dude," says Benjamin, exhaling and looking around nervously.

"I don't believe it. Where did you hear this story?" asks Charlie.

"Hmmm. Can't remember, maybe one of Schoolcraft's journals."

"Interesting."

Both boys are passionate about history, curious about lives and events never to be seen or touched. Nick feels a bond growing with them. That little Benjamin is a nice kid, and Charlie might come around given time. Melina had disappointed him. Though he'd hauled her to historic sites throughout her childhood, she preferred scrambling on monuments and racing around museums without paying much attention to the exhibits. Katie had tried to shield her from Nick's fascination for the past, steered her away. ("You don't want to see another old building, sweetie.") In her freshman year in college, Melina took a deep interest in sociology; living people, busy making their own stories.

"Isn't it time you started your—investigations?" asks Ella, wiping her marshmallowy hands on her shorts.

"Let's put out the fire first," says Nick. "With this breeze a spark could easily carry to a tree and ignite the whole place."

"Hey, look," says Benjamin, pointing to a large rock inscribed with the words: "My dog lies here and someday I will too. God bless Rusty."

"That guy had a sense of humor," says Nick. "But I don't think you're looking for a dead dog."

Ella walks over to the rock. "I remember that dog. Belonged to Stanley St. John, a nice little mutt. Stanley died a month after burying Rusty."

Benjamin stares at the rock a moment. "That's sad."

"Come on, let's go," says Charlie. "You guys coming?"

Ella and Nick exchange looks. "I'd like to take a walk," says Ella.

"Mind some company?" asks Nick. As much as Nick wants to stay on Charlie's good side, an excuse to spend time alone with Ella trumps it.

Charlie scowls. "Whatever."

Leaving the boys behind, Ella and Nick head west along the south shore.

"You're quite the storyteller. You had those boys positively enraptured. How did you know all those facts?"

"I made most of them up, but I suspect Charlie's on to me. He'll probably do a fact check when we get back." He waits for her response but she continues walking. Perhaps she'll tell him more about herself now that they're away from everything. He longs for that truth-telling closeness they once shared, not this furtive, secret-clogged space between them. He glances at her, a northern flower wilting so beautifully. The breeze slaps her gray-peppered curls across her face. She's looking straight ahead, her movements graceful, even here upon uneven rocks, all the angst blown out of her. This is her place, as much as it belongs to the seagulls, stones, and cedars. She fits here, as he once did. If only he could reclaim her trust. More than that, he wants to tell her about his mistakes and losses, how he's squandered opportunities, that his heart carries so much regret. But why burden this woman with his confessions? She isn't a priest, and he's no Catholic; she certainly has not asked for him to barge in on her life, and was less than lukewarm about bringing him along on this expedition. Seems she has troubles, too.

Yet it's such a pretty day. He should put that crap aside and enjoy the simple act of walking in this small wilderness with her, suspend thinking about his smashed-up life back on the mainland.

He smiles and says, "This is great. Thanks for inviting me along." She pauses and smiles back at him. An opening. He links his arm in hers. As they walk he blurts out, "This is one helluva beautiful day."

Ella squeezes his arm and they walk on.

10

How natural it feels to be walking arm in arm with Nick, light and unencumbered.

"Do you still play the guitar?" she asks. One of her favorite times with Nick was when he strummed the guitar and sang, his raspy baritone squeaking over high notes. Sometimes Ella sang too, heartily, flat, a bit hooty, owl-style, Nick called it. She didn't care. Now she feels a tiny rush in her head. *This is getting way too comfortable.* If Nick truly knew her, knew her history, he'd evaporate as quickly as the Mackinac mist. As if reading her thoughts, Nick jerks his arm out from hers, then pushes her away.

"What the—" she starts to blurt, then spots the source of his sudden roughness: a snake several inches from her right foot. She screams, jumps, and clutches Nick's arm.

"Jesus!" he laughs, reaching out to her, lightly patting her hand. The creature, a gray and gold-striped ribbon snake, non-venomous, slithers off hastily. Although the only poisonous snake in Michigan is a *massasauga*, "A snake that can kill a child but not an adult," her father said, this one gave her a scare. Nick picks up a rock and throws it at the retreating critter.

"What are you doing?"

"Sending the little bastard a message," he says.

"*She* won't hurt us."

"Well it just scared the shit out of you, didn't it?"

She doesn't answer, walks faster, not an easy feat on these rocks. Nick can't keep up the pace but doesn't pursue her; instead, he turns to the lake.

"Come on!" she calls.

"You go ahead. I'm a slower machine."

Ella picks up a stone and hurls it out on the water where it skims across the first wave, hops over the next two, then plunks to a halt and sinks. A ways behind her, Nick answers with his own well-executed throw. His stone skips five times in a streak of little bumps before disappearing in the lake. Ella tosses another one, this time eking out six skips. Father had taught her how to skip stones when she was a preschooler. She's good, but Nick's better, a natural. She remembers how he'd always been better at this. Ella walks back to him. "You haven't lost your touch. That was five skips, two pitty-pats and one kerplunk," she says, clapping her hands in applause.

"What's a pitty-pat?"

"In stone-skipping lexicon, the little blips on the water, like the stone is stuttering. The final jump's a kerplunk, the big gulp at the end. Someone on the island made up those terms for the stone-skipping contest. You should enter it."

"What's the prize? A spot on the Olympic team?"

"Better than that—a year's worth of fudge."

"Now that's worth training for," says Nick, picking up another rock. "Plain dark chocolate. I'm starting today."

"Let me see that," says Ella, seizing the stone from his hands. She inspects it—flat, but jagged—then drops it on the beach. "Not round enough, way too big. You want it to be about this size, and as flat as possible." During the many times she and her father had skipped stones on these beaches, he'd advised her to patiently search for the right rock, yet so many times she wouldn't wait, rushing into life with the wrong stones, the ones with jagged edges that would never skim lightly over the curve of a wave. She bends down, examining the smorgasbord of rocks, finally settling on a beige, nearly perfect circle the size of her palm. Instead of throwing it, she hands it to Nick. Yanking his right arm back, he whips it forward with a snap of his wrist.

"Five skips, seven pitty-pats and one kerplunk. Awesome," says Ella.

"Don't forget, I grew up on Lake Superior," says Nick, laughing. "Remember, *superior*."

"Well, it will never be as beautifully blue as this lake," she says, kerplunking herself on an old log washed up on the shore, debranched and satiny from months in the water. Nick joins her, his breathing fast and heavy; perspiration beads his forehead as he scoots closer to her along the log until their shoulders touch. With the stillness of two turtles, they gaze at the lake, listening to the rise and rush of waves on the smooth, gray stones. Ella thinks of the Great Lakes basin as a grand gathering of water, a precipitation party where melted glaciers, frost, hail, rain, snow, sleet, mist, and a few drops of ancient Lake Nipissing mingle in the glacier-carved troughs they now occupy, the ancient ever present in a new combination, an infinite mixture. The past is always with her too, hollowed out deep inside: old wounds and bruises, crushes, prejudices, surprises, joys, the bric-a-brac of daily living and random moments—water moving endlessly over the landscape of her life. Somewhere in this flow, as deep as the drop-off past the limestone shoals of these islands, those days with Nick still swirled.

"Why did you come back here?" she asks, coaxing a wisp of hair behind her right ear.

He turns to her, eyes cast down, avoiding her stare. "That's not so easy to answer because—well, because I'm not quite sure. My research, of course…and I wanted to see the island again."

"Of course."

"Ella, I've thought about you on and off for thirty years. I guess I was curious to see what you'd become." He edges toward her, raising his gaze to meet hers.

"So, what do you think?" She's not sure she wants to hear his answer, but has to ask.

"Look, we're not youngsters. I've taken a few hits from life and I suspect you have too. I wanted to return here, a place with happy memories. The more I thought about it, the more I realized you're totally entwined in those memories." After a long pause he says, "But I don't know you anymore, not really."

She folds her hands in her lap and remains quiet. Finally she says, "Let's walk." The simple act of moving her arms and legs relieves some of her anxiety, helps straighten out her thoughts.

Nick stands up slowly, placing his palms on his thighs to help boost him as he unfolds from a squat to a stand, extending his hand to Ella's. They totter for a moment. "I'm getting to be an old man now, but you, you don't look the least bit sore." Her knees and back ache, but he doesn't need to know that.

Continuing toward the old lighthouse, Ella feels the tension between them slither away like that snake. Longing to run her hand along his face, to stroke his forehead, to trace circles around the edges of his eyes with her fingertips, instead, she unclenches her hands, letting them hang empty at her sides.

***

As they walk, Nick debates whether to ask her what happened, why she'd stood him up, broken that promise they'd made at Friendship's Altar thirty years earlier. Part of him wants to know, the other is embarrassed after all this time to confess what he did. Deciding there isn't much to lose, he asks, "Why didn't you meet me that winter?"

"Winter? What are you talking about?"

"Our promise. We promised each other at that place in the forest—Friendship's Altar—that we'd meet at Mackinac two days after Christmas 1979. You flat-out stood me up."

Ella shakes her head. "You're making this up, right?"

It isn't the reaction he'd expected. "Don't you think it's too crazy to make up?"

"You're a good storyteller. You're saying you actually went to the island in December? Back then?"

"We promised one another. I called your house and talked to your dad. He said you were coming." Nick would never forget. Long before cell phones, the Internet, in a world where verbal promises were made—and hopefully, kept—they'd pledged to one another that on December 27, they would meet on Mackinac. Ella offered to rip a few shutters off her cottage and turn on the electricity. They could do without running water for a day and heap logs in the fireplace. They'd keep each other more than warm. It all sounded romantic and adventurous at the time; now it sounds ludicrous, a fool's errand. He wishes he hadn't brought it up, but now it's too late.

Ella looks incredulous. "Father never said a word. Are you sure?"

"I couldn't make up this stuff."

Crossing her arms on her chest, Ella stares down at the ground. "You concocted a pretty good story back there for the boys."

"I swear this is true." They have arrived at the lighthouse where a brick staircase leads to a concrete walk wrapped around the base of the structure.

"Let's sit down. It will take a while to tell you," says Nick. They lower themselves on the west ledge, buffered from the wind by the lighthouse wall. A ferry passes and tourists on the deck wave as Nick plunges into his story.

It had been two days after Christmas when he'd loaded his car with a pair of cross-country skis, a backpack, a thermos of coffee, a dozen granola bars, and a poem. He knew it was probably stupid to make the trip. She hadn't written to him all fall, only one postcard from her university in Virginia that read, "I miss Mackinac and you, but the world needs me here. Love, Ella."

The drive from Marquette to St. Ignace was a long, slippery zig-zag with icy highways slowing his speed to 45 mph or less. On the twenty-five-mile straight stretch of M-28 near Seney he swerved to avoid a deer, sending his Ford Escort into a tailspin. He ended up in a snowbank on the opposite side of the road and had to shovel out his car. Less than fifty miles from St. Ignace he decided to turn around and head home, but as he began the turn the tape player switched to "You're in My Heart, You're in my Soul," a song he and Ella claimed as theirs.

Surely it was a sign.

A skim of ice had spread across the Straits of Mackinac, but the ferry was still running two trips a day between the Upper Peninsula dock in St. Ignace and the island. The boat hands wore snowmobile suits and fur caps with the flaps snapped down. Only a few islanders were on the boat, huddled in the upstairs cabin where the engine warmed the dull, dark-green space where a metallic odor mixed with the smell of diesel fuel. The windows were covered in ice from the spray as the boat slapped down hard on the waves.

"Who you visiting?" asked a short, solid woman in a black parka. Her jaw was set wide and deep lines crisscrossed her face, the kind earned from lots of time outdoors with wind, sun, and snow.

"A friend from last summer," Nick said. "She's making a special trip over. I'm going to meet her."

The woman shook her head. "Can't think of anyplace you're going to meet except the grocery. Nothing's open, ya know. Well, there's the Buggy Whip Lounge, but they're closed today."

"I'm meeting her up at her parents' place, Cedar Bluff."

The woman stared at Nick. "Son, that place is all boarded up. No one's there. Can't be. There's no water, no heat, nothing on the bluff."

"We made a special arrangement."

The woman rolled her eyes and sighed.

Nick stood up and walked outside, soon splattered by the icy spray and wind. He pulled his jacket hood tighter and covered his mouth with a mittened hand. What would he do if Ella stood him up? Then he realized if she were coming she'd have to be on this boat. *What an idiot I am.*

Through the ice-encrusted windows he watched the people huddled inside. If this boat capsized or started sinking, they'd all be dead in minutes. Hypothermia doesn't care a whit about swimming ability; when it's this cold, there's only a thin layer between life and death.

Suddenly the boat hit something on the starboard side, as ice and the steel hull gnashed with a low booming sound. Jolting forward, Nick lost his footing and fell forward on his face. Blood trickled out of his mouth where his teeth ripped into his lower lip. He stood up, removed a chuck of ice from the rail and nursed his swollen lip. He stayed out there until the boat docked.

As the passengers departed, the woman in the black parka smiled at him. "Good luck," she said.

Nick scanned the dock. No one was waiting there, only one worker who helped moor the vessel and pull out the ramp.

"When's the next ferry back?" he asked the man.

"Don't know if there'll be another one today."

"You're kidding." Nick looked at his watch.

"No, too much ice building up. We may just stay put. Try to get out tomorrow morning if we can."

Nick left his skis propped up against the warehouse, then wandered off the dock onto the frozen strip of Main Street. All the businesses were shuttered and closed, and a few snowmobiles were parked by the grocery a half-block up. In the middle of the street stood a tall pine tree decorated with multi-colored lights, its spire drooped to the left under the weight of the huge plastic star, like a Charlie Brown tree. Had he been in a cheerier mood it would have seemed postcard pretty; now it seemed bleak and depressing.

He walked to the grocery where a weary, middle-aged woman stared at him from behind the counter. She wore one of those big

Christmas sweatshirts with dazzle and sparkles all over it. He bought a cup of coffee laced with the acrid taste from sitting for hours on a burner, but it warmed him.

"I heard you're going up to Cedar Bluff," she said.

How did she hear about that? Nick had been on the island less than ten minutes.

"Is there any way to get up there?" he asked. "Besides walking?"

"If you got a snowmobile it's easy. If you don't you're pretty much SOL, if you know what I mean." She winked. "Unless you're good at walking over frozen snow."

"I brought my skis," said Nick.

She frowned. "Skis? You'll never get up those icy hills."

He remembered Papa scoffing at the sport. "You know what we call guys who cross-country ski? Forest fairies," Papa had said. Nick liked the soft swishing sound of his skis, such a contrast to the roar of a snowmobile. Not that he didn't enjoy rides on the old black Polecat. Papa had dusted it off at the first sign of snow and roared around the trails day and night, often accompanied by a young Nick bouncing on the back seat, his arms around his father's wide waist.

"Say, you working on their house?" asked the woman.

"Not exactly. I was looking for one of their daughters. Have you seen any Hollingsworth girls here?"

The clerk chuckled. "They're summer folks. Haven't seen any of them since Labor Day. Don't waste your time."

"Thanks," said Nick. He left quickly, feeling the woman's eyes drilling into his back, knowing she was about to pick up the phone and tell everyone about this lunatic on a fool's mission.

He'd only walked half a block down the street when he heard someone shout, "Hey, you." Nick turned. The clerk motioned him to come back.

"The guys on the boat just called. They said they're gonna try to make it back to St. Ignace before the ice sets in. Could be a couple of days before they come back and the planes might not come either. I suggest you skedaddle down there."

Nick weighed his options: if he remained on the island he'd have no place to stay unless one of the locals took him in, and he didn't feel like answering their questions for the next forty-eight hours. If

Ella showed up—which looked very, very doubtful—he'd miss her. Oh well, serves her right.

"I'll take the boat. Will you let them know I'm on my way?"

"Sure," said the clerk. "You made a good decision. Happy New Year."

11

A s Ella listens to Nick's story, she can't keep her hands still; squeezes a pebble, scratches her ankle. It seems so improbable, this tale,
so naïve. And a little phony. It's hard to believe she could have forgotten this completely, slammed away in a locked drawer of long-term
memory. Christmas promise? *Bah humbug.* She rubs a smooth, white
stone with her index finger, then drops it with a clatter. Nick looks up
and pauses. She studies him as he speaks, his voice lowered, drawing
circles in the air with big arm movements as he describes the scenes.
Every few sentences he glances at her, then turns his head back toward the water. When he finishes all she can say is, "My God, Nick,
you were such an innocent." He looks hurt, but she presses on. "Why
didn't you call or at least check with me before you roared off to the
island?" *Sure, blame the victim.*

"I already told you that I spoke with your dad."

"Why didn't Father mention it?"

"It's pretty obvious: he didn't want you to know. Just like my mom.
When I got home she was furious. She never liked the idea of you and
me. Said that birds of a feather should stick together."

"But I never met your mother."

"That's probably all for the best."

"Well, I think the whole thing is . . . is hard to comprehend."

Surprising herself, she reaches out and places her palm on top of
his hand. He flips his hand over, and there they are, palm-to-palm.
"This has been quite a day." Nick nods. "The wind is getting stronger. We'd better head back." What a feeble response to his story. This
whole thing makes her feel unbuttoned. And it's true: they do need to
head back. Above the clouds are piling into escaping genies, and the
waves froth at the foot of the lighthouse. She stands up. This time it is
her hand that reaches out to pull up a wobbly-legged Nick.

Only the crunch of their feet on the rocks breaks the silence between them as they walk. Suddenly, Nick stops and turns toward her. "I was just kidding," he says.

"Kidding?"

"About the Christmas rendezvous. I made it up."

"But you had all those details ... the ferry boat, the lady at the grocery. . ." Surely he couldn't have fabricated all that. Nick looks straight into her eyes. "I was trying to impress you, and I'm pretty good at stories. "

Now Ella doesn't know what to think. Rather than impressed, the story has confused her. "But— ", she pauses as she notices Charlie in the distance running toward them. "Something's wrong," she cries, her steps quickening. Charlie waves his arms back and forth above his head, jumping up and down. Ella's maternal instincts fire up and she suddenly feels guilty for leaving him for—what has it been—an hour? She starts running, a baby-step jog with her arms stretched out and bent like the wings of an injured gull. Charlie is yelling something, but the wind churns his syllables into gibberish. As they move closer she discerns his words: "There's someone in the woods! We saw him from the back. And we found a bone! Benjamin is guarding it but he didn't want to be left alone. Come on!" Charlie glances at Nick. "What took you guys so long?"

"Ah, we ran into a phantom soldier," says Nick.

"I'm not kidding. We saw someone!"

"What did this person look like?" asks Ella.

"Not sure. Long, gray hair, camouflage pants and top. He disappeared in the forest heading that away." Charlie points to the eastern end of the island.

"This isn't a private island," says Ella. "Could be someone on their own boat." All true, but goosebumps rise on her arms. The three turn away from the shore, pecking their way through the scratchy branches of white pine, cedar, and Juniper bushes in the center of the island.

"Up here!" shouts Benjamin. They walk toward his voice, then spot his red hair glistening like a pine cone next to a tree. He's holding a whitish object about ten inches long. "I was getting creeped out," he says.

"Let me see that," says Nick, his voice brusque. Benjamin hands it to him a little hesitantly, glancing nervously at Charlie. Nick examines the bone. "Looks like a deer femur."

"No, it's human," says Charlie.

Nick shoots a stern look at him. "In that case we definitely shouldn't be disturbing this place. But I'm certain this is from an animal. You ever hunted, son?"

"No, but I know what a bone looks like."

"Ella, may I talk with you a minute?" he asks, nodding his head to the right. When they're out of earshot of the boys Nick says, "If that were a human bone they'd be disturbing a burial ground. That's not only wrong, it's illegal."

"But you said it was from a deer. And the boys are so excited." More importantly, Charlie seems to be warming up to Nick, and the boy needs a trustworthy man in his life.

"They have to leave the bone here, bury it. Period. If they don't, I may have to report it."

"You wouldn't do that."

"I would."

She knows Nick is right. If only he weren't so Boy Scoutish about it. This is a different side of him. A tight-ass.

"It's the teacher in me," he says. "And the historian."

"No, it's the mean assistant principal." She sticks out her tongue at him before turning to walk back to the boys. Charlie is looking down, his mouth pouty; Benjamin stares at the bone, runs his hands along it.

"Okay, guys, if that's a human bone, we need to contact the state's archeology division," says Nick.

"No way, man!" says Charlie. "They'll take it away. This is our site, our stuff. We found it." Charlie picks up the shovel and resumes digging. "And I'm gonna find more." Benjamin crosses his arms over his chest and stares at Nick.

"Here's the deal: would you want someone digging you up and separating your bones?"

"It would be kinda cool. I mean, people would be really interested in me," says Charlie.

"I'm interested in you alive and in one piece, and I'm sure your aunt is, too." Ella nods her head. The negotiations continue until the boys finally agree to rebury the bone and mark the spot.

"We can always come back here. You know darn well if this ever gets out it . . ." she says, staring hard at Benjamin, "it will be all over the island."

"Like that seagull's going to tell them?" asks Charlie, pointing to a gull squawking overhead. Ella hears his father's sarcasm in his tone.

"It's quite likely. And Benjamin, please don't mention this to your dad."

"I won't," he says. "Scout's honor."

"You're not a scout, dude," says Charlie. Then he shrugs and heads toward the beach, Benjamin trudging behind.

Ella turns to Nick. "Benjamin's dad is on the Historic Council and he can't stand me. He'll probably weasel the info out of Benjamin. By the way, you're pretty good at handling these guys."

"Doesn't look like they're happy at the moment. Just like my students—one minute they're two, the next they're twenty." Nick puts his hands on her shoulders. "Before we go back, I want to tell you I had a great time here today. What happens on Round Island stays on Round Island, right?" he says.

"Right," she replies, suddenly wishing a little more had occurred.

12

~~~

Out on the lake the wind has increased, stoking up two-foot white-caps and Nick's nerves. Ella's boat bobs on swells racing in from the east. "I hope you don't get seasick easily," says Ella.

"We're about to find out," he murmurs. "Maybe we should wait till the wind goes down."

"We'll be waiting all day and night. We've gotta go for it now. I won't do anything reckless. Trust me."

Nick wishes she'd chosen some other words; she, the daredevil who once rode her horse with no bridle; she, who capsized her Sunfish a few yards from a freighter. Now she wants to ferry him back across a quarter-mile of squallish open water—*blue doom*, he calls it.

As if reading his mind Ella says, "The boat can't sink. Let's go."

He salutes her. "Oh, Captain, my captain."

In the boat, Charlie cold-shoulders Nick, averting his glance and feeble, "Kinda windy out here," attempt at small talk. There's a vulnerability about the boy; as precocious as he is, with all his historical knowledge, Charlie only understands the outside edges of the topic; the battles and the glamour, the big stuff, soldier-boy history. Nick can relate to that. When he was Charlie's age he devoured wartime tales, read all the military fiction he could lay his hands on. But there's a spoiled brat in the kid; he certainly has Ella wrapped around his little finger, probably his mother, too. And what if the Historic Council finds out about Charlie's capers? Surely they could ban him from visiting the site again and cause more trouble for Ella.

On the other hand, this Round Island project seems to mean so much to the boy, gives him something to look forward to and most likely steers him away from bigger trouble. He could be doing much worse, like some of his students who spend a lot of time in juvenile detention centers. Maybe he shouldn't have insisted that Charlie put back his treasure. He suspects that Charlie will return soon anyway, once Nick's out of the picture.

The spray from the breaking waves chills them. *Nipply.* The bottom of the whaler is covered with several inches of water. "Shouldn't we bail this thing out?" Nick asks.

"What's the point? We'll just take in more," says Ella. "Put on your life jackets." It must be serious because she's slapping on hers, tugging the white strap and snapping it in place below her breasts. Charlie breaks his silence. "Aunt Ella knows what's she's doing."

Waves slam into their starboard side, their intensity building as Ella steers the boat from the shelter of the cove, zigzagging across the water to avoid the blunt tips of the whitecaps. Nick tries to think about anything but the water all around and below him. His gaze wanders to Charlie who is shouting something, pointing frantically to the west. Looking in that direction, Nick sees a freighter approaching less than two hundred yards away. It seems to have risen up out of nowhere. How could they have missed it? The vessel's at least eight hundred feet long, sitting low in the water and traveling deceptively fast. Staffed by a crew of a scant ten or eleven, the freighters—lakers, as those who live along these shores call them—look like ghost ships, empty and lonely. Nick's Uncle Ted, who worked on one for years, used to say, "It's ninety-eight percent boredom and two percent terror." Nick feels this ride back is ninety-eight percent terror and two percent boredom—and it's not over yet.

The laker sounds its horn—five short blasts for *get the hell out of my way*—startling Ella, who has been so focused on steering into the area directly before her that she must not have noticed anything in her peripheral vision. Instinctively, Nick jumps off his seat and hunkers down in the hull. Later, when he will reflect back on this moment, his action will make no sense; if the freighter hit them he'd be dead whether in the hull or on the seat, but he felt safer there. The same instinct leads a dying animal to a dark and private place.

"Turn, turn!" Charlie shouts.

"We're gonna die!" screams Benjamin, covering his head with both arms, joining Nick in the hull.

"My God!" screams Ella, jerking the steering wheel with both arms to the extreme right. Charlie jumps up and grabs the wheel to help. Nick sits up straight, staring. At first the boat seems glued in place by the power of the waves. The freighter is bearing down on them quickly. *Eyes, take your last look.* The freighter engines snarl and hiss. "Hold on!" screams Ella. Slowly, one wet inch at a time, their boat begins swinging round until the bow faces Round Island and the waves are coming at them from behind. Ella jams the throttle into high; the freighter passes just yards behind them, its huge shadow skimming over them. Benjamin has crawled out from the hull and he and Charlie yelp and laugh, high fiving each other. Ella turns around and slaps their palms. Nick's legs tremble. He almost peed his pants. *A pack of maniacs. High fiving, for God's sake!* Ella smiles at him and raises her thumb in the air. He regrets coming over to this little island with her, regrets his decision to visit Mackinac, wonders what the hell he had hoped to find there. At that moment a four-foot swell from the freighter's wake rolls toward them. "Watch it, watch out!" he shouts, pointing to the wave. The surge shoves hard into their port side. The boat tips at a seventy-five degree angle as the cooler and a paddle scurry across the hull like panicked crabs. Nick watches in dismay as the cooler flips into the lake.

"The cooler!" he shouts. As Ella turns the boat hard to starboard toward the object, Nick leaps off the back. What surprises him, what he would wonder about days later as he looked back upon this moment, is why he did it. What was he hoping to save? Some leftover chips, a few plastic bags, a cell phone and a thermos? No. This was about saving face.

As he jumps into the water, his left foot slips and he barely clears the motor. An odd sensation pierces through his right foot, something sharp. Could it be one of those lamprey eels? No time to ponder, the cooler's getting away. With the help of the freighter's wake he body-surfs toward it, grabs the handle and waves to Ella and the boys, who stare from the whaler. Benjamin mobilizes first, hurling a rope toward Nick. Though it falls a few yards short, Nick powers toward it, barely grabbing the end with his right hand, grateful for the security of the rope, gripping its rough tendrils, trying to block out the thought of the stone-cold depths below.

Hand over hand, Benjamin and Ella yank him in and soon he's next to the boat. "Take the cooler!" Nick yells to Charlie, releasing the rope and grabbing the edge of the boat.

"Move to the other side and keep this thing from tipping!" Ella directs the boys. Then, with help from Ella and Benjamin, Nick heaves himself up, flopping belly down like a beached whale between the back and front seats, his breath coming in short gasps. "Whale on board," he mutters. That's when he notices the pinkish color of the water swishing in the hull.

"Shit, your foot!" yells Benjamin. Nick glances down where the end section of his small toe is cockeyed, streaming blood, the edge of his sandal sheared off.

"The damned propeller," says Ella.

13

Ella switches places with Charlie. "Aim just left of the lighthouse and we'll anchor," she says, grabbing a towel that she tosses to Nick before clambering over the front seat. Easing down next to him she examines his foot. "Lie back and keep your leg up. Press the towel down hard. Jesus, it's sliced as clean as baloney."

"Thanks for the reassurance."

"I think they can stitch it back together at the medical center. It's all there, barely clinging on."

"Oh great. A Klingon." The white towel is now crimson.

"I'm calling 9-1-1. They'll send someone over—if I can get a signal," says Ella, punching in the number. "Nothing. The phone's too wet and I can rarely get a signal over here anyway."

Nick presses the towel down firmly on his toe. The sting has intensified to a feeling of fire. "Don't call—I'll be OK. Let's just get back to the island."

Tapping the keys on the screen she looks up." Hey, I got a signal!" Ella explains the situation to the operator. "Get someone here as soon as you can. Please." Although the boat still heaves on the waves, they are buffered from the wind by the curve of Round Island. Ending the call, she leans toward him. "I'm so sorry."

"It could've been worse, a lot worse," says Nick. "You remember the Bobbitt case?"

"As if anyone would forget about a woman cutting off her husband's penis and throwing it out a car window?"

"Well, think of this as Bobbitt junior," says Nick. The boys are chuckling. At least he hasn't lost his sense of humor. She sure would have. "Don't worry. You'll be walking fine in a few more days."

Nick grips her arm. "Can I call you Lorena?"

"Lorena?"

"Mrs. Bobbitt."

Ella punches his arm. "Get outta here."

Benjamin seems transfixed by Nick's foot. "You want to see it?" asks Nick, whisking off the bloody towel and holding his foot a few inches from the boy's face. Benjamin looks away, but Ella examines it closely.

"Not good. You might get an infection. Keep it covered." Ella gently wraps the towel tightly around his foot, leaving her hands on the cloth and pressing lightly.

"Is there anything to eat?" asks Charlie. "I'm starving."

"I can't believe you've got an appetite," says Benjamin, but he opens the cooler and throws Charlie a bag of chips. "Nick, our hero. You saved the potato chips!"

Charlie sits back in the front seat munching on them, oblivious to the drama behind him.

Despite her reassurances, Ella wonders if the island's small medical facility can perform a Bobbitt-like miracle. The staff is experienced with broken bones and asthma attacks, but this is different.

Soon they hear the insect buzz of a motor as a small rig heads toward them. A big, bearded man in an orange life jacket that adds to his bulk waves at them. Ella recognizes Joe, an islander who works at the marina. *Now everyone is going to know about this.*

"Where's the patient?" calls Joe as he pulls up beside them.

"Right here," says Nick, raising his arm.

"You boys hold our boats together while we get this guy aboard," directs Joe. The waves slam the boats' hulls as they meet with a cracking sound.

"Hey, watch it," says Ella.

"You watch it. I didn't come out here to get my boat wrecked."

Nick crouches to steady his weight, then places both hands on the side of Joe's boat. The towel around his foot unravels, leaving a trail of blood. Joe holds Nick's arm and pulls him in.

"Can I go too?" asks Benjamin. "My dad's gonna get worried."

"Sure. Charlie, you go ahead," says Ella.

"I don't want to leave you alone."

"I'll be fine. Go over and help get Nick up to the medical center. I'm counting on you." From his seat in Joe's boat, Nick wears a sheepish look on his face. "Ella, I'm sorry."

"This is no time for apologies." Both boys climb aboard Joe's boat and the man turns it toward Mackinac, shifting the motor into high speed.

Ella sits alone at the wheel, surveying the jumble of towels, shoes, and trash sloshing around in pink water. She sighs. This is getting messy.

***

The cheerful doctor on duty stitches Nick's toe back into place with a few deft strokes. Nick can't watch. "It's going to heal just fine. You can thank that cold lake," she says, stepping back to survey her handiwork. At first Nick was dubious since the woman looked well under thirty, but as he examines his toe it appears intact, with some colored thread down the side, reminding him of the foot of a stuffed animal.

"Okay, let's cover up the baby," she murmurs, wrapping gauze around it. Nick winces. "I'll get you some pain pills. We have a few freebies in stock."

"How about a shot of whiskey?" suggests Nick.

"Don't mix them with the booze. Trust me. Your toe will start throbbing once the lidocaine wears off; there's no way you'll be able to sleep without painkillers."

As he limps into the waiting area like a spavined horse, Ella bursts in and glances at his bandaged foot. "Guess you'll be wearing only sandals for a while. Come on, I've got a carriage waiting. You're going to stay with us." Now he's in deep.

"That's too much trouble for you. I've already caused enough problems for one day."

She pauses. "You're so right, Nick Pappas. Now come on."

Outside, Ella directs the taxi driver, a handsome, graying man in a red sweatshirt, to the Maples. Not surprising, Ella knows the owner. "Hi, Judy," she says when the woman runs out on the porch as the carriage pulls up. Judy looks from Ella, to Nick, then down to his bandaged foot.

"A little accident," he mutters. "I won't be staying tonight."

Nick limps up the stairs to the second floor with Ella behind him. "In case you slip," she explains. In his room he's embarrassed by the bottle of whiskey on the bureau and soiled clothing on the bed. Ella whisks everything into his duffle bag and lugs it downstairs, then out to the carriage. He hobbles behind her.

Judy clucks. "Ordinarily I'd have to charge you for breaking your stay," she says, handing him a receipt. "But seeing you've got *friends* here and a medical emergency, I'm making an exception. Now take care of yourself."

As he limps to the waiting carriage, Nick feels the eyes of the driver upon his foot. The carriage pulls away from the Maples, where Judy remains on the porch, watching. "If it wasn't already all over town, it will be now," says Ella.

"What?"

"Us," she says.

Make that the lack of us. On the way up the hill, the pain in Nick's foot grips him like a snapping turtle clamping down on a doomed egret's leg. He'd watched one taken down in a wetland once, took nearly four hours before the snapper succeeded. "Damn it," he mutters. "Ella, can I have a hit of water please. Good island tap water?" He removes the pills from the packaging, popping two in his mouth.

By the time they arrive at Cedar Bluff, it's past five. Nick's legs have gone rubbery; a bed is all he wants. They pull up out back near the kitchen door. Using the staircase from the kitchen, Ella shows him to his room. It's small and cozy, with pine beaded board walls and a twin bed with a tartan plaid covering. "I'm wiped out," Nick says, plunking down on the bed. "I'm so sorry, Ella." He's pretty sure his words are slurred.

Putting her hand up she says, "Stop right there. Get some rest. Don't worry about us. We'll be around when you are better." Backing out of the room, she shuts the door softly. He can hear her on the other side whisper, "Sweet dreams."

The room is musty and hot. Opening the window, he sees the barn out back. Stripping off his clothes down to his boxers, he removes a flask from his suitcase, unscrews the top and takes a huge swig, savoring the slow burn down his throat. Yanking back the plaid duvet and white cotton blanket beneath it, he lies down and pulls up the sheet, leaving his right foot out. Below him he hears voices in the kitchen, along with the muffled clang of dishes and silverware. In less than a minute he's out, whipped to shit.

***

Downstairs, Ella makes a simple meal of grilled cheese sandwiches and a salad for her and Charlie.

"This is old people's food," Charlie tells her. He eats half his sandwich before standing up and opening the fridge.

"Get out of there," Ella scolds.

"You should throw out half this stuff. It's reproducing." Charlie holds a plastic tub with slimy lettuce up to the light, dumps it in the sink, then takes a pickle jar in his hand.

Ella shakes her head. "Someday you're going to learn to cook. It'll save money and you'll eat healthier." Charlie sits back at his place at the kitchen table and opens the pickle jar. "So, what do you think of Nick?" Ella asks.

Chomping on a pickle, Charlie says, "He jumped off the boat just to prove his manliness and look what happened. He got—how would you say—toe decapitation?"

"Dephalangated."

"Yeah, he nearly got dephalangated."

"You think that's why he jumped?"

"Yep. And I know what's going to happen next. You're going to smack him down." Charlie stuffs the other half of the pickle in his mouth.

"Come on."

"It's true. You always do."

Later that night, Ella awakens about 1:00 a.m. to tapping on her bedroom window. Moonlight shines on the source of the noise: bats circling outside, touching the glass panes with silken wingtips. A few land on the scalloped siding just above her window, then pop through a minuscule hole that leads to the attic. *They're back.* She smiles. All her life she's loved bats, even when other kids teased her about it and said she was witchy. She remembers the time she and Nick tried to camp out in a little cave on the back side of the island. Turned out they'd taken up residency with a colony of bats.

Wandering through the hallways, Ella hears faint snoring from Nick's room; those pills must have knocked him out. He can't leave for at least a day with that bum toe. She's stuck with him. Ella weighs the pros and cons of the prospect, but her meditation is broken by a thud in Charlie's room. Recently he's been rolling out of bed. Afraid he'll catch her standing there, or worse, awaken Nick, who might find her by his doorway, she scampers to Charlie's door and turns the knob. Locked. She'd told him not to do that. What if there was an emergency? She'll talk to him about that tomorrow.

Back in her room Ella returns to the window, where the bats trace invisible lines across the sky. Whoever said they're just mice with wings has never studied them closely, nor watched their elegant bodies draped in velvety capes glistening in the moonlight.

14

Another misty morning, with Nick up first, sitting on the porch in the wicker rocker, left foot propped on an ottoman, a plaid Mackinaw blanket draped around his shoulders. His head is dizzy from his medication and the whiskey's aftermath. A cup of coffee sure sounds good, but after foraging unsuccessfully for any in the kitchen, he's given up. When he changed his bandage that morning he'd expected a bloody mess, but there was just a line of maroon across the gauze, and his toe was sewn with tight little stitches. Thank God the throbbing had stopped. He'd taken a long bath with his leg hanging over the side, apparently in violation of one of the house rules posted on the bathroom wall in a plastic sheath:

STOP. Conserve water. Please limit showers to 3 minutes, avoid baths.

He hopes Ella will forgive him. *Speaking of Ella, where is she?*

He looks around for something to read and finds the island paper, opening it to the police report:

A white Jack Russell terrier was reported running through the streets near the Beauchamp Hotel last week. Before the police could apprehend the dog, a woman exiting a store said the dog belonged to her. She was cited for letting the dog run loose. A Market Street hotel called the police August 1 to report a man and woman naked in the hotel's public hot tub. When police arrived, the officer discovered the door was locked. The police determined the couple was intoxicated. They were not charged, but were given trespass notices and banned from the hotel property.

A total of 15 bicycle larcenies were reported for the week.

A sound near the side of the yard startles him and Nick looks up. Striding toward him from a gate in the tall hedge separating Cedar Bluff from the cottage to the west is a tiny woman wearing flowery capris, a green striped blouse, and a sun visor. She matches the awning on that mint pistachio fudge shop perfectly. Her bobbed brown hair, cut in a severe angle rising from front to back, gives the impression she's wearing a Roman helmet. She's remarkably short, Nick guesses four foot eleven, tops, and her sturdy build reminds him of a gymnast; rock solid and chest pancake-flat. When she marches over to the porch, arms pumping, he has a vision of R2-D2. "Yoo-hoo!" She stands in the front yard waving.

Nick waves back. "Good morning."

"I'm Darci, next door. You must be a houseguest."

Nick pushes his reading glasses up on his head. "Can't see a thing out there, the fog's so thick. I'm Nick. Friend of Ella's." Given this slight entrée, Darci races up the porch steps.

"Welcome to our bluff." She extends her hand and stares at his foot. "What happened?"

The screen door opens behind him and he hears a soft, "Oh no." It's Ella, looking sleepy, with dark circles under her eyes. Her bare feet protrude from the cuffs of gray sweatpants topped by an inside-out T-shirt.

"Oh, hi, Ella. I'm chatting with your houseguest about his foot." Nicks thinks of a cat with a fresh mouse in her mouth. When he starts to speak, Ella cuts him off. "Just a little cut from a boat propeller. He'll be fine."

"My God, there's been so many accidents this summer," says Darci, her hand flying up to her mouth in shock. "Did you hear about Kitty Sheldon? She fell off her horse yesterday in Soldier's Garden. Was riding alone. Hit her head on a rock and got a concussion. Some fudgies found her and called 9-1-1, thank God. They say there was blood all over her shirt right down to her panties."

"Was she riding Poppy?" asks Ella.

"No, but she should have been. Poppy's a good, calm horse. She had to get fancy and take out her new Saddlebred."

"New what?" asks Nick. Ella scowls at him.

"A Saddlebred, prancy, high-stepping horses. The newest Mackinac equine trend." Turning back to Ella, Darci races on. "Kitty's way too old to start mounting one of those."

"She's only forty-four," says Ella.

"Too old for a Saddlebred. But that's not what I came over to tell you about. There's some bad news: the police found two college kids up above one of the shops last night, unconscious." Darci turns to Nick. "They suspect a drug overdose. Byron heard it on the scanner. Horrible. The island's getting overrun by drugs."

"The next thing you know the cartels will be on the ferry," says Nick with a wink toward Ella. She responds with another scowl.

Darci doesn't notice. "I'm telling you, it isn't safe here anymore," she says. "Ella, you'd better keep your phone with you when you're out jogging."

"Nonsense. I feel safer here than anywhere."

"Two near-dead kids downtown and you feel safe? Things have changed. Trust me."

They'll have a little more substance for the next police report than runaway dogs and naked hot-tubbers, thinks Nick.

"Thanks for your concern. By the way, we were just about to eat breakfast." Turning to Nick she says, "Shall we?" Darci glowers at Ella before turning to Nick, beaming. "So nice to meet you, Nick. Good luck with that toe. Stay out of the manure." Turning back to Ella, Darci nods her head in Nick's direction and winks. "Enjoy." Then she scoots off the porch, pumping her way down the steps and back through the gate.

"Whew," says Nick. "You bluff ladies know how to cut each other up."

"I was polite."

Passive-aggressive is the term he would choose. "So was she. The subtext is everything. Tell me more about Darci. She wears me out just watching her."

"She used to speed skate. A sprinter. Almost made it to the Olympics. She's relatively new here, maybe fifteen years. Her grandmother once owned a cottage here a long time ago, but her father never took to the island. They sold it when she was a child. Her husband's painfully bashful, odd sort of guy. He spends most of his time out back in their carriage house building birdhouses. He runs around the island every morning just like clockwork. Darci's a trust-fund baby, so they've got plenty of time on their hands. Please don't say anything to that woman, not one piece of info, zip—and never ask her a question. If you do she'll go on and on." She looks at him closely. "You're wearing glasses."

"Just for reading. Don't you wear them?"

"Not yet. I'm blessed with perfect eyesight." She flicks a strand of hair off her forehead and shrugs.

"Now that we're stuck inside, how about breakfast?" "I sure could use a cup of coffee. And no offense, but I don't remember cooking as one of your, um, aptitudes."

"I've learned a thing or two."

"I recall you burned the marshmallows yesterday."

"They taste better that way." They stroll back to the kitchen, where patches of sun splash through the wavy-glass windowpanes. "You know what I think?" says Nick, settling into one of the ladder-back chairs at the kitchen table. "This place needs one helluva lot of work."

Ella, who is squatting before an open cupboard and rattling through the pans, pivots around. "You think I don't know that? You heard a bit of my to-do list yesterday."

"I know, I know. Allow me to finish. I was thinking I could help you."

The pan clanging stops as Ella sits back on her heels. "Huh?"

"Yeah, I built a house once, grew up fixing things with Papa. I'm pretty handy." It's true, though he's eliminated the part about hating to do home repairs, especially after all he went through with Katie. "A lot of folks get all out of kilter trying to keep up a place, blow out a joint, fall off a ladder or something. The fixers fall apart more than the houses they're trying to fix." His brother had toppled off the roof while hosing out the gutters just to save a few hundred dollars. After having his head stitched up and being diagnosed with a concussion, the doctors said he could have been paralyzed had he hit the ground on his back instead of his butt.

"Isn't that the truth?" Carrying an omelet pan to the stove, she moves on to the refrigerator where she bends over, shuffling around in the veggie crisper, then walks with a swagger from fridge to sink. He can tell by the lack of lines around her butt she's not wearing any underwear. Probably shot straight out of bed and came downstairs.

"Here's an onion, green and red pepper. Cut," she says, slapping the vegetables and a wooden cutting board on the table in front of him.

Nick smiles. "Do you trust me with this? I might slice off one of my fingers."

"I'll add it to the omelet." She hands him a hunk of sharp cheddar and a grater. "Please grate the cheese, too." Ella leaves the pan on the stove to comb the pantry for spices. When she returns armed with cayenne, basil, and paprika, Nick is standing in front of the stove, nudging the yellow circle of a bubbling omelet.

"What are you doing? I need to add the spices," says Ella. Her eyes sparkle and she seems more relaxed.

"I couldn't resist. Used to make these in my grandparents' restaurant, one of those family joints with an all-day breakfast menu."

"No matter how hard I try, my omelets always turn into scrambled eggs." She hands him the spices. "Add a little of these." Nick looks dubiously at the cayenne. "Mother likes a touch of it in her eggs and I've taken it up, too."

"When will she be back?" He slides the spatula under the omelet, then flips it.

"Not sure. She's causing a stir at the care facility, but I can't handle her yet. Too high maintenance. Orange juice, apple juice, or water?"

"The latter, of course, since it's the best in the world."

"Let's eat in the dining room."

Nick eases the omelets onto a chipped blue and white platter Ella has set out. Carrying their dishes into the wood-paneled dining room, they set them on the long cherry table and take seats across from each other. Nick's omelets are perfect, fluffy semicircles, two half-moons on a blue sky. Ella places one on her plate and takes a bite. "Yum. How did you manage this?"

"I'll show you later." From upstairs comes the sound of feet moving slowly on the wooden floor toward the staircase, then Charlie walks in rubbing his eyes, his hair filled with static. He reminds Nick of a cartoon bird.

"Dining in style, I see," says Charlie. Nick swears there's a smirk on his face.

"We've been waiting for you to get up."

"I'll skip the eggs and go straight for the real stuff." Charlie heads for the pantry.

"I can hear him getting into the Pop-Tarts. He eats way too much sugar. Sara's super-strict about his diet, but as a mere substitute mom I let him get away with it."

"He's a teenager. They all eat like that. And I don't exactly see your sister here to supervise him."

"That's a long story. I'll tell you about it later." She nods her head toward the pantry where the smell of strawberry Pop-Tarts wafts into the dining room. "Hey, cereal killer, do me a favor and drink a glass of OJ!" she calls.

"Don't worry, I won't tell Mom how awesome you are." He strolls into the dining room balancing a glass of juice and a plate of Pop-Tarts on top of a mixing bowl filled with cereal. "I have to be down at the bike shop by ten."

"Don't you usually start at eleven?"

"Bobby's sailing today and asked me to cover for him."

Between bites of his cereal, which he's scooping rapidly into his mouth, Charlie says, "What are you guys doing?"

"Not sure yet," replies Ella, eyeing his toe, "but if Nick's up to it I have a little task."

Nick wonders how he'll manage anything today, then feels the packaging around the pills in his pocket. That'll do the trick.

15

~~~

It suddenly dawns on her: without Charlie, she'll be alone with Nick. She takes the dishes into the kitchen. At the sink she drops a knife on the floor. Since Nick showed up she feels things falling apart inside her. Unbuckled.

When she returns to the dining room, the guys have moved to the sunroom where they are fiddling with her tablet on a white desk near the windows. Sunshine forms little halos around their heads; Ella pauses, taking a mental snapshot of the scene. So domestic.

"You have funny icons," says Nick, staring at the screen.

"Please don't insult my icons," says Ella, walking next to his chair.

"How does this thing work?" He is rubbing his fingers over the screen, clueless to touch technology.

Reaching across the table, Charlie whisks his hand across the device and a screen emerges. "There," he says.

"So you're not into computers?" she asks.

"Not much. I regard my time as too precious for Facebooking, or whatever noun they've turned into a tech verb. As for twittering, I say that's for the birds. I don't want my thoughts truncated at 140 letters."

"I don't do much social media either," says Charlie. "It's a total wasteland."

Nick turns to him. "Ah, so you're a Luddite?"

"Naw. I couldn't live without the Internet for other stuff. I'm just not much into social media. Except gaming, which isn't the same thing at all."

"And his mother wouldn't be able to communicate with him without texting," says Ella. It's true; Sara chooses to text instead of talk with everyone, including her only child.

The landline rings in the hallway, and Charlie moves briskly to answer it. Ella leans toward Nick. "Press enter," she instructs, pressing her finger on a digitized button on the screen. A search box appears. She can feel his hand barely touching hers. In the hallway Charlie mumbles something, and she hopes he'll extend the conversation. Nick has entered a word in the search box and a soldier in a blue uniform rises slowly on the screen. "I want to see if Charlie recognizes this," he winks. "It's kind of a test."

Ella hears Charlie signing off with a "Later, dude." He enters the room with a frown. "That was Benjamin. His dad's all ticked off about the boat accident. Benjamin sort of let slip about the bone. His dad is probably gonna call you. Benjamin had to sneak on the phone. They took away his cell. I'm sorry."

"It's not your fault. Benjamin's dad is an, ah, disagreeable person."

"You can say asshole. I've heard it before."

"Watch your language, young man," cautions Ella.

"John—Benjamin's dad– has a faux Victorian cottage in a development a few miles from downtown that a few bluffers are still simmering about," she explains. "Cut down all those beautiful trees so they could have a view." She hates the development, although she envies its modern conveniences. Unlike the *real* Victorians, the newer houses are better behaved and well insulated, staying cool in the summer and warm during cold days. No rattling pipes or electrical surprises in those places. Not yet. The plumbing will probably be good for the next 20 years. John has substantial clout with the current governor and had wrangled himself an appointment to the Historic Council. Like many of the more recent cottage owners, he's a businessman, not as interesting as the older families, who have had enough years and money to spawn eccentric progeny. Characters were being replaced by coolheaded, investment-minded types who use their cottages as tax write-offs. Ella doesn't fear a showdown with John, just dreads the possibility he'll block Benjamin's friendship with Charlie.

"Charlie, can you identify what kind of soldier wore this uniform?" Nick asks, pointing to the screen.

Crouching beside Nick, Charlie pauses, tapping his fingers on the desk. "Uh, yeah, American soldier around 1800."

"Foot soldier or artillery? "

"Uh... not sure" says Charlie.

Ella settles into an armchair and takes out a notebook, smiling as the two males haggle: "Artillery—see his yellow buttons? "You sure?" "Absolutely."

She begins a list:

- Knock down wasp nest
- Refill Mother's prescription online/call Mother.
- Finish painting porch steps
- Buy 1 cucumber, 2 red peppers, Pop-Tarts, olive oil, eggs.
- Call Billy D. re: tower floor.
- Repair broken screens.
- Recheck company audit.
- Mass e-mail to Save Our Water Now members re: eco-toilets.

She sets down her pencil and turns to Charlie.

"Mom texted me from Colombo last night. She's gonna call Grandma today," says Charlie.

"Did she leave any new instructions?"

"She was in a hurry. Said she'd call you tonight."

"Isn't it time for you to get downtown and take care of fudgies?" asks Ella.

"Yeah. They couldn't possibly make it without me."

"What time do you get off work today?"

"Two o'clock I hope. Will you guys be here?"

"Should be. We'll probably be knocking off a few items on the to-do list." She smiles at Nick. "Now that I have someone here both handy and willing—though a tad maimed—these chores should be manageable."

"Well, see you," says Charlie. "Find me some more soldiers for when I get home," he says to Nick. "Bet I'll kick your butt."

He heads toward the kitchen and Ella hears the back door slam. Nick is hunched over the tablet but his eyes are focused outside, on the view. For a moment Ella imagines that he has always been there, sitting in her favorite place in the world.

16

Leaning backward over the west rail of the porch examining something above, Ella crooks her neck from left to right. She's changed into a pair of jeans and a long-sleeved shirt that says "Crim 10-Miler."

"Come look at this," she says, pointing up at a corner of the porch ceiling. Nick walks to the railing, places his left hand on it and turns his head and torso upward, a maneuver that sends a flash of pain down his spine. There it is, a wasp's nest lodged between the eave and the roof.

"Let's knock it down," says Ella.

"I thought you hated killing anything. You said it would upset the balance of things, like those Round Island snakes."

"This is different." She offers no explanation as to how.

"Why don't we just spray it?" he offers. Ella scowls. "OK, no spray."

"My plan is to smother them. After you knock down the nest, I'll throw a tarp over it."

"After *I* knock it down?"

"Yes. You're strong and handy."

"I'm also handi*capped*," he says, pointing to his foot.

"It won't take much physical effort. Besides, I get a terrible reaction from stings." She hands him the broom, a pair of gloves, and a baseball cap, then waltzes into the house, leaving him alone to commit wasp genocide. Hoisting the broom above his head he takes a swat at the nest. It doesn't budge, but on the second try he manages to knock a off a chunk of it, letting loose a squadron of angry wasps that descend on him from all directions, diving at his head and arms, sending him hobbling across the porch, dropping the broom in the process. "Holy shit!"

A wasp aims for his hand. Ella taps on the front window, cell phone in hand, cheering him on. "Hit it again!" she shouts. "You only got half of it."

Taking refuge in the front hallway, he waits for the insects to calm down. A few wasps circle outside the screen door. Ella has vanished somewhere upstairs; he heard her footsteps running up the staircase when he dashed in. Soon she emerges on the staircase wearing a long trench coat, hat, gloves, and a veil fashioned from mosquito netting, looking like a cross between a Taliban wife and a CIA agent. "Hand me that broom," she says, palm out. At five foot nine, she's just three inches shorter than him, and her lanky arms may be longer. On the porch she takes a whack at the nest, which plummets to the ground and a cloud of wasps emerge. "Throw the tarp over it!" she shouts, running toward the front door.

As instructed, Nick throws the tarp over the railing; as it floats down over the nest, the frenzied energy from the doomed wasps keeps it aloft a few more seconds. "Mission accomplished," he announces as he opens the door.

Inside, they sit in the sunroom, where Ella explains to him why she wants to eradicate the insects. "I had an accident with Sara. A bad one. I blame those damned wasps."

***

She hesitates before telling the story. It resurrects too many feelings. Even all these years later she can still feel a pang down her back where a bolt on their carriage ripped through the skin. She sighs, then begins.

Ella and Sara were in their doctor's buggy with the top down sitting side by side as their horse, Captain, pulled them at a brisk trot. A beautiful Hackney gelding with a fine gait, Captain was an excellent driving horse. Ella was holding the reins casually in one hand, admiring the view from the top of Mission Hill, one of the best on the island. Although she'd seen it hundreds of times, summer after summer, she never approached it without a sense of anticipation. The black flies and other pesky critters were in full force that day due to a wetter than normal June. Ella had noticed a new wasp's nest under the eave of the front porch that very morning.

Suddenly, something spooked Captain and he began to skitter in the shafts. Ella grabbed the reins tighter, pulling back hard. Captain was now cantering in place, a sure clue he was about to bolt. All those years as a tour driver taught her the signals. Beasts of prey, horses are hardwired to run from a predator. And run. And run. It had happened to her a few times, but she was always able to calm her team down before anyone got hurt. She prided herself on stopping a runaway when her horses took off on the hill to the fort. She'd turned them into the park where they stopped just before a row of lilacs. But this was different. Captain had begun running, gaining speed with each stride as they approached a fork in the road a few hundred feet ahead. The stretch of road to the right plunged downhill in an elbow curve; the left went straight and flat. If she steered him that way, most likely she could run Captain out before the road became tricky again. She yanked hard on the left rein. "Whoa, Captain. Whoa." At her side, Sara sat with panicked eyes, her jaw open. She had never taken to horses like Ella and most of the girls who grew up on the island. "Why should I like an animal that poops all over the street and could kill me?" she'd said. Not only that, but she had allergies around them; at least she sneezed and complained, though Ella had suspicions it was an act.

"Hold on to that handle next to you and don't let go!" yelled Ella. "Hold tight. Easy boy, easy."

For a moment Captain's head turned left, and Ella thought she'd managed to steer him that direction. Then his head jerked up and he veered to the right. Ella hoped to God no one was coming up the hill. She had only one trick left, something she'd learned from an old master driver, Harry, but had never tried: loosen one rein, then yank hard on the other, forcing the horse to look back. "Most horses can't look behind 'em and run forward at the same time," Harry had explained. "That will work on a two-wheeler, but it might flip a four-wheeler. If that doesn't work, run 'em into a tree, a fence, anything before they kill you. Consider a tree as a horse brake of last resort."

"But that will break their legs," she'd said.

"So who do you want to die, you or them horses?"

Ella loosened the left rein while wrenching hard on the right, trying to force Captain's head back around.

"Stop him, Ella!" screamed Sara, clutching the side bar with both hands.

"Help me. Pull on this rein with me!" shouted Ella. Sara leaned forward to grab the rein with her left hand; together, the sisters managed to get Captain's head turned slightly back and he began slowing. The buggy suddenly whipped out, its rear fishtailing to the left. The sound of the wooden shaft snapping sounded like musket fire from Fort Mackinac, followed by a screeching of wheels. The carriage flipped over, forcing Captain to slow to a walk, then a complete stop, while ejecting Sara and Ella.

When the paramedics arrived, Ella lay sprawled on her left side. Sara was unconscious on her back, in the middle of the road. Captain was calmly munching grass on the roadside and a group of frightened tourists had gathered around them. Ella remembered hearing voices and seeing the back of Captain's hooves. Her first thought was, "Thank God Captain's okay." Later she wondered why she hadn't thought about Sara at that moment. Pain punched her shoulder and arm, and her back burned. She couldn't move, and passed out.

At the medical center she awoke to a doctor's face staring with concern into hers, his hands gently touching her left arm. "Can you wiggle your toes?" he asked.

"How's Sara?"

"She's fine. Just show me if you can move your toes." Ella wiggled her toes. "Good," said the doctor. "We're sending you to the mainland where they'll put you back together. You have a few broken bones."

Before she could reply, Ella saw her father's face in the doorway, pale and panicked.

"She's going to be OK," said the doctor. Father ran forward, grabbed her hands and kissed them tenderly, with a reverence she rarely saw in him.

"How's Sara?" she asked.

"Pretty bad, my little rabbit. Mother's with her. But she'll make it."

Ella had a broken collarbone and some cracked ribs, a skull gash and a slash down her back from sliding over a bolt connecting the hood to the buggy. It required thirty stitches. But that was nothing compared to Sara, who had a concussion, broken arm, and several cracked vertebrae. Nick, who'd sat quietly though Ella's narration now asks, "How does this tie in to wasps?"

"I think they stung Captain. That's why he ran." Her eyes flash. "I hate them. Not only that, but it's what got Sara started on pain meds. She's had a problem ever since."

17

"We're becoming obsolete," says Nick. Now that the wasps have been silenced, he and Ella are sitting comfortably on the porch, each with a mug in their hand, the sun warm and bright.

"You sound like an old fart."

"Getting there, aren't we? But look at the rift between our generation and Charlie's—it's insurmountable."

Ella smiles. "He doesn't do a lot of the social media stuff, but if there's something that interests him, he's a tech wiz. So are most of his buddies." She takes a sip of tea. "I'm no digital native, but I'm comfortable with it; a good digital immigrant, you might say."

Nick stares at his coffee. "The biggest discipline issue in my classes is kids texting and playing games on their cells. Of course we ban all that stuff in classes but that doesn't stop them. During silent reading I have students—bright ones—begging me to let them go on the computer rather than read a book or even a magazine. I saw a baby—a damned baby—watching a movie on her father's fricking phone at breakfast in a restaurant last week. And her mom on her cell. How much interaction do you think was going on in that family?"

"Oh c'mon, Nick. Welcome to the twenty-first century. You can't stop the younger generation from following its own path."

Nick sighs. "I know, it just seems like everybody is elsewhere. We're not present for one another anymore. Walk around a shopping mall and everyone looks schizophrenic, jabbering away to invisible people. Even here, on this beautiful island, lots of folks would rather see a picture of a tree than touch a real one."

Ella is sitting back on the couch with her legs curled sideways beneath her as Nick talks. *Lecture* is a better word. Does he think this is a classroom? All this talk irritates her because the truth is, it worries her, too. They're in alignment on this, but there's not one damn thing they can do to stop it. "You're afraid that you can't keep up, that you'll be marginalized," she says. Though she shares this fear, she'd prefer to keep that to herself.

"Perhaps. But look out there, Ella, at that lake, that view. Would you rather see that on some electronic screen?" The Straits spread out below the bluff, a shimmering field, each wave a row of blue grain garnished in sunlight. A red and yellow-striped spinnaker blossoms like a rose on the bow of a sailboat tacking off the Round Island lighthouse as the gentle west breeze shakes the geranium petals in the porch flower boxes.

"Of course not." She sighs. "I need the real deal." The drone of departing ferries rises from the harbor, their upper decks stuffed with tourists. Despite the economic downturn, it is a good season. A crow flutters down from a cedar by the porch, hunches its shoulders, and caws.

"This water's a richer blue than Lake Superior, which always has a touch of steel in it," says Nick, settling deeper into the cushions on the rocker.

Now here's a subject she likes to discuss. "You're a Great Lakes kid. Their waters are in your blood, too, just like mine," she says.

"I don't recall either of us being cold-blooded."

She blushes. "You know what I mean. What concerns me isn't so much technology taking over our world, but how we're going to use it to save it, to save this." Ella's hand sweeps out over the lake, leaving a trail of invisible ripples.

"What's the worry? There's billions of gallons of water out there."

"Don't be so sure of that. Water is the oil of the twenty-first century and there's been lots of schemes about stealing all this fresh water. It could happen in our lifetime. And it will certainly happen in Charlie's." Ella stares at her beloved lake, imagining it drained, a moonscape of rocks where hikers scramble across to visit Mackinac, a ghost town, the tallest rock formation in the former Great Lakes. "It's possible. Think about the Aral Sea. They destroyed that in less than fifty years."

"Where's that?"

"In central Asia, Kazakhstan, and a few other *stan* countries. Maybe the worst environmental disaster of our lives. It's barely trickling back. But now we've got the California drought, Colorado's going dry, the whole West . . ."

"We sound like our grandparents."

"We almost *are* our grandparents—without grandchildren." Ella rubs her nose; she will never experience grandparenting. Grand-aunting, perhaps, but never that experience of caring for her children's children.

Nick looks back toward the bridge, bold and majestic today. "Think about our lives as that water out there, the bridge the dividing line, but it's no longer straight down the middle. We've crossed over to the sunset side of the bridge. More water beyond it than on this side."

"Oh, Nick, why did you choose that metaphor? It's worrisome enough to know more than half my life has slipped away."

But he's moved on to a new topic. "Do you know I have kids who wake up and see Lake Superior every day, but they rarely go outdoors?" he says. "That gorgeous lake is staring them square in the face, but they're inside watching TV or playing video games. The science teacher takes a few field trips to the city forest, and we've started an annual trip to the Boundary Waters. It transforms some of the kids, puts the natural world inside their souls."

Ella thinks about Charlie, how lucky he is to have this island, a life-long connection to nature. When he was younger he was outside most all day, a free-range child, riding his bike, hanging out at the barn with the horses, playing in the garden. Even now with his computer games and techy distractions, the island lifestyle forces him to stay outside alot. She studies Nick, how his hands move in wide orbs as he speaks, his eyes blaze. On this subject, he's passionate. It draws her toward him, this shared reverence for the natural world. She'd long ago given up on organized religion, finding her spirituality in the island's beauty, in the fierce power of the Great Lakes, in the wild melancholy of the vanishing outdoors. This is what they've always shared; it remains there between them, unswerving.

Ella imagines him in a classroom, probably the type of teacher who inspires, not in a showoffy way, like one of those Hollywood versions where a stunning young woman or nerdy guy transforms a class of underachievers from impoverished families into calculus whizzes in one semester, but on a fundamental level, one student at a time, the kind of teacher you remember when all the others fade away. "If I were sitting in your classroom, what would I see?" she asks, leaning toward him.

"Hmm. A lot of tables with kids sitting around them, maps all over the walls. And you'd see a middle-aged guy with messy hair walking around from table to table asking questions, maybe saying a little something."

"You mean telling big stories?"

"Well, I have to keep them from texting under the table, don't I?" They laugh.

"What else?" She's eager to learn more, forming a picture of him, firm and in control of a room of horny, distracted teenagers.

"You'd see me struggling to get through to kids like Nathan. He, uh, how can I say this delicately . . . well, the elevator doesn't quite reach the top floor. On a geography quiz he called the Aegean Sea the GNC. I don't have the best and the brightest anymore." He glances at his hands, clasping them together.

"You strike me as the AP type."

"Oh, I used to be before—before I started teaching these more needy kids. I would dress up as a Voyageur during our French explorers unit. That would give you a laugh. I have the whole outfit, used to do reenactments. And I'd take them to visit the state legislature in Madison—"

"Madison? I thought you taught in Duluth." He looks flushed.

"Oh, a long time ago."

"What happened? Why did you stop?"

Nick has slumped forward, squeezing his palms, his gaze toward the floor. "There's only so many years you can teach like your hair's on fire. It's called burn-out."

Something about his look, that distance in his voice, as if he's holding something back.

***

Should he tell her? What would she think of him then? And what if she were to walk into his classroom? Based on the success of his students, he knows his methods work, yet he is far from the inspirational pedagogue of the past who, according to some students, had the *coolest projects ever.* Now at his new school they often spend thirty minutes on the warm-up as he pushes to get a spark from the kids.

Many of them are hungry, a few go to sleep hearing drunken parents fighting, a few are drunk themselves. That or stoned. The smell of weed in their sweaters and jackets is pervasive.

There's no room for charisma where he teaches now. That had faded with the Madison incident. Now it's all structure and worksheets, get their butts in their seats and pass those exams. Graduate. Never mind if much learning's going on. Never again will he be a high-profile instructor who dazzles parents and administrators. On the other hand, he has lit a few fires in some of his students.

In some respect he's working harder than ever, just unnoticed for his efforts. "I help build citizens," he likes to say. His family had pounded this into him. "Niko, you don't know what a great country this is," his grandma Evangelia used to tell him. They'd been purged from Istanbul ("Never say that word!" screamed his grandmother. "It's Constantinople."). A great uncle had been executed during the Istanbul pogroms, leaving his wife with two babies to raise. Nick's parents voted in every election, even one with an uncontested candidate running for school board. Mama once ran for city council and lost by less than forty votes. Later, she refused to speak to a friend who had forgotten to vote. "Mama, even if she had voted you still needed thirty-nine more votes," Nick pointed out to her.

"Stop talking garbage!" she'd screamed at him. "What do you know? You're a child!" Nick was seventeen at the time.

Then there was Stephen, Nick's father. Wide-shouldered with a broad, muscular body and thick bowed legs, he was a hard-working giant who slipped out the door most of Nick's childhood at 4:00 a.m. toting a black metal lunch box to ride up and down the highways of the Upper Peninsula. In the six-month winters he drove a snowplow; during the short warmer months he filled potholes and mowed the right-of-way. During blizzards he often worked eighteen-hour shifts. He and the other drivers would roll into sleeping bags on picnic tables in the Department of Transportation garage for brief naps during the big storms. His dad once told him he'd learned to survive the worst storms through a sort of sixth sense. "Sometimes the whole damn world looks like a polar bear eating a marshmallow in a snowbank. That's when I drive on instinct. I know every bump and curve on US-41 for thirty miles in each direction. Know her better than I know your mama." Papa called the highway "my girl."

In return for his devotion to his girl, Papa developed kidney problems and hearing loss from the bumpy drives and clanging, gnashing of the plow and salt dispenser. But it was a good job with benefits and, in the jobs-stricken Upper Peninsula, one of the only secure ones. "I'm lucky," he'd say. That was before his career ended tragically.

His death made it into all the Michigan media, even a story in *USA Today* with a headline, "Road Worker Flattened in Michigan." It happened when Nick was taking Katie and Melina to Chicago for spring break. Papa, just two weeks from retirement, opted to use a few of his hundreds of unused sick leave days to go fishing when the call came in from the garage. "Can you help us train the seasonal workers in pothole patching?" Papa reluctantly agreed, though he despised the work, said cold patches were nothing but expensive Band-Aids and dangerous to apply, what with all the drivers speeding through the work zones. But Papa felt a sense of loyalty to the men at the garage.

That tragic day he was at the back of the cold patch crew, the most dangerous position. They'd put out orange warning signs and plenty of cones when a trucker hauling a load of auto parts dozed off, slammed into the asphalt truck, flattening Papa into a flesh-and-bone patch in the middle of the road, still warm. To this day, Nick makes a detour to avoid that stretch of highway.

Nick was proud to be the first in his family with a college education. His older brother, Teddy, dropped out his second year to pursue a business—the first of several failed ones—before landing on his feet with a Tastee-Freez. Nick felt his parents' disappointment and vowed to attain the highest degree, a PhD. When he stopped just short of that Papa never brought it up, unlike his mother, Sophia, who had cried, screamed, banged her fist on the kitchen counter before throwing a slipper at him. She'd even called Katie to chew her out, said she was distracting Nick.

Mama never took to Katie and her family with their Finnish roots, their long silences, their downplay of emotion. "They've got ice in their blood; we've got olive oil," Sophia said. "They don't mix."

Nick tried to appease Katie. "Mama considers anything non-Greek as a weakness, as offensive. Don't take it personally." But when their daughter Melina was born—a beautiful mixture of ice and olive oil, with wavy copper hair and skin that glowed but never burned in the sun—Sophia forgave Katie for her ancestry and any other *weakness.* "Moraki mou," she called little Melina. Katie stepped up to "Koukla." Nick glances at Ella and wonders how the course of his life would have run had she been his wife. Whose DNA would have triumphed— assuming they'd had kids (a bit dubious). How would they have divvied up those 23 pairs of chromosomes? Would she have nagged him, resented his touch, his whole presence in the house the way Katie did, forced him to look elsewhere? With Ella, he's pretty sure he'd have stayed put; surely she would have badgered him, run hot and cold (as she's now doing), but always kept his interest. Without worries about tuition costs, he'd probably have earned his PhD years ago.

"What do you think about me dropping my graduate program?" he now asks her.

"How do you feel about it?"

"I've pretty much put it out of my mind. I'm too old to get hired by a university now anyway. Age discrimination."

"Have you ever considered finishing it?"

"On a teacher's salary, paying college tuition for my daughter and me, too?"

"You could get a loan."

"Easy for you to say." He looks at the sprawling cottage, her second home, far grander than most people's first and only house. That morning he'd counted out fifty paces as he walked from the kitchen to the front porch; his rental in Duluth was less than 1,500 square feet. He wonders what her other house looks like. Probably twice as big.

"In case you haven't heard, the term 'rich American' became obsolete in 2008," says Ella.

"In case you haven't heard, the credit crunch that started then would make it tough—if not impossible—for regular folks like me to get a loan." He's annoyed, thinking of the joke that you can tell the student parking lot from the faculty one because the nice cars are in the student lot.

"If you really want to do it you'd find a way. Somehow."

He rubs the back of his neck vigorously, holding back the words he wants to hurl at her: limousine liberal, elitist, out-of-touch with America. His suppressed diatribe sounds like a clip from one of those right-leaning commentators. There's a bitterness in his mouth as he remembers his father, all those early mornings when Papa tiptoed out into the dark so as not to awaken his children, his rough hands wrapped around his lunch bucket handle. Even in the blind selfishness of childhood Nick had realized that it was for him and his brother that his father did this. Nick hadn't known the word at the time, but he understood the meaning of sacrifice. After Melina was born he learned firsthand why parents abandon their dreams, wear shabby clothes, leave their homelands for distant places, work seven days a week. For Melina he would do any of these things, and happily. Looking at Ella sitting there scowling at him from her pretty little sofa, he realizes she has no idea what it's like to be average. She in her expensive, eco-friendly clothes complaining about the burden of a cottage. On a fundamental level, she is blind to her privilege.

He stands up, sweeping his hands down the front of his thighs. "I don't think you'll ever understand some things about me and the average American. Even when you drove a carriage around and hung out with the locals, you could always come back here, to your perch on the bluff."

She springs from the sofa, raising her head, a salt-and-pepper hooded cobra.

"You always had a chip on your shoulder, didn't you? An inferiority complex. Stop implying that I'm some sort of out-of-touch snoot because you don't know what I am."

"That's for sure." He crosses his arms and stares at her. "I don't even know what you do anymore except try to hold this place together."

"Like it's any of your damn business."

So this is why they'd gone separate ways: this tension between two worlds that divided them may be partly to blame, but a bigger issue was her tendency to close down, get nasty, and when that happened, he couldn't connect to her. No one could. Like that night near summer's end thirty years ago when Ella totally shut down.

They'd gone out to the gazebo, Nick leading, when he saw Ella's mother, Audrey, standing in the shadows near the doorway, a candle inside illuminating two wine glasses on the coffee table before the sofa, the sound of someone walking through the wooded area, the crack of twigs underfoot. Nick had glimpsed the outline of a man in the shaft of light before he disappeared into the woods. Audrey's eyes locked with Nick's and she put her index finger to her mouth, signaling him to shush. Nick was walking in front of Ella and prayed she hadn't seen her mother. He immediately turned around and put his arm across Ella's shoulders, pushing her back toward the house.

"Stop being so rough," she'd protested. "What's going on?"

Glancing back he saw the lights in the gazebo die. Audrey must have blown out the candles.

"I'm getting allergies," said Nick, faking a series of sneezes.

She looked at him quizzically. "What's going on?"

"Let's go downtown and, and check out the park. I'll get my guitar."

"Huh?"

She glanced back at the gazebo, her mouth drawn taut. Then she claimed to have a headache and dismissed Nick who walked dejectedly back to his little room downtown. Later, when he tried to bring the incident up, she changed the subject. He brought it up again and she'd snapped, "Why do you keep talking about that?" The event became taboo for the few weeks left of that summer, the first icy inch between them. When the family packed up and left the island abruptly the last week of August, a distressed Ella showed up at the dock. "Father's insisting we leave. He won't let me stay," she said. Just then a ferry pulled in and Nick's boss signaled him to get over to the vessel.

"I'll see you at Christmas. Right here. I'll write," said Nick.

But things didn't go as planned, neither then nor now.

He feels the window slamming shut between them again. "I'm sorry. It isn't my business and I probably have no right to be sitting here on your porch, a rude, prying houseguest. I had originally planned to leave today anyway." He stands up, coffee mug in hand.

"And your research? When, if ever, were you planning on doing that?"

Uh-oh. "I, I've had to change my plans a bit since the accident."

"Of course." She begins pacing back and forth, slapping the outside of her thighs, left, right, left, right. Nick feels like slapping her smack on her ass. "So you're going to go home? Just like that?"

Now what in the hell is he supposed to do? He sets his mug on a porch table and walks toward her, aching to wrap his arms around her. If only she'd stop, chill out, put her feet up, rip off her clothes. But she's backed up all the way to the railing with her arms crossed over her chest, a tightly closed box. "I'd rather stay," he says softly, planting a kiss on her forehead, just below her hairline. To his surprise, she doesn't budge, and they stand silently, within inches. Nick feels her warm breath near his cheek, but he keeps his hands at his sides, afraid to break the spell. To the east, the breeze lifts the flag on the cottage next door and it beats out a steady *tap-tap, tap-tap*. There's a surge inside him; not lust, something with greater power, a sense of finding himself home at last.

The moment is wiped out by the sound of the cellar door banging and the tinny rattle of aluminum as a man rounds the corner of the yard holding an extension ladder, dressed in paint-splattered jeans and a T-shirt.

***

"Hey, Annie Oakley, I'm ready," says the man, then stops abruptly. "Oopsie." As he turns around the ladder crashes into a corner of the house, knocking him to the grass where he lies rubbing his head. "Damn!" he yelps.

Ella jumps up and runs toward him. "Are you all right?"

"Yeah, yeah. I'm fine." His eyes look crossed, confused.

On her knees next to the man, Ella looks up at Nick and shakes her head. He joins her on the lawn. "Nick, let me introduce you to Boon." Nick knows that face, high cheekbones, its former handsomeness lurking beneath a lined leather map, one of the islanders who used to hang out on the park wall where he'd first met Ella. And he'd seen it somewhere else.

"Let's get you a drink of water," she says before turning to Nick. "Looks like I've got another patient."

Rushing into the house, Nick soon emerges through the front door with a glass of water in hand. He limps down the steps and hands it to Ella.

"Here you go," she says, passing it to Boon, a forced sweetness in her voice. "Come on up onto the porch."

Boon gulps the water, smacks his lips together and tries to stand. "I'll be fine. These old bones just need to cooperate. You two go back to whatever you were doing." He smirks.

Turning to Nick she asks, "The day is young. Is there anything you'd planned?"

"There's your to-do list. We haven't gotten too far on it."

Ella shakes her head. "Let's forget that for a moment. How about a little picnic?"

"I think I'd prefer to keep my other toes in tact," laughs Nick.

"No boats this time, I promise. And I know a perfect place."

18

Ella can identify all the songs within the island's medley of winds: wind in the cedars, gentler than wind in the beeches with its dark undertones; wind on the bluff tops, gustier than back in the forest; November winds, filled with longing and admonition (*The lake, it is said, never gives up her dead, when the gloomy November winds come calling*). She began naming the winds after learning that the island's first people, the Anishinabe, had names for dozens of winds, reflecting their belief that their ancestors' spirits rode in these gusts. Today Ella hears the wind in the cedars, lithe and light-hearted—a good sign— blowing at their backs as she and Nick bike through the center of the island. She's taking him to Friendship's Altar on the backside, one of their old haunts. She wonders if he'll remember it.

The journey is all downhill and they can take the flat shore ride back, which will be easier on Nick's bum toe. Only toward the end will they have to mount the hills. Surely Nick can manage that. She duct-taped a plastic bag over Nick's foot and he can favor the left pedal. Not that they're doing much pedaling at the moment as they coast toward British Landing, a tunnel of trees arching into a lush canopy above their heads.

Just before reaching the shore road, Ella's shouts, "Turn right!" and she heads onto a dirt road overlaid with a load of white stones. The wind vanishes, leaving only the sound of their tires grinding through the stones.

"New gravel!" she shouts. "Watch it!"

Ella scans the woods for the path back to Friendship's Altar. She hasn't been here for several summers. It used to be marked, but with budget cuts, the Historic Council has abandoned upkeep of minor tourist sites such as this. Ella doesn't mind, preferring to keep the place a secret.

"Slow down," she says, hopping off her bike and pushing it into the woods. The remnants of a path are marked by sprigs of cedar and small rocks. Nick follows closely.

"Look," says Ella, pointing to the ground where, littered by leaves, a wooden sign lies, still attached to a broken post. "Someone must have busted it." They lean their bikes against two trees. Nick brushes the leaves from the sign and reads:

Friendship's Altar: An isolated stack of brecciated limestone. A close examination of this stack will reveal many angular fragments which have been cemented together with calcium carbonate. This reformed conglomerate is harder than the surrounding rock and soil. As a result, the waves of ancient Lake Nipissing (about 2000 BC) washed away the softer materials and separated Friendship's Altar from the ancient coastline or cliff to the left.

He looks up. "I remember this place." Then he winks. "Don't you?"

She can feel her face reddening. Whatever was she thinking when she decided to bring him here? "Yes, we visited here once." *Visited* was a euphemistic verb: *got it on* was more accurate.

He looks at her unabashedly. "Well, where is it?" he asks, looking around at the trees.

"Follow me." They continue about a hundred feet when Ella halts. "There it is," she says, pointing to a stack of limestone that rises high above their heads. Mossy, with a small cowlick of cedar sprouting from its top, its lime-hungry roots have jabbed deep into the rock, a firm anchor for the tree. Combined, the rock and tree create a distinct presence, like an old man turned to stone. Ella catches her breath. She had forgotten how this modest little sanctuary never fails to thrill her.

Ella picks up a crisp brown leaf from the ground and carries it to the rock, holding it as if it were a delicate work of art, then places it on a ledge.

"We need some tobacco leaves for a proper offering," says Nick, selecting a cedar sprig and placing it next to Ella's leaf. Two crows, their raspy cries preceding their entrance, flutter into the cedars above them. "They say when a crow gets this close, it's an old friend who's passed on coming back to pay a visit. At least that's what Grandma told me." One of the crows jumps from branch to branch, *caw-cawing*. "I think that one's Ella."

"But I haven't passed on." She gestures toward the second crow huffing itself up to look bigger. "That must be Nick."

"And I haven't passed on either." Nick sighs. He stares up at the trees, his profile outlined by the sun; his nose, with its little twist, brings his face a subtle dignity. His thick hair is a delightful mess. She remembers how he used to do this, gaze at the lake through the tower windows, or on a bike trail, pull over and watch the water. Funny how it's all coming back, these memories, bringing them out the way water washes over a dry stone to reveal its patterns and colors. She feels light, girlish. "Come on," she says, tugging at his shirt. There's a lookout just above the path with a beautiful view of the north end of the Straits she wants to show him. Nick doesn't budge. His hands are on his hipbones, his eyes closed. A shaft of sun radiates his face. She wonders if he's praying.

Finally, he opens his eyes and says, "Don't you wish that everything would just stop so we could savor it longer?"

"That's why we invented cameras."

"Cameras don't even capture ten percent of it. I just wish . . . well, to somehow escape living in time. You know what I mean?"

"Not really."

"I thought you, of all people, would understand. You used to. It's like, like we're always losing something, giving something up, then grieving for it. What can we preserve? The big moments—a few of them make it into museums and history books—but the beauty of this place, this day, the so-called small stuff, what happens to it?"

She's drawn closer by his earnestness. "I guess it lives in us. Here and now. When we go, it goes." They stand silently, Nick surveying the sky, she, the ground. The crows have departed in a trail of *caw-caws*.

"Have you ever thought about what you'll leave behind?" asks Nick, turning toward her.

"I don't like to look back." She feels weighted down by Nick's sudden sobriety. She watches him warily. Nothing like a light conversation. "You want to know the basic biologic truth of it? In my humble opinion, the best thing we can do is make a hell of a good addition to the compost heap."

"That's it?"

"That's it."

"Oh, come on. What about the caskets? You could have the deluxe model."

"For God's sake, I'm not going out in some fancy bronze box. I want a natural burial. Dump me on the manure pile; that is, unless I can come up with a totally biodegradable casket."

Nick smiles despite the gruesomeness of the topic. "I believe that is called a pine box."

"Why are we talking about this anyway?"

"You brought it up." She shrugs and casts her eyes downward where pine cones lie scattered on the forest floor. Ella grabs one, thrusts back her right arm and slings it at Nick. "Watch out!" she shouts, ducking behind a tree.

"What the—oh, now you've done it," says Nick, scooping up two cones. "You can run but you can't hide." He walks toward her tree as she aims another cone at him, this one hitting him in the gut. Out of ammunition, she rushes out and grabs another just as Nick's hits her square in the butt. The war continues for a few minutes until Ella gets a side stitch from laughing so hard. Just like old times.

19

"Truce!" cries Ella, emerging from the protection of a white pine between spasms of laughter. "Let's check out the view." She strides toward a set of stairs leading up the hill into a grove of balsam and cedar. Nick watches as she lifts one leg, then the other, hustling up the stairs with athleticism; her butt looks firm, the ass of a young woman. He wants to grab it, but he can't keep up with her and is winded before reaching the top.

The stairs end two flights up at a wooden lookout, entirely secluded, with a treetop view of the lake, like one of those window shades that raise and lower from either the bottom or top, providing privacy and the full light of the sky. A soft wind stirs in the balsam branches that lift like little green skirts to expose the brown tree trunks; out on the lake, a St. Ignace-bound ferry drones its way past.

Ella sits down on the deck, crossing her legs, right leg over left. Nick sets the basket on the deck, then eases himself down next to her. The boards are splintery. "Be careful or we'll be pulling toothpicks from our southern halves," Ella warns.

"How can you sit like that?" His knees ache and his injured toe throbs.

"Some natural flexibility, and Yoga classes to keep it going."

"I don't remember this lookout."

"It wasn't here back then. They built it about twenty years ago. Now it's so grown over the fudgies can't find it. Which I like." Turning toward him she says, "When we were talking down there, you didn't tell me what you wanted to leave behind. Well—?" Now she's got him.

"As a dad, I guess I've already left my magnum opus, Melina. As a teacher, I hope I've stirred up a wellspring of curiosity, opened a few minds. But as for me, hmm, well . . ." She's looking at him earnestly. Under her direct gaze it's hard to suppress the truth. "I'd like to finish my dissertation."

She uncrosses her legs and scuttles crab-like on her butt to the lookout's edge, swinging her legs over the side. "You know what? I think you should do it."

He's thought about it, dreamed about it, hell, even written the first half. It's the discipline he lacks. Katie was always reminding him of that. "You never finish anything, Nick." It wasn't entirely true: he'd built a house, gotten his master's degree. Okay, it took him two extra years and lots of nagging by Katie, but he'd done it. He shrugs. Why think about that now? He's sitting in the treetops, surrounded by the most beautiful things in the world: the lake, the woods, the sky, and his old lover. Anything is possible. He scoots up to the rail, also swinging his legs over the edge of the platform. They sit silently, two old crows in their secluded aerie. To his west he can make out the outline of a roof nearly hidden by the trees.

"Is that a house?"

Ella turns and surveys the area where he's pointing. "Sure is. Jake's place."

"Must be peaceful way out here."

The sounds of feet grinding over stones, the snap of twigs, then voices float up from below.

"Shh." Ella's index finger is pressed to her lips as she points with her other hand toward Friendship's Altar. Below, a male voice booms, "Not much back here. Just a bunch of trees, a big rock." A bulky man wearing a Detroit Tigers baseball cap and a green backpack appears below.

A woman's voice says, "But it shows right here on the map there's an altar. I wanna see it." A short woman with dark roots staining her platinum hair comes into view. Nick notices the words *Handcrafted by God* curved across her jumbo breasts. "There ain't no altar. Just a bunch of trees and rocks. Same old, same old." The couple looks up and waves to Nick and Ella. Nick waves back. *They better damn well not come up here.* For a moment they stand staring up, then the man puts his arm around the woman's shoulders and they turn away from the lookout.

"Now those were two full-blown fudgies," whispers Nick.

"Shhh," she hisses. "They're leaving. We've got the place all to ourselves again." She pumps her legs and opens her arms wide. "Isn't this a perfect spot?"

Glancing at her from the corner of his eye, he wonders what this is about. She's certainly gotten all perky, but he's not quite ready to trust this sudden openness.

"Do you still play the guitar?"

Nick shakes his head. "I sold my last one about ten years ago." He'd stopped playing when Melina said his music was boring. That, and Katie complaining about too much clutter in the house. She'd never cared much for his music anyway.

"You should've kept it. You have a great voice. Remember that song, the Bee Gees, I think." She hums a few bars. Nick picks up the words, "In the morning of my life the minutes take so long to drift away." Ella joins him for the next two lines, "Please be patient with your life/ It's only morning and you've still to live your day."

She sings with her head thrown back; beads of spit pop from her mouth, caught in the sun's glare. It's the same old off-pitch voice he remembers, loud and unabashed.

"La la la la la la la . . . damn, I can't remember it," says Nick, his shoulders slumping. The words, with their youthful optimism, deflate him. That and the thought of Katie belittling his music. "Who do you think you are, anyway? A twenty-something rocker?" she'd mocked.

"You okay?" Ella asks, her singing stopped. She's studying his face and has inched closer.

"Yeah, just a little tired," he mumbles. She uncrosses her legs, stands up and removes two plastic containers from the picnic basket. "This will perk you up." She's opened the picnic basket. He's starving, but what he really wants is a drink.

"Here, try this." She hands a container to Nick. A strong whiff of garlic rushes out as he pries off the plastic top.

"What is it?"

"Roasted red peppers marinated in garlic," she says, biting into her sandwich. He would have preferred ham or beef, but after one skeptical bite he finds the sandwich surprisingly good. Ella hands him a linen napkin embroidered with a delicate vine and small white flowers; he traces his finger on the threads. He would have used a paper towel—that you could toss out. But this thing must be washed, ironed, and folded. He dabs a trickle of olive oil from his chin. Extracting two

metal bottles from the picnic box, Ella hands him one. Before lifting
it to his lips he says, "Let me guess, Mackinac tap water, purest in the
world." Then he takes an impressive swig. "Anything else in that box?"
He hopes she's brought cookies or chips, but she pulls out a box of
dried fruit mix and an overripe banana.

"I know, I should've brought some fudge." She reaches back in the
box. "Perhaps this will cheer you up." She hands him a bottle of beer,
some sort of microbrew with an artsy label and the edgy name "Lovely
Bastard."

"Thanks." Ah, perfect. His hand brushes hers on the bottle's cold
glass. She doesn't flinch, and smiles. He swigs the beer. "Good choice."
He swills the rest and belches. Ella's eyebrows arch up. "'Scuze me," he
says. "Can I ask you something?"

"You can ask, but I might not tell," she says. Her toes are
pointed as she swings her legs back and forth like pendulums.
"Fair enough. How long were you married?"

"Five years, plus two more sloshing through a divorce. I like to say
I had one good year of marriage."

Nick eases himself down on his back, swings his arms behind his
head with his elbows sticking out and squints at the sun. "And in all
these years did you ever think about me?"

Ella sets her beer bottle on the deck. "To be honest, not much. But
there's something I want to tell you."

He sits up.

"Remember that painting you made, a dock porter with a puzzled
look on his face?" Only vaguely. He'd stopped painting after dropping
art as a minor his sophomore year.

"I kept that piece. Every now and then when I was decluttering I'd
run across it, just couldn't throw it out."

The thought that Ella has kept his painting all these years startles
him. More than that, it delights him.

"Uh-huh. It's up in the attic at the cottage. Remind me to try and
find it when we get back." They sit digesting their lunch and this new
piece of information. Above, the lacey edges of the trees brush against
the sky, a northern Michigan blue, clean and clear. No humidity today,
no pollution. A cedar sprig floats down, landing on the hem of Ella's
shorts. She plucks it off and pops it in her mouth.

"The world's best after-dinner mint," she says. She's wrong. The best after-dinner mint is her. He remembers the taste of her, the salty spiciness of her skin. His hormones are rushing back like the waves breaking on the stony shore below. He turns on his side, watching her, the fractured light on her silver earrings, two small teardrops falling from the pink edges of her earlobes.

"OK, it's my turn to ask something," she says. Nick tenses. "What happened to your marriage? Why did it all fall apart?"

Where could he begin? That Katie was Barbie Doll pretty, petite, surface-sweet? That he'd fallen in love with her for the shallowest of reasons, flattered by the attention she'd given him, excited about screwing her, ignored the warning signs. "Friends, Niko, best friends through the thick of it. That's what a husband and wife must be because life will throw *skata* at you," his mother had advised. But he didn't listen.

And there'd been plenty of skata.

"We shouldn't have gotten married in the first place. I'm not sure she ever loved me."

"Really?"

"You know, it sounds kind of crazy, but the one time I felt close to her was in a forest—in the night."

Ella pulls back her shoulders, but she coaxes him on. "And?"

"Ah, you don't want to hear about all that."

"Maybe I do."

He sighs and begins his story. It was the night Katie came out with Melina to pick him up from a long inline skate run he'd made while training for a skating marathon along the Lake Michigan shore. At thirteen months, Melina was a plump cherub, rosy from breast milk, a singer, talker, endless babbler, practicing for the language to come. She turned phonemes into songs: *Da da, da a,* and *ma mam mam ma.* Sometimes she'd put them together. *Da da ma ma da da.* Her parents felt she was phenomenally bright. *A phenom*, Nick called her.

Katie's approach to motherhood was para-militaristic. Melina's infancy was highly scheduled; Nick's fledgling fatherhood was equally regimented. That fall he'd signed up for the marathon and trained on weekends, pushing young Melina in a jogging stroller along a spectacular paved trail paralleling Lake Michigan. Katie always insisted they be back early for Melina's dinner and bath.

In mid-September, a week before the race, he wanted to get in one more twenty-two-miler so he had slipped away from school at three, picked up Katie from work and Melina from day care. Katie dropped Nick off at a spot on the trail with three commercial buildings, a kay-ak rental, auto repair shop, and Susan's Mini-Mall—a mom-and-pop grocery with a trickle of customers and country kitchen décor (Nick loved their Rice Krispies treats, all buttery and oversized). Besides a house or two, there wasn't a lick of development for the next twen-ty miles. The forest marched to the trail's edge, blocking out all light once darkness arrived. Nick's goal was to be back before dark and Ka-tie would meet him with the car. She had agreed to modify Melina's schedule *just* this one night.

Nick was having a grand ride, achieving a perfect rhythm, hum-ming along with one arm pumping, the other resting lightly on his tailbone with the grace of a speed skater. He passed two joggers and one other skater heading the opposite direction. Deer crossed the trail twice, and at a rocky overlook he saw the outline of a bobcat disappear into the woods.

Then he remembered to call home; *Shit,* it was after seven, pitch-dark. He dialed his messages. *Call me,* Katie's crisp voice rammed through the static-y connection like an axe. He picked up the pace. Less than a mile from their designated pick-up point, at seven thirty, he heard something ahead, a babbling baby sound, then Katie's fear-filled voice shouting, "Nick! Nick!"

So she does care.

"I'm here, Daddy's coming. I'm here!" he'd shouted, skating faster. "Katie, Melina!" He saw the flashlight ahead, then the stroller and the white of Katie's T-shirt. He skated into her arms, swirling her in a circle like ice dancers.

"You're OK. Thank God. I was terrified," said Katie. He felt mois-ture on her cheeks. This moved him more than anything, for he'd only seen her cry twice: once, during labor, another time when her father died.

Nick took the stroller, skating slowly behind it while Katie jogged next to him. Melina sang to the trees, to the black, starless sky. When Nick looked back on his marriage, this moment emerged as one of the best.

"Well, at least you had that," says Ella when Nick finishes. She's looking at her hands, tracing a line of veins on her left hand with her index finger. Nick reaches over and places his hand on hers.

In a soft voice she breaks the stillness of their newfound intimacy. "Remember when you showed me that little cave beneath Arch Rock?"

"How could I forget? I must have gotten fifty mosquito bites on my ass."

"Touché," she laughs. "By the way, I've always wondered how you knew about that cave."

"I bet that's kept you up nights for thirty years. I never told you this, but one of the guys on the dock knew about it." Working on the dock with all the locals, Nick had learned a lot about the island.

That night, wearing a backpack in which Ella had stuffed a blanket, matches, a candle, and a couple of bottles of beer she'd swiped from the refrigerator, they'd scaled the bluff below Arch Rock. Then they'd crawled belly-style like guerilla warriors until they found "the cave," a small pocket about eight feet deep and less than six feet wide hidden by a cedar clinging miraculously to the cliff. Ella spread out a blanket, where they sang and toasted the moon, then slept in snatches, wrapped together in an S-figure, changing positions every half-hour or so to relieve the hardness of their rock mattress. Hours later they were awakened by the dull wingbeats and squawking of a great blue heron, its head hunched into its shoulders, winging against the slate-gray sky. Sitting together, their bones chilled and sore, they watched dawn roll up on the eastern horizon, sliding from misty gray to florescent pink.

"That was the best sunrise I've ever seen," she says, pulling her legs up and wrapping her arms around them.

"Me too." Once again, Nick feels his companion of long ago back beside him, his lover and his friend. As he reaches over to place his arm around her shoulders, he's pleased she offers no resistance, instead laying her head upon his shoulder. Closing his eyes, her hair tickles his cheek, resurrecting that old feeling of contentment, that yes, life is good.

A few moments later Ella pulls slightly away. He feels her eyes upon him, but refuses to break the spell by opening his.

"Nick," she says softly.

"Yes."

"Look at me."

Opening his eyes slowly, there she is, with a pine needle poking through her bangs, a half-circle penumbra beneath each eye, something he hadn't noticed until he was this close to her.

"What do you see?"

"I see *you*."

"I'm not the same person you used to know. You need to understand that. Take off those rose-colored lenses. I'm not a girl anymore."

"You are to me."

"There's so much—too much—between then and now, water beyond the bridge, gone forever. We can't go back."

"Okay then, let's stay here, here and now, like you said earlier."

She shakes her head gently and moves away several inches. As he reaches over to take her hand his watch band scrapes her shoulder. He hadn't fastened it properly and a little piece hangs off the attachment. "Ouch," she says. Then, clasping his arm, her head a few inches from his watch she asks, "Can you read the time?" Nick raises his arm close to his face. "Four-o-seven."

"Four-o-seven?"

"Yeah."

"I have to get back."

"Why?"

"Charlie. He doesn't know where we are. I didn't leave a note. And I forgot to bring my phone. And Mother, she'll be expecting a call from me." Ella is already standing, brushing off her shorts, running her fingers through her hair with a jerky motion.

"What's the rush? Charlie's fourteen. He knows we can't be far. Your mother's in good hands." Ella is gathering the lunch basket and backpack.

"Charlie has pulled some big ones, and Mother freaks out when she doesn't hear from me."

Nick straightens his shoulders, puffing himself up like that crow she'd pointed out earlier. Damn it, he's not going to lose her again. *She cannot do this to me.* As she turns toward him, pushing her bangs back from her forehead, he notices a brown spot on the pale underside of her arm. He stares at it transfixed as she says softly, "I'm really sorry."

"I understand." But he doesn't.

20

~~~~~~

B ack on their bikes, Ella directs Nick to turn up the hilly road they'd so easily descended earlier. "I thought we were taking the shore road," he says. "My toe's throbbing." Along with his thighs and hips and back. And heart.

"Changed my mind, too many fudgies this time of day," she replies. "And they're complete morons on bikes."

Nick sighs and pats the pocket of his shorts where he feels the little plastic casing around a pain pill, his third-to-the-last. "I'll try," he says, popping the pill in his mouth and swallowing it with no water. The bitterness burns his gums.

They pass a log cabin, more forest, and then a house set back from the road, shrouded by trees. He hadn't noticed it on the way down, but at this tortoise pace he can take in the scenery. Stained a honey brown rather than painted, it's unlike the island architecture with its faux and Victorian homes in whites, greys, and greens. Nick stops his bike, easing over to the side of the road and stares at the house. "What's up?" asks Ella, pulling to a halt beside him.

"I built a house. Looked a lot like that."

"Nice."

Nick's eyes remain focused on the house. "Built it with my hands, took over eight years. Had to sell it during the divorce." Not exactly the whole truth, but so what? He'd moved out after the Madison incident and quit-claimed the place to Katie so Melina would have a sense of stability and continuity. She'd suffered enough. Ironically, Katie sold the house within a year. She wanted something conventional, with banks of light switches, granite countertops and bright paint, not a place that blended into the landscape with wood and stones. Their house was small but elegant, like a white bowl of organic fruit. Everyone who visited admired it—except Katie. A friend who stayed there told Nick, "I feel like this house just wraps its arms around you."

The house had gotten between them, becoming an extension of Katie's growing resentment toward him; she considered his love of old things sentimental, his favorite clothing shabby; he thought her penchant for everything shiny and modern as mindless, consumer-driven blindness.

This little jewel in the Mackinac woods reminds Nick of all that he's lost. There's an air of abandonment about this place, with layers of brown pine needles coating the roof, the unmowed lawn, weedy flowerbeds.

"A foreclosure?" he asks.

"Not yet, but the guy who owns it, has fallen on hard times. He has some kind of cancer and spent all his money on treatment, you know, without health insurance or anything. The community's rallied behind him, held fundraisers, but he needs a lot more money."

Nick feels a bond with this stranger. "Poor fellow."

Ella is quiet, studying the house. "I showed you the roof from Friendship's Altar. Haven't heard much about Jake recently. Think he's downstate with his mother. Maybe he'll sell the place before the bank gets it. Wouldn't that be a shame? It was his dream."

Nick knows all about that; dreams delayed and dreams destroyed.

***

Nothing comes easy on this island, you have to earn every inch, and Ella sets a lickity-split pace once they hit the road again. A group of tourists wheel towards them on the wrong side of the road. Ella swerves to avoid them; Nick brakes hard, nearly crashing into her. "Watch it, move over!" Nick shouts to the group, repressing the *Fuck you* forming on his lips. "Idiot fudgies!" shouts Ella, raising her left hand in the one-finger salute. They cycle on, fudgie-free for the next quarter-mile. The pain pill has kicked in and Nick pedals next to Ella, their legs pumping in unison, up down, up down, wishing it was the movement of their hips, not their legs, that they were back up on the deck, he on top, she grinding into the wood, to hell with the splinters.

"Hey, isn't that Charlie?" Nick points ahead to a bicyclist moving quickly toward them.

"Sure is."

Charlie sees them and waves, signaling them to pull over. His face is ruby-red.

"Aunt Ella. Why didn't you answer your cell? I've been calling and calling you. Grandma's fallen again."

"I left it at home, damn it. Is she OK? Did she break anything?"

"I don't know. The nursing home called and said they were taking her to the hospital. That's why I came out to find you guys. I've been all over the place." He scowls at Nick. "Darci said you'd left with a picnic basket so I figured maybe you'd gone to British Landing."

"Darci?"

"Yeah, she saw you two leave. It must have been a pretty long lunch," says Charlie, eyeing the basket. "Where'd you go?" Nick sees the suspicion in his eyes.

"Up in the woods near the Landing."

"Oh. Had a good time, huh? Your toe must be feeling better." He hops on his bike and starts pedaling.

"You must be worried about your mom," says Nick, riding next to Ella. Charlie has pulled far ahead, pumping his legs furiously on the hills.

"Yes. I'll have to go over to the mainland with Charlie. I'm so sorry."

"Why don't you go on over and leave Charlie with me? We can do some investigation, some male bonding. I've adjusted my schedule and I don't have to leave until late tomorrow."

Ella takes a few more strokes before answering. "Let me think on it."

Back at Cedar Bluff, Ella's arm brushes Nick's as they dismount their bikes. Nick smiles at her.

"I think I'll take you up on your offer," she says.

21

The news from the nursing home is mixed: a fall in the dining area, lots of confusion, nothing broken. They've brought Mother back to the facility, where she demands to speak to Ella every few minutes.

"We need you to go over some forms and reassure your mother," advises the director. At $250 a day, they'd better take good care of her.

Ella throws a toothbrush, a change of underwear and a shirt into a tote bag. She writes out notes for Nick and Charlie:

Genevieve comes in the morning. Watch Boon carefully. Food in fridge—charge account at grocery. Feed Jed before 6:00 tonight and by 8:00 tomorrow morning. Charlie can explain. I should be back by 10:00 or 11:00.

She hands the paper to Nick. "Take good care of my boy. I'll see you tomorrow morning." She squeezes his wrist.

"How much should I feed Jed?"

"Two flakes of hay, plus some pellets—maybe a couple of cups. His teeth are grinding down and he needs a supplement. It's in the barn." She notices a look of confusion on Nick's face. "A flake is about this much," she says, holding her hands apart about eight inches. "Charlie can show you. Charlie, be good to Nick. And no shenanigans."

On the ferry to Mackinaw City she chooses a seat facing the stern of the boat with a view of the island. As it rounds the break wall, she can see Cedar Bluff, a spot of blue in a sea of green. Maybe she shouldn't have left Charlie there alone with Nick. What's she gotten herself into? And what was that all about back at Friendship's Altar? How could she have let herself be so silly, practically letting him seduce her on the lookout? She has way too much on her plate to have time to dabble around in a romance. *For goodness' sakes, hold yourself in.* It would be nothing but a heap of trouble. As they pass Round Island Light she remembers yesterday's accident. The trouble has already started.

***

He feels a little nervous about being left with a moody kid. And what if Ella finds out about the mess-up in Wisconsin? He'll do a pre-emptive strike, tell her first, as soon as she gets back. In the interim, what should he do with this boy who has explicitly demonstrated a distaste for him? Despite the picnic less than two hours ago, he's ravenous—the fresh air and constant exercise on Mackinac have whetted his appetite like a knife blade. "What should we do about dinner?" Nick asks. He and Charlie are sitting face-to-face at the kitchen table, Nick with some reheated coffee, Charlie with a glass of juice.

"I don't know. Check out the fridge," says Charlie. "Aunt Ella is the queen of leftovers, although it's pretty bad stuff. She's a terrible cook. I have a stash of macaroni and cheese. Do you know how to make that?"

"You don't?"

"Uh-uh."

What a shame that the kid can't even boil water and throw in a few noodles. At fourteen, Nick cooked in his family's restaurant on weekends and could make just about any item on the menu from spaghetti to steak sandwiches. Opening the fridge, Nick sees shelves stacked high with unlabeled mysteries tucked into little plastic circles and squares. Removing a container with a red lid, he opens it and sniffs. *Ugh.* Tiny blue blobs float in the top of what appears to be lasagna.

"Gross, right? My aunt saves everything. Mom always warns me to check the expiration dates on stuff, especially the salad dressing. How about ordering a pizza?"

"Now there's a plan."

"I'll go get it," says Charlie. "Except there's one problem."

"What?"

"Money."

"Don't worry, pizza's on me." He removes a twenty-dollar bill from his wallet.

"Uh, that's not enough."

"How much does a pizza cost around here?"

"About twenty-five dollars. Minimum."

"Twenty-five?"

"It's Mackinac. Everything's jacked up."

Nick's cash supply is dwindling. He'd earmarked $800 for his entire trip around Lake Superior and hasn't gone halfway, yet he's already spent $450. There's still seven more days of camping, overnights, and driving. He hands Charlie an additional ten-dollar bill.

"Bring the change."

Charlie looks at the bill. "Uh, have to give a tip."

"Okay, forget the change."

Once Charlie's out the door, Nick scurries back to the refrigerator. He pours the leftover lasagna down the garbage disposal and reaches for a switch above the sink. No response. Opening the cupboard beneath the sink he presses the reset button and tries the switch again. The disposal blades screech and clank, reminding him of a snowplow blade scraping pavement on his father's highway rig.

Nick removes a jar of fancy mustard from a shelf on the refrigerator door and turns it upside down; the expiration date is a month ago. He returns to the sink and dumps that too.

Katie wouldn't allow for leftovers. She tossed out food that was perfectly safe and edible. "You're wasting food," Nick argued for years. But Ella, it seems, is the polar opposite, saving food that may not only sicken, but kill you. He wonders how she's lived this long. Must be the pure water that's saved her.

Opening the kitchen door, Nick frowns at a large hole in the screen. That and the loud squeal of the door, its hinges hungry for oil. He makes a mental note to fix it. As he walks off the back porch into the yard the evening air feels warm, without the thread of cold that often scissors through summer nights this far north. The cottage sits on a small knoll, with the garden and a walkway terracing down out back to a gravel drive and a barn. Nick hears a soft crunch on stones by the barn. Must be old Jed. He'd better feed the boy.

Walking toward the barn, he passes a rain barrel beneath a downspout at the rear of the house, then another by the barn. To his left he notices a clothesline with plastic baggies pinned to it flapping in the breeze like awakening bats. *So she saves her baggies.*

Jed snorts expectantly in the dusty paddock next to the barn, his head poking over the wooden rail fence, eyeing Nick. Whistling, Nick tentatively approaches the gelding, who nods his head up and down, ears cocked in a friendly forward position. Nick hesitates before reaching through the fence to stroke the horse.

"Are you hungry, old man?" Jed snorts again, pacing back and
forth, his hooves scraping the loose rocks below the fence line. "I'll get
you something. Just you wait."

Nick hurries into the barn. In a shaft of sunlight through the window, he sees a set of saddles hanging on pegs to his right, their stirrups
bundled on top like handcuffs. He kicks a pail with his left foot, glad
it isn't his right one. Reaching down, he feels the hard metal sides of
the bucket and pours pellets in it from a plastic container sitting next
to the pail. He turns toward the door where Jed stares over the fence.
Should he just dump the food on the ground? How the hell do you
feed a horse anyway?

A sound from the old groom's quarters overhead startles him, and
he remembers the time he and Ella went up there and discovered Sara
hiding in the hay bales, erupting in sneezes. The kid was allergic to hay
and everything associated with horses. Nick had to bribe her with the
promise of candy so she wouldn't rat to her parents. Even after deliv-
ery of a large bag of M&M's she'd demanded more candy.

Scanning the rafters he decides it must be bats, maybe a squirrel.
Anything could be hanging around up there. He shrugs, then walks
into the paddock, where he notices a food crib with a wooden holder
on top. *So that's where I put the pellets.* Jed races over, nearly knocking
Nick down. "Whoa, boy," but the horse is pulling on the bucket with
his teeth. Nick sets it down while Jed lowers his head and sucks up the
pellets with the efficiency of a shop vac. Now there's only the hay to
fetch. He never knew feeding a horse was so much work; dangerous,
too. Searching in a stall behind the pail he spots bales of hay stacked
against the wall, one half gone. Nick grabs an armful, hoping it's two
flakes.

Jed stands at the fence staring at Nick as he walks toward him, his
ears pointing up in excitement. "Here you go." Nick pushes the hay
between the fence rails, careful to avoid the electric wire stretched over
the top rail. Jed lowers his head and rips at the bundle with his teeth.
Nick leans into the rails, petting Jed's head. The boards feel loose, another item for the do-do list.

"Is that you, Ella?" someone yells. The voice sounds like it comes
from a barn a little up the road to his left, and Nick sees someone

approaching. Drat, it's that damned woman. Darci's figure scuttles toward him in robotic style. "Nick, right? Don't want to overfeed that horse," she says, eyeing Jed. "He'll bloat up and then you'll have a mess on your hands."

"I'm kind of a novice at this," says Nick.

"Why isn't Ella doing it?"

"She had to go off the island. I'm the designated horse sitter."

"Charlie went too?"

"No."

"Of course he couldn't feed the horse, right? Ella enables that kid if you ask me, but it really isn't any of my business. Where'd she go?"

"To see her mother. Minor emergency."

"Oh dear. Is she hurt again?"

"Don't know the details."

"Such a shame. Audrey is a tough woman. Hate to see her going downhill—and this place, too." She extends her hands out toward the cottage. "Place is in shambles."

"I think Ella's got it under control," says Nick.

"You don't know the half of it. Ella cares a lot about living things—and I would never speak against my neighbor—"

"I'm sure you wouldn't." *Yeah, right.*

"But around here you've got to care for the nonliving things too. And she's carrying this environmental thing too far. People are getting annoyed. More than annoyed."

"I'm not sure what you mean," says Nick. He'd noticed the rain barrels, the laundry, the broken door and fence.

"Look at this—like some kind of eco-experiment." Darci's palms are face up as she makes a sweeping motion with her arms. "She's been experimenting with her manure pile out back, attracting every varmint and fly on the island."

"Well, it's her property," says Nick.

"No, it's the Historic Council's land. We lease it. We own the homes, not the land. They've got some strict rules and the power to enforce them."

Nick recalls someone, probably Ella, telling him this. "Perhaps the Council needs to reexamine its rules, be more broadminded," he says. "This is the twenty-first century."

"And our job is to preserve the nineteenth. Look, the laundry is one thing, but this composting has got to go. And the garden. Have you seen what she's done to Audrey's garden by the gazebo?"

Nick doesn't respond, hoping the squall will blow over and she'll go back to her barn. She plows on.

"Audrey had the best perennial garden on the bluff back there. Some of her plants date back to the late 1800s. Heirlooms. The most gorgeous irises on Mackinac—purple like velvet, flagship for sure. But Ella's ripped out most of the plants—wouldn't even give them to her neighbors—said they weren't *native* and will cause a botanical disaster. Do you know she even called those irises an invasive species? Invasive—can you believe that? Now the place is a pile of weeds. Audrey's going to flip when she sees it." Darci looks down at his foot. "Say, how's that toe?"

"Getting better."

"Keep it clean, use loads of hydrogen peroxide. Wouldn't want gangrene or something to set in. They'll have to amputate it. And stay away from that manure pile." She glances toward the back of the barn. "It's been a pleasure." Extending her hand she gives Nick a vigorous handshake, then turns and scoots away to her property.

Nick exhales deeply, then inhales, noticing a stench from behind the Hollingsworth barn. He walks around to two huge piles of compost. A banana peel lays next to broken eggshells on top of the first pile, glowing in the sun. The other pile appears to be plain old manure.

He chuckles. So this is where Ella will be someday. Right on top.

22

~~~~~

Ella walks down the hallway to the euphemistically named "Memory Care" unit, a double-wide door separating it from the rest of the facility, locked down by an electronic code. Ella wonders why they bother; none of the residents except Mother can remember a sequence of numbers for more than a few seconds. The only reason Mother is on this side is she requires extra care. The hospital wouldn't keep her and she needs more attention than they can provide on the "Active Seniors" side of the building.

Ella punches in the code and pushes the door wide, wincing at the sweet scent of air fresheners, an attempt to mask foul odors. The carpet is discolored where residents have dribbled, and cleaning staff have scrubbed the color out of the fibers. Ella remembers wiping feces from the bottom of her shoes the last time she was here.

A startlingly thin man in diapers clutching the arm of a robin-shaped caregiver crosses the hallway as Ella walks toward the lounge. "Now, Mr. Peterson, just come this way," coaxes the woman.

A scene from *Singing in the Rain*, with a young Debbie Reynolds swirling in the arms of Gene Kelly, plays on a wide-screen television in the lounge. A tiny white-haired lady hunched over in a wheelchair giggles to herself, and in a wingback chair next to her, another woman sings along, improv style: "*I'm swinging on a swing, just a la de da da thing.*" Snoring, his mouth open, a lanky man in a plaid shirt snoozes on the sofa, one side of his face pushed in where the pillow presses against his cheek.

And there, like a queen, sits Audrey in a wheelchair, a lavender cardigan draped over her shoulders, wearing a little feather hat crafted from a pheasant that flew into their front window in Ann Arbor years ago. Soft pink lipstick outlines her mouth, and a touch of rouge gives her a theatrical look. Encircling her gaunt neck is a diamond necklace, a gift from Henry on her fiftieth birthday. She's clutching a Cape Cod handbag, fiddling with the clasp, opening and shutting it. She reminds Ella of an elegant turtle in a pond of deformed amphibians.

"Mother." Ella rushes to her side, hugs her gently.

Looking up, her blue eyes ablaze, Audrey says, "It's about time you got here. I've been waiting all afternoon. Let's go home."

She was so fragile after her last fall, and now all this. "Mother, you know you can't leave until you're completely healed."

"Well I'm damn-near healed."

"Mother, you fell again today."

"Nonsense. I'm not hurt, just hungry. Let's get dinner."

Touching Audrey's shoulders Ella says, "Mother, it's August. Even up north it's way too hot for cashmere."

"But I don't have a coat here."

"That's just the point, Mother. It's 82 degrees outside. You don't need a coat. Besides, we're dining in." Tonight Ella hasn't planned to take her out.

"No. I'm not eating another meal in this dump."

"Not here, Mother, in the dining hall on the other side." Fortunately, the facility includes a large dining room with crystal chandeliers and linen-covered tables in the outer section where the *regular* residents dine on bland food from china plates, sip weak coffee and wipe their mouths with cloth napkins. Although the food consists of canned cuisine and frozen food packages, it's elegantly presented on glass platters with a sprig of parsley or rosemary, a dollop of sauce. High school students in black pants and white shirts serve the residents. Better than the tables in Memory Care, where staff gently coax and spoon-feed their charges, or the shaky journey of meat and vegetables from plates to mouths by the few still able to wield a piece of cutlery. The last time Ella ate there with Mother, two of their tablemates fell asleep during the meal, their heads cocked forward like silver bells. Even Mother dozed off briefly between the salad and the main course. The place is rubbing off on her.

"All right. But I'm keeping my sweater on." Audrey waves to a staff member wearing a polka dot smock. "Como está usted, Yanci."

"Muy bien. I see you have your *hija* here." Yanci hugs Audrey. Ella winces when she hears her mother speak Spanish, remembering that night years ago when she saw Mother hiding by the gazebo, and the figure of a man retreating in the woods. She'd always suspected he was a Mexican gardener from one of the hotels.

A charmer, Audrey has regaled the staff with stories, most of them exaggerated. Ella's learned her mother told one of the attendants she could have been the first woman to attempt Mount Everest had she stuck with it. Although Audrey had flirted with mountain climbing in college, she'd only scaled a few minor peaks before she married Henry. "I gave it up for love," she'd said. As it turned out, her marriage came with an equally steep summit.

"My mom, the jock," Ella liked to say. Audrey also excelled at distance swimming. Fearless, with the stamina of an island drayhorse, she'd swum many miles in the Great Lakes. Ella and Henry escorted Audrey in their outboard on her first successful swim from Mackinac to Round Island. Wearing a black wetsuit to stave off hypothermia, Audrey stroked through the waves for half a day. Ella jumped in and out of the boat, swimming with her mother for short stretches.

At forty-five, Audrey took up golf, soon trouncing most of the women at the golf club. She'd spent the off-season at driving ranges, once carted her clubs to one during an ice storm and was annoyed the establishment was closed. She preferred to pull her bag rather than take an electric cart. Not until age sixty-eight did she succumb to a cart, and only then because the younger women she played with insisted. Sometimes she teed off the men's tees to show off.

"My daughter is taking me back to my cottage on the Island," Audrey tells Yanci, emphasizing the capital *I*. It doesn't impress the staff; to them the island is a place to visit once a year when the ferry companies offer free boat fare on Labor Day.

Ella dreads reminding Audrey she won't be going to the island today, perhaps not at all this season. "Beware the wrath of Auddie eruptus," Father would warn. Even if her leg mends by the end of August, it's too risky, way too much trouble. Cedar Bluff is filled with hazards and temptations: slippery staircases, loose floorboards, and then all the social events. Unlike Ella, Audrey maintains a brisk social calendar. Just stepping up into a carriage requires some agility. Ella knows Audrey will try to ride a bike, golf, anything. She'll get out her electric chariot, maybe crash into another tree. Even a full-time caregiver wouldn't be able to keep her under their thumb: Audrey could charm or lie her way into trouble.

But tonight is Ella's turn to charm and lie.

The dining hall is deserted. Ella had requested a late meal and the staff will accommodate her, provided she pays hourly wages for two workers. That pushed the cost of a $15 meal up to about $50, but the expense would be worth it. Besides, she has a few questions for Mother.

Ella glances at her watch, 7:00 p.m., three hours until the last boat. Given some luck she could speed and hit the dock a few minutes before the ferry made its final run. She wonders how Nick and Charlie are getting along. She wheels Mother down the hall rapidly.

"Slow down, Ella. This isn't I-75."

In the dining room Ella picks out a table near the bay window with a view of the lake and moves a chair to make room for the wheelchair. When she tries to tuck a napkin in Mother's neck, Audrey snatches it away.

"Stop treating me like an infant."

"Sorry, Mother."

"I wish Sara were here."

Ella frowns. "Sara's on business in Sri Lanka, remember?"

"Who's taking care of Charlie?"

"Me, Mother. Me. For eight weeks."

"It's a wonder you have time for that, what with all your social activities and work." *Right. A big date with a paint scraper and a manure shovel.* "But who's watching him right now?"

Should she tell her? No, that will cause way too much trouble. "He's a big boy, Mother. He can handle a few hours by himself."

Audrey rolls her eyes. "Charlie our little troublemaker? Remember last year?"

Regretfully, she did. Charlie played a prank by exchanging the horses from a neighbor's barn with those in a stable down the road. Thank God it wasn't Darci's. He was caught when a taxi driver on the graveyard shift shined his spotlight on him. "I miss that boy."

Changing the subject, Ella asks, "Do you remember any of the guys I dated?"

"You had lots of beaux. Some of them were dreadful. Remember that one with the high forehead who shaved his legs?"

"He was a swimmer, Mom, like you."

"And that boy Daddy liked so much who you despised. Going to law school."

Ted, the jerk who'd deflowered her.

"Henry was so upset when you broke up with him." Mother gazes above with her fingers stroking her chin. "Didn't you date someone from the yacht races? A sailor, nice-looking, blonde?"

"Please, Mother. He hated horses, remember?" This was beginning to sound like the top ten list of Ella's crummy boyfriends. "Do you remember one named Nick? Nick Pappas?"

Sitting up straight, Mother turns to Ella. "Heavens yes. The handsome Greek." She purses her lips staring ahead, a furl forming on her brow. "Something . . . something about him."

"What?"

"Father didn't like him, thought he wasn't appropriate for you."

"Not appropriate, huh?"

"You know what he meant. We felt he was using you, but you seemed so unaware, so happy with him."

"What do you mean?"

Mother pauses, her unsteady hand chasing down a piece of lettuce with her fork on the salad plate. She stabs at it, misses, tries again. This time she impales it and draws it toward her mouth. She chews the lettuce staring straight ahead. "He worked on the dock. Played a guitar." Audrey swallows and a shadow crosses her face. "Oh, you were two little love birds, always running off to the lake, the forest. Nature worshippers." Audrey winks. "Thank God Father put a stop to it."

"What?"

Audrey nods her head. "I think he ran him off. We left the island early that summer. When your beau called the house looking for you a few times Father told him you were gone. I think he sent back a few letters, too."

"You're kidding! Why didn't you tell me?"

"Darling, your father was determined. And it probably wouldn't have worked out. A Greek Yooper." Audrey stabs another shred of lettuce and knocks a cherry tomato on the white tablecloth, leaving a trail of brown dressing. "Can we get some dessert?"

"Did he call around Christmas, say he was supposed to meet me on the island?"

"What?"

"Nick, did he call at Christmas?"

Mother draws a blank. "Christmastime? No, I don't think so." She shakes her head. "But I'm not a very reliable source."

"What else?"

"I don't know, dear. I'd like a slice of that pie a la mode." Audrey points to the menu.

Ella pushes back her chair to find someone to place the order. When she returns Audrey has dozed off, her chin resting on her chest, mouth open. Ella pulls out her chair to sit down and Audrey's eyes flutter open.

"When's Sara coming back? I miss her."

A young woman plops two plates of pie on the table. The cherries leaking from the crust remind Ella of blood clots. A phone in the girl's apron rings with a hip-hop tune, and she scurries off, giggling.

Audrey devours the pie, but Ella has no appetite. She glances at her watch. Nine o'clock. She can still make the last boat. "Time to get you back, Mother," she says with the forced brightness of a nurse poking a needle in her patient's arm. Ella maneuvers Mother's wheelchair around the tables and pushes her down the hallway.

"Please don't leave me tonight. I get scared." Ella stops, walks around the chair and looks at Mother. Rarely has she seen her scared, though Audrey would never admit it if she were, all pluck and etiquette. Is this Audrey the drama queen or Audrey being real?

"What are you afraid of, Mother?"

Audrey squeezes Ella's hand hard. "Being here. Sometimes I wake up in the dark thinking, 'I'm going to die all alone tonight, never see the cottage again.' It makes my heart race. Like this." Audrey shakes her fist rapidly, knocking her purse to the floor. "That would never happen if I were at Cedar Bluff."

Ella sighs, walks back around the wheelchair and pushes hard. Mother grabs the arms. "Whoa!"

"Sorry."

She'll have to stay, but leaving Nick and Charlie together is worrisome: Charlie might pull one of his pranks and stay out all night. Or—a big or—they might hit it off. "All right, Mother. I'll stay."

Once Mother is tucked in, Yanci enters and hugs Audrey. "Buenos noches," she says.

"Buenos noches," whispers Audrey, her voice trailing. Ella pulls up the bedding and tucks it tightly around the mattress, shaken by the sight of Audrey so frail, vulnerable. Leaning forward, Ella kisses her on forehead where her skin glistens in a bluish tone. "Goodnight, Mother." She turns to head out of the room, but Audrey's eyelids open and she calls, "Ella?"

"Yes, Mother."

"Are you trying to poison me?"

"Why on Earth would you ever ask a question like that?" Ella is on her knees at Audrey's bedside.

Turning her head slightly toward her daughter Audrey says, "To get Cedar Bluff."

"Oh for God's sake, Mother, that's a horrible thought." Father's will specifically stated that the girls inherit Cedar Bluff only after Audrey's death. Perhaps that's what she was thinking.

"Do you honestly think I value that old place over you—that I would poison you?"

"It's crossed my mind."

"Jesus."

Audrey doesn't speak as she squeezes Ella's hand. Once Audrey is asleep, Ella tiptoes toward the door.

"Ella?"

"Yes," she sighs, turning back to the bed.

"Father was right. That Nick fellow, he wasn't your type. It would have never worked."

A few minutes later, assured Audrey is truly asleep, Ella hurries into the hallway where she dials the cottage on her phone. It rings until the message comes on with Father's voice. It sounds downright ghoulish. *I'm going to make a new message when I get back.*

Into the phone she dictates, "This is Ella. Please feed Jed breakfast first thing in the morning and make sure Charlie's up by nine. There's lots of food in the fridge. Charlie, you stay put, hear? Genevieve's coming over in the morning, and Boon too, but that's always iffy. I'll be back around ten thirty. Bye." Then she realizes Charlie's unlikely to listen to a message—such hard work!—so she types the whole thing into a text and clicks "Send." Oops. He won't reply without a threat so she types, "Please acknowledge this message or you'll be in trouble." Within twenty seconds a ding sounds on her cell. "Got it," it reads.

In Mother's room, Ella pulls out the sleeper sofa and strips to her underwear. She hasn't brought any pajamas and the room is stuffy. She lies in the dark, wondering what Nick and Charlie are up to. Playing a guess-the-soldier challenge, Trivial Pursuit? Or is Charlie sneaking off to cause more mischief?

A few feet away, Audrey snores softly. When Ella closes her eyes, she sees Nick standing next to her at Friendship's Altar, his eyes closed, the sun on his face. She feels more alive, less numb than in months.

Later, long past the time she'd finally faded into a dream, Ella is awakened by her mother's voice.

"Is that you, Ella?"

"Yes, Mother."

"Come over here."

Ella pulls herself up on legs wobbly with sleep, and kneels by her mother's bedside. Grasping her mother's hand, she feels the big diamond ring flopped sideways on her shriveled finger.

"That Greek boy, did he ever talk about me?"

"Well, I'm sure we talked about you sometimes."

"I mean about me specifically."

Ella drops her hand. What is she hinting at? "Don't know, Mother. He said I shouldn't be so oppositional around you. Think he took your side on a few matters."

"Really?"

"Why are you asking?"

"Just curious. I'm sorry I woke you up. Sweet dreams little rabbit." Ella squinches her eyes to hold back the tears. That was Father's term of endearment, something she hasn't heard in years. She holds her mother's hand until it goes limp, like a small bird shot out of the sky.

23

Entering Charlie's room, Nick finds a montage of clothing, pictures, boyhood toys, books, and electronics, the vortex of childhood's end and horny adolescence. It's a large space with white beadboard walls. On one, a framed map of the island highlighting the battle sites, and next to it, a poster of the USS *Enterprise*. Two twin beds, one coated in t-shirts and pants, sit parallel to one another, a double sash window between them. A dream catcher flutters above it. A large red and white oval braided rug covers part of the hardwood floor. On the other side of the room is a desk with a laptop computer and an open copy of *MAD Magazine*. What catches Nick's eye is a miniature diorama on a low table near the desk. He recognizes the toy soldiers: Brits and Americans.

Nick walks to the diorama and squats before it. The soldiers are beautifully crafted. He's seen them at shows and knows they're pricey. Whistling, Nick picks one up. "Quite a collection."

"I've kind of outgrown those," says Charlie.

"How about a battle?"

"This is the Battle of Saratoga." Charlie moves a tiny soldier wearing a red uniform.

Nick moves a British soldier toward Charlie's American and shouts, "Eieee!" The two clash, and Nick's man prevails. They continue fighting until Nick surrenders. "Take it. Take everything. It's yours."

Charlie smiles. "Aunt Ellie hates war games. She'd rather be bag snagging or studying her hydrometer," says Charlie. "Her only interest in war is how it affects the ecosystem."

"Bag snagging?"

"One of her weird hobbies. Not here, cuz there's no litter; in DC where she used to live, Detroit, any place with lots of trash blowing around."

"I don't get it."

"She didn't tell you about it? About her invention? You walk around with this big claw-like thing on the end of a pole yanking plastic bags out of trees. She patented it, did this big launch, but Uncle Kevin took her to court and won the patent."

"Uncle Kevin?"

"Yeah. My ex-uncle. I can't say the K-word around my aunt. You know what she did at my tenth birthday party? She made up a game called Get the Cans, dumped cans all over the yard, hid them in bushes, behind plants. The kid with the most cans won a prize. It was pretty embarrassing."

"So, your Uncle Kevin likes trash too?'

Charlie places a soldier on the diorama. "I don't know. He was the kind of guy who would do whatever it took to get what he wanted. You know. Mom said he was an opportunist. He wasn't very interested in me. Didn't like kids. Well, he didn't back then, but now he's got a couple of stepkids, so maybe he's changed his mind."

"Stepkids?"

"Uh-huh. He married some lady with little kids."

Nick isn't sure how far he should push. "So where is Kevin?"

Charlie looks annoyed. "I don't know. I don't keep track of him."

"So what's the deal with you and your dad?" asks Nick, switching the subject. Maybe he can get back to the Kevin topic after this. "I don't have a dad. I have a sperm donor."

"You mean your mom never married him?"

"Oh, they were married, but he left us. Never tried to contact me. And you know what? I don't want to see him."

He's had students like this, abandoned kids, bottling up their feelings, acting out. He understands Charlie's desire to pretend his father doesn't matter. Men like that infuriate Nick; he has an urge to hunt down this man, this sperm donor. Punch his lights out. *You've got a beautiful boy and he needs you, asshole.*

"Do you have any kids?" asks Charlie.

"One, a daughter," he says, surprised Charlie has taken an interest in him. "She's twenty. Studying in Honduras—a work study thing."

"Cool. My grandmother speaks Spanish. Used to spend her winters in Costa Rica. What's your daughter's name?"

"Melina." Just saying her name makes Nick ache to hear her voice.

He wonders how her experience in Honduras is going. He should call Katie to check on news from her, but then he'd have to go through all the BS with her, all the fake *how are yous*, immediately followed by requests for more money. Still, he's burning to hear about any scrap of news about Melina.

"Does she like history?"

"Not all that much. She says it's a guy thing."

"Maybe she's got a point." Charlie seems to have lost interest in his soldiers and is looking at his computer. "You a gamer?"

That, he is not. He'd played Pac-Man, what was it, a hundred years ago—had skied a little on one of those platform games where you held gizmos in your hand.

"I can do a little Wii."

Charlie snorts. "I don't mean that family friendly crap. I'm referring to serious gaming, like Shooters, Legends, stuff like that."

"No, I'm pretty illiterate in advanced gaming."

"Well, I need to get on it now so . . ."

Nick gets it. Time to butt out. He can't relax with the boy anyway, keeps his guard up. And he could really use a nightcap. "'Scuze me a minute," says Nick. "I need to check in with someone." Charlie doesn't look up as Nick slips out the door.

In his room he discovers his cell phone is out of juice; he'd neglected to charge it. Plugging in the charger, he strums his fingers waiting for the phone to return to life. The phone finally lights up and Nick taps in Katie's number. Her voice sounds friendly for a change, eager to share news about Melina. "She met a little boy with no shoes who was living under a bridge," says Katie. "She wants to bring him home. I told her she can't save everyone. She's growing up a lot on this trip."

After hanging up he walks past Charlie's door where the booms of guns and explosions resound. In his room Nick takes out the flask of Jack Daniels and heads for the kitchen for ice. On the staircase he hears Charlie calling him. "Hey, Nick, what are you doing down there?"

"Getting a little refreshment!" he shouts. "I'm going on the porch, check out the stars. Could use some company."

Out on the porch Nick chooses the rocker he sat in on Saturday, his first day on the island. It seems so long ago; hard to believe it was just two days. The scene tonight is glorious; to the east the moon swings low, spreading a neon orange path across the water.

Behind him the screen door opens. "Do you think it's wrong to be messing around over there?" Charlie asks, pointing toward Round Island, a black hump behind the moon's path.

Nick swirls his glass slowly. "Sure do. I know you love the adventure of it. I do, too. History gets in your blood. But suppose you find something and disturb it, mess it up? People have methods, they sift through dirt for days, months, years. Painfully slow, to be safe. They're trained to do that.

"But there's a more important reason to leave it be. That island—heck, this island—is not ours. The Odawas, or Anishenabes, were here long before us. The land is sacred to them. There's pretty clear evidence they buried their dead there too, long before any cholera victims showed up there. It's a matter of respect for that."

"Hmm. I guess you've got a good point."

They sit quietly, the boy looking toward Round Island, Nick toward the mainland, wondering what Ella is doing. The moon is nearly three-quarter size, soon to become the red Sturgeon moon of August.

"Can I ask you something about Aunt Ella?" asks Charlie.

"Fire away."

"She was your girlfriend, right?"

Nick clears his throat. "That was a long time ago."

"Is she still?"

"We're friends. And now, with this—" he points to his toe and chuckles, "we're getting to know one another better than I believe she wanted to."

Charlie laughs. "Man, you should see the way you look at her. I think you're whipped."

***

Hours later, long after Charlie had left him with an unexpected friendly slap of the palms and a "Night, dude," Nick stirs and finds he's still on the porch. Must've fallen asleep in the rocker. A chill has set in and he stumbles into the house. The door to a room on his right is ajar. Ella hadn't taken him there on her "house tour." Pushing the door open, he flips on a light switch. The room, a library, smells mustier than the rest of the house, layered in the odor of old books and paper, topped with a hint of lemony furniture polish. Two walls of floor-to-ceiling bookcases harbor an array of books from collector-grade hardbacks to contemporary paperbacks. Sprinkled on the bookshelves are photos and knickknacks. A bright little ceramic cart that looks Spanish catches his eye. On a large mahogany desk centered before the opposite wall, file folders, envelopes, and paper are stacked in neat piles. Though exhausted, he's curious. When will he get a better chance to snoop? Nick sits down in a cracked leather chair and pulls himself up to the desk. The chair feels comfortable, well suited to his back. He imagines Henry, perhaps even old Oscar sitting here.

He picks up a bronze paperweight shaped like a coffin sitting atop a stack of papers. Embossed across the base are the words, "Hollingsworth Casket Company, Quality Forever." His watch reads one fifteen. *I'll just peek at one paper.* Mostly bills. *Trash pick-up, seven bags, $18.50.* Seems reasonable. Nick opens a drawer on the right where a jumble of safety pins, business cards, three AA batteries, and a wood ruler lie amidst a tangle of paper clips. Toward the back a rubber band holds together a stack of old letters. Nick pulls out the letters and removes the band. The first is a sympathy card to Audrey on the death of Henry. "Such wonderful memories we share, my dear. He is now one with the Island." Nick picks up another and a photograph falls out. It's one of the resort hotel types where groups or couples line up in evening clothes on the Grand Hotel's massive porch overlooking the Straits. Ella, her mother and father, and a good-looking man with light-brown wavy hair topping an oval face stand together, smiling. The guy can't be a day over forty. His arm is around Ella's waist, his hand reaching out of sight but definitely to her glutes with a she's-mine-dudes sense of proprietorship. She's wearing a white dress and sandals, the man a beige sports jacket with a cream-colored shirt opened two buttons. He has a small, trim beard. Kevin? He drops the photo, burning with envy.

Slamming the drawer, he hears a creak of the floorboards. "Who's there?" A chill runs down his spine as he jumps to his feet. Then he hears a skittering sound. *Damn mice.*

24

Loud knocking on the back door awakens Nick early. He stumbles into his pants and shirt, then walks barefooted down the back stairs into the kitchen where he opens the door. A woman in a black blouse and skirt smiles at him.

"Hello. Is Miss Ella here?"

"No, she's on the mainland."

"I'm Genevieve. I do some work around here, ironing, cleaning." She walks past Nick into the kitchen. "Don't you worry about me. I'll get started now." She opens a door in the pantry that leads to a small room with a washer and dryer that Nick had not noticed before, then drags an ironing board through the doorway.

"Here, let me help you with that. By the way, I'm Nick, a friend of the family."

"Nice to meet you, Nick."

Genevieve sets up the ironing board in the kitchen and hauls in a basket of clothing from the laundry area. She flips on the radio, steering the dial to a station with Christian music.

"Don't mind me," she says. "I'll be working my way through this for the next two hours. You just make yourself at home." Nick's feet feel cold and he craves a cup of coffee, not only for the caffeine, but the warmth of the cup in his hands.

"Do you know where Ella keeps her coffee?"

"Sure, mon. I'll make it. Like a cup myself, too."

"Thanks."

He walks upstairs, showers for less than the three minutes recommended—that's only twenty-one gallons, tops, he calculates. He shaves using a few spurts of water, proud of his newfound conservation measures. In the sunlight pouring through the window he pulls the bandage off his toe and examines it. The skin is paler than his other toes, all wrinkly and chicken-skin white, the swelling gone. Gingerly he swabs alcohol on the wound and cringes as the liquid bites into the skin. He wraps fresh gauze over it, then new tape. Looks like it's healing quickly.

All his clothes are filthy. Since he'd only planned a two-day stay on the island, he hasn't brought much with him. He gathers up two soiled shirts, underwear, and a pair of shorts, and walks down to the kitchen where the smell of coffee pierces the cool morning air along with the song from the radio, *"I will give you all my worship, I will give you all my praise."*

Genevieve sings along as she navigates the iron in and out of the shell buttons on its ride across a linen shirt. A clean cup and saucer, a sugar bowl and creamer sit on the table.

"Coffee's ready," she says.

"Thanks. It smells delicious."

Genevieve notices his armload of clothes. "Here, I'll take those and wash 'em up."

"No, I can do it."

"This is my second job. Helps me pay for my little ones back home."

Genevieve tells him about her three daughters in Jamaica, ages 6, 11, and 14, and about her husband who is taking care of them while she's here from May through October. Her job as a chambermaid at the Trillium Hotel supports her immediate family and a few more relatives, but she needs to moonlight to pay for decent schooling for the girls.

"You don't know how I miss my babies." Genevieve stands up and pours more coffee. "Thank the Lord for Miss Ella and her laundry. All this cotton wrinkles faster than a mushroom in a microwave."

Nick sips his coffee, an extra-strong and bitter brew, exactly what he needs. On the counter he notices a plate of cookies covered with plastic wrap. Darn that wallpaper; he's been craving cookies every time he enters the kitchen. Genevieve looks up. "Go ahead and help yourself. That neighbor lady brought these over while you were in the shower."

"Was she short, with hair like this?" Nick makes a straight slicing motion below his ears.

"That would be her. Miss Darci. Says she's sorry about your accident and Mrs. Hollingsworth, thought Ella's too busy to take proper care of her guests right now."

"She is busy."

"Between that boy, her mother, and all her projects, she never sits down. If you ask me, she needs a man to help around here. A good man." Genevieve's arms halt for a moment and she looks directly at him. Nick wonders if she'll burn a hole in the blouse she's ironing. "Are you a special friend?"

"Oh no, just an old friend."

"Hmm." The iron hisses as Genevieve jabs down on the steam button. "Miss Ella never, ever leaves that boy with anyone, not even with her mama. And I've been working here for four summers. She must trust you a lot."

"She seems very fond of Charlie. Treats him like a son."

"You're telling me! Last summer she had a man up here, a special friend,"—she winks—"but Charlie didn't take to him. He was gone in a day."

"Oh."

"That boy gets his way. Look at him, still up in bed, not doing any chores."

"Teenagers are like that."

Genevieve sets down the iron and stares at Nick. "Not where I come from."

He needs to get started on those projects. "Do you know where they keep the tools around here?"

"In the pantry, bottom cupboard on the left. You gonna fix something?"

"Thought I'd start with that screen," he says.

"Then you better plan on staying here all summer," she laughs.

As Nick hunts for screen repair tools he hears a loud thump against the front of the house. He hurries to the front door and sees a ladder running from the front yard to the second story, and Boon standing on the porch. Nick opens the door.

"Just to let you know I'm starting now," says Boon.

"Starting?"

"Painting. Ella said to start today."

A trace of booze wafts from him. "With this weather? Looks like a storm's on its way."

"I'm just scraping today."

"Well then," says Nick, scratching his head. "Don't you think you should straighten out that ladder?"

Boon squints at it. "Looks straight to me."

"Maybe you should wait until Ella returns. She'll be back soon."

"Nope."

"Well, let's straighten it out so you won't fall." Nick walks to the ladder, then pushes on it until the top rails rest upright against the siding. "Isn't that better?"

Boon grunts. "I better get started before that rain you were talking about comes in."

Nick holds the ladder while Boon ascends. Inside the phone rings, and Nick hurries up the steps and answers it before Henry's voice can come on the answering machine.

"Hollingsworth residence," says Nick.

"Hi, Nick, it's Ella. How are things going?"

"Busy. Genevieve's ironing and Boon's trying to kill himself on the ladder."

"Drinking?"

"Maybe."

"Well there's no point in arguing with him. How's Charlie?"

"Asleep, I assume."

"You'd better wake him up. Could you make sure he eats something before he goes downtown? I'm running a little behind. Mother got panicky and now she's insisting on coming with me. Did you feed Jed?"

He'd forgotten all about the horse. "No."

"Give him two flakes of hay. Better do it soon, the old boy needs his breakfast and it's late. Oh, a guy named Mike might come by to check out the damage in the tower. Just let him in."

"Anything else?"

Her voice softens. "How are you? Did you sleep well?"

"Pretty well. We missed you." There's a pause at the other end.

"Um. I'll be on the ten o'clock ferry, back home by about ten thirty. Bye."

He places the receiver back on the phone. Despite his aching toe and stiff knee, a feeling of contentment moves over him. In the kitchen Genevieve is singing, and there's an occasional *thump, slide, bang* from Boon, who has somehow managed to stay on the ladder. The rhythm of the house, everyone at work... except Charlie.

Better go wake up the boy. Finding Charlie's door closed, Nick puts his ear to the door, listening. Hearing nothing, he knocks softly. "Charlie, you up?" No response. "Charlie?" Slowly, he turns the knob; the old hinges squeak as he pushes the door inward a few inches. Nick can see one of the twin beds where the plaid spread is tucked in neatly. The other bed is unmade, with the spread hanging over the side, the sheet and blue blanket twisted, a pile of t-shirts on the floor.

Nick walks down the back stairs to the kitchen.

"Have you seen Charlie?"

"That lazy boy is still up in bed."

"No, he's gone. Just wondered if he'd slipped through here."

"Not one sign of him."

"Guess he just went out to do whatever kids his age do, but I'll check the barn."

Outside, the yard is quiet. Nick walks toward the barn, looking anxiously to the left for signs of Darci. She could pop out from that hedge at any moment. "Charlie!" he calls. Jed trots to the fence. Nicks pulls a few handfuls of grass growing by the fencepost and holds his hand flat for the horse. Jed's warm mouth presses Nick's palm, leaving a trace of slobber. In the barn he takes two portions of hay and runs it out to Jed. Conquering his squeamishness, Nick strokes the old gelding's head, noticing he has one blue eye, one brown. His father used to joke about a dog one of his uncles owned with eyes like that, "Down a quart on shit."

He walks by the compost piles past the little paddock where the horse has gnawed down every blade of green and it's now mired in manure. Better tell Ella it needs mucking out.

The gazebo sits on a slight rise behind the barn. Nick remembers the night he discovered Audrey there, how he'd shielded it from Ella. Coated with a layer of pine needles, the gazebo's roof is deteriorating, and the white wooden door badly needs painting. Pushing it open, Nick smells the familiar sweet traces of marijuana. He jumps back, shaken. This is what brought him down in Madison, young men and marijuana. "Charlie?" he calls, his voice breaking.

Only silence and the rush of his heart. "If you're in there please answer me."

Through the doorway he sees a coffee table in front of a wicker loveseat, where a paint-splattered blue and white work shirt hangs over one arm. On the table, a roach clip rests in an ashtray. Dismayed, Nick wonders how he will break the news to Ella: her darling Charlie, a pothead. In the shadows toward the back of the gazebo sits a cot with a lump on top. *Ah ha.*

"Charlie, get up. Your aunt will be home in less than an hour."

Silence. Nick walks to the cot and lifts a bunched-up blanket that has created the illusion of someone lying there. Nick turns and walks out of the gazebo. Thank God it wasn't the boy, but where is he? And who'd been smoking weed in there?

Back in the cottage, Nick makes one more search for Charlie, opening the doors to all five bedrooms on the second floor except Ella's. Standing before her door, his hand on the glass knob, he pauses, hesitant to poke around in there. He turns the handle and the door squeals, opening to what appears to be a recent police shake-down. Stuff's strewn everywhere. A periwinkle blue quilt hangs over the side of the unmade high brass and iron bed; the fitted bottom sheet loosened from the left corner, top sheet in a wad beneath a pile of clothes strewn on the bed. Had a family of squirrels partied in here last night? "Barbarian," Nick mutters. On the floor, clothes are strewn in layers: black pants—ironed by Genevieve?—numerous pairs of white and beige shirts and shorts decorate the window seat, bed posts, and the floor. The closet is open with a long flannel nightie draped over the door. If Charlie were in here, Nick wouldn't be able to find the kid.

On a mahogany highboy with a few drawers partially open, a white candy box sits next to a family photo with a younger Audrey—an Ella look-alike for sure—holding a cherubic baby in her arms. She's next to a severe-looking man in a Stetson hat. It must be a young Henry. In another photo, a towheaded boy in a white sailor suit who looks about two, stares out with a worried look. Charlie. *Well, kid, I'd be worried too if someone stuck me in an outfit like that.* Nick opens the box where a few chocolate-covered candies remain, takes one out and bites into a raisin. Delicious. He eats one more, then picks up a crumpled beige blouse from the floor and buries his nose in it: woodsy, with a hint of musk; Ella's scent. He suppresses an urge to sniff her panties.

Through the windows, the lake, now a dull pewter scrolled with whitecaps beneath a darkening sky, fills the view. Two windows are open. and the lace curtains slap the window frames like frantic bumblebees. He'd better close them before the rain.

Thump. Out the window Nick sees Boon pushing the ladder up against the house, fiddling with the extension unit. Several more thumps and Boon begins climbing toward Ella's window. Nick ducks down. *Thump.* "Whoa, boy, don't you buck on me," Boon barks at the ladder, his head crowning the bottom of the window. Nick dives under the bed. Good thing it's one of those old-fashioned extra-high types or he'd never fit. He stares at the debris gathered around him: dozens of dust balls, a nightie, a pair of tall riding boots, one white ankle sock, and a book flipped open, facedown. He shakes his head and shuts the book, dismayed to see a perfectly good book getting ruined like that. *Great Lakes Water Wars.* He smiles. Did he think she'd be reading a romance? Lying there, he wonders what would happen if Ella were to discover him. Probably put on those boots and kick his ass right across the Straits.

A good ten minutes pass before he hears Boon moving down the ladder—"You hold still, boy"—and Nick crawls out, tiptoes to the door and sneezes hard. All that dust. He can't quite believe what he just did, can't stop thinking about the pungency of her clothing. Then he remembers Charlie.

25

Ella opens the back screen door. "Charlie? Nick?" she calls. She'd had a devil of a time leaving Mother. First Audrey had thrown a fit, threatened to hire a private plane and fly to the island. Then she cried. Ella sneaked out when Audrey dozed off sitting in the lounge in her wheelchair, barely making the ten thirty ferry.

"When she wakes up, tell her I just stepped out. If she has another fit, well, do your best. I'll call from the cottage. Thanks," says Ella. The deception should buy Ella a few days of peace.

On the porch she notices a half-empty cup of coffee and a glass of water with a dead fly floating in it. She calls up the stairs, her voice echoing on the wood paneling, reverberating down the dark, long hallways. "Nick?" Walking toward the kitchen, Ella picks up and sniffs a cocktail glass on the dining room credenza; the faint reek of booze.

In the kitchen, the counter is scrubbed, the sink clear, and a pile of freshly ironed clothes hang on hooks in the pantry. Thank God for Genevieve. Opening the dishwasher she notices a few plates and empty plastic containers. She smiles. *Nick ate my lasagna.*

She glances at the door to the back staircase and walks up. Nick's room is at the back of the house, furthest from Ella's. They call it the green room, now painted yellow. The family identifies every room by its original color, and all but Ella's room have long since changed hues. She loves this room for its coziness, but most of all for the secret staircase connecting it to the kitchen. Growing up she'd claimed this room, but was forced to move back to a front bedroom when he father caught her sneaking out one night. When Ella moved away, Sara took over the room. As the youngest child, Sara escaped the 24-7 parental vigilance that stalked Ella's growing-up years, the lucky second child who slips under parental radar with acres of freedom. Sara said she'd sneaked a boyfriend to her room while her parents slept.

As she places her hand on the white porcelain doorknob Ella hesitates, then opens the door slowly. The bed is made, a green army blanket neatly folded at the foot. On the oak dresser lays a planner and a small photo of Melina, like the one Nick showed her from his wallet. Ella opens the planner to August 3. Blank. She flips backwards, scrolling her finger down the lined pages, the details of days before their reunion. Some are bursting with notes: "Faculty meeting, bring class lists," "Grad Standards due," "Meeting with T. Olson's mom," "Dry cleaners," "DDS," "Melina's break," "Anne for dinner," "Lunch, Anne," Who's Anne? She closes the cover, carefully placing the planner back at the exact spot on the dresser, then opens the slim top drawer, the one used to fill with odds and ends from pockets, wallets, and purses. In a nest of change sits a silver cell phone. She quietly shuts the drawer.

Glancing around, Ella notices a pair of navy blue boxer shorts and a T-shirt folded on a plaid ottoman. She picks up the T-shirt and presses it to her face. The soft cotton smells like laundry soap with a hint of fresh grass. Closing her eyes, she remembers the feel of Nick's leg when she leaned over him to wrap the towel around his foot in the boat: rock-solid, the tendons taut, circling his calves like vines. Downstairs a screen door slams.

"Ella?"

It's Nick's voice. Hurriedly she refolds the T-shirt—was it sleeves in first, or sleeves last?—places it on the ottoman, then tiptoes from the room. The sound of footsteps on the front staircase move closer. As she rounds the corner of the back hallway she nearly crashes into Nick.

"Ella."

"Hey."

"You're back." He reaches out to hug her. "This place was Grand Central Station this morning. How's your mom?"

Relieved that he hasn't asked her what she'd been doing in the back hallway, she sighs. "Better. No, worse. I mean, she wasn't really hurt badly, but she's slipping. And cranky. She was asking for Sara. At one point I had thoughts of matricide and fratricide." She pauses, taking a breath. "She's desperate to come here. I more or less tricked her out of it, but I don't know how long I can put her off."

"Why don't you let her come home? Either that or take her back to Ann Arbor. Why this halfway stuff?"

The nerve of him second-guessing her. She pushes her hair behind her ears. "For starters, Mother will do some stupid thing to mess herself up again. I'll have to watch her night and day, and she'll spew vitriolic speech half the time. Under our current arrangement she's close enough that I can shuttle over there every few days and Charlie can have island time."

"Oh yes, island time."

"Please, Nick, don't get sarcastic on me."

"How about getting someone else in your family to help? Can't you get Sara back to at least watch her son?"

"Not in a blue moon."

"How about some cousins or an auntie who'd like to come up here? My family would be fighting over a chance to stay on Mackinac."

"My family's not like yours." She knows she seems unsympathetic about Audrey, but Nick doesn't understand. "Look, what would your family do if you were thrown in jail for doing something really awful, like armed robbery or murder?"

"Mama would start cooking and set up a schedule for family visits."

"Well there's the difference: mine wouldn't even visit. They might send a card, one of those things from the Coping section that says something like 'We understand the pain you are suffering.'" What's the use of her trying to explain? Theirs are such different worlds.

"Did you wake up Charlie?"

"I knocked on his door but he'd already left."

"What?"

"At about nine, a little after you called. I knocked and he didn't answer so I opened the door. He wasn't there. I was worried, so I checked everywhere, the barn, the bedrooms, I even looked in the gazebo."

"The gazebo?"

"Yep." He wants to tell her about his suspicions someone has been staying there, but decides to wait. "Guess Charlie left early."

"He never gets up early."

"He's fourteen years old. Probably off on some historic investigation. I'm sure he's fine."

"You don't know this kid."

***

Ella rushes down the steps. "I'm calling Benjamin. I hate dealing

with his dad, but I've got to find out if those two are up to something."
Last summer Charlie and Benjamin had sneaked out in the middle
of the night and bicycled up to Fort Holmes at the top of the island.
They'd stuffed their backpacks with food, flashlights, and a sleeping
bag. They planned to come back before anyone was up, almost got
away with it, but were caught building a campfire. Benjamin's father
blamed Ella for being too lenient. No surprise that Sara wasn't around,
and when she heard about it, she chewed out Ella.

She dials the McDowell's number and a male voice answers, "Hello." Her heart sinks. It's John. She'd hoped to get Jane, his obsequi-
ous wife with her long flowered sundresses and nervous giggle. "Good
morning, this is Ella Hollingsworth. Is Benjamin there?"

"Funny you should ask. Jane went up to wake him for a tennis lesson and he wasn't there. You don't think that—"

"Of course not. Just wondering."

"Where's Charlie?"

"I thought he might be with Benjamin. They're probably both at the
bike shop. Not to worry."

"Jesus Christ. If those boys are out in your boat, I'm holding you
responsible."

"I'm sure they aren't, and I don't appreciate your lack of trust in my
nephew and your son."

"I'm calling the Coast Guard."

"Whoa, John, talk about putting the cart before the horse. Let's first
see if the boat's here."

"Look out your window; see that storm moving in? Didn't you
catch the weather report? Small craft warnings. If they're in the boat
we need to get them back here now. I'll meet you at the dock." He
hangs up.

"Damn." He's right about the weather. On the ferry Ella had noticed the darkening sky and Curt, the boat captain, had mentioned
something about it. "Gonna be a big one. Getting back just in time."

Ella slams down the receiver and swirls around, facing Nick. "Why
didn't you check on him earlier?" He should have been more responsible. She shouldn't have run off. If only she'd hidden those boat keys.
The kid couldn't be trusted.

"Get a grip. You keep treating him like a little boy. Charlie is growing into a young man. Even if he's in the boat, he's had plenty of experience on the water, right?"

"Easy for you to say. He's not your son."

"He's not yours either."

If she weren't so fearful about Charlie she may have slapped him right then and there. No time for that now. Rushing to a small oak desk in the front hallway, Ella opens a drawer and bangs it shut. The boat keys are missing. "Come on, let's get to the dock." Grabbing two yellow rain ponchos, she tosses one to Nick and pulls the other over her head. "We'll be needing these."

Zipping down the hill on bicycles, they hear the rumble of thunder west of the Mackinac Bridge. The storm will arrive in minutes. By the time they reach the dock, Ella's shorts are soaked, but the poncho has kept her top half dry. "No!" cries Ella, pointing to the empty boat slip in the marina. Standing on the dock above it, a cellphone at his ear, is John McDowell. He sports a yellow rain jacket, a University of Michigan cap and a black umbrella.

"I just called the Coast Guard and filed a report," he says.

"This is Nick, a, a friend of mine," says Ella. He shakes Nick's hand in a fist-crushing squeeze.

"I'm sure the boys will be fine," says Nick. "Just some mischief gone awry."

John's eyebrows rise. "You think? Benjamin is easily influenced, but that will stop as of today. If we find him."

"*When* we find them. Not much we can do but wait," says Ella.

"I'll wait up at the club," says John, nodding toward a white building across the street with a red-striped awning. "Care to join me?"

"Thanks, but we need a decent cup of coffee," says Ella, nudging Nick with her elbow. Once they're out of earshot she adds, "I can't stand that man, such a pompous ass."

"His handshake borders on brutality," says Nick, rubbing his hand.

26

Ella steers them to a coffee shop overlooking the dock. It's a shoe-box of a structure with a large puddle of water covering the welcome mat, but inside it is cozy, with tables and a sofa in the corner where two bearded men are absorbed in a game of chess. Ella nods to one and he smiles. The clerk, a tall woman with short gray hair and a pale face, says, "Good morning, Ella. The usual?"

"No, I'll have a soy chai please, with extra foam, extra hot."

"Black coffee," says Nick.

"Six fifty-two," says the clerk. Nick gulps. He's used to paying a buck at the local gas station for his coffee. Ella removes a ten-dollar bill from her pocket. "Let me get this," says Nick.

"Nonsense. You're my guest."

Nick takes off his poncho, tossing it over the back of a wrought-iron ice cream parlor chair. Water pools on the floor beneath it. Ella does the same. Nick looks around. The coffee shop has an unfranchised feel to it, unique and homey, a vanishing breed. He glances out the window where rain cascades in sheets, pushed by the west wind. Waves race toward them, slapping the retaining wall holding up the coffee shop, leaving beads of water running down the windows. Not a good day to be out on the lake, not even for a duck. He wraps his hand around the warm mug and studies Ella's face. She's staring into her cup, all the swagger and primness blown out with the storm.

"Worried?"

"Of course, but deep down, something's telling me they're OK."

Nick has his doubts. "That McDowell guy is sure intense. Benjamin doesn't look at all like him."

"Charlie's right, John is an asshole. Pure and simple. There's no polite way to say it. I didn't want to hang out at the yacht club with him barking orders." She pulls her phone from a pocket in her sweater. "I've tried to dial Charlie's cell and texted him, but it's nearly impossible to get reception over there. I just keep hoping."

"He has a cellphone on him? Why didn't you tell me?"

"Didn't think about it." Nick puts his hand on top of hers. "You love that boy a lot." Ella lowers her head but he sees the tears, translucent tiny pearls piling in the corner of her eyes. "Ella, you don't need to hide this from me. We're friends. Loving someone so much can hurt like crazy." He squeezes her hand; she squeezes back so hard that his middle fingers crunch.

"Thanks." She removes her hand and brushes it across her eyes, then checks her phone again. "Nothing yet." In the daylight from the window the lines in her face appear deeper, and for the first time, Nick notices the circles around her neck. It makes him sad.

Then, a chime pipes from her phone. Ella grabs it without checking the caller ID. "Yes?" As she listens, her face goes pale. "We're on our way," she says, jumping up and yanking her wet poncho over her head. "Come on." Half her chai, a circle of gold, glistens in her cup; Nick still has a few good sips of coffee.

"Charlie?"

She shakes her head. "No. That was John. He said someone found a boat and reported it to the Coast Guard. A white Whaler. Empty."

Empty? Nick's heart drops. That means the boys must be in the lake. How long could they last in that cold water? An hour? He hardly dares look at her, but when he does, he's surprised by a sunny expression on her face.

"Don't you get it?" she says.

"Huh?"

"I bet he didn't secure the boat properly at Round Island and it got away. That means—"

"-—that he and Benjamin are sitting on Round Island." Nick hopes she's right, but he's dubious. Even safe from the water, they'd have to dodge the lightning and trees that were sure to blow down in a storm of this magnitude.

"Come on, come on," says Ella, halfway to the door. They slosh down Main Street to the yacht club with its huge anchor planted in the front lawn, up the long steps to the front door. As Ella puts her hand on the knob and turns to Nick she says, "Please help me not fly off the handle."

Inside, they find John in the foyer on his phone. He tucks it in his pocket as they approach. "The Coast Guard says they found three life preservers, some soda cans and a book in the boat."

Ella's upper lip trembles. "Oh."

John presses her. "How many life jackets do you keep in that boat?"

"Five." Nick does the math. The boys must be wearing the other two.

"Are you sure there was nothing else in there?" asks Ella.

"That's what they said. Let's get over to the dock and check with the Coast Guard." John keeps a pace ahead of them and they fall into step behind.

At the dock they are met by a young officer in uniform with a well-scrubbed, serious face and a solid handshake.

"Officer Moore. First name is Sean."

John reaches out his hand first. "John McDowell, Benjamin's dad. He's one of the boys. This is Ella and her, ah, friend."

"Nick."

"So, Sean, give it to us straight," says John.

"Yes, sir. This storm is bad. We'll send our chopper over as soon as it's safe."

"Why not now?" asks Ella, her voice shaking.

"Too rough, but the radar shows the storm's clearing up soon."

"I don't think you heard me. I said why not now? There are two boys' lives on the line."

"Ma'am, let's go in there and talk." He points to the rescue craft moored next to them.

Nick follows Ella onto the boat that's tossing at seasick magnitude, even here in the harbor's protective arms. Officer Moore is all business. "There are other lives at risk too. And if these boys are alive—as I'm sure they are—they need strong parents because right now, they're probably peeing their pants."

"I'm his aunt."

"Well, whatever, aunt, mother, you get my point?" He continues without waiting for a reply. "I want you to tell me exactly where you think he is." Ella sketches the island and places an X by the south side where they picnicked Monday. "Or they might be at the sandy beach by now, waiting for someone to rescue them," she adds, plopping another X on the sketch.

There's a clamor as John descends the ladder. "Excuse me," he says to Nick, brushing past him. "I need to be in on this."

"So we're doing a full-court press," continues Officer Moore. "I've seen these situations turn out good . . . and not so good . . ." His voice trails off. Nick notices how pale Ella's knuckles appear, little knobs glowing in the table lamp. He sits beside her as the boat rocks violently in its ropes. Nick has to clutch the rail on his seat to prevent sliding off. The movement presses him against Ella, the heat from her body warms his right side.

"I don't know about you fellows, but I'm going to get some help," announces Ella, rising to her feet.

Jumping up, Officer Moore says, "All in good time, ma'am. We'll get them once we determine their location. Looks like the lightning's gone so the chopper can take off in a few minutes. When they locate the boys we'll send this boat over. If you go out in this squall now you're risking your life."

"And you're risking the lives of two boys." Ella pushes past the officer and Nick follows. On the dock she pleads with him. "Look, I'm going over there now. You can stay here or help, but you're not talking me out of this."

"The officer said they're going soon. Besides, you have no way of getting there. Let's wait. Please." But his last words are futile, blown away in the squall, yards behind Ella's retreating back.

Within minutes he hears the *clackety-clack* of the helicopter blades. The rain changes from the cats and dogs variety to a light patter; enough to soak you, but slowly, one drop at a time. Nick sees Ella spin around and run towards him. Thank God.

During the following nail-biting minutes, Ella glances at her phone constantly while John paces the dock, silent and grim. Officer Moore's radio is alive with chatter, so when the call from the chopper finally comes in announcing it has spotted the boys on the shore of Round Island, they can barely discern it.

"All right, everyone off while we go get 'em," Officer Moore orders.

***

Soggier than towels on a locker room floor, the boys emerge from the rescue vessel, hair plastered down around their moist faces. They

appear so much younger wet than dry, like puppies, but not so innocent. Charlie's mendacious side has emerged.

Benjamin comes first, walking with slumped shoulders, his eyes to
the ground with one quick glance at his mother, Jane, who has joined
her husband on the dock.

"Benjamin!" she cries, shaking off her husband's attempt to restrain
her as she runs to embrace her sopping wet son. John grabs Benjamin
by the elbow. "Come on, son. We've got some talking to do." As they
move down the dock, Jane takes a windbreaker from a backpack and
throws it over Benjamin' shoulders. Charlie doesn't look up, but Nick
notices a trace of a smirk on his face.

"Thank God you're OK," Nick says, stepping aside to let Ella come
at Charlie with hugs and thank Gods. But she doesn't budge, not one
inch; her feet remain rooted to the dock, her eyes ripping into the boy.
Nick strips off his poncho and hands it to the kid. "You must be freezing."

"Thanks," says Charlie, slipping it on.

Ella moves toward him "For God's sakes, what were you thinking?"
she erupts, her face granite, her blue eyes gray. Nick expected this reunion to be joyful, with punishment put aside for later, or forever.

"I could eat a horse," says Charlie.

"Don't say that too loud," says Nick, cocking his head toward the
street where a carriage is passing.

When they're out of earshot of the McDowells, who have walked
off the dock heading toward the street, Ella charges toward the boy
and grabs his wrists. "What in the hell do you think you were doing?"

Charlie shakes his wrists free, yanking down forcefully. "I didn't
know it was going to storm!"

Ella backs away, arms flailing. "What's that supposed to mean?
How about an apology, some remorse?"

"Look, everything turned out OK. Benjamin and me, the boat—"

"Oh shut up. Stop justifying it." Ella steps toward Charlie as Nick
gently touches her arm to steer her away from the boy who has turned
his back on them and begun walking up the dock. She shouts, "The apple doesn't fall far from the tree, does it? You're just like your father!"

"What? What did you say?" asks Charlie, spinning around, his head
bucking up. "I can't believe you said that." Neither can Nick.

"That's it. I'm outta here," shouts Charlie as he breaks into a jog.

"Damn it, damn it, damn it!" Ella is knocking her fist against her head.

"I'm going after him," says Nick, breaking into a run, not an easy feat with his injured toe. At the curb by the street he catches up with Charlie, who has paused for a group of bicyclists.

"Don't say a word. I don't wanna hear it," says Charlie without looking at Nick.

"Just give me a minute, please."

"It's not your place. I wish you'd butt out, go back to the UP."

"I totally understand where you're coming from." Charlie shoots a quick glance at Nick. "And I'll leave soon, trust me. But first I want you to know that your aunt was out of her mind with worry about you." He searches for the words. "She's not angry—she's terrified. Terrified of losing you. She loves you so much."

"She sure has a crazy way of showing it."

Tell me about it. "That's just the fear in her, fear borne from her love for you. Why, it could fill all the Great Lakes and then some." It rings cheesy, but he knows her fierce affection for this kid is genuine.

"Yeah, right." The bicycles pass, and Charlie starts walking rapidly across the street, Nick right at his side

"Listen, why don't you go up the hill and get a hot shower and then have a talk with her. Think you can do that?"

Charlie shrugs and walks toward a bike rack. Yanking the handlebars as he pulls his cycle from the rack, he glares at Ella, who has reached the curb across the street. Nick makes a feeble thumbs up sign and smiles as Charlie pedals off.

As he walks toward Ella, Nick wonders why, of all the things she could have said, she chose the worst words possible. Charlie is a confused kid; he doesn't know his dad, doesn't know what it means to be "just like him." The jerk abandoned him, for Christ's sake. It's senseless, toxic to talk like that.

"I gave it my best shot. He's going to get warm and eat. Then he might be ready to talk with you. I think you two need to work it out."

"I see you've appointed yourself family mediator."

What a bitch she can be. Katie would go all silent, never slamming, just shutting the door quietly, not speak to him for hours, sometimes days. It drove him crazy, but this haughtiness of Ella's, mean and sarcastic—why does he fall for such pissy women? With difficulty he suppresses the urge to chew her out—all those years with moody teens come in handy—and this situation requires a good amount of tongue-biting. At the moment he needs to put a vice clamp over his mouth. "Charlie just told me to butt out too."

"And?"

"I will if that's what's required." Her chin's stuck up a few inches and she is looking straight ahead. On her arms, a patch of goose bumps add to the aura of chill rushing from her.

"Hmm." She removes her cap, shaking off the water. A few drops fall on his arms.

"Why don't you go home now, take a long, hot bath and forget about water levels for a change? After that, you could try talking to him."

Ella places her arms across her chest, shivering. "Water levels are the least of my worries right now. Tell me straight up, do you think I blew it?"

Nick places his hands on her shoulders. "For the moment, yes. But he'll come around if you talk to him. But do it soon. Don't put it off or pretend it never happened. Tell him your feelings."

"That's not exactly my strong suit."

"So I've noticed. But what have you got to lose?" *Her fucking pride.*

Ella bites her lip, then straightens her shoulders and forces a smile. "Well, I'm off to the tub and a confession. You should come up and get warm too. I bet you're freezing."

"In a bit. You need some alone time with the kid." *And I need some time away from the Hollingsworths.* Watching her pedal away, a spot of bright-yellow against the gray, he wonders if she can pull it off. If she'll even try. "Remember what I said, talk to him!" he shouts through cupped hands around his mouth. Ella doesn't look back.

He craves a hamburger, the juicy type where the fat squirts out and rolls down your chin, the kind Ella would never serve up at Cedar Bluff. He heads toward the greasy burger joint of his youth, the Mack Shack, a few doors down and still in business. Inside, orange-ponchoed tourists sit in plastic red seats hunched over the matching Formica tables. The place is vintage '70s, from the décor to the large volume of senior customers. If they're all getting an AARP discount, the Mack Shack's profits will be low today. It feels good to be one of the younger customers for a change. A perky teenage girl, her blonde hair slung into a ponytail, greets him at the counter with a look of puzzlement that breaks into delight. "Mr. Pappas!" She looks familiar, but he can't place her.

"Hi," he says, studying her face, pink and pretty, German or Scandinavian roots for sure.

"Don't you remember me? Staci Stroud, from your government class?" It hits him. She was in his AP class in Wisconsin, a fine student—she was also there on the trip to Madison. *Shit.*

"Staci, of course." He reaches his hand over the counter and shakes hers, hoping she doesn't notice the shock on his face. "Great to see you. So, where are you in school now?"

"UW Madison. Starting my sophomore year, majoring in public policy."

"Wow."

"You had a lot to do with that, Mr. Pappas. We missed you my senior year."

"I missed you too. So glad you're doing well." *And can we change the subject now* . . . "I'd like to get a big, nasty, greasy double burger. I'm cold and wet." Staci surveys him.

"You look frozen." She glances down. "And what happened to your foot?"

"Looks worse than it is. Just an injured toe."

"What brings you here? The tourist thing?"

"I used to work on the island years ago. I'm visiting old friends."

"Oh my God. You worked here too?"

"Yeah. Before you were born. I was a big strong dock worker."

"Unbelievable." She turns and shouts the order to a man standing at the grill behind her. "Daddy Mack with fries! I'll bring the burger out. Maybe we can talk later. I'm slammed right now." Nick's legs wobble as he waits at the side of the counter, scanning the crowded dining area for a table. He notices an elderly couple preparing to leave and catches the eye of the woman, a stubby little thing with a yellow-toothed smile. "You can have our place, laddie," she says. Nick nods, grateful for a seat and her kindness. He sinks into a chair, watching Staci flit from table to table, a fast-food butterfly. *So she remembers.*

Breaking his reverie, she marches toward him with a burger in a yellow plastic basket, the bun a golden egg in a nest of fries. She plops it on the table, then sits down in the chair opposite him. "Mr. Pappas, I want you to know that that whole thing back in high school was bogus. I mean, they totally screwed you with a capital 'S'. Everyone said so."

Nick glances down at his food. "Thank you, Staci."

"That guy—what was his name—oh yeah, Matthew—he got expelled spring semester for drugs. The other one, I forgot his name, switched to regular government. He graduated in my class." Despite the chill from being outside for so long, Nick begins to sweat. "Hey, are you on Facebook, Snap Chat, anything?"

"No. I'm not much into social media. Don't need another universe to tend." He's been saying this a lot recently.

"Well, if you ever are, I'd like to friend you." She takes a pen from her apron pocket and writes *Stroudandproud* on the back of a blank receipt. "Search for me under that."

"Don't forget your tip." He points to the two quarters the couple left. "Live well and prosper."

A man stands at the counter scowling at them. "Just a minute, sir," she says. Turning back to Nick she asks, "Hey, where are you staying?"

"With friends. They have a cottage."

"Oooh, a cottage, huh?"

"Yes.

"Where?"

"One of the bluffs. Old family place."

"Awesome." She rushes back to the counter. The burger and fries stare at Nick, but his appetite has vanished. This is shaping up to be one crappy day.

27

As she bikes home, Ella kicks herself with every pedal stroke. Charlie doesn't know what it means to be like Matthew, a man who paid neither child support nor any attention to his own flesh and blood. As if abandonment by his father weren't enough, Ella has dumped extra anguish by comparing the boy to that sonofabitch who cast him off like a pair of torn-up old tennies. Charlie most likely sensed the truth of it: if those words were at the tip of her tongue, they must have been stored in the center of her heart. The boy had no say over the strands of DNA that had predetermined part of him. Neither did she. She'd have to love Charlie for himself, whatever and whoever he was, the good, bad and the ugly, not what she wished he was. Isn't that what she'd always longed for from her own parents? Things were so much better when Father was around; he took Charlie under his wing, the son he'd never had. Even on Father's dark days he would rise up out of depression for the kid. And he didn't put up with his crap. Now Nick had witnessed the lousy way she'd handled the situation, hurting Charlie and embarrassing herself.

So distracted is she by her concerns, she reaches the top of the big hill without realizing it. The sun has broken through, the storm rumbling to the east over Lake Huron and bothering folks on Bois Blanc Island. She peels off her poncho as a familiar elf-like figure bikes past, going down the hill: Darci.

"Hey, Ella!" she calls. "Did you find Charlie?"

"Yes, everything's fine. Crisis over."

"You poor thing."

At Cedar Bluff Ella rushes through the back door, letting the screen door slam behind her. This is going to be a tough conversation. "Charlie?" There's no reply, but he's left a fresh trail: a mixing bowl with a ring of milk around the bottom, and two circles of cereal floating in the center, golden life preservers in a white sea. The scent of strawberries lingers above the toaster, and sprinkles of hot chocolate mix darken the counter. Walking up the back stairs she passes Nick's room before walking down the hall to Charlie's door.

"Charlie?" She taps lightly on his door, wishing she had Nick's skills at talking with adolescents. It doesn't come naturally. Then she hears water from the shower down the hall. The talk will have to wait.

In her room she strips off her wet clothes and dons a maroon velour bathrobe that was Father's. The thing is so large it hangs off her frame like a tent. Ella seats herself in Grandma's old walnut rocker and looks out the window. Down the hall she hears Charlie's door bang shut. She waits a minute, then taps on his door.

"Whaddya want?" Charlie mutters.

"I'd like to talk to you. Please." Silence. "Charlie, I owe you an apology. I'm sorry. Please let me in." She pulls the robe around her tighter.

Charlie grunts and unlatches the door. Without saying a word he shrugs, turns around, and walks to his desk, where he plops down in the oak captain's chair and inserts ear buds in each ear. Ella walks toward him.

"Could you please turn off that thing?" Charlie sighs, removing one bud from his right ear. "Listen, Charlie, I didn't mean it, what I said. You are not like your father. Not one bit. You're better than any of us, unique and wonderful. But you can't go sneaking around in the boat. It scares the heck out of us."

Charlie spins around in his chair. "Oh, me sneaking around, huh? What's been going on here? You creeping down the hall at night, then that guy snooping around. When's he leaving anyway?"

"I thought you liked him."

"For like, maybe a day."

"He's leaving tomorrow."

"The way he looks at you . . . and me."

"What?" Her pulse quickens. Surely she must have misheard him. "Please repeat that."

"There's like something a little creepy about him. Benjamin thinks so too."

"Did he bother you? Did he—"

"No, no, nothing like that. It's hard to explain . . . just a vibe."

"He's an old friend—" Charlie looks incredulous. "OK, more than a friend, a long time ago, long before you were born."

"He was going through stuff in the library."

"Nick loves books, especially history. Like you."

"Yeah, but he was looking at stuff in your room too."

Oddly, the thought brings her a ripple of pleasure, like being happy that a classmate read a well-written entry in your diary. Her face reddens, remembering that earlier that same day she was snooping through Nick's belongings.

"Well, well."

"That doesn't bother you?"

"Of course it does. But I didn't come in here to talk about Nick. I want to talk about you. About the whole boat thing. It definitely wasn't cool, but I shouldn't have said what I did. I was way wrong and I'm very, very sorry." Charlie blinks, turning his head away for a moment. His eyes have dark circles beneath them.

"Okay." He sighs.

That's as good an acceptance as she'll get. She walks toward him for a hug, but he swirls back around in his chair toward the desk and picks up the ear buds. "What do you think about seeing someone to talk about things?" she asks.

"You mean a shrink?"

"If that's the word you prefer, yes."

"You think I'm crazy?" Charlie flings the ear buds on his desk.

"No. But there are times that professionals can help us."

"You're calling me a nut job? Like I was the one who said there was a bomb in a building? Like I'm some sort of freak? That's what Mom says you are. And Benjamin's dad, too."

Charlie's fighting dirty, but it's understandable. After all, he's had plenty of role models, herself included. "Charlie, I've explained it over and over. The police totally overreacted."

If she could only take back those six words, "There's a goddamn bomb in there." That's what she'd said that day in Maryland last year. That's what got her fired. She worked in an old EPA building as a consultant on water quality in the estuaries around the Chesapeake Watershed. The building, vintage 1950s, with little windows that you couldn't open, traces of asbestos in the ceiling tiles, chemicals in the basement, and two people in the same office with lung cancer, was a health menace. Ella referred to it as a time bomb. They'd had a fire drill that day and marshaled everyone out front. Ella stood with a group waiting for the all-clear signal to return to their offices. A man who worked a few offices down from her said, "If there was a fire that place would probably blow up."

"Tell me about it, it's like a damn bomb."

A security guard walking behind her spun around and said, "What did you say, lady?"

"I said there's a damn bomb in there," repeated Ella. "The place is a health hazard waiting to explode. Asbestos, poor ventilation, chemicals—"

"Don't move," he commanded, hailing another security officer, a beefy guy wearing a shiny badge and packing heat. "This woman says there's a bomb in there."

The large guard grabbed her arms and pinned them behind her. As they handcuffed her Ella yelled, "It was a metaphor—don't you get it? The place is about to kill people with poor ventilation, crap in the walls. A metaphor."

"Four what?" asked the security guard. "Four bombs?"

The story blazed through the media, forgotten by most at the end of the twenty-four-hour news cycle. But before that, the news escaped into the blogosphere and social media, where it hit the Mackinac rumor mill. Some folks still look at her funny, but most seemed to have forgotten. She'd been downgraded from a nut job to merely eccentric. Now that she holds the honor of being the weirdest Hollingsworth, social invitations are few and far between. When she accompanied Mother to a party in June, a family *friend* came up to her and asked, "Found any bombs in your cottage recently? Ha ha."

After the incident in Maryland, Ella got the axe. Her supervisor said it had nothing to do with the "mistake." No, it was her work, her figures were off, her research "flawed." She was never charged with a crime, but a judge ordered Ella to attend counseling for three months. She'd faithfully marched into a psychotherapist's office weekly, but most sessions were consumed in wonky discussions about pollution levels in the Chesapeake Bay watershed. Betty, the psychotherapist, a pleasant woman who looked like an LL Bean cover with her plaid jumpers and bobbed brown hair, had a vacation home on the Bay and was impassioned about protecting its marine life. When they did get around to talking about Ella, Betty looked at her and asked, "Why did you really come here?"

"Because I was ordered to."

"Let's discuss that."

Grudgingly, Ella told about the misunderstanding during the fire drill, her relationship with Kevin, her divorce, her family. Betty said, "I think you needed a baby a long time ago."

"It's a little late for that. But I'm in no position to be a mother. Besides, there's Charlie."

Betty sat very still and looked at Ella kindly. "He is your sister's son. Don't forget that."

"Well?" Charlie is staring at her; defiance so unbecoming on his bright young face. She pushes a strand of hair behind her ear. "Look, I went to therapy, and I'm sorry if that whole mess embarrassed you."

Charlie cracks his knuckles. "Can I ask you a question?"

"May—not can."

"OK, may I ask you something?" Without pausing he continues, "Is my dad as big a prick as he sounds?"

"I wouldn't use the word *prick*. How about, say, misplaced priorities? Because anyone who doesn't make you Number One will come to regret it. Someday your dad will realize what he's missed by not including you in his life."

Charlie looks at his hands. "Oh."

She remembers her first moments with Charlie. She'd flown to Chicago where Sara and Matthew lived in a small apartment. Sara handed her the two-week-old infant, donned in a cotton onesie sprinkled with a pattern of puppies. Charlie's eyes were closed, his fists furled up by his tiny ears, reminding Ella of a cross between an elf and Buddha. As Sara slipped him from her arms into Ella's, he squeaked and his head wobbled toward her chest like a kitten sniffing for milk. Ella felt a new sort of tingling in her breasts; felt surely, impossibly, that she was lactating. And in that moment she understood a mother's blind love.

Although she's certain he'll abhor it, she walks over to this big Charlie, this naughty boy, and plants a kiss on the top of his head. "Okay, kiddo."

Exiting Charlie's room, she exhales deeply, her legs shaking beneath her robe. The thought of immersing herself in a hot bath, though breaking one of her self-imposed rules on water use, feels irresistible. In the bathroom she turns on the water, triggering a moaning noise in the wall. Their plumber, Jerry, liked to say a litter of baby pigs lived in the pipes. "Can't you hear 'em squealing?" he'd laughed. "It's your 110-year-old plumbing that keeps me employed."

As the windows and mirror steam over, Ella feels a mixture of delight and guilt, like taking the last cookie. This is a rare treat, an indulgence. In this big tub she'll probably use at least fifty gallons of water. She pushes the window up; it sticks stubbornly to the casing, but finally budges. The screen is missing. Another item for the to-do list.

Lying back in the white porcelain tub, the water rises over her belly until only the tips of her breasts protrude above the water, two pink islands in a sea of steam. Her thoughts slip to Charlie. Poor kid. Embarrassed by his loony aunt, estranged from his dad, wondering who he is. She lies back, letting the infusion of warmth encase her body; it's impossible to hold onto baggage when you're melting.

She's awoken by a stabbing pain in her left breast. Opening her eyes she sees the source: a wasp plunging its stinger into the soft flesh of her nipple, like an oil rig drilling into a wetland. It must have carried its grudge from yesterday's massacre all the way to the second floor. She screams and swats at the wasp with a towel. Leaping from the tub, she slams down the window, cursing.

There's a knock at the door. "Are you OK?" yells Nick.

Stark naked, holding a towel in her left hand like a whip, she stands at the window, her back to the door.

"Fine, fine!" she yells as a second wasp circles the room and stings her on her left buttock. Grabbing a bar of soap she throws it at the wasp and misses, meanwhile knocking her knee against the toilet. "Damn!"

The door bursts open. She'd forgotten to latch it. Nick stands in the doorway, staring. For a second, every lump, bump, and piece of her backside are on exhibit before she yanks the towel around her.

Their eyes lock for a moment, and then Ella bursts into laughter, one of those laughs that start deep in her belly and then explodes. Bending over, roaring, she holds her stomach. It's infectious, and Nick's soon laughing just as loudly.

"The wasps!" cries Ella between bursts. "The wasps made a beeline for me. Get it? A beeline!"

"What's going on?" she hears Charlie shout. He appears in the doorway behind Nick, puzzled, then scowling, elbowing Nick out of the way. When he sees Ella howling in her scanty towel a look of disgust crosses his face. "Geez. Aunt Ella, you okay?"

"Just a little sting. I'm over it. The wasps have found their revenge," she says between guffaws, then slams the door. "No need for help, I'll be out soon." She pulls the lock shut, lies on the floor, and continues chortling.

28

Nick sits on the bed in his room, shocked and yes, excited. Ella's body has changed, and that slice down her back like a mountain ridge on a topo map. Despite all that, seeing her naked has aroused him. Grabbing a towel and dry clothes, he rushes to the bathroom near his room, where he turns on the shower and stands under the spray for less than the three-minute shower requirement, keeping the temperature on cold. After toweling off he pulls on a long-sleeve cotton shirt and pants, and opens the door to the hallway. He hears Ella and Charlie down in the kitchen. Their voices travel up the back staircase. At least they're talking. Good start.

"I love it here, you know that, but I think I'm kind of in your way. A nuisance." It's Charlie's voice.

"A nuisance, never," replies Ella.

"Come on, be straight with me. I mess up everything."

"No, no—"

"You never get any time to relax or hang with, uh, guests. I think I should go with Mom."

"Kiddo, I don't need to spend a lot of time with Nick. The only reason he's here is because of the accident. Would have been rude not to offer a place after my boat cut him up."

Nick snaps the towel against the wall. He's heard enough. Ella said it plain and clear: she doesn't want to be with him. *What a frickin idiot I am.* Were she forced to choose between him and the kid, Nick knows she'd pick Charlie. The boy knows how to play his deck.

On tiptoes he moves to his room, hauls out his duffle bag and begins packing. Then he strips the bed, gathers up the dirty towels and the washcloth, and rolls the whole thing together in a wad. His stomach hurts from dejection and hunger.

Once packed, he plunks down on the bed. His fantasy of reconnecting with Ella is shredded, his silly plan a washout. Where will he go from here? He has an inkling, and one thing's for sure: he must get out of here fast. He glances at his watch—almost 3:00 p.m. If he hurries he can catch a three thirty ferry and drive to Mama's in Marquette.

Ripping a sheet of paper from his planner he scrawls,

Dear Ella,
    I think it best I leave now. You've been a great hostess and nurse. I feel you and Charlie need time alone together. I am, and always will be,
    Your friend,
    Nick

He places the note on the bed next to the roll of dirty laundry, takes a last longing look around. As he leaves the room he pauses, cocks his head and listens. The talking in the kitchen has ceased, replaced by some banging of pans and opening and closing of pantry doors. He hears the sounds of a carriage pull up out back and wonders who's arriving. Nick quietly moves down the hall to the front stairs, where he walks down the steps awkwardly with his left foot leading. As he exits through the front door he sees Charlie standing on the porch, gazing at his phone. Hearing the door, Charlie turns around and asks, "Are you leaving? Aunt Ella didn't say anything about it."

"Yes."

Charlie puts his hand up and slaps Nick's. "Dude."

"I've caused enough trouble around here. Your aunt doesn't need some injured guest hobbling around. Take care of her for me, will ya? And let me know about your latest discoveries. And keep those wasps away." Charlie doesn't reply. "Here's my number and address." Nick scribbles it out on a piece of paper, hoping the kid will pass it on to Ella. As he passes the paper to Charlie, he looks him in the eye, lowering his voice. "Don't let your aunt get too frazzled. Know what I mean?" He winks as Charlie nods.

Out on the road, Nick turns and waves, but the boy walks into the cottage without responding. A curtain moves in an upstairs window of the house next door, probably Darci. Nick wishes Ella would look out her window, race out of the cottage and beg him to stay. Glancing back one last time he sees only empty windows and the front door, now closed. Another unfinished project. The story of his life.

The trek downtown will be painful on his bad foot. He regrets not calling for a carriage, feels a little cowardly sneaking out like this. Halfway down the big hill he looks back once more. Maybe she'll have read the note by now. No sign of her, only a carriage bulging with tourists, and a kid that looks like Charlie trailing on a bike.

The journey takes longer than expected, more than 45 minutes. He'll now have to catch the four o'clock boat. Near the dock he finds Staci in front of the burger place, sitting on a bench, fiddling with her phone.

As he approaches she looks up. "Hey, Mr. P, you leaving already?"

"Gotta get home, put in some summer hours at school."

Patting the bench she says, "Sit down. How's your foot?"

Lowering himself to the bench he says, "Killing me."

"You shouldn't be walking on it so much."

"Tell me about it."

"Mr. P, I've decided I'm not coming back here next summer. I'm going to apply for an internship with a state rep in Madison. And you know why? Because of you, that class. Getting our bill passed. That's my inspiration."

At least he's done one thing right. "You don't know how much that means to me." Nick glances at his watch. "Well, I'd better move on. Boat's almost here. Good luck with your studies. And let me give you one word of professorial advice: don't fall in love this summer."

Staci smiles. "Your advice may be coming too late. It's hard to avoid a summer romance on the island." She jumps up and hugs him.

The ferries have begun their every half-hour honking concerto. "Gotta scat. Study hard!" he yells, hurrying toward his boat. Once aboard he looks back at the burger place, where he sees Staci sitting on the bench talking to someone. Squinting, he could swear it's Charlie.

***

As she bangs around in the kitchen deciding what to serve that night—soy burgers (Charlie and Nick will probably hate) or chicken salad (Nick will like that) and sweet corn (they'll both like)—she hears a carriage pull up out back followed by a sound that almost knocks her off her feet.

"Hellooooo. Anybody home? Ella? Could someone please help me?"

No one on the planet sounds like that except Mother. Mother!

Charging out the door, she sees a figure in the back seat waving her arms around. Ella doesn't recognize the driver, a slight young man with sandy blonde hair looking none too pleased with his passenger.

"Ma'am, could you help her?" he asks. "I can't let go of these horses."

"Mother, what are you doing here?" cries Ella, now standing at the side of the carriage facing Audrey. Dressed in her favorite lavender sweater, a pair of gray slacks and a leg cast, Audrey glares at her daughter as an electric lift on the back of the carriage carrying a motorized wheelchair lowers.

"What am I doing here? I'm coming home—to *my* home. Now would you please give me a hand?"

"Charlie, Nick!" Ella shouts, looking toward the house. Where have those two gone off to when she needs them?

Audrey taps her cane on the carriage floor. "Just help me down, dear, and bring my chariot over here."

Ella pulls the wheelchair off the ramp, then strains under the weight of her mother (punning to herself, *She's not heavy, she's my mother*), but manages to carry her down the two steps to her vehicle. Next she lifts off two matching leather suitcases, both heavy, making Ella even more cross at the guys for abandoning her. "Charlie, Nick!" she shouts again.

After paying the driver (adding a hefty $10 tip), she turns to Audrey. "Mother, you shouldn't have come. Not yet. Your leg isn't fully healed. By the way, how did you get here?"

Looking smug, Audrey says, "I signed myself out—after all, it wasn't jail, you know. Yanci's son drove me to the boat and helped me down the ramp. The dock porters were very sweet, of course. So—" she wipes her palms together in a brisk movement, "voilà, here I am." Turning on the chair controls, she points the electric wheelchair toward the back door and races along the walkway.

"Whoa, not so fast, Mother. You're going to break your other leg." Of course it doesn't slow Mother down one whit. Ella has to run ahead. Once inside the kitchen, Audrey looks around and declares, "It's so good to be home. What's for dinner? And who is this Nick?"

29

As he pulls out of the ferry parking lot, Nick glances at his watch: four thirty, still plenty of time to get to Mama's, and if he's lucky, he'll be in time for supper.

Three hours later he pulls up to her house.

"Niko, what happened to you?" asks Mama, staring at his foot.

"Nothing a little home cooking wouldn't cure," he says, kissing her cheek.

She has the cure; a feast she's prepared for a birthday party for Uncle George who is there with Aunt Margarita and a few cousins, some great-nieces and Nick's big brother, Teddy. They chat until the meal is ready and a splendid spread it is. Mama serves *horiatiki salata*, which he hasn't eaten in months. She's bought Kalamata olives, his favorite, and made fresh bread with *tsatziki* sauce for dipping. When Mama serves a steaming *moussaka*—"Your favorite, Niko," he already feels stuffed. Although he'd grown tired of moussaka years ago, his earlier fondness for it stuck in Sophia's head; every time he came home she greeted him with a fresh one and sent him on his way with another from the freezer. "Have some more, son," she says, piling a whopping slice on his plate.

"Mama, if that serving were a T-shirt it would be extra-extra-large."

But there's more: *lahanodolmades* (stuffed cabbage) and much too soon for his overstretched alimentary canal, *milopita* (apple pie) for dessert. It is aerobic eating. But rather than being good for your heart, like exercise, it could stop your ticker in one massive jolt.

Once the dishes are cleared away, they sip Greek coffee in demitasse cups. Laced with cardamom, its sharp taste bites into his tongue. As they finish the coffee, Aunt Margarita insists on telling fortunes by reading the patterns of coffee grounds in the bottom of their cups. "For you, George, I see a big parasol. New lover?" Everyone laughs. At eighty-three, George recently survived a triple bypass and is devoted to Margarita, his wife of fifty-three years. Lifting Nick's cup, Margarita stares at the grounds a few minutes before turning to him and declaring, "I see a rabbit. You need courage, my boy."

Mama points to his toe and says, "He is brave. Look, he doesn't complain about his foot. You never told us how it happened, son."

Nick tells the story but keeps it vague: "some friends with a boat," "A friend with a cottage." He remembers how upset his mother was years ago when he told her about Ella. Mama distrusted non-Greeks, and wealthy WASPS in particular. "Island princess," Mama had called Ella. Of course, after all this time, he doubts she'll remember. He is wrong. Mama's eyes grow suspicious. "You were seeing that lady again, that island princess, weren't you?"

"Mama, a boat motor nicked me—not Ella."

Mama turns to her audience. "This is a smart boy but when it comes to women he is a stupid man."

"She's certainly not a princess. She paints her own steps."

"Niko, just remember, birds of a feather flock together."

Later, having eaten himself into narcolepsy, he collapses on the twin bed in his old room that he's sharing with Teddy, who's taking an extended break from his wife—they have been separated for two months—under the auspices of helping Mama. Not much in the room has changed since the boys were teenagers. Two beige chenille spreads cover the beds, and the walls are decorated with a high school pennant, a poster of KISS, and some childhood art Mama had framed. Also sleepy from the food overload, Teddy comes in and lies on the bed next to Nick's.

A loud dinging sound penetrates the room. "Crap, it's my cell, a text," moans Nick. "Can't read 'em."

"Give me the phone," says Teddy.

"Can't be important. Anyone I want to hear from knows I don't text." True, but what if it's Ella? Maybe Charlie showed her the number.

"Okay, little brother, let me introduce you to the twenty-first century," says Teddy, picking up the phone from the bureau. "How can you live like this?" Easing himself onto the end of Nick's bed, Teddy looks at the message and whistles. "Oh man." Sitting up, Nick tries to grab the phone. "Give that to me."

"Google play is ready when you are. Dial 937-5340."

"That's all?" asks Nick.

"Gottcha," says Teddy as he hands the phone over. "Yep. Now let me show you how to work this thing." Teddy gives him a mini-lesson on texting. "Now, brother, let's get some sleep." He removes his pants and climbs under the covers.

"I could never understand what Mama has against Ella," says Nick. "She's never even met her."

Teddy glances at Nick. "Can I tell you a deep family secret?"

Nick sits up. He's grown weary of secrets. "Are you going to say Papa isn't my dad?"

Teddy laughs. "Whoa! No, nothing like that. Oh hell, it was so long ago it doesn't matter."

"Maybe I shouldn't hear this."

"Ah, it's nothing, but it might help you understand Mama's attitude. When she worked in Grandpa's restaurant, this guy used to come in. He was good-looking and rich, up from Chicago. His parents had that big place on the lake near Middle Island Point."

"The Castle?" Nick remembers a stone mansion by the point with gates in front and a big *No Trespassing* sign. Everyone called the place the Castle. It was torn down years ago.

"Yeah, that one. Anyway, this guy and Mama fell in love. He wanted to marry her, but his folks told him she wasn't good enough. Next thing you know they've packed up and gone. Mama gets a letter from him later saying she's his true love, that he wants to marry her and all. They write back and forth, then the letters stopped in the winter. The next summer he comes back engaged to some debutante or something. Wouldn't even look at Mama when they passed on the street. Broke her heart."

Nick whistles. "Poor Mama. But she loved Dad. I know she did."

"True. But there's nothing like that first big love."

30

He'd left just like that. Without a word. Well, with no word to her. He'd told Charlie, who didn't bother to pass along the information to her for hours. He'd disappeared too, and when he popped up in the back drive on his bike Ella was fuming. She'd met him at the back door, hands on her hips.

"Well guess who's coming to dinner?"

Charlie looks puzzled. "Who?"

"Your grandmother. She's back."

"You're kidding. Where?"

"Resting in her bedroom for the moment. I had to help her off the carriage, get all her stuff inside, and there was no sign of you or Nick."

"Oh, he's gone," says Charlie. "He took the three thirty ferry, said to tell you he was causing too many problems."

"Are you making this up?" Charlie shakes his head. "He didn't say anything else?"

Charlie nods his head. "No, just said I should help you."

Nothing else? Why did he have to leave so abruptly, secretly? Charlie certainly contributed to it. She's growing weary of his antics. "I need your help right now."

"I've got stuff to do." He heads toward the back stairs.

"Wait a minute. You've got *stuff* to do right here in your very own kitchen," she says, yanking out a chair and patting the seat. "Sit down."

Within minutes Charlie sits before a pile of fresh corn, a trash can on the floor beside him.

"So where did he go?" asks Ella, trying to sound casual.

"Nowhere, just walked straight to the dock. That's when I turned around and came home."

"You sure he didn't say anything?" she says, tossing an ear of corn in the trash. "That one's spoiled."

"The only person he talked to was a really hot girl from the Mack

Shack." Ella stops shucking. Charlie chuckles. "I think she was a student of his or something because I heard her say, 'Good luck, Mr. P.'"

"What do you have against him?"

"Nothing."

"Charlie—"

"Okay, okay. He wore those nasty sandals and a fake leather belt
like he'd got it at Wal-Mart or something. He just doesn't seem like
your type." Weren't those the words Father used, *not your type*? Ella
reaches for a piece of corn, snapping off the stem so forcefully it stings
her palm. "I thought you liked him. He knows a lot of history."

"Can we talk about something else?"

"Sure." For a moment only the sound of the ripping of husks fills
the space between them. Charlie avoids her glance. What's happened
here? This was supposed to be a long stretch of halcyon summer days,
a respite for both of them from the storms in their lives. If this month
had been an opportunity for her to nurture her nephew, she'd blown
it. Charlie did not need another fickle, confused adult in his life.

"How did Grandma get here?"

"She talked and bought her way. Don't know how I'm going to
manage. I'll need your help, Charlie."

Charlie stares into space, scratching a mosquito bite on his fore-
arm. "I think you should ask Mom to come."

"Impossible." She's surprised at how the word had just rushed out,
how stern her voice sounds. The thought of Sara giving up her travels
and actually lending a hand at Cedar Bluff is a joke. Leave it to Sara to
screw something up. Like the time she'd accidentally left Charlie at a
gas station when he was eight, then driven more than five miles before
realizing it. Charlie was sobbing outside; the attendant had told him,
"Sonny, looks like your mom left you with me." The maddening thing
was how Mother defended her. "Sara occupies another dimension,"
Mother explained. At least she didn't pretend to be good mommy material. "I love the kid. That's why I'm letting you all do so much of his
upbringing," Sara had told her.

Ella sighs and sets down a husk. Sara hasn't called or texted in three
days. Ella has a mind to tell her she's going to make videos of Charlie
and place them on YouTube so Sara can see her son and, if she so
chooses, write comments beneath them, thereby setting up a line of

communication with her kid.

"Okay, kiddo."

Breaking from his reverie, Charlie fumbles for a moment in his pocket, extracts a piece of paper and hands it to Ella. "I forgot about this. Nick gave it to me. Said I should take good care of you."

31

"I can't believe you didn't sleep with him," says Beth, her feet propped up on a green-striped ottoman. Her short, brown hair, round face and broad shoulders are a sharp contrast to Ella. Beth dresses impeccably, like a sorority girl, her colors matching. A pair of blue earrings dangle from her earlobes, and complement her turquoise sandals and the tiny flowers on her shirt. Ella's wearing a beige V-neck blouse with a missing button and a pair of jeans. They're sitting in the sunroom, the late August sun splashing over the white bead board walls in shadow cutouts of the window panes, the fourth straight day of fine weather since Beth arrived. She's staying for a week. The first three days were fun, but Beth has a way of wearing Ella down, and truth to tell, Ella will be glad when Beth leaves.

"Sleep with him? Why do people always have to inject sex into things? What would be the point of that? It would just get complicated and not solve anything," says Ella.

"Solve anything? What's that mean? You might have just enjoyed it. Maybe fallen in love."

Ella snorts. "You're a hopeless romanticist. The typical old love plot: guy and gal fall in love and live happily ever after. Look, Nick's a friend and that's it. He's going through a rough patch." She shrugs. "And you wouldn't believe how busy it was around here."

Beth's eyebrows arch. "Busy?"

"Well, things were just happening all at once. We've already been over this, Beth. Like Nick practically getting his toe sliced off, people working on the house, Charlie going off on the boat, and scaring the heck out of us, everything." She pauses, sweeping her hair back. "Stop looking at me like that." She and Beth go way back; it's impossible to pull something over on her.

"Be straight with me; were you attracted to him?"

"Yes. No. Oh, c'mon. It's not like he's the same old Nick of yesteryear."

"Like you're the same Ella?"

"I know, I know. It's hard to explain, but sometimes I'd look at him and think, what did I ever see in this guy, and a few minutes later I'd be practically panting for him."

Beth shoots her a smile. "Panting, huh? At our age, I thought chocolate was the only thing that could make us do that."

"Or kitchen makeovers," laughs Ella, glad she is spared from one of Beth's theories. She has lots of them, little life prescriptions: "Write a worry journal and cluster all your worries into one hour." "Gorge yourself with a quart of flavored water when you're craving cookies." Her latest, "Keep that gallon of gross crap you have to drink before a colonoscopy well refrigerated and drink it with a straw to prevent gagging." Thank God Ella has escaped that procedure. Beth, a liberal arts major at the University of Michigan, took a lot of psych classes, not that she ever practiced them. She's been a full-time homemaker and now, with her kids gone, she's started a special events business that has blossomed into a full-time operation.

"You wouldn't believe what he remembers—things I forgot, like the songs we sang up on the wall at the fort, how we paid off Sara with M&M's for not ratting on us—everything."

Beth looks her in the eye. "Anyone who remembers that much is totally in love."

Ella looks away, rubbing her nose. "Don't you think that what we remember is pretty damn subjective, a personal spin on the truth?"

"If I'm following you, I think you're saying that our memories are hogwash."

"Something like that."

Beth shrugs. "You're hopeless."

Ella rises on her knees, folding her legs under her. "Can we talk about something else?"

"Did you tell Nick about the bomb incident?" asks Beth.

"Of course. He was very understanding."

"You're lying."

"OK, I was going to tell him, but, well—stuff got in the way."

"Oh yes, that stuff again. Did you talk about Kevin?"

"A little."

Beth looks skeptical. "Ah hah!"

"There wasn't time to tell him much. I doubt if he'd want to hear about it anyway."

Beth snorts.

"No, seriously! After Charlie took the boat all hell broke loose. Oh, and then, when he just left, what was I going to do?"

"You're one of the most private people on this planet. Sometime you've got to let us in."

Ella stands up and walks to the window, her gaze resting on the Round Island shore. Had she been too private the day she and Nick walked there? She swirls around, facing Beth. "After all these years, how can you say that? You know me."

Beth shrugs, shaking her head. "I'm not so sure of that anymore. All I'm saying is let this guy in the door a teeny weenie bit. Can't hurt, you know."

From downstairs, a bell rings faintly. Ella sighs. "Guess who?" Since Mother came back, she's tyrannized Ella. She needs water with a bit of lemon, please, and help to the bathroom—*please close the door.* Find her purple cableknit sweater, put fresh flowers in the dining room. *Not that vase, Ella, the crystal one.* But Ella has to admit, the island is working its magic; Audrey's sharper, and more so every day. Getting her out of the nursing home has re-energized her. But they have to watch her every minute. Charlie was canned from the bike shop after the boat incident, but he's a big help with Audrey, although he's been spending more hours on a new computer game while Audrey naps, usually twice a day. Genevieve found another woman to help a few hours a day, adding an extra pair of hands and eyes. Even Beth has pitched in, although she spends most of her time biking and on the phone arranging events back home. And then there's Darci, with her offers to help, frequently bringing over baked goods. "I made her this little raspberry torte; handpicked the berries out by Lilac Ridge." "Yoo-hoo, anyone here like warm chocolate chip cookies?"

Ella rises and shouts, "Coming, Mother!" Turning to Beth she says, "We'll have to resume this conversation later."

The bell rings again. "Hold your horses."

"You are a dutiful daughter," says Beth with an eye roll.

"Tell that to Mother. She keeps begging for her darling Sara."

Ella wheels Mother into the bathroom and helps her to the toilet.
"I can take it from here," says Audrey, lowering herself slowly while
clutching Ella's arm.

Wandering into the dining room, Ella picks up the mail Charlie
brought up from the post office. In the corner of a white business envelope she sees a handwritten address: N. Pappas, 1601 Oakwood Dr.,
Duluth MN. She rips the envelope open, unfolding a note.

Dear Ella,

*Now that I'm back home I've had time to reflect on my Mackinac
visit. I'm sorry to have left like I did, but under the circumstances felt
it was best for you and your nephew. Little Bobbitt has healed beautifully so you don't need to worry about him. I'm also sorry I caused
so much trouble. I hope Charlie has straightened up and stayed away
from Round Island. Hope you two are able to talk about stuff. Put some
boundaries around that boy before things get out of control. I am sending him a separate package with some information on the Cholera epidemic and more dope on the soldiers of 1834.*

*I'm sure it wasn't easy having me barge in on your life. You certainly
have more than enough complications now. Perhaps at some future date
things will be simpler and we can meet again.*

Your old Luddite friend,
Nick

The letter sounds rehearsed, as if he'd rewritten it multiple times.
Perhaps at some future date. Maybe Beth is right. Part of her wishes
he'd come back and they could replay the whole visit. For starters,
she'd forget about the drinking water and keep Boon away, even ship
Charlie off, something she's feeling more like doing every day.

"Ella, I'm done!" Mother calls from the bathroom. Ella sighs and
folds over the letter.

Beth walks into the dining room and eyes the letter in Ella's hands.
"Everything all right?"

"Uh-huh."

"What's that?" Ella shoves the envelope into her pocket. "Something from the Greek?" Beth extends her hand. "Let me read it."

Mother calls from the bathroom, her voice shrill, "Must I wait forever?"

"One more minute!" says Ella, relinquishing the letter to her friend. Beth reads the note, chuckles, and hands it back to Ella, beaming.

"I told you. The guy's smitten. So, what are you going to do?" Mother pounds on the wall. "You should invite him here when this place empties out."

"Get out of here. Go ride a bike," Ella says, marching toward the bathroom. "Here I am, Mother." Turning to Beth she says, "On second thought, give me a minute and I'll join you."

***

Beth has returned to her husband and their comfortable life in a leafy Victorian neighborhood in Atlanta where she is in charge of a neighborhood fall festival. Her parting words were, "Contact that guy soon. You've got nothing to lose but your pride, and that, as they say, goeth before the fall."

At Cedar Bluff, Charlie is spending more time in his room on his computer, which annoys Ella, but he has a knack for making Mother laugh, a skill Ella has yet to develop. The other day she heard the two of them chuckling. "What did the horse say when it fell?" asked Charlie.

"I don't know," said Mother.

"I can't giddyap."

This set Mother into a roar. Ella remembers it from one of those kids' joke books that used to crack up Charlie.

Boon's been more reliable, repainting trim on the second story, replacing a porch column that had severe wood rot. One morning Ella was surprised by the hum of the lawn mower. Boon must have finally caved in to her pleas to mow, but as Ella walked around the house toward the sound she saw Charlie behind the mower, a first.

"How'd that happen?" she asked Mother.

"I have my ways, my dear," she'd laughed.

Later that day she found Mother on the porch wearing a sports halter top, exposing a good six inches of midriff, bare arms and shoulders. "Mother, you shouldn't be wearing that." Though she looked better in it than most seventy-eight-year-olds, the point was, no seventy-eight-year-old should wear one. When Ella brought her a white short-sleeved blouse Mother folded it neatly over the arm of her chair and said, "You're so conservative, my dear." Then she pointed to a spot on her shoulder. "I'm thinking of getting a tattoo right here. Maybe a little butterfly."

Ella is bracing herself for Sara's return in a week, breaking short her work abroad to "protect Charlie." That's how Sara described her new-found motherly role in her last text to Ella. "I need to protect Charlie. Obviously you have been negligent, letting him take off in the boat and leaving him with your boyfriend." Though the words infuriate Ella, she has to admit they bring her a sense of relief. Charlie is a handful, and it's time for Sara to step up to the plate.

This morning Mother is napping while Ella sits in the sunroom with Charlie, absorbed on their separate laptops. She'd threatened taking away his computer if he refused to join her. Ella has opened two screens: one, the Hollingsworth Casket accounting report, the other a Great Lakes hydrometeorological dashboard that tracks lake levels on a weekly basis. Both screens indicate decreases, one in profits, the other in water. Ella sighs and turns to Charlie, who is wearing ear buds.

"Have you heard from your mom?"

"What?"

"Take out those ear buds."

He stretches his arms slowly before pulling the bud from his right ear.

"Remove the other one," says Ella, her voice rising. "Now." Charlie obeys with a look of annoyance. "Have you heard from your mom?" she repeats.

"Yeah, this morning. She texted that she bought me new shoes. Ha ha." He's looking at the screen. Sara always buys Charlie shoes on her trips, the trendy types that he never wears.

"Anything else?"

"She's arriving Friday night, last ferry."

"Umm." The kid's still staring at the computer, his ear buds lying on the table.

Snapping her fingers in front of his face Ella shouts, "Have you heard a word I've said?"

He looks up. "I have something to show you. I don't think you're going to like it."

Pulling up a chair beside him, she leans close to the screen and reads, "Teacher Perverts in Wisconsin." What's this about? A headshot of Nick appears next to the words "Nicholas Pappas, Perch Harbor High School."

"This can't be right. Nick teaches in Duluth."

"Now. He used to teach there. He left under questionable circumstances."

Ella's head snaps up. "How do you know this? And how can you be sure this isn't the work of some disgruntled kid?"

Charlie turns his chair toward her. "I've been checking it out. The site is written by students. I finally tracked down the guy who sent in Nick's name. But it's the real deal. Staci, this girl who works downtown, she told me. She said that after Nick got caught trying to do something to a kid on an overnight field trip, the kid reported him to the school. Nick went on paid vacation leave before taking early retirement. I have e-mails from the guy."

"You've been doing all this (she wiggles her fingers to for two quotation marks) "investigation" without letting me in on it?"

"I wanted to be sure." Charlie performs a series of rapid-fire clicks punctuated by type strokes. "There." On the screen, an e-mail from someone with the address of andyo@stt.com of appears.

Dude, that teacher, Nicholas Pappas, is hardcore. Tried to rape a student on a field trip in Madison. School didn't fire him, but he took "early retirement." I was there and everything I am saying is true. Don't know where he went and I haven't tried finding out. Stay away from this guy.
Andrew Olson

Ella reads the note twice, three times, her stomach tensing on each. It had felt like this before: the day Kevin told her about Laura; the day they wheeled Grandma from Cedar Bluff, begging the medics not to cover her face. "She needs to see the Mackinac sky!" Ella had yelled; the morning in August when Charlie went missing with the boat. Now this. It must be true. How could she have been so deluded? *What a frigging idiot I am.* Pervert, predator. Then a darker thought. "When he was here, did he—?"

"No, nothing like that. But like I told you, I felt there was something, um, something just kinda weird about him. It's one of the reasons I left that night in the boat."

Ella frowns, then pounds the table, making the computer shake. "Hey, watch it," says Charlie as his screen flashes to black momentarily.

"Damn him. Has he contacted you since? Did he send you a package?"

"Nothing incriminating, just some stuff about soldiers and some history. Don't worry."

"Where is it?"

"In my room."

"Bring it to me." Charlie hustles up the stairs two at a time and is back in a minute holding a large manila envelope. He dumps the contents on the table. On top of a pile of photocopied sheets and printed materials is a handwritten note that includes Nick's e-mail and the words, "Call me anytime if you have questions."

Ella snatches it. "Don't respond to him ever, and let me know if he tries to contact you."

"Okay. Calm down. I'm fourteen, I can handle this."

"Yeah, you're fourteen, a kid, a minor. I'm going to take care of this right now—permanently."

Snatching the paper and shredding it with her hands, she marches toward her bedroom where her phone is charging on top of the dresser. She snatches it up with such force that the phone drops from her hand and the battery flies out.

32

Sitting at his school computer, Nick leans back in his chair, hands crossed behind his head, feet propped on the desk, unable to focus and disinterested in school matters. Around him lay unpacked boxes of books, posters, and materials for his upcoming classes. His room, a plain gray box with rows of desk chairs and an empty whiteboard, contrasts with his colleagues' classrooms with their cheery signs—"Welcome back" "I want you to succeed" "Fall into Reading,"—spruced up blackboards with lists of learning objectives and class rules. Nick hasn't even posted the school mission statement, and soon will have to answer to his department chair as to why he hasn't completed a new curriculum piece on the Civil War. A stuffy, pent-up odor pervades the place and dust coats everything. The room overwhelms him. Too much to do. And outside it's another perfect day, way too few of them in these parts to be wasted.

Leaving the building, he drives across the lift bridge to Duluth Point where he parks, then heads east on foot along the shore. He removes his sandals, glad to be walking normally again on his right foot. The sand is warm. After about fifteen minutes he plops down a few yards from the water's edge and removes a flask from his backpack. Unscrewing the cap he peers inside the flask where several ounces of Jack Daniels slosh inside, holds it to his mouth and takes a swig. The whiskey burns the wet flesh of his inner cheeks.

Leaning back on his elbows he surveys the view before him. Superior Bay sits calm for a change, and he can see cars rolling along US-2 in Superior, Wisconsin, to the south. Letting his imagination spin over the Upper Peninsula, it glides across the Straits to the island, then up to Ella's porch. There she is; not the Ella he'd left a few weeks back, but the one he'd left thirty years ago. She smiles as a breeze through the cedars lifts her hair and she sweeps a strand from her eyes. "Is that you, Nick?" she asks. And then it all fades, leaving nothing but a man alone on a deserted beach, a piece of driftwood delivered by the random waters of life.

***

After his walk, Nick returns to his Subaru, where his phone shines in a pool of sun on the passenger seat. While rolling down the windows to cool off the car he picks up the phone and a *Missed Call* alert pops up on the screen. He doesn't recognize the 734 area code. The car is hot and the call can wait.

Instead of heading back to school, Nick steers the car toward home. When he enters the living room, the sectional sofa with its wide, soft cushions looks incredibly inviting. Just a short nap and he'll return to the school.

Later he awakes sweaty and sandy, with a groggy, post-nap light-headedness. He's always been a lousy napper. Stumbling to the kitchen, he retrieves his phone from the counter to check the time. Three in the afternoon, too late to get back to his classroom. Then he remembers the missed call. Picking up the phone he hits Call Back. After a few rings a woman answers. "Hello." Ella!

"Hey there," he says in as casual a voice as he can fake. "It's Nick. How's it going?"

"Listen, you can cut the small talk and don't ever call Charlie, write, or speak to him again. And don't call me, either. We don't want any contact with you. Understood?"

"Whoa there. What's going on?"

"Wisconsin Teacher Predator." She enunciates each word slowly. "Why did you lie to me? What happened when I left you with Charlie?"

"Oh my God, I can explain everything. Ella, it's all a mistake, a lie. Bogus."

"Let me be clear. Do not contact me or anyone in my family, ever again."

"Ella, wait, I can—just hear me out—" He stares at the screen where only a small red light remains. Immediately he dials again. No answer. One more time. The same.

Shit. If only she'd listen to him. If only she were not so pigheaded, so, so proud. Why, when the word *predator* appears, does everyone assume guilt before innocence?

Attempting to speak with her by phone is a dead end. Sending a letter will probably yield the same result. Just forty-nine cents more. He can picture her reading the return address and ripping the envelope in shreds and, oh yes, tossing it in the recycling bin. How can he convince her to listen to his side of the story? And how the devil did she stumble onto that predator list? Did such a thing exist?

***

At first she was tempted to hit "delete" without reading a word of Nick's e-mail. An intruder, that's what he is; what had she been thinking—or drinking? It came the day after Charlie showed her the predator list. Must be the subject line that grabs her—"In America one is presumed innocent until proven guilty."

So she reads as far as "please hear me out" before hitting the delete key. It isn't enough: she must demolish all temptation. Opening the Trash Folder she clicks Nick's e-mail, then scrolls to "Delete forever."

Beth doesn't agree. "You need to hear him out," she says during a phone call.

"What?" says Ella, as Beth mumbles something to someone at her end. It is like this with Beth. "Who are you talking to?"

"Just a sec," says Beth. "The flowers on the logo need to be smaller, coral-colored. Oh, sorry, Ella, but they are destroying a perfectly good logo with too much detail. Anyhoo, you should hear him out. What kind of friend are you? Are you going to do this to me someday?"

"Whose side are you on anyway?"

Beth sighs. "Truth's side. And there are two sides to everything. Listen. I know how protective you are of Charlie, but everyone's got an agenda. Think about it. Charlie's been known to lie quite a bit—that's according to you—and he's endured some not-so-great men in his fourteen years."

"True but—"

"So why not read his damn message, then make a decision."

"I deleted it."

"You can request he re-send it."

"But I deleted it forever from the trash thing."

Beth sighs. "Text him, call him. Just a suggestion."

"I don't think he texts." She hears Beth's exasperated groan.

"Then call him for God's sakes! Listen. Gotta scoot. Think about it."

Perhaps she's right. This whole episode is filled with the angst of a young adult novel. Someone in this mess has to transcend adolescence. Opening her e-mail she hits *Compose* and types in his e-mail address.

What should she write in the subject line? She settles for "Please resend." Her message is terse: "I deleted your explanation in your last e-mail. Please resend." Nothing could be read into that. Even if it were, so what? With one quick keystroke she hits the "Send" button.

***

Resend? The hell he will. Not after her refusal to speak with him, her pigheadedness. It had taken two hours to compose that e-mail. He's done with her. Resend? No. Rescind his feelings, his obsession, his misguided love, yes.

The sweet spot of being able to reject her (ha!) is soon soured by the high-burning intensity of loss. This is the second time he's lost her; first, 30 years ago, lost her to the wide geography between them. Lost her to the fears of parents, their secrets, concerns, and that invisible dividing line, class. If only she'd been a little more generous, a little more open to hearing him. But no, she didn't just close the door, she'd slammed it shut. Now he has to lock it on his side, forever.

Resend, my ass.

Under the circumstances, his normal course of action would be to head to the bar, but recently he's found a healthier outlet on the seat of his bike. He had his 21-speed retuned with a spiffy new derailleur, even bought a pair of biking shorts with a padded crotch panel for long rides. The quiet hauls over long distances help him sort things out with the side benefit of whipping him back into shape.

Nick happily discovered this during the better weeks of the crappy Duluth climate: its extended fall, thanks to the warmth of Lake Superior. All summer the lake gathered heat, and the region stayed warmer until sometime in November, when all hell would break loose. Today, a balmy 62 degrees in October, Nick opts for a long bike ride.

He heads out toward the Bong Bridge where he will pick up the bike trail to Wisconsin Point at the east end of Superior, Wisconsin. The bridge crossing is windy, but when he arrives at the Wisconsin end sweat rolls down his shirt and he peels off his windbreaker, tying it around his waist. Establishing a rhythm, he feels a tingling course through him, endorphins blunting the edge of his depression. He misses Ella with a pain that embeds itself in his upper back, spreading down his arms to his hands. He remembers her standing at the helm of her boat, wind slapping the tail of her shirt around and a strand of hair slanting across her face, her smile. He remembers her singing at Friendship's Altar, the wonderful sound of it even when it cracked on the high notes. Now even her initial peevishness over his water bottle pulls the corners of his mouth into a smile. Wait a minute. What is he thinking? *Get her out of your mind. Baby steps. Think about someone else.* Images of women flash through his mind: that hot substitute teacher in the pencil skirt in the choir class last week. No, she's almost Melina's age. Or Whitney's mom, who attended her IEP meeting wearing a tight, short dress and flirted with him as they discussed ways to help her daughter cope with a severe spelling problem. On a recent essay Whitney had spelled "Got" for "God" and "thing" for "think." ("I thing about Got a lot," she'd written.)

Hitting a straight stretch, he shifts into a higher gear and his mind follows suit, switching from women to students, which leads him to the issue of completing that curriculum piece on the Civil War. By the end of the ride he has a full set of lesson plans.

Back home he takes a shower, then fills a pitcher with ice water and sucks it down, sitting naked at his desk in front of his computer. He has to capture those thoughts before they vanish. Fireflies. He's surprised at his energy, his ability to complete this task he'd put off for weeks. It feels good to be naked. It feels even better to be writing.

It occurs to him: he hasn't thought about Ella for hours.

***

Melina notices the change in Nick. He suspected she would. Nothing like one's own flesh and blood to see things others don't. She returned from Honduras and spent a week with him before going back to Madison for her junior year.

"Are you on meds or something?" she asked.

"No, why?"

"Well, you just seem different, happier. And you've lost weight."

Leave it to modern kids to ascribe any positive change to pharmaceuticals. Still, she had a point. He is biking nearly every day, and on Duluth's steep hills, it is a hell of a workout. He'd also looked into

completing his dissertation, and had spoken on the phone with a professor at the University of Minnesota-Duluth, an earnest man about
half Nick's age. "You'll probably have to repeat some courses and do a
major rewrite of your dissertation," the man advised.

"I'll be rewriting history."

"Isn't that our job?" They both laughed.

And then there's Jodie. Nick could always rely on her, his buddy,
a special ed colleague in charge of the resource room at his school,
the kind of woman who'd give you the shirt off her back provided
you play straight with her. The kids respected her, rarely gave her any
crap like they did that new hire in her department, some sweet young
thing the kids walked all over. Jodie is the best teacher in the building,
and as far as he is concerned, in the district. He's had plenty of chal-
lenging students this year. "The elevator doesn't reach the top floor on
a few of 'em," Jodie kidded. Yet it was Jodie who stayed after school
when Alex's dad got too wasted to pick him up, Jodie who escorted a
screaming 14-year-old pregnant teen to the hospital after her parents
kicked her out, Jodie who took one of Nick's Asperger's students under her wing and tutored him during her planning period. The kid had
graduated, a miracle to all.

No wonder it was to Jodie whom Nick had blurted out his whole
heartbreak story one night after downing a few too many drinks at an
after-school social. They were sitting at a table in a seedy lounge on
3rd Street, best known for serving the captain of the ill-fated *Edmund
Fitzgerald* weeks before his ship sank in a November gale in icy Lake
Superior. The place was a smoky dive with a carpet reeking of stale
beer. He sat across from her as Mike, a business teacher, told stupid
jokes: "The surgeon asked a heart transplant patient, 'What kind of
heart would you like to receive?'

"'How about one from a statistician?' the patient says. 'That way, I'll
know it's never been used.'"

Jodie couldn't stop laughing, practically snorting. "How about
changing the word *statistician* to *Norwegian*?" she guffawed.

One by one, teachers peeled off, leaving only him and Jodie. Nick
leaned forward and started talking. All the booze had loosened his
tongue. Soon the name Ella rolled out of his mouth, like a marble.
Once he started, he couldn't stop.

Jodie listened attentively. "So, this is your true love?" she asked.

"Soul mate. At least I used to think so."

"You are so full of shit. I've seen you hit on a few women."

"Not since I went to Michigan, since I rediscovered her."

"Well, she's never gonna read your e-mail, I can guarantee that," Jodie yawned.

"Then what should I do? Tell me."

Looking up from sagging eyelids she whispered, "Go to her."

He felt Jodie's leg bump his beneath the table. One bump could be attributed to clumsiness, but not two. Glancing at her face he became intrigued by her mouth, had never before noticed how full her lips were, and below, her big boobs pushing against her blue sweatshirt. Beneath the table he felt her hand on his knee, her fingers creeping up his thigh. *Jesus, she'd better stop.*

Nick jumped up so quickly, his chair fell backwards to the floor. Jodie looked from the chair to Nick's face and broke into laughter.

"What's so funny?'

"You passed the test!" she roared.

"What test?"

"The test to prove you must really love this woman," muttered Jodie. "Good for you."

Then he escorted her out into the cool night, glad Jodie didn't know how close he came to failing her exam.

33

L ike a ghost on amphetamines, the outside bangs on the cottage, biting at the siding, swirling around the chimney, licking at the windowpanes, seeping under the doors. The thin cottage walls offer no more protection than a paper bag. And it's cold, so cold for late October. She's armored in layers of thermal underwear and a heavily pilled wool sweater and socks. The electric floorboard heaters spit out pitiful amounts of heat, delivering about as much warmth as she gets from peeing in the cold lake. Despite the chill, something about days like this draw her to them, a happy sense of isolation. Long gone are the cries of "Marco Polo" from the hotel swimming pools, the chatter from hordes of seniors stacked up on the big buggies, and the every-thirty-minute honks of the ferries, replaced by the wind's lonely ballad, a lone taxi here and there. The ferry schedule is whittled down to three boats a day, most of the shops are shuttered, and only two restaurants remain open downtown. Outside a few perennials linger on—a hosta, a sunny splash of Brown-Eyed Susans—while the ferns rust on the hillside. And now it's just Ella on the bluff with the house to herself, a frosty palace of her own.

Mother, Charlie, and Sara returned to Ann Arbor the day before Labor Day, Sara in her newfound protective mother role fawning over Charlie—"Isn't he handsome?" "Charlie and I are having quality time now" (Ella saw him roll his eyes on that one), and adding to it, a stint as a dutiful daughter. Fine with Ella. She could use a break and hopes it will last. As for Mother, Ella was surprised how vulnerable, scared she seemed when Ella left Ann Arbor to return to Mackinac. Mother—now able to walk again—followed Ella to the car and squeezed her hand. "Don't stay up there too long," she'd murmured, and kissed her on the cheek.

Ella could barely suppress her excitement to be returning alone to the cottage. "I'll miss you," she'd fibbed. Now the luxury of uncluttered time in complete solitude awaits her. She should be able to take a close look at the business records, and prepare a presentation on water levels in the Lake Huron watershed. She's thrilled, asked by the National Council for Water Conservation to speak at their conference in December.

Poring over the casket company accounts, a familiar anxiety returns. Although she kids that it's a dying business, sales are dismal, down three percent thus far this year, just like last year. All those cremations; and now this rent-a-casket trend, with folks cutting costs by renting a casket for a viewing and funeral, then hauling the corpse off for cremation. There's new competition from the big box companies: Wal-Mart has joined the business, buying low-cost caskets from overseas and making them available for in-store pick-up. The thought of a family driving up to Wal-Mart in their van and going through checkout with a casket seems so undignified.

How she hates this business, profiting off the dead and turning cemeteries into toxic dumps filled with embalming fluid and tons of metal. If only they could find a buyer.

Out on the porch, a crashing sound breaks Ella's concentration. She jumps and hastens to the front window where a wicker chair has blown over. She should have brought in all that porch furniture long ago, fooled by wishful thinking that the weather would improve.

Seeking a warmer place, she gathers up her notes and computer and moves into the kitchen where she turns on the oven and sets the tea kettle on a burner. Soon its shrill whistle pierces the room. Instead of tea, she slips a shot of cognac in the cup along with a spoonful of honey. Settling into a chair she takes a big sip. Ah, warm at last.

Over the sounds of the frenzied symphony outside, she hears chimes pour from her phone. "Hello," she answers, her throat tingling from the cognac.

"Hi. It's Sara. So how's the weather up there?"

"High winds, rain, a nasty Mackinac day."

"Got plenty to do on the inside, I'm sure."

"We'll never run out of work at Cedar Bluff." *Not that you do any, little sis.*

There's a pause. "Just wondering if you made up with that old beau."

"No. Why would I do that? Besides, we aren't, uh, communicating. And like you said earlier, he's a pervert."

There's a snort. "Ha. Well, wait till you hear this. Charlie told me he sort of fudged the truth."

Ella grasps the phone tighter. "What do you mean?"

"He didn't tell you the full story. See, there was this girl on the island, guess she was a former student of Nick's. Anyway, Charlie saw Nick talking to her so he introduced himself to her."

"Wait, slow down." It must be that girl Charlie met downtown somewhere. "Who was she?"

"I don't know her name. All I know is that she told Charlie that Nick had been her teacher—her favorite, I might add—and then she said how he'd gotten this false accusation at his school by some kid and resigned voluntarily."

"Hold on. Are you saying—?"

"Let me finish. So, Charlie being Charlie, you know, well, after talking to this girl he starts fishing around on the Internet. He finds some kid who writes him back that e-mail you read. And he makes up the rest. That's it."

Exhaling deeply, Ella says, "But that doesn't mean it didn't happen."

"Well, it seems pretty clear to me the kid in Wisconsin has an axe to grind. That, and Charlie told me that Nick was nice to him that night you left him—they even played soldiers together."

"But what's in it for Charlie?"

"C'mon Ella, our track record with men hasn't been exactly sterling. He's trying to protect himself and us too."

"Sounds like you're taking Nick's side. What's up with that?"

Sara sighs. "You've always been paranoid. Charlie told me this in family therapy. I thought you should know, that's all."

"Oh."

"We're making lots of progress. You should go, too. It's really helpful."

"We'd blow a million dollars if we hauled everyone in our household into family therapy," laughs Ella. "How's Charlie?"

"Academically he's doing fine, but the therapist says he has to learn to take responsibility, says Charlie has a scapegoat problem."

And this is something new? "He may be right about that. Just have to keep working on it. Oh, and Sara—"

"Yes?"

Taking a deep breath Ella says, "I'm sorry about everything that happened with Captain, the runaway, everything."

"Our old horse? Why are you bringing up ancient history?"

"I just wanted you to know. That's all."

"It wasn't your fault. You did everything possible to stop him. I don't hold you responsible. Never did." A pause. "But thanks."

She sets the phone down and drinks the now-tepid cognac tea in one gulp. Outside a cedar branch bangs on the roof. Suddenly the house feels unbearably lonely.

34

Nick debates the idea during another bike ride, a long one, where he maintains a blistering pace up and back on the Munger Trail, his mind focusing solely on moving ahead to get home to a hot shower. Maybe Jodie's suggestion has merit: go to the island and confront Ella in person. On one hand it makes sense; she may honor his effort if he travels all that way. On the other hand, it's ludicrous. Ella will have every reason to slam the door in his face; she may not even be there. It could be a repeat of that day in December when he'd been a young fool. Now he's an old one.

The ride ends with no decision and he nearly falls asleep in a steaming shower, letting gallon after gallon of water pour over him. Toweling off, he notices a subtle leanness in his mid-section; tightened abs, less flab. No six-pack, but improvement. He marks the tiny victory by slapping the towel on the sink and making a muscle pose in the mirror. *Watch out, Ella, here I come!*

He draws up a plan: he'll take off Friday, leaving at sunrise to catch a mid-afternoon ferry.

When he tells Jodie he'll be gone Friday she breaks into a smile. "You're gonna do it?" Nick nods. Jodie jumps up and high fives him. "Way to go, guy!"

"Thanks. You gave me the idea." His eyes rest for a moment on her chest.

The plans don't go smoothly. Though he's had all week to prepare for his long weekend, he's put off getting a sub, and now all the decent ones are booked. He'll have to hedge his bets on the unknown, a big risk, since he's under evaluation this year and the administrators hate it when classes get rowdy, even if he is not there and it's the fault of some clueless sub. The last time he had a bad one she'd written five student referrals to the office, was unable to stop a fight and left him a terse note: "You have the WORST kids ever. Please don't request me again." Dialing the school district's automated sub finder line, he selects "no preference" and crosses his fingers that it will be a good one.

The reality of the Mackinac trip hits Nick when he opens the garage door, where his yellow toolbox glows in the light of a single bulb, surrounded by stacks of boxes and plastic tubs. After a good fifteen minutes foraging through them, Nick uncovers his drill, a box of bits and a skill saw, circles of rust on its blade. Nick sighs. God knows if Ella will even let him in the door, but coming armed with repair equipment can't hurt. He'd once heard Mama advise a niece that the way to a man's heart was through his stomach; with Ella, the way to her heart is through her cottage repair list. He tosses a jacket and a sleeping bag in the back seat of the car, just in case.

As he rolls the garage door down a white minivan pulls up in the drive and Jodie jumps out from the driver's side.

"You might need a few of these for the trip," she says, handing Nick a plastic bag filled with cookies. He examines it and smiles. "Oatmeal chocolate chip, my favorite." He hugs her.

"Get that frickin woman to listen to you, ya hear?" she says, whacking him on the arm and turning toward her van. Nick follows. "Jodie, thanks. Thanks for everything!" he shouts as she backs up. He stands watching her retreating van roar off into the gray Duluth evening.

Back in the house, he sets both his cell phone and radio for 5:00 a.m. Better not take any chances of oversleeping and missing the last boat. In the bathroom he looks in the mirror where his four o'clock shadow underscores the dark circles around his eyes. He runs hot water over his face and scrubs vigorously. The circles remain. It will have to do.

35

Though early afternoon, the day looks more like dusk: mouse-gray clouds paper the sky, the glint of the Mackinac Bridge barely visible to the west, the water a sheenless pewter, cold and formidable. Earlier she wished she could extend her autumn stay, but today Ella concludes it is time to go. The place is getting to be downright uninhabitable.

The year Ella turned sixteen, Mother decided to spend Christmas at the cottage. *It will be splendid, a real old-fashioned Christmas and an enduring memory for the girls,* she'd announced. Mother sold many of her ideas on the greater good of the girls. Father thought the idea halfbaked and harebrained, but Audrey had her way. After an uncomfortable journey on a ferry whose steel hull hammered against slabs of floating ice the entire trip, followed by a frigid carriage ride, they'd arrived at Cedar Bluff.

Inside, a trickle of heat from the fireplace and stove provided the only warmth. They melted snow on the stove for water, huddling around the fireplace rubbing their hands together, and drinking lumpy hot chocolate from a mix in tepid water. All the windows remained boarded except the front one and a door. Sara and Ella slept together under a stack of blankets wearing wool hats and two pairs of socks, their breath forming smoke above their heads. Ella remembers waking up in the middle of the night and touching Sara's cheek, smooth and cold as a moonstone. Father gave Audrey a diamond bracelet for Christmas that year, but she accidentally tossed the box in the fire as they were clearing away the mess of gift wrapping.

When Henry knocked the smoldering logs around with the poker in search of the bracelet, a spark shot over the fire screen, landing on the Oriental rug where it proceeded to burn a hole. The bracelet was salvaged, but it ruined the rug and their Christmas morning. Then Sara got so sick with stomach issues—probably all the hot chocolate—and they had to rush her to the medical center, ruining the doctor's Christmas, too. That afternoon they caught the ferry back to St. Ignace and stayed in a motel room with smelly orange shag carpeting and no pool.

"Don't romanticize a Mackinac winter," Cindy, a year-round resident who'd weathered sixty island winters had told Ella. "Most of us spend it drinking to drown our boredom and stay warm." However, Ella knew that Cindy, like most all the real islanders, loved the hidden winter season and could scarcely wait to rid the place of summer folk, mount her snowmobile, and reclaim her island.

Cedar Bluff was too large to winterize. If Ella wanted to stay through the winter, she'd have to rent a room or a condo in town. She'd flirted with the idea before, even suggested enrolling Charlie in school there during Sara's worst times in and out of rehab. None of it panned out.

These late fall days are the most Mackinac-to-herself times she's ever had, but she finds it hard to get in much thinking. Reading spreadsheets and creating presentations isn't easy when you're wearing a coat and hat inside the house and still shivering. In four days she'll take Jed down to the ferry and he'll cross the Straits to St. Ignace, where a trailer will await him for his winter at a farm in the Upper Peninsula. It may be his last, and Ella has already put it off too long. She'd wanted to get in one last drive, but by the look of the sky today it may be too late.

Putting on a pair of recently-purchased reading glasses, she checks the weather on her phone: a rainstorm and possibly ice tonight, clearing tomorrow. Next she clicks on the weather in Ann Arbor; rain, of course. All this moisture has been a blessing for the Great Lakes. The levels were beginning to rise and with them, Ella's spirits. On a whim, she clicks to the Duluth weather. Crummy there, too.

Out back she hears the sound of horse hooves. Who would be out today? Pushing the glasses up on her head, she walks to the kitchen to see a team of wet Percherons, their coats glistening in the rain, with a carriage behind them. Ella recognizes Mary Jo, who's driven island taxis for years, hunched over the reins, her yellow raingear as slick as her horses' coats. Remembering those miserable cold days on the front seat of a carriage, her hands as brittle as someone with severe arthritis, Ella empathizes with the woman.

Now, who in the heck could be in that carriage? Stepping away from the window over the sink, she watches as a man shrouded in a hooded rain poncho steps down from the back seat, his face shielded by his hood as he hands Mary Jo some money and says something. Finally, he turns toward the house. She gasps. *Nick.* What in the hell is he doing here?

Steadying herself she grips the kitchen sink, staring in disbelief. Her initial instinct is to duck. Too late for that. He waves and walks toward the back door. Running her fingers through her hair, Ella hesitates, then straightens her shoulders and marches to the door, flinging it open before Nick can knock. She's shaking; not sure if it's with fury or excitement, or a mix of both. Drawing herself to all of her five feet nine inches, in a crisp-apron tone she says, "Yes?"

She can tell by the look of his eyes that he's apprehensive, like a soldier ready to poop his pants as he runs into battle. She should probably tell him to go to hell and slam the door; instead, she stands silently staring him straight in the eye.

"Ella, I have to talk with you, please. Will you do that for me?"

What can she say? The rain is whipping around out there and poor Mary Jo's freezing; it's too late for a return boat, and this man she hung up on, deleted forever—for the second time, in fact—is standing right here before her like that song, "And The Cat Came Back." Opening the door wider she declares, "Damn it, Nick, come on in."

He glances at the carriage, then back at Ella. "I've got a few things in the carriage. Mind if I bring them in?"

"What kind of things?"

"Tools, mainly. For your to-do list."

This is insane: he can't just come up here, barge in on her and expect to work on the house as if nothing happened. "Where you staying?"

He rocks back and forth on his heels, rubbing his hands together. "I was hoping you'd invite me, but if that didn't work out I was going to check with the Maples."

"You mean you haven't made a reservation?" Ella glares at him, but inside she has loosened. "You thought you could stay here?" All the starch has gone soft in her apron.

Nick sighs. "Yep."

"Well, get your things and let poor Mary Jo be on her way."

Nick turns and walks to the carriage, returning lugging an orange and yellow box and a bulging duffle bag.

Mary Jo picks up her reins, and the carriage disappears up the drive.

In the kitchen, Ella surveys Nick's face, senses something different about him, that he's somehow changed.

"You can set those over there," she says, pointing to the pantry. "Let them dry off."

Nick doesn't budge, just stands planted with his hands at his sides, water dripping off his poncho onto the linoleum and his belongings on the floor. "You're wearing glasses."

"No, I'm not."

Nick chuckles. "Then a pair has sprouted on your head."

Patting her hair she feels the glasses. "Only for reading."

The puddle beneath him is expanding. "Ella, I came all this way to explain in person. Will you hear me out?"

She'd already heard Sara's explanation, but she's not about to tell him that. Will the two stories match? Even if they do, he should have been more forthright earlier. "All right, Nick Pappas, but first you need to take off that wet jacket before you flood the place. Move your stuff while I make you a cup of coffee."

Obediently, he takes off his poncho, places his duffle bag and toolbox by the pantry and plunks down in a chair at the kitchen table, shivering. Ella bounces around the kitchen pouring water in a coffee pot and dumping grinds in it. She's averse to measuring things, so this will be a strong cup of coffee. Pondering what's ahead for the evening, she makes a cup for herself, breaking her rule of no caffeine after 11:00 a.m. It may be a long night indeed.

36

Suddenly he's afraid to tell her; not only that, but he hates repeating it. The whole thing makes him feel soiled. Such a sordid little tale. Fortified by a mug of her two-alarm coffee and the expectant look on her face, he leans forward. "Well . . . this may take a while."

"I've got time."

He takes a sip of coffee and sets the mug on the table. "It was in February, nearly two years ago," he begins. "I had started this tradition of taking my students to Madison to lobby for legislation they'd written."

He continues, first explaining how that year his students wrote legislation to ban the killing of cats in Wisconsin. It was the centerpiece of his AP Wisconsin government class, and he was proud of it. Students received authentic, hands-on learning by meeting not only with their own legislators, but many others from around the state. Nick took it another step: he'd received funds from the school, the PTO, and a few student-led carwashes to fund the trip. The money covered hotel rooms, meals, and transportation.

After a busy day lobbying, the students returned to their hotel rooms, where they were required to bunk down by 11:00 p.m. The boys and girls slept on separate floors, chaperoned by parents and another teacher. This year they were stretched thin on chaperones when one of the moms cancelled at the last minute due to a virus, and a dad bailed out, too. Nick considered postponing it, but a group of parents persuaded him to go ahead with plans.

At 11:00 p.m., after determining everyone was safe, sound, and present, Nick slipped down to the hotel bar. Although against school rules, he didn't see any harm in one cocktail. Trouncing around the capital with nineteen teenagers had worn him out. The day had gone well. A state representative had taken Nick aside that afternoon and said, "This is the best damn learning tool I've ever seen. You're brilliant."

The hotel bartender, a baby-faced man with a high forehead, placed the Manhattan on the bar and said, "Long day, huh?"

"Sure was."

"You with that group of kids?"

Nick hesitated for a moment. He didn't want the guy to rat on him. "Uh, yeah."

"You got my sympathy. Teenagers, little shits." The bartender plunked a second drink on the bar. "This one's on me."

Boozy and tired, Nick exited the elevator on his floor and noticed one of his students, Carlos Martinez, pounding on the door of the room across from Nick's. "Let me in!" Carlos shouted.

"Get the fuck out of my room!" a voice inside the room yelled.

"Hey, it's my room, too. You can't kick me out. Open up!" Noticing Nick, Carlos turned red and said, "Mr. Pappas. Hey, ah, hi."

"Who the fuck are you talking to?" said the voice on the other side of the door.

Nick knocked on the door and said, "It's Mr. Pappas. Open the door right now and cut the profanity." Carlos was staring down, his hands clenched. It took a good minute before the door opened; there, in BVDs and a T-shirt, stood Andrew Olson, a kid with a short temper, a sense of entitlement, and an overbearing dad. A smart guy with lousy study habits, he aced his exams, but flunked most of the paper assignments because of failure to turn them in. The odor of pot permeated the crisp winter air blowing from two windows opened wide despite the bitter February temperature.

"OK, guys, what's up?"

"This ass—I mean-—this dude, his shoes stink," said Andrew.

"And that smell," said Nick, sniffing the air, "sure doesn't seem to be coming from foul feet." Neither boy responded. "Looks like I may have to talk with your parents."

"Hey, if you're accusing me of smoking dope or something, go ahead and call my dad. He's a lawyer." Nick was very aware of Mr. Olson's occupation. At parent-teacher conferences he was arrogant and demanding, and had challenged Nick once for marking Andrew down for a stream of sloppy grammatical errors on one of the rare times he turned in a research paper. "I would love to talk with your father, and yours, too," said Nick, looking first at Andrew, then Carlos. "Let's call now. What's the number?" Neither boy answered. "I've got the numbers in my room, but it would be easier if you'd tell me."

"It's 414-405-7985," said Andrew.

Nick repeated it aloud. "Wait right here." In his room, Nick grabbed his phone and began touching the numbers before he forgot them. The phone rang as Nick walked back to the boys' room. After four rings a male voice said, "You have reached the Olson's. Please leave a message."

"Mr. Olson, this is Nick Pappas, your son's history teacher. I'm calling at 12:02 a.m. on Saturday. We have a big problem here. Please call as soon as you hear this."

"You're making a big frickin' deal out of nothing," said Andrew. A boy of privilege without a grain of responsibility, thought Nick. The worst. Over the years he'd watched kids like this in his classroom squander their talent with the help of enabling parents.

"This is grounds for suspension," replied Nick.

Andrew laughed.

"Now listen up, guys. I'll give you a choice: either you work out whatever it is between you or . . ." he suspected these two would probably argue ". . . or one of you can stay in my room." It was an old teacher trick: give them a choice to give them a sense of control. Carlos looked at Andrew, who was glaring at him, arms folded over his chest, then turned to Nick. "Are you sure it wouldn't bother you?"

The last thing he wanted was a kid in his room, but what were the options? "It's not my first choice, but I don't want to have you two fighting all night. And I've got to speak with your parents, too." Andrew was smirking. "Get whatever you need and come across the hall. There's two double beds. The rule is you have to go to sleep after I make that call." Nick turned to Andrew. "As for you, get to bed immediately. I'll be checking."

Within minutes, Carlos stood in the doorway clutching a pair of PJs, a toothbrush, and a pair of shoes. His lower lip was trembling. "Mr. Pappas, please, please don't call my parents. My dad'll kill me. For real." Nick had met Mr. Martinez at a parent conference, a proud man who emigrated from El Salvador and had a crappy job at an oil change shop. He ached for his son's success, imposing a rigid set of restrictions and rules around his life. "He doing all his work? Call me if he lazy."

Carlos was certainly not lazy. A hard worker, he struggled to maintain a C-minus in the class. Nick was committed to recruiting more minority students into AP classes, but dismayed that those for whom English was a second language had such a struggle.

"I'll tell you what. I have to call, but I'll wait until tomorrow."

"Thank you, Mr. Pappas," he said, raising his hand in a high five. "Thank you." Nick pointed to the empty bed, the one closest to the bathroom. "I'll be back in a few minutes, and when I am, I expect you to be in bed. Understood?"

"Yes, sir. Mr. Pappas, I'm sorry about this, but I really had nothing to do with that weed."

In the hall Nick closed the door and took a deep breath. Incidents like these were never easy, but after a long day and two drinks, his judgment was clouded. Maybe he should get Tom, the other teacher. He walked to the end of the hall, trying to remember if Tom's door was to the left or the right. He couldn't remember. *They don't pay me enough for this bullshit.*

Back in his room, Carlos was already under the covers. "Good night, Mr. Pappas."

"Good night. We'll talk tomorrow."

Nick flipped off the bathroom switch and the room darkened, leaving only a smudge of city light from below the hem of the draperies. "Can you leave the bathroom light on? I kinda hate the dark," said Carlos.

"Okay." Nick turned on the bathroom light. Although he usually slept in the buff, now that the boy was there, he pulled on a pair of pajamas in the bathroom, then sat reading the newspaper on the toilet until he'd consumed the front page, editorials, and sports section. When he emerged, Carlos was lying on his side, his eyes closed. Nick left the bathroom door open an inch, but the slice of fluorescence rankled him; he preferred total dark, like the woods with a new moon. He stretched out on his bed and thought about what he'd say to Carlos' father before falling into a deep sleep.

***

Hours later, Nick awoke in a sweat. The heater next to his bed had been turned too high, cooking the room to at least 80 degrees. Back home he always cracked the window and kept the thermostat below 65 at night. After all, he was a Yooper. Nick stripped off his pajamas, throwing them on the floor. A while later he woke again, this time with the urge to urinate. He had a headache and felt dizzy. Padding softly to the bathroom, he saw Carlos in the other bed. Damn, he'd forgotten all about the kid. The boy's legs were curled up with his thumb touching his bottom lip. He reminded Nick of Melina, fully developed but so innocent, so perfect and beautiful. Carlo's eyelids fluttered, then opened. Nick fled into the bathroom, praying the boy hadn't noticed him. Quietly, he wrapped a towel around his waist before emerging and tiptoed past Carlos, back into his own bed, where he struggled to slide into his pajamas under the covers.

When he woke the next morning at 7:00 a.m., Carlos was gone. Given teenagers' penchant for sleeping in, Nick thought it odd, and when he didn't find Carlos or Andrew in the restaurant at breakfast, he was sure they were pulling a fast one on him. He cornered Carlos in the lobby after a cup of coffee and toast.

"You're certainly an early bird," Nick said. Carlos backed away. "I'm calling your dad now."

Carlos shook his head, shrugged and said, "Whatever."

Nick took his phone from his pocket and dialed as Carlos left the lobby. A woman answered. "No speak Ingles," she kept repeating. Finally he simply said, "Tell Mr. Martinez to call me, Señor Pappas, por favor." Slowly, in his best Spanish, he said his number.

The bus trip back was uneventful, although Carlos and Andrew sat way back, whispering and laughing together, now best buds. Nick scanned the group of waiting parents for Mr. Martinez and Mr. Olson, but when he stepped off the bus he was bombarded by delighted parents shaking his hand, thanking him and asking so many questions. "Did you meet our senator? What did he say?" "Did Alison behave?" Nick completely forgot about the previous night's incident until he was driving home.

As matters turned out, they had not forgotten him. He had only been home a few minutes—time to greet Katie and hug Melina—when the phone rang. It was Mr. Martinez. "You pervert. You should go to jail," he said.

"Excuse me, this is the Pappas residence."

"Yeah, no more perverts. Carlos change classes. You never teach my boy again." The man hung up before Nick could respond. Andrew's dad called next. He was already planning legal action against Nick. "But first I'm taking this before the school board." Olson was a friend of the school superintendent.

"Don't you want to hear my side? Your son was smoking weed and cussing at his roommate. Didn't you get my message? I called you at about midnight."

"Do you have proof? Do you have a witness? And why in hell did you invite that kid to sleep in your room?"

"The whole thing is one huge mistake," Nick muttered into the emptiness of the hung-up signal.

After that it was one myth exploding into another, the frying pan to the fire to the blast furnace. Rumors grew from, "Mr. Pappas walked naked in front of Carlos," to, "Mr. Pappas tried to rape Carlos after luring him into his room." " Sex predator. Perv." Fortunately, his principal, Jane Woodson, believed Nick. "I've got your back," she assured him. Unfortunately, the school superintendent didn't. "Your only witness is Carlos, and he's not going to come clean, not with that dad of his," said the superintendent. "And we haven't even touched on Bob Olson's arguments." That was the catch. Bob Olson, highly connected attorney, political ally of the superintendent.

"I'm sorry. This isn't going to work," Jane told Nick a week later. "Come spring, I'll be looking for a new job in a different school district too."

"Meaning—?"

"Meaning you're being screwed over and I'm going to leave too. I think you should resign. For your own good."

"I can't do it, Jane. I'm 100 percent innocent and this will ruin my reputation. I have to fight this. Do you know how it's already eating up my little girl?"

"You're absolutely right, but it doesn't matter. Fighting back will destroy you. Trust me. If you think it's hard now, just wait."

Nick hired an attorney. "I want to fight this," he said. His attorney shook her head. "You'll lose." She didn't charge him a cent and he dropped the idea, but things became complicated quickly. A photo of Nick appeared on a student blog with the caption: "New addition to

Teacher Pervert list." The tech chatter spiraled into a roar, although many of his students rallied behind him. Nick resigned a week later on the condition that there would be no further action and that he'd receive a letter of recommendation with full pay until the beginning of the next school year. Apparently satisfied, Bob Olson did not pursue the case.

It was Nick who had helped Carlos get into his AP class; it was Nick who stayed after school to help him; Nick who softened his first semester F to a D+. But when Nick tried to talk with Carlos in the hallway a few days after the Madison incident, Carlos said, "Get away from me or I'll call security."

Although hard on Nick, it was tougher on Melina. She didn't understand why a group of kids suddenly turned on Daddy, why Daddy had to leave. He and Katie's stay-together-for-the-kid marriage was dissolving quickly, but neither wanted to file for divorce until Melina graduated the following year. Katie, a speech therapist at an elementary school, loved her school and the community. Unable to work in the school district, and blackballed throughout Wisconsin, Nick applied in neighboring states, finding a job as a history teacher in Duluth, Minnesota. Not at the good high school, but that other one.

"I'll work there for just a little while," Nick had told a weeping Melina. "When all this blows over I'll be back."

He was hired to help failing students pass a standardized history test required for eligibility to graduate. "This job, I hate to say, is teach-to-the-test," the assistant principal conducting the job interview told Nick. "Nothing fancy." Nick did as he was asked, bringing the scores up remarkably quickly, but still tried to inject deeper thinking skills into his students. Most resisted it. "Come on, Mr. Pappas, can't we just have a worksheet?" students would ask.

Katie filed for divorce two months after Nick moved to Duluth, insisting that Melina remain in Wisconsin with her and that she get the house. Having lost so much—his job, reputation, respect, self-esteem—Nick, the historian, looked backward for solace. Those happy days with baby Melina snuggled in a carrier, her tiny back resting upon his heart, visiting the First Capitol near Belmont, their first big historical excursion. Later, they'd made a pilgrimage to Williamsburg, where he snapped one of her favorite photos: a six-year-old Melina with her head locked in wooden stocks. He wanted to peer through time with her, to inculcate this child with a desire to remember.

37

"Well, that's my sordid little story," says Nick, leaning back in his chair, afraid to look at Ella in her seat across the table. It may as well be the other side of the world. He's told too many tales. Why should she believe the truth now? Daring a glimpse, he looks up. She's staring past him to the wall behind, with a puzzled look. He wishes she'd say something, anything, but all she does is sigh and shrug her shoulders, then push back her chair.

"Well, hmm, wow," she says. "I feel so, so—"

"So what?"

Looking at him he sees moisture welling in her eyes. It takes his breath away.

"So badly that you didn't tell me before. So terrible for you."

"You believe me?"

"Yes, but I don't believe a few other things. Will you tell the straight-up truth about something?"

"What?"

"When you came here in August, that first day, were you just dropping by and doing some research, or had you planned the whole thing. I mean, did you come to the island solely to see me?"

Geez, she isn't giving him any wiggle room. "Straight-up truth, huh?" Ella nods.

He readjusts his position in the chair. "Remember what I told you over on Round Island, that I'd thought about you on and off for thirty years? It's true, but it wasn't until last spring that I started thinking about you—about us—constantly. It haunted me."

"An obsession."

"You can call it that, but I'd choose a different word—quest, a quest for happiness. I checked for you on the net, but I'm not good at that. I found someone with your name, your age. I called the house and heard that recording by your dad. And yes, I'm guilty as charged. The only research project I was conducting was to find you." He waits for her response, certain she will order him out the door. He is surprised she is staring intently at the table.

"What did you think you would gain if—well, if things all fell into place?" she asks.

What is there to say but the truth, even if it means losing her forever? Reaching across the table for her hand he blurts, "I thought the whole world would shift."

Miraculously, her palm opens to receive his. So warm and moist. They sit for what seems to Nick a very long time, the sound of their breathing subsumed by the ticking of the old kitchen clock, the song of the wind through the cedars out back.

Standing up abruptly, Ella pushes back her chair and walks around the table toward him, then thrusts her arms around him, laying her head against his back below his neck. "And did it?" she whispers.

"I think it's about to," he says, kissing her hair, moving his mouth toward her ear. Strands of her wavy hair rise toward his mouth, an electric current feeding straight into his groin.

***

Later, Ella would look back and laugh at the scene: two horny middle-aged adults yanking off layer after layer; long underwear, damp socks, vests, and sweaters puddled on the floor as they tore into one another. First he pulled her to him, ran his fingers up her chest and squeezed her left breast until her nipples stood out like the tip of a soft-serve ice cream. She reached beneath his undershirt—the last barrier between their flesh—and shoved her hands lower. Nick's tongue held a taste of chocolate chip cookies and his chest hairs tickled her breasts as he placed his fingers on her inner thigh. Slowly, in upward strokes, they found their way home.

Ella didn't notice the cold air seeping through the linoleum, nor the prickly fibers of the sweater beneath her left arm, nor even Nick's thick leg wrapped over hers. Curled into one another they formed a nest, there, on the kitchen floor, satiated and fast asleep.

A noise on the back porch awakens Ella. Outside the sky is dark; only the light from the open door on the oven illuminates the kitchen. Nick's mouth forms an O shape, his eyes closed. She sits up and he stirs.

"It's freezing," she mutters, sorting through the clothes for her thermal long underwear bottoms. Nick reaches out and pulls her toward him by the wrist.

"Don't desert me."

***

When Nick sits up, he feels disoriented. Is this real? He and Ella, together at last on Mackinac Island? And on the kitchen floor of all places. He grins at the cookie-baking woman on the wallpaper, then at the woman next to him hustling on her long underwear. Pulling her toward him, he feels the bones in her shoulders, close to her flesh, a little grasshopper. She feels so fragile, but he knows she's firm and tough, not easily broken.

"What time is it?" she asks, yawning. The oven clock reads "PF" again.

Peering at his watch he says, "A little after nine."

"Let's go up to bed and treat ourselves to a mountain of blankets and a soft mattress."

In Ella's bed they snuggle beneath three blankets. Nick gently nips her neck, growling like a bear cub. They fall asleep with her spine tucked into the curve of his chest, her buttocks against his groin, his right arm flung across her ribs with his hand ending in hers, much warmer than Nicolet's Watchtower and without one damned mosquito.

Later, he awakens to an empty bed; only the indention in Ella's pillow gives testimony that she's ever lain there beside him. The apprehension he's carried for months rushes back: has he lost her again? A noise somewhere outside the room sounds like crying. Hastening from the bed, he opens the door and listens. The sound comes from the bathroom directly across the hall. He hesitates before knocking. "Ella?" he says softly.

"I'm fine," she mutters.

"May I come in?"

At first she doesn't reply, then says, "OK."

As he opens the door she is wiping her face with a hand towel, and he approaches with his arms opened wide. Ella rests her head on his shoulder. He can feel her trembling, and moisture soaks the sleeve of his T-shirt beneath her eyes.

"There, there." He rubs her back, kissing her hair.

Nick doesn't know how long they remain like this—as far as he's concerned it could be forever—but eventually she looks up and says, "Thank you."

They slip back beneath the blankets as if this had never occurred.

38

They awaken to light splashing through the big windows. Ella's eyelids flutter, then open fully as she turns to Nick, who is beginning to stir. Ella sniffs the air, tastes her foul breath.

"What is it?" mumbles Nick.

"I haven't brushed my teeth."

"So what," he whispers, kissing her. He wants to ask about last night, decides it would be best if she brought it up. "Kiss me." She pulls away from him. "Is this the manure-loving Ella Hollingsworth speaking? Madam, I submit to your wishes."

Heaving himself out of bed, Nick pulls on plaid boxer shorts as Ella yanks the T-shirt she'd cast off last night back over her head; she doesn't want him staring at her body in the morning light. The darkness hid the patches of lunar landscape on the back of her thighs and the scar. Nick walks around the bed to her side, yanking on the bottom of her T-shirt.

"Lady Godiva, where art thou?"

"Please, Nick." Grabbing a pillow, she stands on the bed and whacks him on the head. He wrests the pillow from her hands, then heaves it at her as she leaps off the opposite side of the bed, snatching another pillow on the way down. On the floor she dives under the bed. Nick's pillow sails past the spot where she'd stood an instant ago before smacking into a table. The antique lamp teeters, its fringed shade quivering on the brass stem. Nick thrusts himself belly down on the bed with a pillow in his hands, his head peering over the edge.

"I see you."

Ella scuttles crab-fashion on the floor but Nick grabs her ankle, pulling her toward him.

"Stop it." Twisting around, she extricates her legs from his grip, then, sitting on her knees, strips off the T-shirt and beats on her chest. "Aah Eee ahhh!"

Nick reaches his arms out and pulls her up.

"We're still good animals," she whispers afterwards.

***

Well, good *older* animals, thinks Nick. Lovemaking at fifty takes more effort, but can still provide equally satisfying results, if less frequent.

"I'm famished," he says.

"Me too. I could eat a horse."

Nick looks toward the window, clicks his tongue and calls, "Here, Jed." Ella bops him lightly with her fist.

"Speaking of horses, I better get out there and feed the poor boy," she says.

At breakfast, Ella reminds him of a little mouse in her long gray sweatshirt (inside out with the label showing) and a plaid wool scarf tied around her neck in a jaunty knot. She's pulled her hair up into some sort of ponytail fastened with a barrette contraption, exaggerating the size of her ears that poke out, adding to the mouse image. He's pulled on long underwear beneath his jeans, and a turtleneck under a maroon sweater. Heat blasts from the open oven door but vanishes instantly through the cracks around the windows. Ella and Nick huddle at the kitchen table with their hands wrapped around their mugs, their steaming mugs of tea and coffee losing warmth in nanoseconds.

"For someone so concerned about saving water and energy, that's the least efficient way to heat your house," he tells Ella, nodding toward the stove.

"But it's the fastest way to get out the chill."

"So is this." Nick reaches across the table and takes Ella's hands, rubbing them vigorously.

"Last night in the bathroom—" he begins.

"Oh, that was nothing, just a case of nerves. I've been a bit overwhelmed."

"Of course." He studies her face, imagines a "No trespassing" sign appearing in her eyes. He can wait. Searching for a new topic he asks, "When are you closing this place?"

"Very soon or the pipes will freeze. We've already dipped below thirty-two a few nights."

"And you, where will you go?"

"First I'm going to Ann Arbor to help Mother. Oh, I didn't tell you this—how could I have?—I've been asked to make a presentation to a national organization about conserving water in the Lake Huron watershed and—" she pauses, "we may have a buyer for the company. Fingers crossed."

"So you need to sell it?"

"Mother's medical issues are costing more than expected. That, and Mother's generosity binges have ripped a hole in our investments."

"Generosity binges?"

"That's what I call them. She is recklessly generous, has been for years. Just last month she donated $900 for a new organ at a Jamaican church—Genevieve's—and she recently gave $500 to the Humane Society in Petoskey. Mother doesn't have a dog or cat and doesn't even live there," says Ella, shaking her head. "She was having tea with some lady from there and got talked into it. And Sara has been raiding the family trust for Charlie's private school, and to top it off, my profligate little sister has been using the Hollingsworth company credit card for items over her company's per diem, such necessities as massages, waxings, and floral arrangements."

"Wow." Nick leans back in his chair, clearing his throat. "I've been thinking about something. Let me run it by you. There must be a boatload of hydrologic issues up my way. Lake Superior has something like three trillion gallons of water in it—"

"Quadrillion."

"Whatever, quadrillion. That's a lot of water. You could come up and investigate. Duluth sits on one giant bluff with a great view of the lake, even has a few beautiful bridges."

"I remember driving through there as a kid on a family trip across the UP. I saw a lot of the lakers that pass by here anchored by massive grain towers. Duluth had a muscular, industrial feel to it."

"You're right. The water is a steel-gray blue, not like out there." He nods toward the harbor. "The people of Duluth are the same color."

"Gray?"

"Norwegians; cool, like ice cubes, a different tribe than mine." He walks around the table and begins rubbing her shoulders. "Did you ever hear about the Norwegian farmer?"

"No."

"After ten years of marriage he told his wife he loved her." Nick lifts his hands from her shoulders and slaps his thigh, laughing. Then his voice goes soft as he leans over and whispers, "I am not Norwegian. I love you."

Instantly, she stiffens beneath his hands. It had just slipped out, so easily. Of course it spooked her, this woman who shies at the sight of love, but someday she will pick up the cue and say, "I love you, too." He can feel it growing inside her.

He feels her watching him. "Nick, I . . ."

"Yes?"

"I, uh, I checked the weather app and they're calling for sun by noon."

That's it? The weather report? "Great. Let's go for a swim over on Round Island, and you can run the propeller over my other toe."

"Enough of that. I have a better idea," she says, pushing her chair back. "Just a little repair." She points to the kitchen door. "That screen door is driving me crazy. Flies getting in all summer and then the banging. Think you could you fix it?"

"You call that a better idea? Alright, but it will cost you five kisses."

By noon the clouds have fled east and the temperature has risen to fifty-one. The screen door is fixed, and Nick's moved on to a minor plumbing issue involving a drippy tub faucet upstairs. "It was driving me out of my mind," says Ella, watching from the bathroom doorway.

Nick stands up, wiping his hands on his pants. "My uncle Ted's a plumber. His motto is, 'Your shit is my bread and butter. Maybe I should give up teaching and become a Mackinac plumber."

"We can keep you in business for a whole season. But let's get out of here. It's beautiful out there."

39

After washing up, Nick goes downstairs, where he finds Ella in the kitchen yanking a bag of carrots from the refrigerator. They're long and unpeeled, not the stubby little ones everyone eats nowadays. She extracts two, takes them to the sink and washes them.

"What are you making?"

"Nothing. These are for Jed."

"Washing carrots for a horse?" he asks.

"Don't want Jed ingesting any chemicals," she says, plunking them on the counter and taking up a knife in her right hand. She slices the carrots horizontally into two-inch pieces. "Jed's teeth aren't what they used to be."

When his carriage pulled up yesterday Nick was surprised to spot the old horse by the back fence neighing to the taxi team. Even with a plaid blanket strapped around him Jed appeared thin, his whinnying forlorn.

"When will you take him back to the mainland?"

"Day after tomorrow. But first I was hoping to get in one more drive. He needs to get out of that soggy paddock before he gets thrush, plus he could use some exercise."

Remembering the scar on her back, Nick shudders. Jed could drop dead pulling the buggy. "How about biking instead? You could tie Jed up in the front yard and he could graze his heart out."

"It's a little cold for biking, and it's not good to let him graze too long."

"Fifty-one degrees? Shame on you—that's a summer day in Duluth."

Soon Ella tethers Jed to a long line in the yard. The horse looks content, now on a sniffing quest for the best fodder.

Standing beside her bike, Ella's donned a winter jacket, thick gloves, a wool hat and neck warmer; Nick's jacket is zipped halfway. He's hatless, and his bare hands rest on the handlebars.

"You're going to be sorry," says Ella disapprovingly.

"Got my gloves right here," says Nick, patting his bulging front pockets.

As they turn northwest from the drive, the wind slams into him full force, reddening his face and stinging his ears. Still pedaling, Nick reaches in his pockets, one at a time, and extracts the gloves, hoping Ella won't notice. They pass by cottages, their windows blindfolded, doorways gagged by winter boards, some painted to match the trim, others plain weathered plywood. Without their people, these old houses lose their sight and speech. It's eerily quiet, such a lonely place.

When they turn north, the wind subsides. Pulling up next to Ella, Nick asks, "Where to?"

"It's a surprise."

They pass the airport, now planeless, past Wawashkamo, the old golf club with its Scottish links, also deserted, its sign singing a creaky tune as it swings below a cedar archway. Nick enjoys the ease of the nearly all-downhill ride, takes his feet off the pedals, and pulls beside her. "I'm a badass," he shouts. Ella turns her head, flashes him a huge smile, and races ahead. Conditions today are perfect—no kids, no Boons, no mothers, no peevish Ella. So immersed in thought is he that he doesn't notice that Ella has pulled over and he brakes forcefully, a move that almost catapults him over the handlebars.

"Geez!" she shouts, jumping a foot onto the grass, still holding her handlebars. "What were you thinking?" They're in the front yard of that house near Friendship's Altar that he'd admired back in August. A black and yellow For Sale sign rattles in the wind.

"Aw, I thought that might happen. You said the guy was having financial problems."

Nick remembers his connection to this stranger, their shared heart-break of losing a dream house.

"More than that," replies Ella. "He's very ill, needs to sell soon, though that will be hard to pull off. The real estate market here's less than flat—it's a mine shaft."

Nick stares longingly at the place, which appears more abandoned than earlier, with a new dusting of brown cedar on the roof, the bushes overgrown. "You think anyone will come this way to see it this late in the year?"

"No, but the real estate market doesn't work like that anymore. People shop on the web. They've posted pictures of it on their web page next to about twenty-five lots that won't sell."

"Maybe he'll get lucky." Sweat oozes down Nick's back and chest beneath his layers of clothing and he wipes his forehead with the back of his glove-encased hand.

"Want to go inside?"

"Inside?"

"Yes. Come on." Ella pushes her bike around to the back of the house where a weathered red Adirondack chair and matching table topped with a pot of dead geraniums deepens the aura of hasty abandonment. A splintery deck on the back extends east; behind it, a small garden abuts the woods. Ella stands in front of a window to the right of the back door, the sill a few feet above the deck. Grunting, she thrusts her arms upward and the wood midsection of the window eases up the sash.

"What are you doing? We'll get busted for B and E."

Ella chuckles. "Are you kidding? This is Mackinac. Jake will appreciate someone checking on the place."

"How did you know that window was unlocked?"

"No one locks their windows around here. Most of us don't even lock our doors. Anyway, I've known Jake for years. He did some work for Father, and I've gotten some native plants from him. He knows more about them than anyone around here."

Nick wonders how well she knows him. Was he another one of her island interests? "Let's take a peek," says Ella, already halfway into the house, straddling the windowsill like a saddle. Nick follows.

The interior impresses him immediately with its simple beauty: a series of not so much rooms, but spaces that flow into one another, all wood and stone. In the main area a pine floor-to-ceiling bookcase covers an entire wall; next to it a fireplace of stones, like those on the shoreline, rise to a wood mantel at eye level. Shafts of light enter the rooms at angles from skylights in the ceiling and small windows are strategically placed to capture the light in which dust motes now dance. Even inside the house Nick feels he's still in the woods.

"I feel like I'm in a church, " says Ella.

"Then let's pray we don't get caught," says Nick, looking around. "Just look at the way he's kept everything natural." He's walking around grinning, his arms open wide.

Nick plops down in a leather chair, leans back, stretches his legs out and sighs. It feels like a place he belongs, comfy and peaceful.

Ella begins to pace around the room. She reminds Nick of the lions at the National Zoo he saw on a field trip years ago, all pent up on a little concrete island separated by a moat and high wall, yearning for a romp in savannas they'll never see. "What do you think?" she asks.

"It's awesome."

"But it doesn't have a view of the water."

"Bet you can see the lake from upstairs. Let's take a look," he says, rising from the chair. They ascend the stairs, where a dark hallway ends at a window. Nick turns left and opens the first door to a modest bedroom with only a queen-size bed with no headboard. Windows on the west and north walls are darkened by window shades. Nick pulls one up and the snapping sound echoes through the upstairs. Through the trees they can see a patch of blue. "There's your lake," he says.

"I can't see much at all," says Ella.

"Bet you could with a three-story tower here," he says, moving toward the northern window where Ella yanks on the shade. The movement awakens a fly, which begins to buzz desperately at the window glass.

"Look at that," she exclaims, pointing out the window. "You can see the lookout."

Nick joins her and makes out the top railing of the lookout above Friendship's Altar. Squeezing her hand he says, "What are we waiting for?"

They descend the stairs and clamber out through the open window. Although her movements are nimble, outside, in the full light, Ella's face looks lined and tired.

As they near Friendship's Altar, an uneasiness creeps over him. He should be delighted, rebuilding a relationship with the Ella he'd—what was it?—reclaimed. Lovers and best friends once more. But a whiff of that August afternoon, the sweetness so palpable, then snatched away in Ella's uppityness, her guarded privacy, followed by one thing after another, here it is gnawing at him again.

They turn their bikes up the gravel road, the path to the Altar less than a hundred yards away. Nick takes a deep breath, trying to focus on the happiness inside, pushing away the forethought of grief ahead, the remembrance of sorrow behind.

This time the sign is back up announcing "Friendship's Altar" in white letters inscribed on brown wood, like frosting on a gingerbread man.

"I wish they hadn't fixed that. I wanted to keep it to ourselves." She glances at him over her shoulder. "Come on."

Nick follows until Ella halts in front of the chunk of limestone. The humble little altar. With the sugar maples and elms denuded, the space is brighter, less intimate than back in summer. The cedar sprouting from the formation's top has browned at the edges, the rock is coated in yellowed sprigs. No birds cry, only a lonely autumn wind whooshes through the cedars.

Nick moves closer to Ella, reaching for her hand. "Remember when I said I wanted to stop time? I've changed my mind. I want time to keep marching forward so I can anticipate all the days ahead with you."

Ella squeezes his hand. "Let's take what we've got. Nothing more is guaranteed."

"I refuse to go along with that. I'm greedy. I want more and more of this." Turning to Ella, pushing her bangs away from her eyes, he kisses her forehead. Above the altar, the blue sky cuts so clear Nick swears he can feel oxygen pouring out of it. From the corner of his eye he sees the stairs leading to the deck. Tugging on Ella's hand, he directs her toward it. This time he's the leader.

At the top, he steps carefully onto the deck, the boards greened by lichen, slippery from the autumn rains. With so many leaves gone, the view through the trees has magnified; to the north they can see the rocky cliff and tower over in St. Ignace, the bold silver signature of the Mackinac Bridge gleams across the horizon. Nick throws up his arms. "It's frickin' beautiful!" he shouts.

On the other side of the lake, the green ribbon of mainland is another world, one they no longer inhabit. Not today.

***

Up on the lookout the air is colder and Ella pulls her scarf tighter. They sit on the wooden bench, shoulders touching. "About last night," she says.

"Which part?"

"The, uh, the bad part."

"I don't recall any bad parts."

"Come on, you know what I mean. It's weird, I hardly ever cry. Don't take this the wrong way, but last night it all kind of hit me and—"

Pulling her close to him Nick murmurs, "I don't take it the wrong way."

"Charlie—what a mess he's become—and I thought I could be some kind of perfect aunt mom."

"You do your best."

"OK, but I'll never have kids now. Thanks to Kevin. See, he swore he didn't want kids. Ever. That was a surprise, but I refused to get my tubes tied. That was his preference, but it's so, so permanent." She looks at him. "And a whole lot more complicated than you guys getting a little snip."

"Well, I'm not so sure about that." He'd come close to having the procedure until he heard about a guy whose scrotum turned blue for weeks following a routine vasectomy.

"Anyway, I told him, 'I won't go down that road.' So I come home from work one day and he's in bed moaning, cursing. Says he got a vasectomy and it's all my fault."

"And?"

"Well, he recovered in a day or two, but he was angry at me for—I guess the rest of our marriage. And then he went off with a woman who had two kids. I mean little kids, not full-grown teenagers or something. No, a three- and five-year-old. Boys. Like two little puppies you have to housetrain, the whole nine yards."

"Sounds like a real prick." Ella doesn't respond. "How did you ever hook up with this guy?"

***

Ella cringes at the memory. The way she'd met Kevin was an impulsive act with lifelong consequences, as damaging as packing a Saturday Night Special in her handbag and blowing away the first person who ticked her off.

"I put a note on the windshield of his car."

"You what?"

"Put a note on his windshield with my name and number. He called. It was spring, April in Washington, DC, drop-dead gorgeous. I lived near the city and stayed outside as much as possible when I wasn't working. I even biked to work on a trail along the Potomac River."

"You just can't stay away from bikes and water, can you?" says Nick.

Ella wonders if she should continue.

"So what happened?" asks Nick.

Ella recounts how early one Saturday she left her townhouse on her bike, heading south on the trail toward Mt. Vernon. After several miles the trails passed some older suburban residences that reminded her of her parents' neighborhood in Ann Arbor, yards blazing with pink, purple, and salmon azaleas. On this ride she was staring at a particularly bright azalea in the yard of a red brick two-story when a man emerged on the front porch. Slowing down she shouted, "Gorgeous azaleas!"

He smiled. "Thanks." As he walked toward her she noticed he was very good-looking, cleft chin and wavy hair, the way Robert Redford looked back in the day. She slowed her bike and hopped off. "But I can't take any credit. I'm just a renter," he said.

He looked extremely fit, bulky forearms protruding from the casually rolled-up sleeves on his blue shirt. His eyes held hers for a moment. She knew that look, the way a man who's aware of his effect on women makes eye contact with a female. A player. She usually avoided his type, but something about this man drew her to him.

"Well, enjoy," said Ella, resuming the seat on her twenty-one speed and pedaling off.

That was all.

But she kept thinking about him.

For the next several weeks she biked past his home regularly, but never saw him again. She noticed a car—a silver Honda—twice, and figured it was his. The next time she passed his house she was armed with a plan. She scribbled out a note on some paper she had stuffed in her saddlebag.

My name's Ella, the azalea admirer. 703-435-2984.

She placed it under the windshield wiper of his car and sped off on her bike, instantly regretting her action.

That evening she jumped when her phone rang, but it was only a telemarketer hawking a credit card. She felt ludicrous, exposed.

The phone rang the next evening. This time it was he, Kevin Ra-nier, a young attorney. "Is this the azalea admirer?" he asked when she answered. Turned out they had a lot in common; he was doing environmental law for the EPA's hazardous materials division, and she was beginning a program to design environmental curricula for schools. They were decidedly the minority in those conservative years.

For many evenings after that and every weekend they were insep-arable. When June rolled around she dragged him up to Cedar Bluff. Father took to him immediately, his sense of style, his smooth good manners, but Mother never warmed up to him. Something phony about him, she'd said.

"So do you have any contact with him?" asks Nick.

She laughs. "Are you kidding? You know what he did? He called me early this summer to ask if he could bring Missy—that's her name—here with the kids."

"And you said?"

"What do you think I said? Sure, bring 'em up, I'd love to entertain all of you. How very nice that would be." Ella's face flushes. She can feel the burn from her neck to her eyebrows. Nick rubs her shoulders gently.

"Thanks for sharing that. It must have been awful."

Ella sighs. "I'm over it."

Turning toward her, Nick takes her hands in his. "Would you ever place a note on my windshield?"

"No need to."

"You found me." Standing up and tugging her arm he says, "It's getting colder than hell up here, even for an old Yooper."

It's true, but she's reluctant to leave. Cold as hell it may be, but what a heavenly place.

40

On their bikes, they pedal casually, like tourists, crossing over the yellow line and chatting. Ella's chosen to head west on the shoreline road to have the wind at their backs. The scenery is spectacular: the rolling blue lake on their right, the yellowing forest to their left. A patch of fancy nouveau Victorian homes emerge, most gray and white, tasteful, dull, and expensive. On an empty lot a construction crew circles a hole in the ground like hyenas. All the trees have been hacked into pieces, stacked like Lincoln Logs in the corner of the lot. Ella remembers the days this place was all sugar maples, beeches, cedar, and balsam.

Rounding a bend a mile farther, they see the Round Island Lighthouse they'd walked to in August, when Nick told her that story about his fabricated Christmas visit.

"Hey!" she shouts, letting up on her pedals until she is even with Nick.

"Hey."

"I was thinking about that Christmas promise. Why don't we try it for real, meet up here this winter? I won't stand you up. Promise."

"Scout's honor?"

"I got kicked out of Girl Scouts for putting shaving cream on the leader's homemade pie. How 'bout pinky swear?" says Ella, reaching over to encircle her pinky finger in his. Her front wheel swivels into Nick's bike.

"Watch it!" he shouts, barely able to keep his bike upright. When he steadies it he pulls even with her again. "Can I tell you something?"

"I'm all ears."

"That Christmas promise stuff—I didn't make it up."

Ella's brakes squeal as she halts, nearly taking Nick down again. "What? You mean it wasn't BS? You made up a story about making up a story?"

"Yep."

"But why?"

"You looked so flummoxed when I told you it, I felt like such a friggin idiot."

"Saving face, huh?" His confession has put into play—once again—the possibility he has lied about other things: his marriage, his ex, maybe even the Madison fiasco. That it's all hogwash. And what else might fall into that category? The line between a good storyteller and mendacity is a thin one. She glances at him to see if his nose has grown longer.

"Are you ever going to believe me again?" he asks.

"Good question." She'll have to leave it there for now. Grabbing the handlebars, she jumps back on her bike, pedaling hard. But this time she can't leave Nick in the dust; he rides right next to her.

***

As they approach the western edge of the village, a lone figure, hood pulled over his head, slouches toward them along the board-walk, leaning into the wind. A few houses are festooned in Halloween décor, a string of plastic jack-o'-lanterns prattle between two trees in the front yard of the O'Shays, and small cloth ghosts dance from the branches of a crabapple tree. Ella turns her bike up a side street to one of the few eating establishments still open, the Great Turtle. "Let's get some coffee," she says.

Chilled and famished, Nick feels a backache coming on. Coffee with a slip of hooch sounds perfect.

Pushing the door open, it takes a moment for his eyes to adjust to a dark, wood-paneled room. A trace of grease scents the air; on the television, two talking heads shout at one another on a cable network. "Wall Street can't be blamed for everything," says a plastic-perfect looking blonde on the screen.

A rangy man with a long face in a plaid shirt whom Nick judges to be in his mid-seventies turns around on his bar stool to greet them. "Well if it isn't Miss Hollingsworth."

Ella nods. "How are you, Danny?"

"Weather's awful, business down, laid off my crew, can't complain. So what brings you down here today?"

"Long bike ride, ended up here. Cold and in need of coffee."

"Coffee I can do. Unless you want one of those fancy Star-five-bucks types."

"No. Regular old coffee will do. Two please."

"Make mine an Irish coffee," says Nick with a wink. "My back's hurting."

Danny chuckles. "I've heard that one before." The man's eyebrows, Santa Claus-bushy, remind Nick of Papa's.

They seat themselves in a booth away from the bar, but the prattle on the television is still audible. Nick's famished. No way to lose weight on this island. Even with all the exercise, the fresh air and biking intensify the appetite. He picks up the menu, a small laminated rectangle featuring a list of heart-attack-friendly choices: Big Dan's Fries, smothered in melted cheese; nachos and beef with spicy peppers; deep-fried mozzarella sticks; a fried pizza, and the obligatory hot buffalo wings.

"Do they have any soup?" asks Ella, squinting at the menu.

Nick scrolls down the column to the soup entries. "Chili."

"Loaded with red meat, I bet, probably straight from a can." He'd had his eye on those nachos, but Ella would likely be turned off by the oily cheese and piles of ground beef. "I don't eat anything with four legs," she'd told him earlier.

Danny brings two mugs of coffee. "Regular for you,"—he sets a mug in front of Ella—"and Irish for you. We don't have much of what's on that menu right now. Pretty much out of everything. Too late for leaf peepers and Halloweeners, too early for snowmobilers. Almost ready for deer season, which means no one will be here so I'm closing it up in two weeks."

Pointing to the menu Ella asks, "Got any salad left?"

Danny smiles. "That we can do." He stands there, shifting from one foot to the other. "And you, young man?"

"Chili."

"I can do that too. It's your lucky day."

Danny shuffles off to the kitchen. "His family's owned this place forever. Danny's second-generation. Father liked to come here for a late-night sip of hooch." Ella reaches across the table and squeezes Nick's hand. "A penny for your thoughts."

"I don't want this weekend to end." The thought of mainland life with all its tedious tasks, its demands, its Ellalessness, depresses him. But he can't picture Ella in his mainland life; he's unable to take her out of this context. She and the island are tie-barred, not to be transported elsewhere in his mind. But of more immediate concern is that elephant plunked there beside them, his worry she doesn't believe him since his confession about the Christmas story.

"I'm thinking of joining the BSA," he says.

"The Boy Scouts of America?"

"No, Bullshitters Anonymous of America."

Ella cocks her head and holds his gaze. "Answer these two questions and I might believe you."

"Shoot."

"When you came over that Christmas, what was the name of the boat?"

The boat? That was a cinch. He'd help unload the thing hundreds of times. "The Mohawk."

"That was too easy. Second question: what was the first or last name of the woman at the grocery store?"

"Wait a minute. Unfair. How would you know? You weren't there," Nick laughs.

"True. These are stupid questions. I'm just going to have to believe you Nick Pappas."

"Thanks." He takes her hand and rubs it.

"Scuz me," says Danny carrying a small salad of iceberg lettuce topped with a few tomato slices. The dressing choices are French, Thousand Island, or Italian in plastic pouches. "Miss your Pa," he says, plopping the plastic bowl in front of her. "Tonight's the last night for the Grand Hotel. I remember seeing Henry and your mom up there. Millie and I were celebrating our anniversary, sitting at a table next to the dance floor, and I looked up. There goes Henry and your mom, waltzing right past us. Your dad was humming, your mom's eyes were near closed, a smile on her lips. They circled the floor like two swans. It was a sweet sight. Millie just about knocked me out of my chair to get me onto that dance floor. She said 'Why can't you dance like Henry Hollingsworth?' Then she dragged me out on the dance floor." Danny rocks back on his heels. "Funny thing is, I started liking it. Matter of fact, Millie and I are going up there tonight for the last dance. You two should go." He smiles and extends his hand to Nick. "Danny."

It's about time. Ella had forgotten her manners. Nick shakes his hand. "Nick. Old friend of the family."

Danny winks. "Let me check on that chili."

***

Ella pushes the lettuce around with her fork, thinking about Father out on the dance floor. Dancing always cheered him up, and he moved with a natural grace. Back in Ann Arbor, folks had more or less forgotten him, but here, in this tiny community, he lives on in small ways: the man Danny remembers, humming as he waltzed around a ballroom with a gimpy leg; the old guy who still rode his bike down the Grand Hill at age eighty; the fellow who stopped his bike at the bottom of the hill to chat about the weather with a manure sweeper. Snippets of a happier Henry.

"Now it's my turn. A penny for your thoughts," says Nick.

She brushes her hair off her forehead and spears a tomato slice. "It's just—well—you can't get away from memories here. There's a porous membrane between the living and the dead. Much more than anywhere else."

He leans toward her. "And I thought I was the rememberer."

She chews on the tomato, then swallows. "Perhaps we love the dead too much here."

Danny is back with the chili, a big, steaming, white bowl. "Your Father's favorite was a cheeseburger with a big pickle. He always ate the pickle first. Don't know why I remember that," says Danny, scratching his head. "Of course he had to have it with a shot of brandy."

"Thanks, Danny." When Danny's out of earshot Ella leans forward and whispers, "See what I mean? We're remembered here, even for the silly little things."

"Is that so bad?"

Ella pauses. "I think it's one of the many reasons I love Mackinac."

"Aha! Caught you being nostalgic."

What is it about grief, she wonders, how it follows you around silently, shapelessly, only to punch you in the gut when you're sitting down in a bar, or leaning back in the tub, standing in line at the post office; like fruit flies, unseen, but always present, appearing out of nowhere at the scent of a rotting piece of memory, a grief subsiding. Betty, the psychologist, told her she had "displaced grief" when Ella told her how she barely shed a tear at Father's memorial service, but broke down in sobs at the funeral of an elderly cottager a year later. And Mother, of that generation that so admired Jackie Kennedy for not screaming as she held the bloody head of her dying husband on the lap of her pink suit.

Ella scoops a spoonful of chili from Nick's bowl. "Hey, that's mine. Order your own," he says bending forward, straining his neck to kiss her above the bowl.

When Danny checks back on them, Nick says, "Another chili, please."

As stealthily as it had arrived, grief slinks off to the corner.

41

As they leave the restaurant Danny shouts, "See you two on the dance floor tonight!" Outside the wind has picked up and the sun plunges behind the bridge, the sky flaming orange, streaked with flamingo and indigo lines.

"What do you think about going to the Grand tonight?" Ella asks.

"Are you serious? I thought you were just humoring Danny." First, he hasn't any dress clothes, and second, he doesn't dance that traditional stuff very well. He'd rather go up to Nicolet's marker and romp around beneath the stars, cold as it is. It's their last night together and it calls for something special. "They'd never let me in," says Nick. "No suit, no tie. Not even a pair of good dress shoes."

"You could wear some of Father's clothes. We've got a closet full of them."

Nick's never been one to wear dead people's clothes. Only Papa's shirt and a few of his ties. The rest he wouldn't touch.

"But I don't have good shoes, just sneakers and boots," says Nick.

"What size are you?" asks Ella, surveying his feet.

"Ten."

"I think we can find a pair," she says.

As they wheel their bikes into the backyard, Ella looks up and cries, "Jed! I forgot all about him." Dropping her bike she runs toward the lawn, where a big circle of chewed-down grass has appeared, but no trace of the horse "He's gone!" she shouts, hitting herself upside the head with the base of her palm. "Whatever was I thinking—or not thinking? I can't remember a damn thing."

"He's probably in the barn chowing down on hay."

"That would just about kill him, and how in the hell would he get in there?" she shouts, racing toward the barn. Nick retrieves her bike and wheels it to the porch as she yells from the barn, "He's here!"

Nick sighs with relief and walks toward the barn, where he finds

Ella in a box stall rubbing her head against Jed's while she strokes his neck. "Someone found him, probably all wrapped around the tree. Who in the heck?"

Nick shakes his head. "Some good Samaritan I guess."

"A good Samaritan who knows horses, and our house," she says, pointing to the lead line, tied neatly to the bars above the stall door in a perfect set of loops. Turning to the horse she mutters, "Jeddy, poor boy, I'm so sorry."

"Maybe there's a note at the house," suggests Nick. "Or a message on the phone."

"Not many neighbors are left. I suppose it could have been the barn boy up at the Anderson's, but that's a ways. Or a worker boarding up one of the places."

"Call the police and file a good Samaritan report."

"Ha ha."

"I don't think I can go dancing tonight; I mean, the clothes and everything," he says.

"Nonsense," says Ella, rubbing Jed's neck and then kissing it. Turning to Nick she says "Come with me." He follows behind as she marches to the house.

Upstairs she opens the door onto the room next to hers; Nick vaguely remembers it from his search for Charlie in August. Painted a pale mint green with a floral rug of pink flowers, the room feels distinctly girly. A tall brass bed covered by a pink and green duvet with decorative pillows looks like a throne, and, unlike Ella's room, the place is neat and tidy. Ella proceeds to plunge through the closet, emerging with several shirts, jackets, and trousers. They smell musty, with a hint of soap. "I don't think these will work," he says, examining a shirt. "A button's missing."

"Try this one." This one is light blue with narrow white stripes and a thread line of maroon. All the buttons appear attached.

The shirt fits, though the neck's a bit tight, the sleeves an inch too long. Ella hands him a maroon tie with a small blue design. Examining it closely, he sees the pattern is made of tiny skulls. "I don't think so," he says, tossing it on a chair.

"You're so superstitious. Here, try this." Nick's relieved to see plain red and black stripes crossing a deep-blue background.

Next he slips into a navy blue jacket with brass buttons. He turns around to show Ella the back view. "There's moth holes in it," she says. "Hold on a sec, there's one more."

In a moment she's back, toting a nearly identical blazer. "No holes." Nick sneezes as he buttons it. He sticks his hand in the pocket and pulls out a dime and two pennies. "I'm going to make money on this."

The shoes are more problematic. Henry's feet are a half-size smaller, and every pair Ella lugs out pinches Nick's toes, especially his small right one that was injured in the accident. "Can't walk in these, let alone dance."

"Don't worry. Be right back." She leaves him alone in the room, and Nick's back begins to itch. No telling what might be in a shirt after two years in a home that's boarded up seven months of the year. Removing the jacket, he begins unbuttoning the shirt when Ella sweeps through the doorway with a pair of pink suede shoes in her left hand.

"You've got to be kidding. I won't wear those even if they fit," says Nick, staring at the shoes. "Your dad wore those?"

"I found them in another closet. Come on, try them on. I bet you can dance better in them."

It's not that he's homophobic, but come on, pink suede? "Ella, I can't."

"Oh try them on, please."

Sitting on a dressing table stool, Nick inserts his right foot into the shoe. It's soft, immensely comfortable.

"Perfect," says Ella, beaming as she hands him the left shoe.

His foot slips in with ease and he ties the laces. Standing in his half-buttoned shirt, gray pants and pink shoes seems to delight Ella, who throws her arms around him.

"Can you dance?" she asks. "I mean, like old farts."

Katie had insisted they take ballroom dance lessons. He'd messed up the fox trot, stepped on her toes in the cha-cha, felt more confident with a waltz. *All you have to do is count one-two-three, one-two-three and swirl around,* said their instructor.

Lightly cupping his hand behind her back and taking her right hand in his, Nick begins waltzing. "Shall we dance?" He swirls her around the room.

"I didn't know you could dance like that," says Ella.

"Must be something in these pink suede shoes."

They never make it to the ballroom.

***

Something wakes him. Sniffing the air, he realizes it's his own gas. Must be that chili. He rolls toward Ella, finding only a warm spot and an indentation in her pillow. Where the devil has she gone off to this time? Sliding his legs over the bedside, his feet touch the cold wood floor. Wearing only a T-shirt, he searches for his underwear and socks, then moves quickly to the bathroom. "Ella?" he calls, his voice bouncing off the windowpanes that rattle in their frames like wooden dentures. Back in the bedroom he plunges his hand in the pockets of the pants he left hanging over a chair, retrieves his phone and reads the time: Nine twenty-five. The night is young. This, their last night. He's spent more than the last ten thousand days of his life without Ella; damned if he'll pass another one without her, not even a minute. Grabbing a sweater, he hurries down the front staircase. Through the foyer, past the library door, into the dining room. The uneven floorboards squeal with every step. Such an old house. Turning into the kitchen he hears the back door slam and he finds Ella leaning into the counter, breathing deeply, wearing sweats, a hand-knit blue sweater and a necklace she'd put on for the Grand. "Ella."

She looks up, startled. "I was checking on Jed. He was lying down and his nostrils looked dilated. May have colic from all that grass so I walked him."

"Is that serious?"

"Can be. It's killed many a horse. He seems fine now, but I'll need to get up one more time and check him. I'll set my cell phone alarm."

"I thought my gas had driven you away."

"I thought mine would drive you away," she laughs. "That chili works quickly."

Enclosing her in his arms, Nick flicks away a piece of hay from her sweater and runs his hand down her back, forcing away all thought that this may ever end.

42

They decide to walk to the highest point of the island. Despite his tired legs, Nick goes along with the idea. The fort offers the best damn view on the whole island, a perfect way to end the weekend.

With gloved hands held tight, palm-to-palm, they walk, two figures on a dark road beneath a canopy of cedars, a crescent moon overhead. Past the shuttered mansions, dark hulks rising from empty flower-beds, past the near-vacant big barns whose tenants are off wintering on horse farms in the UP, past the Grand Hotel golf course where they hear water spilling from a fountain on the ninth fairway.

"My parents used to play there," says Ella, nodding toward the dark expanse to their right.

Nick had shied away from the sport. Too expensive, a time stealer. Where he lived the season was too short anyway. He wonders what it would be like to have an athletic mother, finding the thought of Sophia with a golf club or jogging shorts amusing. The most exercise he'd witnessed Mama do was some kind of workout in the school pool for older ladies when her doctor said it would help her bad knee. He glances at Ella striding beside him with such strength and muscle. *She'll probably outlive me by a decade.*

They move up a hill past the governor's summer home, a three-storied white abode near Fort Mackinac, and arrive at the vacant field behind the fort where the galaxy blooms above them. "There's Orion," says Nick, head tilting back and finger pointing to the sky. "The Greeks called him a hunter, but the Chippewa called him Winter Maker." How he dreads the celestial appearance of Orion, knowing the long UP winter will soon arrive. "Look how clear his belt buckle is tonight."

"See that star in his buckle, the reddish one? That's Betelgeuse," says Ella. Father had first pointed it out to her years ago. "Did you know it's disintegrating?"

"Even the stars are falling apart, like me," laughs Nick. Especially his right knee, which is throbbing. "Let's sit for a minute," he says, plopping on a white concrete bench at the fort entrance. Above, a rope on the flagpole bangs against the metal, a ghost longing for attention; moonlight dapples the fort's white stone walls.

"You OK?" asks Ella, lowering herself beside him.

"No, I'm way beyond OK. A-plus." He turns and kisses her, thinking how cold her face feels in contrast to the warm cave of her mouth.

They pull apart slowly. She stands, tugging on his hand. "Well come on then. We've miles to go before we sleep."

"The woods are snowy, dark and deep," Nick chimes in.

They follow the road north into the woods where the overhang of trees blots out the stars. Deeply dark. Nick feels a chill. They plod on until they arrive at Skull Cave and turn right on the carriage road, until they arrive at a set of stairs.

"Stair-stepping Trail, one hundred thirty-seven steps," Ella announces.

"What do you do, go around counting the steps?"

"Sara and I used to fight about it so we started counting them."

Steeling himself for the upward climb, Nick grabs the wood railing. Halfway up, his breath comes short and he pauses. Ella has moved ahead and doesn't notice; her feet thumping on each stair in perfect rhythm: five steps and a platform, another seven steps and a platform. *Damned if she'll beat me up there.* Charging the stairs, Nick catches up to Ella, who begins jogging. The race is on. By the time they reach the top—she, panting, three seconds ahead—he, gasping, doubled over, holding the rail with both hands—they are so hot they have to unzip their coats.

"You're too macho," he exclaims.

"Oh, me? If that's not the pot calling the kettle black."

Recovering quickly, Ella strides ahead onto the gravel loop around the old redoubt. Only its earthen walls and a wooden gate remain of the fort built by the British in the War of 1812.

"This place is eroding fast," says Nick, who hasn't been up to the site in thirty years. "That side is going to wash away in a few years. They need to fix it."

"The Historic Council is broke, so don't count on it," says Ella. "But who cares about history tonight? We're here for the view."

And she is right about that; from the top of the old walls, the Straits spread out below them, a bright silver skirt wrapped around the island. A crescent moon rides across the sky, and to the west, Big Mac's red and green lights blink on its two towers like an early Christmas tree. Beyond the bridge, the water disappears in the dark. Through the forest's edge the lights in the Grand Hotel's cupola glow for the last time this season; tomorrow the hotel will join the league of phantoms of summers past, shuttered and deserted.

Sprawled on their backs on the wood platform over the fort's entranceway, Nick feels the spaces between the huge logs under his spine. He points to the sky. "Some day we'll discover a planet out there as pretty as Earth. It will have forests and lakes, yes, plenty of lakes. Now you don't need to worry about water anymore," he says. She moves tighter against him. Overhead, the entire galaxy brightly burns, the stars so close Nick feels he can reach up and pluck one. Tonight there is no past, no future, only the two of them, beyond the limits of time.

Nick turns to Ella. "This is the closest to heaven I'll ever get."

43

The walk back to Cedar Bluff is freezing. Once home, Ella declares they must build a fire "to get this cold out of our bones."

Nick totes in logs and kindling from the basement while Ella fills two brandy snifters from a bottle of brandy she found in the credenza. "This'll warm you up," she says, handing Nick a glass. They sip them before the fire, now robust and crackling, Ella in one armchair, Nick in another. Neither says a word.

Basking in the bittersweet glow of this last night, Ella stares at the flames, feeling the liquor burn in her blood. Nothing beyond this is guaranteed, not one second. Her inner rememberer is out in full force, gathering all the materials for a new memory: the flickering light from the flames, the musty smell of the rug mixing with the smoke from the logs, the rattle of wind at the window, and Nick's profile illuminated by the firelight. He sits in the chair Father favored, his head back, eyelids drooping, an empty glass on the table beside him. She imagines them growing into one of those elderly couples who have been together so long they look alike, holding hands, the man carrying his wife's oversized purse. Her parents never attained that state of senior intimacy. Although their marriage extended a full fifty-three years, they held one another at arm's length, withheld secrets of the deepest sort. And she's the same strain—has she told Nick anything about the humiliation and shame of her arrest, the drudgery of looking over the family finances, the burden of being the strong one, like one of those dray horses slogging up the big hills? Tomorrow, before he leaves, she'll pour out buckets of truth. After breakfast, yes, they'll talk then.

Taking one more swill of brandy—the stuff's too fiery for her to finish—she stands and picks up the fire poker. Opening the fire screen, she knocks the logs down to prevent them from rolling, then tugs the metal handles of the screen tight. Nick groans from his chair. She kisses his forehead, now warm and slightly moist. His heads rolls to the right. "Uuhhh?"

"Time for bed."

Grunting, Nick sits up, rubbing his eyes. "You gonna finish that?" he asks, pointing to her glass.

"No."

He reaches down and quaffs the contents. "Let's go upstairs."

Hand in hand they ascend the staircase, the wood creaking with each step.

Ella helps him remove his shirt and pants before he tumbles onto the bed in his undershirt and briefs. She pulls a flannel nightie over her long underwear. Remembering Jed, she sets her phone alarm for 3:00 a.m. before climbing in beside Nick.

Sometime in the middle of the night, Nick's snoring awakens her. *Oh God, we are getting old.* After she nudges him with her leg the sounds stop, the snarly wheezing sliding into smooth breathing. She holds her breath, anticipating his next eruption, but only soft, methodic puffs of air course in, out, in, out. She rests her head next to his and matches his rhythm, pictures the oxygen swirling in their blood, rushing through their pulmonary arteries into their lungs before moving out to feed every cell, a perfect exchange between their circulatory and respiratory systems.

"Nick," she whispers in the dark, the air so cold she exudes smoke as she speaks.

He rolls over, moans, "Umm."

Taking his hand in hers she brings it toward her mouth and kisses it.

Nick's eyes flicker, then open, and he pulls her towards him. His chest is warm, a furnace. He kisses her forehead, closes his eyes and relapses into slumber.

Ella lies on her back, wishing sleep would come to her so easily. His wheezing has resumed. Rolling on her side she studies Nick. His left hand is curled beneath his head, his right resting just above his thigh. The shadow of a windowpane falls on his face and his mouth gapes open, exposing his teeth that glow in the moonlight with a pearly florescence. Still unable to sleep she turns on her stomach, but it hurts her neck so she rolls onto her right side, curled first in a fetal position, then straight out. Not one position is comfortable. Damn it. She'll have to get a cup of herbal tea and endure the cold all the way to the kitchen and back. Sitting up with her feet over the edge of the bed, she surveys the room. If it wasn't messy before, now a state of anarchy has taken over. Nick's clothes lie strewn on the floor by Father's shirt and trousers, on the closet door hang two ties over several pairs of pants, and the rug is layered in her shirts and bottoms from the entire week. She jumps down, landing squarely on the two pink suede shoes Nick placed by the bed before diving in with her. She didn't tell him they were Kevin's. What did it matter, anyway?

Her nipples stand at attention in the frosty air and the hair on her arms salutes. She pulls a sweater over her head, then yanks on a pair of pants that scratch from slivers of bark from the logs at Fort Holmes. The darn things are inside out.

Leaning over, she kisses Nick on his forehead and whispers, "I'll be right back." He doesn't stir. "My love," she murmurs.

Hurrying toward the kitchen she trips, banging her right knee hard on the wooden floor. In the kitchen the oven clock flashes PF. Another power cut, probably from some animal. The last one went on for seven hours, the cause discovered by a worker near Stone Bluff: a snake had crawled in a generator box. In her hand she carries her phone; the glowing digital numbers read 1:45. She sets it on the table.

Outside she hears Jed's neigh. Poor boy, she had thoroughly abandoned him today. At twenty-seven, his days are numbered, and he definitely overate today. Grabbing a jacket from the peg by the door, she slips her feet into a pair of rubber boots and hurries out the door. Outside the sky is still twinkling with stars and a planet or two. There's Venus, and just below, Jupiter.

Waiting anxiously by the fence, Jed snorts and thrusts his head up and down. Unlatching the gate Ella mutters, "What is it, boy? Has Mama neglected you?" She has always talked to horses like children, forging a kinship with them stronger than those she's developed with most humans; to her, horses *are* people. She runs her hands over his face, checks his nose for fever, then picks up each leg to examine his hooves. Nothing. Stroking his head, Ella stares at the dark hulk of the cottage, a Cyclops with its single eye formed by a nightlight in an upstairs bathroom across the hall from where she left Nick snoring contentedly in a nest of exhaustion. Nick. Yes, Nick. Nick and Ella, two aging lovers, one acting like a fresh mare, the other, a stallion. Once she let down her guard it had been so easy to open the gate that led him back into her life. He's a full-grown man with baggage. And Lord knows she has baggage too, enough to fill a dray and then some. But they would always have this weekend, just as they'd had that summer. Beyond that, who knows?

"Jed," she says, leaning her head into his neck. "What have I gotten myself into?" The horse snorts softly as she strokes him, his mane tickling the top of her hand.

"Let's walk." As she reaches for his halter, something moves above them. Jed lifts his head and Ella goes taut.

Standing still, her hand tensing on the horse's neck, she listens: a pine bough slapping against the old wood siding, Jed's soft snorting as he nuzzles her, the scrape of his hoof on the floor—nothing more.

"Not to worry buddy," she whispers, rubbing his neck with her knuckle. Her hand is shaking. Then a loud moan from the loft cuts through the barn. Ella's stomach tightens and she shouts, "Who's there?" She debates whether to stay and approach whatever is up there, or hightail it back to the house and get Nick. She glances toward the house as more sounds erupt above. Jed, however, looks perfectly relaxed.

"Who's up there?" she calls again, lowering her tone to sound intimidating.

"Holy shit," exclaims a voice from the loft. Holy shit is right! As she stands clenching Jed's mane, a face appears just over her head; a scabrous chin, blackened eyes, hair every which way. It's Boon. She hasn't seen him in weeks.

"What are you doing here, Boon? You scared the wits out of me!" Although angry, she's relieved it's only him. She catches a whiff of booze and sweat. "You've been drinking."

A carriage blanket wrapped over his shoulders, pointy cowboy boots coming down first, Boon descends the steps. At the bottom they meet face to face.

"I couldn't make it all the way home," says Boon, "No harm done." Turning toward Jed he continues, "And I fed your boy. Unraveled his line from that tree today, too. Seems you and your boyfriend were too busy to concern yourself with poor Jed."

"So that's who it was. Thanks for helping. Now it's time for you to go home."

"I don't think so. Cold as hell out there."

"Well you can't stay here."

"Calm down, pissy mare," Boon laughs.

"Boon, I'm serious. Go."

"Anyone ever tell you that you look like your mother?" he says, stepping towards her.

"Stay back."

"Don't worry. You're not my type. Your mother, on the other hand—"

"What would you know about my mother?"

"What the hell don't I know? Audie and I go way back."

"What are you talking about?" She'd always suspected that Mother had a dalliance, but with Boon? She thought it was that gardener from Mexico.

Looking suddenly sober, Boon stares at Ella. "Why'd ya think I lost my job?"

"For starters, showing up smashed, throwing a bucket of paint all over Mother's peonies," Ella's voice is rising, "among other things!" She takes a few steps back, but Boon closes the gap between them. The foulness of his breath is overwhelming.

"That was your Father who did it. He threw the bucket. Blamed it on me." Moving within inches he snarls, "Because your mother and I got caught that night and he was pissed off—you were there with that boyfriend of yours—he saw us."

She can feel her breath coming in short gasps. Impossible. The pieces don't fit. And Nick? If he'd known all this time, why hadn't he said something?

Staggering, she presses her hand against her forehead and grabs the side of a stall for support. Boon backs away slightly, but his reek fills up the space between them.

"Go ask him," he taunts.

She turns to run back to the house and wake up Nick, find out the truth of this. "I don't care. That was all so long ago. Just go, go away. Get out of here."

Boon spits on the floor by her left foot. "Henry knocked me upside the head. After that he watched your mother like a hawk."

"Enough!" she shouts. "Get the hell out of my barn!"

Boon turns toward the door, takes a few steps and stops. "Holy shit," he whistles. "Would ya look at that?" Wheeling around, Ella looks toward Cedar Bluff. Smoke billows through the window edges on the first floor while a knot of orange flames flicker within. Later, she would wonder why she thought it, but for a split second she felt everything would be all right since the cottage was filled with fire extinguishers and smoke alarms. Father had been paranoid about fire, "We never have to worry about earthquakes and tornadoes, but fire, that's our enemy." He took great care to keep an extinguisher and a smoke alarm in every room. Then something at the back of her mind rushes forward in high alert: she hadn't put new batteries in the alarms, kept forgetting to buy them. That was in July. And those extinguishers, no one had checked them since Father died.

"Nick!" she screams, breaking into a sprint. To her astonishment, Boon is running too, even quicker than her. He's shed the blanket and is racing toward the house a few feet in front of her. Her feet flap in the rubber boots and she trips, sprawling on the ground. "I'm right behind you!" she cries. Boon looks back but doesn't stop. She crawls to her knees and sprints to the back door where Boon has already disappeared. Pulling open the door, she feels a rush of heat and smoke. From the corridor connecting the kitchen to the dining room Boon shouts, "Stay back!"

Ella rushes forward into Boon, who stands at the pantry hallway. He pushes her away with a bolt of force. "You stay out, ya hear me?"

Pounding on him with her fists, she screams, "Get out of my way! We have to get Nick!" Kicking hard at Boon's groin, her foot misses. She kicks again.

Boon pushes her hard and her head cracks against a cupboard. A white bolt of light, and then Boon leaning over her asking "What room's he in?"

"The tower bedroom." She clutches her head as Boon disappears up the back stairway in thick smoke. It is only a moment, but later she will remember every frame of it, a blow-by-blow slow-motion replay. Steadying herself she tries to follow him, choking on the smoke, clasping her sweater over her mouth before retreating to the kitchen, where she turns on the sink faucet and throws a dish towel beneath the flow, then covers her head and face with it. She'd heard about people doing this, but she can't get past the pantry because the flames are now raging in the staircase. How will Boon survive that? And Nick. Surely he must be struggling to breathe. He sleeps so soundly, would he even hear a smoke alarm if it were working?

Remembering her cell phone on the kitchen table, she gropes about frantically until her hand touches the smooth sheen of the phone. It's baking in the heat. She dials Nick's number but the words of his voice mail come on immediately, indicating it's turned off. There's only one option left—the front staircase.

Racing out the back door and punching in 9-1-1, she continues around the house toward the front porch.

"I'm reporting a fire, a fire at Cedar Bluff. Mackinac Island," she gasps.

"What'd you say?" asks a man's voice.

"A fire. I'm reporting a fire."

"You calling from the Island?"

"Yes. There's a fire at Cedar Bluff. Big blue Victorian place. The crew will know it. Tell them it's the Hollingsworths'."

"Someone's already reported it, ma'am. Crew's on the way. You be careful, stay away from the fire. Remain outside."

"I'm going in!" she screams, flinging the phone on the wicker rocker next to the front door, the one Nick sat in that day in August. Charging into the front foyer, screaming "Nick!" over and over, she can make out the stairs ahead, but the smoke is hopelessly thick. Still she moves forward, into the flames, the dish towel over her mouth already drying. The crackling sounds intensify as she moves toward the staircase, no longer shouting Nick's name, not now when she can scarcely breathe. Better to save what little oxygen the fire hasn't stolen.

Through the smoke, at the top of the stairs she sees Boon pulling Nick by the legs. He makes it to the top step and pushes hard on Nick's shoulders, succeeding in getting Nick down a few steps. Boon pushes again as the body rolls down the stairs, *thunk, thunk, thunk*—stopping a few steps before the bottom. Rushing toward Nick, Ella reaches out to grab his arms, his legs, any part at all, but is overcome with coughing, can't breathe, can't breathe at all. She crawls toward the front door and collapses.

44

So vicious is the pain—worse than after the runaway accident years ago—that the pounding in her head, the throbbing in her arms, supplants all other thoughts. Then Ella notices bandages, sheaths of gauze wrapped over her arms. Reaching for her hair, she pats down on a bald scalp. Equipment surrounds her bed, beeping, swishing, humming. The place is louder than a casino. A woman appears beside her wearing a flowery, cheerful version of a uniform. "You're awake. Well, good for you," she says.

"Where am I?" asks Ella.

"At the hospital. McLaren, in Petoskey. They flew you over last night. I'm Eileen. You have some serious burns honey, but nothing that won't heal up. What a mess you were before we cleaned you, all covered in soot. Had to shave off your pretty hair."

"What happened to the house?" Her first thought. "And Nick, how's Nick?" She tries to sit up, but Eileen restrains her. "There, there. Don't get up. Your family's coming soon. They'll explain everything." Her stonewalling is not a good sign.

"And Boon. What happened to him?"

"I'm sorry, but I don't know those people. Now just lie back and drink some water," says Eileen, holding a white foam cup with a straw next to Ella's lips. Ella takes a long sip before pushing it away. "Sorry, but I can't wait. I'm leaving." She flings off the bed covers and yanks on a needle from a hill of gauze they've constructed on her right hand. Eileen must have stealthily signaled for help because a man in scrubs rushes in.

"So, Ella, I understand you want to leave," says the man, a sturdy young fellow with a pleasant smile that reveals a set of sparkling teeth. His hand rests firmly on her arm. Cheeky young man, using her first name, and now this. She pushes against his hand and he tightens his grip. "You need to wait for your doctor to release you." Something about the look in his eyes, pitying it seems, signals something very wrong.

"I am just fine. Now if you'd please remove your hand I promise to stay put…" reading his name on his hospital ID, adds, "Alex."

He walks with the nurse to the hallway, where they confer. The nurse returns quickly and fusses with the IV. Then there's no resisting as the medicine flowing through the tubes begins to take over. But not before Ella sees Mother, Sara, and Charlie enter. Charlie is holding tightly to Sara's arm, and Mother reaches over and kisses Ella on the forehead. "My little rabbit," Mother whispers.

45

Out in the garden, Ella bends over a spade, digging a home for a new milkweed. The soil is rocky and stubborn, so different from the flowerbeds at Cedar Bluff, with their decades of worm-filled dirt and manure. She pauses, takes a deep breath and lifts her eyes from the ground, feeling something watching her. On the fence around the new turn-out, a crow turns its head and stares at Ella, caws and flies off. Jed emerges from the run-in shed and trots up to the fence. He'd survived the fire and long winter.

"Hey Jeddie," she calls, just as her cell phone emits a single chime from her back pocket. *Mother.* Ever since Ella taught her how to use a smartphone last winter, Mother, ever the good student, has become a texting nuisance. *We're out of toilet paper; I'm taking a nap. Please wake me up in thirty minutes; I forgot our ZIP code,* she'll text.

What on earth is it now? Scrolling to the message, Ella reads "Some girl named Melina is here." Ella gasps, reads the message again and runs her hand through her hair, completely gray and spikey since they shaved it at the hospital last fall. Melina has rebuffed all of Ella's overtures.

When Ella tried to get information about Nick's memorial service during a rare phone call when Melina actually answered, Melina said, "Under the circumstances, we think it best if you don't attend." Ella sent a flower arrangement and donated $500 to a scholarship fund the family established in Nick's name. She had never received even a thank-you note. Now the girl is here. *How did she find our place?*

Ella crosses the backyard, hoping to eavesdrop on Mother and Melina on the porch, but the noise of hammers and a radio blaring soft rock from the construction crew working on the house drowns out all other sounds. Ella slips in the back door, scrubs dirt from her hands, then runs a comb through her hair. Her legs wobble as she crosses the living room and tiptoes to the screen door. The girl sits in a chair facing Mother, and Ella gets a full front view of her. Melina's long, brown hair, haloed in the sun, creates a Madonna effect. She's wearing a teal tank top and brown shorts, and her tanned legs remind her of Nick's, firm and powerful. Ella leans into the door for a closer look as Mother asks, "You sure you're not one of those native plant gals? Ella is very involved with those folks."

Melina smiles, shaking her head. "No, no. Not me. I can hardly tell a rose from a violet."

"Then you must be from the water group."

"Huh?"

"That group that makes such a fuss about saving water." Mother leans forward, lowering her voice. "They save their flushes."

Melina sits straighter, covering her mouth with her left hand. "Really?"

That's enough, Mother. Ella thrusts the door open and strides toward the girl. "You must be Melina," she says. "Such a pleasure to finally meet you. I'm Ella."

Melina reaches out and shakes Ella's hand with a limpid grip. "Hi," she mutters, staring at the porch floor. Melina's eyes move to Ella's forearms, a patchwork of large red splotches from the burns, and Ella wishes she'd worn a long-sleeved shirt. There's something compelling about the girl, with her thick glossy hair and olive complexion, but it is her eyes—Nick's eyes—that light, golden cognac, warm and bright, that draws Ella to her. Even though her lips are too thin, her nose a bit long and angular, somehow, the whole mix adds up to an attractive face, a face with so many of Nick's features. Ella tries not to stare and she fights the impulse to take Melina in her arms and hold her.

"I've heard so much about you. Your father bragged about you, called you his magnum opus," says Ella.

"His what?"

"Magnum opus, means masterpiece."

"Oh."

"I know you two have been chatting, but let me officially introduce you. Mother, this is Melina Pappas."

"Popeyes?"

"Pappas, Mother," corrects Ella.

"Then you must be related to that Greek fellow who died at our cottage."

"Mother, this is Nick's daughter." Ella takes Melina by the elbow and steers her toward the front door. "I want to show Melina around the house. We'll be back soon," she says, whisking Melina into the house. "I'm sorry about that. Mother can be, uh, difficult."

"I understand. So can my grandma." Melina bites her lower lip. Looking around, her eyes widen. "Wow, this reminds me of my old house. Daddy built it."

"Your father said the same thing."

"He was here?"

"Once, yes."

"Oh."

"Since Cedar Bluff was destroyed, we've moved on."

Melina halts and looks Ella straight in the eye. "I—I saw it. I mean, the place where it was. It was awful."

"Here, have a seat," says Ella, pointing to a long leather sofa facing a stone fireplace. Melina chooses an armchair, the farthest piece of furniture from where Ella seats herself. The girl is obviously distressed, making the grim pilgrimage to her father's death site. People do it in search of some closure, but Ella knows there's no such thing as closure, not with those you love.

Rubbing a tear from one eye Melina says, "What a beautiful view you had at your old place."

"Yes, we surely did."

"When I was up there, some woman came out and asked me what I was doing. She told me you had moved here. That's how I found you."

"Was she about this tall,"—Ella holds her hand palm down at shoulder height—"short, brown hair, and very hyper?"

Melina giggles, "Exactly."

Darci. Well, no surprise there. On Mackinac there's no getting away from old neighbors. After the fire, Ella found out that it was Darci who first reported the fire, even though she was back at her home in Bloomfield Hills. Turns out she had a video camera on the top story of her cottage pointed toward Cedar Bluff, and just so happened to glance at it that night. Ella shudders at the memory. If only she had put batteries in those smoke alarms. If only she hadn't poked those logs. If only she hadn't left the house. She wants to confess this to Melina, who sits quietly, but of course she can't burden the girl, who is already suffering.

"I saw his grave. Lady in the post office told me where it was," mutters Melina.

"Whose grave?"

"Boon's. I owe him. He died trying to save Daddy."

"Yes he did." But it was too late; even Boon's heroics couldn't save Nick. They sit quietly. The sound of hammers and saws ceases, and with it, the radio. Lunch break.

"What are you building?" asks Melina, studying a blue tarp that seals off the construction area on the left side of the room..

"A third floor and a tower, your dad's idea. It will have a sitting room and a bedroom. Can I get you something to drink? You must be thirsty."

"Sure."

Ella walks to the kitchen and returns with two glasses of fresh, clear water. "Your father had a fondness for Mackinac water. It's some of the best in the world."

"Oh."

Resuming her seat, Ella jiggles her glass in her hand. "I suppose you want to hear about, about that night."

"Well, I—"

"Horrible, the worst moment of my life. I am so, so sorry."

"You don't have to tell me."

"I think it would be best if you knew, at the very least, knew that he died peacefully, probably had no inkling. Smoke inhalation does that."

"But he was badly burned, too. Mom said so. She didn't want me to see."

"Of course not," says Ella, leaning toward Melina. "But he was gone before any of that—that horror—occurred. The firefighters told me." Not all the truth, but enough. She'll never know if Nick was alive when Boon heroically dragged him down the stairs. Ella shudders.

Melina stares at her. "Did you see him, I mean . . ." Her voice trails as she glances at the burns on Ella's arms. "When you went in?"

"The last I saw of him he was sleeping contently, even snoring."

Melina's face brightens. "Daddy was a horrible snorer." She pauses. "Thank you," she mumbles. "He left lots of notes, e-mails and stuff.

He really, really wanted you to hear his side of the story, you know, the whole thing about that kid in Wisconsin was pure crap. Did you believe him?" Her eyes look defiant.

Ella holds Melina's gaze and takes a deep breath. "The truth is that at first, no. I wouldn't even talk to him. I have a teenage nephew and I—"

Melina hits her fist on the arm of her chair. "I knew it. Where is that kid? I want to tell him to his face how wrong he was."

"Wait, please hear me out. My nephew's away this summer and he's very remorseful, trust me. And I regret more than you'll ever know not believing your father at first. But then, I found out otherwise. He came here and told me." She looks at the floor and pauses.

"He came here and got himself killed."

"Yes, and I will regret that the rest of my life." Tears form in the edges of her eyes. The room is still, save for the soft flapping of the plastic tarp.

Ella stands. "There's something I'd like to show you." Ella pulls back the tarp where a set of stairs with no backers and a shaky, temporary railing leads upward toward the sky. She gestures for Melina to join her. Melina hesitates.

"Come on, come on."

Melina eyes the stairs dubiously.

"Don't worry, they're as solid as Mackinac." Ella bounds up the steps with Melina right behind.

At the top of the stairs they arrive at a small platform. Ella stops, pointing west where the Mackinac Bridge rises from a pool of liquid silver, the sun riding directly above it. Melina stands next to her, staring in that direction. "The bridge?" she asks.

Ella laughs, turning toward the clear blue water north, the green line of the Upper Peninsula stretching to the horizon.

"The UP?" Ella shakes her head and points into the woods behind the house where a set of stairs leads to a lookout.

"What's that?" asks Melina.

"Friendship's Altar, one of your father's favorite places. I'll take you up there."

They stand together, surveying the spot as the tarp slaps against the side of the house like a sail fluffing in the wind, readying the boat to come about on a new course.

Ella's gaze is fixed on the lookout, but Melina turns back toward the lake.

"This will be a million-dollar view when you finish," she says, her eyes sparkling. "The bridge, and all that beautiful water."

ACKNOWLEDGMENTS

Thank you to all who have supported me in this endeavor – there are so many of you – with a shout-out to these people in particular: Rebecca Johns and her fine workshop at the 2008 Iowa Summer Writing Festival; Ann Hagemann for inspiring me to write a novel; Sandy Harris and Bill Castanier for reading that first draft and giving me hope; Monica Hogan for her fine edits; my children Glenn and Ginger for their belief in me (and Ginger's wonderful sales enthusiasm), and Don Hinman, my kind and patient husband who is also an excellent editor. Also, Jennifer Wohletz of Mackinac Memories for pulling the pieces together and bringing it to print, and Lily Porter Niederpruem for her beautiful cover art.

The St. Ignace/Mackinac Island Town Crier supplied information and inspiration, and the Mackinac Island State Park Commission provided me with such wonderful sites and markers for my characters to visit.

Above all, I want to thank my parents for giving me a home on Mackinac.

AUTHOR'S NOTE

The idea for this novel came when my daughter found a handwritten note scribbled on the back of a business card in the front door of our family cottage on Mackinac Island, Michigan. When she read me the name I faintly remembered a boyfriend from a summer long, long ago. Curious, I called him. Turns out he had brought his wife to tour the island and they passed by our cottage. We filled one another in on more than three decades of our lives, its losses and its joys. Both of us were happily married, and that was that.

The following spring I signed up for a novel writing class at the Iowa Summer Writer's Workshop. As time drew closer —I had no novel and was feeling panicky —the idea of two former summer lovers resurrecting an old relationship began to brew. It blossomed from the teeniest flicker of my imagination into the full-grown adults who people these pages. I've grown to know them very well. I hope you have too.

ABOUT THE AUTHOR

A lifelong Mackinac Island summer resident, Sue Allen wouldn't trade her beloved island for any place on Earth. A former teacher in Fairfax County, Virginia, she splits her time between Mackinac and northern Virginia where she resides with her husband, Don Hinman, and two persnickety cats. This is her first novel.

ABOUT MACKINAC ISLAND

Rising from the waters of northern Lake Huron, Mackinac Island is an exquisite jewel of the Great Lakes. Just eight miles in circumference, it covers 3.8 square miles and is officially in Michigan's Upper Peninsula. It appeared when glaciers melted at the end of the last Ice Age about 13,000 BC, and its human history stretches back to Anishanaabe settlements around AD 900.

Home to French missionaries during the 17th and 18th centuries, the site of two battles during the War of 1812, and a once thriving fur-trading hub, Mackinac Island is now a popular tourist destination. The movie *Somewhere in Time* was filmed there in 1979. Its most distinctive feature is a ban on motorized vehicles, thus making horses Mackinac's reigning kings and queens.